Cold winds sang through the valleys, low clouds hid the rising peaks, and spitting snow had begun to dust the marchers on the Stoneforge trail when those in the rear of the great caravan heard running hoofbeats behind them. A single rider, wearing the colors of Hammerhand's personal guard, the Ten, came into sight.

Then he was among them, dropping exhausted from his horse. A crude sling held his right arm close against his armored breast, and the right side of his face was crusted with dried blood.

"What is it? What's happened?" The Chosen gathered around him, their eyes bright with concern.

"The truce was a trick," the dwarf told them, his voice thin with anger. "Lord Kane attacked with his entire garrison. They used seige engines . . . catapults . . . We didn't have a chance."

"And Derkin? Is Derkin . . . ?"

"Turn your column," the messenger rasped. "We're going back."

The DRAGONLANCE® Saga

DragonLance® Saga

**Dwarven Nations Trilogy
Volume Three**

the
Swordsheath
Scroll

Dan Parkinson

DRAGONLANCE® Saga
Dwarven Nations
Volume Three

THE SWORDSHEATH SCROLL
Copyright ©1993 TSR, Inc.
All Rights Reserved.

First Printing: December 1993
Printed in the United States of America.
Library of Congress Catalog Card Number: 92-61108

9 8 7 6 5 4 3 2 1

ISBN: 1-56076-686-7

TSR, Inc.   TSR Ltd.
P.O. Box 756   120 Church End, Cherry Hinton
Lake Geneva, WI   Cambridge CB1 3LB
53147 U.S.A.   United Kingdom

Dedicated to the Captain and his Lady,
Rob and Marianne Little.

And dedicated
—as always—
to the lady who lives
in all of my memories.

KAL-THAX

ELVEN FOREST

THE EMPEROR'S ROAD

REDROCK CLEFT

KLANATH

SKYWALL PEAKS

KLANATH MINES

DERKIN'S WALL

THARKAS PASS

THARKAS MINES

THE KHAROLIS RANGES OF KAL-THAX

WILDERNESS MOUNTAINS

STONEFORGE

SKY'S END PEAK

ANVILTOP RANGE

SHEERCLIFF

NORTHGATE

THORBARDIN

SOUTHGATE

Prologue
The Slave

In the centuries following the "Wizards War," the mighty achievement of the dwarven nation of Thorbardin was to establish a golden age in which the embattled thanes of Kal-Thax came together under a council of chiefs to construct the subterranean fortress of Thorbardin. This was a time of relative peace and prosperity. It was, though, a short-lived age. Without serious threat from beyond the dwarven realm, old jealousies and unresolved rivalries once again began to surface among the thanes.

It had been resolved long since that there would be no king of Thorbardin. Thus all of the thanes within the fortress nation went their own way, held together in common cause only by the inspired wisdom of an aging group of chieftains serving as the Council of Thanes. But by the fiftieth year after Thorbadin's completion, the Council of Thanes had begun to lose its force. Some said the old order ended the day Willen Ironmaul of the Hylar, who had once served as Chief of Chiefs, quit. He resigned his seat in disgust when, following the death of the old Theiwar chieftain, the Theiwar proved unable to agree upon a new chief and instead divided themselves into two warring camps.

Olim Goldbuckle, the Prince of the Daewar, had died years earlier, and his successor was far more interested in enhancing the grandeur of Daebardin—the huge Daewar city on the northeast shore of the Urkhan Sea—than in the workings of the overall realm.

The Daergar, no longer led by the wisdom of old Vog Ironface, had withdrawn to their mines and their smelters and rarely bothered even to send a representative to council. Within three years of the death of the old Theiwar chief, Slide Tolec, Thorbardin had become a dismal, dangerous place where steel rang on steel almost daily as rival bands of Theiwar stalked one another along the subterranean roads. Daewar and Daergar tribal leaders withheld their tariffs from the council coffers to maintain their own separate guard units for their own holdings, and even the wild, unpredictable Klar—who had surprisingly maintained their loyalty to the Hylar concept of a united nation longer than some other clans—were drawn from central concerns by the necessity of defending the farming warrens from becoming battlegrounds.

Thus when the Hylar, Willen Ironmaul, resigned, the Council of Thanes all but ceased to exist, and the managing of Thorbardin's mighty systems—its defenses, its waterways, its roads and ventilation systems, its stores and even its trade with the outside world—fell to the wardens, whose only authority consisted of continuing to do exactly what had been done before.

The fortress nation, sprawling in dissolution beneath its mountain peak, became hardly more than a collection of squabbling cities and rivalrous tribes, bound together only by proximity.

The dark ages of Thorbardin began then, and little would ever be known of those next centuries except for the occasional scribings of Hylar and Daewar scrollsters who kept sporadic records of the times.

All through the turmoil of the Theiwar conflicts, the dark-sighted Daergar stubbornly continued their mining and smelting of ores, and the jovial, wily Daewar maintained a semblance of trade with the Neidar settlements beyond Thorbardin and with some of the human and elven traders who came to their borders. The Klar kept the farms going, and the wardens somehow kept the roads clear, the water flowing, and the lifts operating.

But only among the Hylar, in their growing city of Hybardin, delved into a gigantic stalactite rising above the Urkhan Sea, were records of lineage kept which would survive the "warring times" of those centuries. And as time passed, even the Hylar records became sparse and less reliable.

Of the four children of Colin Stonetooth, the visionary first chieftain of the Hylar who initially brought the mountain thanes together, only one had remained in Thorbardin after the Wizards War. Cale Greeneye was gone, preferring the Neidar life outside to the Holgar life within the fortress. His brother Handil had long since died and was buried beneath the rubble of the ancient city of the Calnar in the far-off Khalkist range, while the second son, Tolon Farsight, had remained there as leader of the Calnar. Only the old chieftain's daughter, Tera Sharn, lived out her life in Thorbardin as wife of Willen Ironmaul.

Their only child, Damon, married a Neidar girl soon

after the Wizards War. Damon's first son, Dalam Fire-blend, became chief warden of Tharkas, far to the north of Thorbardin. Dalam's younger brother Cort succeeded Willen Ironmaul as chieftain of the Hylar, then passed the role to his own son, Harl Thrustweight.

Harl Thrustweight became known in Thorbardin as "The Iron Fist." It was his stubborn intervention—backed by grim companies of armed Hylar streaming out of Hybardin—that finally put an end to the anarchy of the Theiwar battles and once again restored a semblance of order to the undermountain realm. With angry efficiency, Harl Thrustweight reestablished the Council of Thanes and the Halls of Justice.

Beyond Thorbardin, among humans and elves, this dwarven leader—whom none outside of Thorbardin had ever seen—was known as Hal-Thwait. Many humans, and others, in surrounding lands came to believe—from comments passed by traders—that Thorbardin was a kingdom and "Hal-Thwait" was the name of the king of the dwarves. Even among the outside-dwelling Neidar, scattered throughout the protectorate of Kal-Thax, there were many dwarves who accepted that Thorbardin now had a king. Those who knew otherwise made no effort to correct the human and elven traders who referred to King Hal-Thwait. The humans and the elves were outsiders, and as far as the dwarves were concerned, outsiders could believe anything they wanted about Thorbardin. It was none of their business, anyway.

The "Hylar Peace" in Thorbardin and the mountain realm it protected, enforced by Harl Thrustweight, lasted more than a hundred years, which was forty years longer than the reign of Harl Thrustweight as chieftain of the Hylar and senior member of the Council of Thanes. In the Year of Iron, of the Decade of Willow, Century of Rain, the great chieftain and seven of the ten members of his elite guard were crushed in a rockfall near the entrance to the city of Theibardin.

A Daewar leader, Jeron Redleather, and a Hylar soldier, Dunbarth Ironthumb, took over the coordination of events in Thorbardin following Harl Thrustweight's death. Through sheer determination, the two of them kept the Council of Thanes going and maintained a troubled peace in Thorbardin.

Unfortunately, Harl Thrustweight's only child, a grown son named Derkin Winterseed, disappeared on an expedition to Tharkas Pass.

* * * * *

The iron shackles they had placed on his ankles, hammered into place and secured with hot rivets in the manner of bonds intended never to be removed, had been an agony to him for a long time. First there had been the deep burns from the riveting, then the open, bleeding sores caused by the constant rubbing of the rough iron against his skin. But what had lasted longest were the aches in his back and his legs, from hobbling around each long day, dragging the loose, eight-foot length of heavy chain which connected the shackles. That, and the deep, patient anger within him.

He had borne the pains in stubborn silence, just as he bore the welts on his back from the overseers' whips, and eventually the wounds had healed over and the pains had subsided. Now his ankles were toughened by bands of heavy callus that had formed over the scars there, and his legs and back had grown accustomed to the awkward weight of the chain clanking behind him as he labored up and down the dim reaches of rough-delved mine shafts, his hod filled with raw ore from the digs below, or with tools and torches on each return trip.

Most knew him by his deep anger and stubborn silence. Neither the slave masters in these mines nor the other slaves knew more about him than that he was a sturdy, level-eyed young dwarf with a dark, backswept beard, that his name was Derkin, and that he would make trouble if he could.

Three times in two years, his back had been striped until it bled, twice for trying to escape from his bondage, and once—the most recent time—after one of the human guards fell to his death in a refuse pit near the mine's entrance. He had not been the only one whipped that time. The human slavers had whipped every slave within sound of the refuse pit, just on general principle. There was the suspicion that the dead man's fall might not have been an accident, and the slave masters knew that a smartly applied whip sometimes loosens tongues. But they had learned nothing. Most of the slaves were dwarves, and bore their punishment stoically. The few human slaves in the area had nothing to tell their tormentors, because none of them had been nearby when the fall occurred.

Like the other dwarves, all of whom he had ignored since his arrival as a captive of slave hunters, Derkin bore the torment in stony silence. The angry shouts of the humans, the crack and sting of their whips, he simply endured, and never made a sound.

But later, when the mine slaves on that shift had been secured in their dungeon for a few hours' rest, there was cautious movement in the shadows, and another dwarf crept close, to hunker down beside him. In the murky cell, Derkin could barely see the newcomer, but he recognized him. It was the one they called Tap, a young Neidar from one of the hill settlements. Tap had the broad shoulders and long arms of Theiwar ancestry, and his back, like Derkin's own, was striped with bleeding cuts.

For a moment, the hill dwarf simply sat beside him, gazing around furtively. Then he whispered, "I saw what you did."

Derkin ignored the whisper, pretending he had not heard.

"I understand," Tap whispered. "I'm not asking you about it. I just wanted you to know that I saw you kill that guard. You used your chain on him. I only wish I'd had the chance to kill one, too."

Still he made no response, ignoring the other dwarf.

After a moment, Tap shrugged. "You're Hylar, aren't you," he whispered, "from Thorbardin?"

"I am," Derkin admitted, still not looking around.

"I thought so. You look like a Hylar. And I've heard you called Derkin. That sounds like a Hylar name. What's the rest of it?"

The Hylar sat in stony silence, ignoring him.

"No other name?" Tap prodded. "Just Derkin?"

"I'm called Derkin," the silent one muttered. "It's name enough."

"I'm pleased to meet you, Derkin." The other nodded. "I'm Tap. I've heard them talk about you. They say you've tried twice to escape."

"Obviously, I didn't make it," Derkin growled.

"You never will, alone. You'll need friends."

"I need no friends, and I have no friends."

"You could, though," the Neidar said. "I wasn't the only one who saw what happened to that human guard. Think about it."

When the Neidar had gone, back into a far corner of the big, low cell, Derkin sat motionless for a time. It disturbed him that anyone had seen how the human guard died. He had thought the incident went unobserved. He had waited and planned for a long time before the right moment came along—a time when the shift was late and the guards were sleepy, and more importantly, when one guard stood alone on the ledge above the pit as a line of hod-carriers plodded past, carrying tools to the lower shafts. It seemed that ages had passed while he waited, but finally the moment came. One guard, alone on the ledge, and a line of hod-carriers.

In the shadows, Derkin had stepped aside and dropped back to the end of the line. Ahead of him were a half-dozen laden dwarves, their shoulder packs and hods filled with tools.

As always on the ledges, the guard stepped back, away from the edge, forcing the slaves to pass precariously around him. Derkin stooped carefully, picked up a large rock, and went on, toward the guard.

With little interest, the man watched the dwarves passing him. Derkin was almost to him when he saw the human's face turn away, distracted momentarily. And in that instant, the Hylar heaved his stone—not at the guard, but in a high arc toward one of the hods ahead. The stone hit the laden hod, and tools rattled from it as it tipped. The guard stepped away from the wall, peering ahead to see what had happened, and Derkin set his own hod aside, flung his ankle chain against the man's ankles, and jerked.

It was very sudden. The man toppled over the ledge, screamed, and disappeared. Derkin retrieved his hod, skipped past several dwarves who had turned toward the scream, and eased past the spilled hod where a dwarf was crouched, trying to retrieve his load.

Only seconds had passed. By the time other humans reacted to the guard's fall, Derkin was far along the line, just one of many dwarven slaves looking back at the commotion behind.

Still, he had been seen by Tap. The Neidar had witnessed everything, and so, apparently, had others. Would they tell? So far, it seemed, they had not.

"Friends?" he muttered to himself now, shaking his head. "I need no friends."

When all was quiet in the big cell, he retrieved the chisel hidden in a fold of his kilt and went to work on his shackles. It was the reason for it all—for the death of the human guard, for the fresh welts on his back and the backs of others. And it was worth it. Once before he had tried to steal a chisel, but it had been tricky. All tools were counted and accounted for.

But not this time. It was unlikely that anyone would ever know that a chisel had disappeared, among all the commotion of a spilled hod and a dead guard.

Far back in the shadows of the cell, other slaves squinted in the murk, and one—a young dwarf with the large, contemplative eyes and foxlike features of Daergar ancestry—grinned. "So that's what it was all about," he muttered.

Beside him, Tap squinted. "What is?" he whispered. "What do you see, Vin?"

"A chisel," Vin said. "The Hylar has a chisel. He's working on his shackles."

"Ah," Tap mused. "From the spilled hod. He's a lucky one, isn't he?"

"You think that was luck?" The Daergar face creased in a sly, sideways glance of reproach. "Luck had nothing to do with that. He planned that out and executed the maneuver as skillfully as a captain in the field. I think we should get to know this Hylar, Tap. I like the way he thinks."

Tap glanced around as a shadow moved nearby. "Hush," he whispered, then squinted and shrugged. It was only the old one-arm who carried the slops.

Tap returned his attention to the Daergar. "It won't be easy, getting close to that Hylar," he said. "He's a cold one. No one has ever gotten close to him that I know of. Just now, I as much as invited him to join us. I'd have gotten as much response from a wall."

"Join us? In what? We have no plan."

"But maybe he has one. He's Hylar. From Thorbardin. As I hear it, those people have no shortage of plans."

Vin scratched his whiskers thoughtfully. "Then maybe we should join *him*, whether he likes it or not. He has a chisel, but he has no hammer."

"Neither do we," Tap reminded him.

The Daergar gazed at him with ironic eyes. "No, but if that Hylar can get a chisel, I can get a hammer. Or a pry-bar or maul. Let's spread the word, Tap. Tell those with us that we wait for a signal from the Hylar. He is readying an escape."

"How do we know he's planning an escape?" Tap frowned. "Maybe he's just easing his cuffs."

The Daergar gazed at him thoughtfully, his large eyes seeming—as Daergar eyes usually did—to see right through him. "Call it a hunch," he muttered. "I know, half the dwarves here have tried to escape at one time or another. But that Hylar is the only one of us who may yet succeed. It's why he wears that heavy chain."

If Derkin was aware of their watchful eyes upon him, across the great, crowded cell, he gave no evidence of it. The chisel in his hand made almost no sound as he began the tedious cutting of rivets, driving the cutting edge of the tool methodically against the softer metal of the binds, using his free fist as a hammer.

It would take time, but he was in no hurry. In his two previous escape attempts, he had learned much of the pattern of the shafts and the terrain beyond the mines. And he had listened to the talk in the shafts. In a few weeks, they said, the next grand tour of inspection would begin.

Through the rest period he worked, pausing only to swill down a wooden bowl of slops when the old, one-armed pail tender came by. When the horns sounded, he buried his chisel in a chink in the stone floor, rubbed soot on the spots of bright metal where he had worn down the rivets, and lined up with others on his shift to file out of the cell for another day's grueling labor under the eyes of armed human guards. Each step of the way, as always, his loop of heavy chain dragged and clinked behind him. The chain was nearly eight feet long, with heavy iron links an inch and a half in diameter. It weighed almost forty pounds. Most of the slaves in the mines—certainly all of those young enough or strong enough to ever pose a threat to the human taskmasters—wore ankle cuffs and chains. But most of the bonds were smaller and lighter than Derkin's. The big, heavy chain dragging behind him was his "reward" for his second attempt to escape.

Most slaves in the mines dreamed of escape. Some, particularly among the stubborn, surly dwarves, had even tried to escape at one time or another. But rarely, if ever, did anyone try it more than once. The punishment was more severe and painful each time. Derkin's second lashing had been with a special flail, its thongs tipped with balls of lead. Such a beating would have broken the ribs of a human or an elf. It was after that beating that he had been fitted with the heavy chain.

At the end of the day's labors, after another bowl of slops, he retrieved his chisel and went back to work. Today, and tomorrow, and for as many tomorrows as it took, he would prepare for his departure from bondage.

He knew the way now, and he knew the time. He had seen the fortifications at the north end of Tharkas Pass. The time to make an escape, and possibly succeed, would be when the human delegation from Daltigoth arrived, when the masters and guards of the mine complex were preoccupied with welcoming their visiting dignitaries.

Part 1:

Master of the Pits

Klanath

Century of Rain
Decade of Cherry
Summer, Year of Copper

1

The Mines of Ergoth

The mines of Klanath, under the direction of three successive emperors of western Ergoth, had become a huge, sprawling complex of pits, shafts, and digs extending for miles along the vertiginous slopes of the peaks that rose like a wall of ranked monoliths above the deep forests to the north and west. Named for the first true emperor of the human realm of Ergoth, Klanath the Conqueror, the mines —and the entire region they commanded—had become a sizable outpost of the empire's center in far-off Daltigoth. Even before the recent discovery of rich new lodes of metallic ore in the wild mountains south of Tharkas Pass, the Klanath mines had supplied more than half of Ergoth's treasured iron, nickel, and coke, as well as copper and tin in smaller quantities. But since the discovery of the Tharkas lodes, the complex of mines had nearly doubled in size.

Sakar Kane himself had led the human forces that thronged through the pass to attack and defeat the dwarven miners at their village of Tharkas. He had claimed all of the lands south of the pass for the empire. Now the dwarves who had survived, along with thousands of others captured by slavers raiding through the mountain lands, were Lord Kane's slaves. They worked in the shafts and tunnels, the caverns and sumps, the pits and the slag heaps, the slopes and the scours.

Among the slaves were other races as well—humans, goblins, mightily bound ogres, and even a few elves. But the most numerous of the slaves, and the most prized by their masters, were dwarves. Stubborn and unrelentingly hostile, often as ready to fight among themselves as against others, the thousands of dwarves imprisoned here were a constant nuisance to the overseers. But when it came to working in mines, every dwarf was worth five of any other race. Adept at tunneling, climbing, delving, and the shaping or breaking of stone, the dwarves were natural miners.

The mountains south of Tharkas Pass were full of dwarves. Legend held that there had once been a mighty nation of dwarves there, protected by the huge, subterranean fortress called Thorbardin. But Thorbardin no longer exercised power over the mountain lands. Village after village, mine after mine, and valley after valley, the raiders had swept down in massive attacks until most of the dwarves north of the wilderness ranges were now dead or enslaved, or had simply vanished into the wilderness.

With the growth of the mines of Klanath, so had grown the population of humans there. What had been a scattering of overseers' villages and headquarters shacks had become a fair-sized city, sprawling across the flats at the north end of Tharkas Pass, and it was here that much of the empire's wealth was assembled.

Thus it was not unusual for various high personages from the emperor's court to accompany the annual visits of inspection by the Grand Master of Mines. Many of the great court had visited Klanath in the past, though usually only once. Rich they might be, but the sprawling warrens of Klanath were unsightly and reeking, lacking any of the civilities and trappings of Daltigoth, the opulent city they served.

In recent years, though, there had been changes. The changes had come with the repeated visits of Sakar Kane, the tall, brooding man who was better known as Lord Kane. Three times in as many years, Kane—a cousin of the emperor, some said—had passed through Klanath on his way to and from the conquered mining regions south of Tharkas Pass.

Since his second visit, hordes of craftsmen and slaves had worked to construct a new fortification in the midst of the spreading encampments. Now the compound of Lord Kane, dominating the north approach to Tharkas Pass, was the most formidable structure in the region. The rumors had circulated through Klanath—and even among the slaves—that Lord Kane's next visit would be permanent. It was said that he had been given command of the region—even to include authority over the Grand Master of Mines—and that Klanath would be his base.

It was whispered that the emperor intended to extend his realm eastward, maybe even as far as the elven lands of the Silvanesti. It was said that Lord Kane's authority was part of a grander plan, and that Lord Kane's fortress would serve as more than just headquarters for the empire's mines.

It was suspected that Klanath would be a stronghold for the assaults to the east, a link in a chain of conquest that would take in all of southern Ansalon.

Shalit Mileen had heard all of the rumors and had savored them. As chief of pits, Shalit Mileen was one of a dozen deputies of old Renus Sabad, the Master of Mines. One of a dozen, but in his own mind not like the others who were his peers. Most of them seemed perfectly content with their lot, each having a bit of authority in one area of Klanath, and each ready to clean the boots of old Renus, to sing his praises or fetch his tankard, to secure their positions in his favor.

Most of the operation of the mines rested with these deputies. Just as Shalit Mileen ran the soft-ore pits, giving commands and keeping records, driving his overseers to drive their slaves to increase production each year, so did each of the other deputies run an operation. Yet each season, when the high-borns came from Daltigoth, arriving in splendid entourage to inspect the emperor's resources, it was not the deputies who received them and had the honor of reporting the latest successes. No, when the inspectors came, the deputy mine masters were sent deep into their respective works. It was the Master of Mines, old Renus, who each year met with the dignitaries and humbly took full credit for all of the fine works that had been done.

Only when things went poorly did any deputy stand before the dignitaries. That was because, as Shalit Mileen had noted, when things went well it was the Master of Mines who received the credit, while if something went wrong, it was always one of the deputies who took the blame. Shalit Mileen had seen four of his peers so used in past years. Three of them now were slaves, though not in the same mines they had once ruled—a master become slave would last no time at all among the slaves who knew him. The fourth had been blamed for a cave-in that so displeased the high-borns that the man had been executed where he stood.

Rarely did the various deputies ever meet in a group, but Shalit Mileen had heard their individual comments from time to time and shaken his head in disbelief. Each deputy was, like himself, a strong, brutal man. But unlike him, the others were no better than sheep. They lacked the ambition to scheme for better positions for themselves, or the courage to make such schemes work.

All of which suited Shalit Mileen very well. He had no such lack. He had heard that there would be a new ruler in Klanath, and he intended that new ruler's favor to fall on him. One way or another, he intended to make himself look good to Lord Kane, and to make old Renus look like a fool.

If he had his way, Shalit Mileen would soon be Master of Mines and have deputies of his own.

He kept his plans to himself, trusting no one, but as the season of inspection approached he governed his pits carefully, preparing. The best ores he withheld, hoarding them in unworked shafts, waiting for the time when he could "discover" rich new lodes. He guarded the energies of his slaves, plied his overseers with the best of food and drink, bribed the captain of the guard company assigned to his pits, and stockpiled the best tools. When the inspection came, the inspectors would hear from Renus a report of hardly better than average production in the soft-ore pits. They would hear that the pits were producing, but only at quota. Then they would see a far different thing. They would see riches rising from Shalit's mines, far beyond what Renus had reported.

Renus would be shamed, maybe even suspected of stealing metals for his private use. And Shalit would make his move then. He would make his own report to the new ruler, Lord Kane.

Days passed, and Shalit busied himself at the ore pits. In this area there were four deep, wide pits, a rectangle of great scars on the slopes below Tharkas. They had begun as scour mines, where armies of slaves had worked with sledges and skids to haul away the soil overburden from the stone below, exposing veins of ore that were then mined with spike and drill. But the pits had expanded in recent months. As the veins were followed, deep tunnels had been delved downward and outward from the bottoms of the pits. Now there was a vast network of shafts deep in the mountain's underbelly, and the "pits" were only the staging areas for deeper mine operations.

The layout was well suited to slave mines. The four pits were interconnected by large tunnels, where guards and overseers went to and fro. Each pit had its own slave contingent of about two thousand, and each had a single, delved "cell" large enough to contain all of that pit's slaves. But there was only one access to the entire complex —a steep, narrow ramp that was always heavily guarded. For the slaves brought to the pits, the world lay beneath the surface. They spent their lives there and escaped only in death, when their bodies were hoisted out for disposal.

Now Shalit Mileen stalked the floors of the pits, reading his charts, checking his calculations, readying his plans. He spoke only to his overseers, but their words carried to the throngs of slaves coming and going among the shafts and were passed along in whispers.

"The pit boss is misdirecting his digs," a broad-shouldered dwarf laden with ore buckets told another. "In that seventh shaft, and in the ninth, he's hoarding the best ores from all the shafts. The sappers say there's a fortune in fine, rich ore just waiting there."

"Maybe he doesn't know what's there," the second dwarf surmised. "Or maybe the sappers lie. Maybe they're just making trouble."

"Not them," the ore carrier frowned. "Those deep-delvers are all Daergar. They might lie about what day it is, or who got what bowl at slops, but they don't lie about ore. Where mining is concerned, the Daergar are all fanatics."

"Then the pit boss is up to something," another dwarf whispered. "Maybe he wants to save the good stuff for himself."

The ore carrier shrugged and went his way, but the rumors spread, as rumors do, and at the midday break for feeding, Vin edged close to Tap. "You heard?" he whispered. "The pit boss is hoarding the best ores."

"I heard." Tap nodded. "What does it mean?"

"I think it means the inspection is coming soon." The large-eyed dark-seer squinted as he spoke. "I think the humans are plotting against one another."

"Means nothing to us," Tap said. "I'm more interested in what that Hylar is doing. I've been watching him. He's been busy with his chisel, but for the past two days he hasn't touched it. I think those rivets are gone, and he's ready to make his move."

"Ah." The dark-seer nodded. "Good timing. He's planning to break when the inspectors are here. In the confusion, he just might make it. The humans will be diverted then."

"He might succeed," Tap agreed. "One dwarf alone might slip away. But what of the rest of us?"

Vin stood silent for a moment, thinking. "With enough of a diversion, we might escape, too. Of course, such a thing could spoil all of the Hylar's plans, if he *is* planning a break as we believe."

"To rust with his plans." Tap frowned. "I tried to get him to include us. He refused. It would serve him right if we let *him* be *our* diversion."

To one side, an old, gray-bearded dwarf paused, set down the slops pail he was carrying, and wiped sweat from his brow with his only hand. Old, crippled, and slow, Calan Silvertoe no longer wore chains. He had been a mine slave as long as most there could remember, and had become as much a part of the pits as the stones themselves. He went about doing trivial jobs such as dishing

the slops for the mine slaves' meals, and hardly anyone
ever noticed him. Where his left arm had once been, now
was only a short stump, and the weathered features of his
face, where not hidden by his whiskers, were as dark and
creased as old leather.

Only the clear blue eyes squinting from what might
once have seemed a shrewd, jovial face, and the traces of
gold in his silver hair and beard, marked him as what he
had once been—a full-blooded Daewar dwarf, a person of
note. And only the sharpest of ears might have noticed the
slight traces of accent in his speech that said that this was
no hill dwarf, but one who had once been of the undermountain realm of Thorbardin.

In fact, few in Klanath had ever noticed any of that, and
it had been a very long time since anyone—master or
slave—had really noticed Calan Silvertoe at all. He went
his own way, he spoke little and stayed out of the way of
others. In many years as a slave, he had learned much. He
managed always to be busy and never to be conspicuous,
and he attracted no attention to himself. And always, he
watched and listened. And he waited.

Now, though, he suspected that his waiting was at an
end.

Inconspicuously, he made his way to one of the shadowed walls of the pit, where he hung his basket from a
peg and glanced around. No one was watching him, so
with a quick motion, he stooped, stepped into shadows,
and ducked behind an out-thrust shoulder of rough-hewn
stone. The opening there was virtually invisible. Had anyone been watching, the old dwarf would have seemed to
disappear into the stone wall.

Beyond was a shallow, dark niche, no more than a
wind-scoured hole in the porous stone, but as he hurried
into the opening, it seemed to extend ahead of him,
becoming a narrow tunnel. A few yards into the stone, the
tunnel widened, and there was faint light from a high

crevice above. A person sat cross-legged on the floor there, staring into a shallow, dark stone vessel where cloudy liquid reflected the faint light. In the dimness, it was impossible to see more of the person than the outline of the loose-fitting garment that covered him from head to toe. He could have been human, or elf, or any of a dozen other races of Ansalon. It was obvious only—in the length of his back and his shrouded arms—that he was not a dwarf.

"You have seen and heard?" Calan asked the shadowy figure.

"I have been watching," the quiet answer came.

"Do you think he is the one, then? The Hylar, I mean? Is he the destined one?"

The bowl-watcher did not look up. "He is the one," the soft voice said. "Zephyr has observed him, as I asked. The Hylar has the soul of a leader. I believe he is Harl Thrust-weight's son."

"So is the time at hand, then?"

"He intends to wait for the inspection," the hooded figure murmured. "But if he does, the others will be ready to go with him . . . or to try."

"Will they mess things up?"

"They might, but the Hylar must act now. You must help him, old one."

"Should I tell him of the others?"

"Tell him what you must," the hooded one said. "Let him know of his situation. Then get him free of these mines. As we have discussed."

"Should I tell him his destiny, Despaxas?"

The hood moved then, and the shadowed face within its folds turned toward Calan. "No person really accepts another's words regarding destiny," the low voice said. "No, he must see it for himself as time passes. But let him understand about the other slaves, that they know of his plan, and that they may endanger him."

Calan looked away, thinking he had heard sounds in the tunnel. The dim light from beyond the tunnel seemed to flutter, as if shadows were dancing in it, and there was a faint, eerie sighing. His hackles rising, the old dwarf scurried aside as something appeared in the tunnel's mouth—something that could not be seen clearly. It was a large thing, but insubstantial. It neither walked nor flew, but seemed to undulate in the air, as though swimming. It came to rest at the entrance to the cavern, settled soundlessly, and shrank as it wrapped itself in wide, transparent flaps that were more like bat-fish fins than wings.

Calan had never gotten used to the "pet shadow" that Despaxas called Zephyr. The creature appeared to have no substance at all, only a random texture of shadows that fooled the eye. It was nearly invisible, and Calan had often suspected that if he were to touch it—which he never had —he would find that there was nothing there at all. Yet, at the same time, Zephyr emanated a sense of great strength, and Calan often had the impression of long, narrow, needle-sharp teeth beneath slitted, slanted eyes.

"I wish you'd leave that thing outside when we meet," the dwarf growled. "I have nightmares for a week every time it shows up." He shook his head, grimacing, and turned toward Despaxas. But there was no one there. He turned back, and found that he was alone. Both Despaxas and his weird creature had disappeared.

"Despaxas?" the dwarf whispered, then shuddered. Few dwarves ever became comfortable with the presence of magic, and the old Daewar was no exception. "Rust," he muttered, "I wish he'd quit doing that. I don't know which is worse, his pet shadow or his vanishings."

Back at the pit, old Calan paused for a moment in the shadows, in what was once again only a shallow hole behind an outcrop, then slipped out and retrieved his slops pail. Filling his pail at the steaming caldron where sullen human slaves worked to make food from whatever scraps and leavings the guards allotted, he returned to the cells below the ore shafts and wandered among the slaves there, pausing here and there to ladle slops into bowls for those just returning from the pits. He saved the last bit of stew for the young Hylar squatting in his shadowy corner, and when he arrived there he set down his pail and made a pretense of filling the wooden bowl.

But he whispered as he lifted the ladle, "Are your shackles weakened, young Derkin? If you intend to escape, the time is now."

The Hylar glanced up, startled. "What?"

"Unless you make your escape now, tonight, many others will try to go with you. They know you intend to escape. They have decided to make you their leader and follow you. But a plan for one will fail for many."

"You speak in riddles, old one," Derkin growled. "What do you want of me?"

"I want to go with you when you leave here," the old dwarf whispered. "Just me, and no one else."

"Were I planning to leave here, I'd take no one with me."

"Oh, but you will, or never leave at all. You need me, Derkin. I can help you."

"Help me? What can you do for me?"

The old dwarf squatted beside him, tilting his pail as though to scrape out the last bit of contents. "I can help you escape. Have you seen what is beyond these pits? The defenses there? I expect you to try to slip up the ramp and escape, but you'll never make it that way."

"I don't need your help," the Hylar hissed.

"Stubborn." Calan smiled faintly. "Would you rather succeed in escaping from this place, *with* my help, or find yourself the leader of a failed mass escape by all the rest of these slaves? You will be followed, Derkin, whether you intend to be followed or not. There is little choice in such matters."

"Riddles," Derkin growled.

"I've heard it said that wisdom is in letting those help you who want to help you," the oldster said. "Accept friends, and they will serve you. Reject them, and they will use you."

Derkin glanced around, his eyes bright with sudden curiosity. "I've heard those words before. Who are you, old one?"

"I'm just an old dwarf." Calan shrugged. "But you're right. The words are not mine. I heard your father use those words, many times. So did you, I warrant."

"You knew my father?"

"I knew him, and I know you. Will you hear what I have to say, Derkin Winterseed?"

"How do you know my name?" Derkin hissed.

"I know much more than that. Will you listen?"

"I'm listening," Derkin said grudgingly.

"Then believe what I say," the old dwarf urged. "Tonight, when you are returned here, I will come to you. Be ready to leave then. I know the way past the pits."

"If you know a way out, why are you still here?"

"I've been waiting for you," the old slave said.

"Why? What do you want from me?"

"You ask too many questions for someone with no choice in the matter, Derkin Winterseed. Be ready tonight. I know a way out."

2
Escape from Klanath

In the near darkness of a nighttime cell, where the only light was dim reflection from the low wick of the guard's lamp beyond the grate, Derkin raised himself carefully from the stone floor and turned his head this way and that, listening. For more than an hour now, there had been no sounds of movement in the wide cavern. Only the breathing and occasional snores of hundreds of sleeping dwarves broke the silence.

There had been no sign of the crazy old one-arm, and Derkin half suspected that the old dwarf had either been having a joke at his expense or, more likely, had forgotten all about his promise to help him escape. Probably, he thought, the oldster was as addled as he seemed. Long years in service to humans as a mine slave might well have robbed him of his senses. And just because the old dwarf knew his name, and the identity of his father, it did not mean that he knew some secret way out of these pits.

Still, some of what the old slave had said troubled Derkin. He had sensed for some time that others among the slaves were watching him carefully. He had seen their glances in his direction as they huddled among themselves.

The old dwarf had said that other slaves knew he planned to escape, and that they intended to try to go with him. He sensed the truth of that, and it troubled him. His "plan" was hardly a plan at all. He had sabotaged the shackles on his legs—had cut the heads from their rivets so that only the curve of their iron held them in place—and now he was simply waiting for an opportunity, a moment of confusion such as the arrival of mine inspectors, to slip away from his work gang and either steal away unnoticed or, at worst, make a dash for the ramp and take his chances.

Not much of a plan, he admitted, but it was the only plan he had. One dwarf, alone, just might make it to freedom in such a way. But if others tried to follow him, they would certainly be pursued, caught, and thrown back into the pits. And he would be branded as their leader.

In the near darkness he grimaced, seeing the shadows of all the other slaves who shared the cell. He wished them no harm, but neither did they mean anything to him. They were as capable of escape as he was. If they wanted to try it, let them try it alone, as he intended. But he didn't want them messing up his chances.

The old dwarf had convinced him of one thing. He could no longer wait for an opportune time. He had to try it now, before he found himself encumbered by throngs of "followers."

For long moments, he listened to the sleeping sounds

around him. Then with a sigh of aggravation he sat upright, grasped one of his ankle cuffs with strong hands, and pried at it, his wide shoulders bulging at the effort, short, thick forearms rippling like heavy cable. For a long second, the cuff did not respond. Then, with a tiny pop, the beheaded rivet gave way, and the seam spread an inch, then another and another.

When the gap was wide enough he slipped the shackle from his ankle, moving carefully so that the attached chain would make no sound. Then he went to work on the other cuff. Vaguely, it occurred to him that he was lucky these bonds had been fashioned by humans. It would never occur to a human that a circlet of half-inch iron could be pried apart with bare hands. Few humans were strong enough to do that, and it was the nature of humans to see dwarves as inferior to themselves.

The second cuff popped quietly, then slowly opened as stubby hands nearly as hard as the iron they grasped pried its ends apart.

Breathing carefully, making no sound, Derkin got to his knees, lifted his tunic around his shoulders, and slowly, carefully wrapped the eight-foot length of chain around his waist. Its length encircled him three times, forming a cold, heavy belt of links, with enough spare to loop the shackle ends in a clumsy half-knot. With his tunic lowered, the chain was hidden.

The heavy chain and his worn chisel were the only things he had that might serve as weapons or tools, and he did not intend to leave them behind.

Standing then, he took a deep, slow breath and turned toward the closed grate at the entrance to the cell. The crossed bars of the wooden portal were silhouetted by the dim glow of a guard's light beyond. There were no guards in sight, but he knew there were at least two just beyond the grate—burly humans armed with clubs and whips, and with swords that were never out of reach. Beyond was the narrow corridor out to the open pits. There would be other guards there, but he must think of the nearest ones first. With any luck, there would be no more than two humans beyond the grate, and they might be dozing at this hour.

With his chisel in his hand, he started for the portal, moving as quietly as he could. His only idea was to some-how slip the bar that held the grated gates, get past the opening, and then, somehow, with only his hands and a worn-down chisel, silence the guards there before they could raise an alarm.

With a grunt of anger, he glanced back into the sleeping cell. Rust take you people, he thought. Why couldn't you all just leave me alone? Because of you, I must do this the hard way.

As though the air had read his mind, a quiet whisper sounded at his shoulder. "It isn't their fault," the voice murmured. "They want out just as much as you do."

At the slight sound, Derkin started, peering about.

"I'm right here beside you," the voice continued. "I told you I'd come."

It was the voice of the old, one-armed dwarf who called himself Calan. Derkin squinted in the gloom, straining to see.

"Don't worry," the voice said. "You can't see me, but I'm here. Look."

The empty air seemed to shift slightly, and a shadowy face came into view.

"How do you do that?" Derkin hissed.

"I don't exactly know," Calan admitted. "It's magic, of course. It's a sort of robe that fools the eye. I have one for you, too. How do you intend to get us out of here?"

"I thought you said you knew the way," Derkin growled.

"Oh, I do, once we're past that gate."

"Where's my . . . my magic robe?" He held out his free hand.

There was a faint rustling, and the old dwarf's shadowy features seemed to come and go. "Right here," the specter said, and Derkin felt something in his hand. He couldn't see it, but it felt like very soft fabric. Feeling foolish, he unfolded the invisible thing and draped it around himself.

"Pretty good," the voice said. "Be sure to cover your head, too. It only hides the parts it covers."

He pulled the fabric over his head, forming a cowl, and found a two-button catch with his fumbling fingers. When it was in place, he raised his arms beneath it and looked down. Indeed, it was as though he had disappeared. He could see nothing of himself.

"Your face will show, of course," the old voice whispered, "so keep your head turned away from anybody you don't want to see you. Now, let's get going."

At the grated portal, Derkin peered out. The guards were not in view, but he suspected where they were. A few yards to the left of the portal was a plank table with benches, where warders worked in the daylight hours, keeping enscrolled logs for the master of the pits. The guards would be there now, probably asleep. At least, he *hoped* they were asleep.

Bracing himself against the heavy grating of the door, Derkin reached through and grasped the hardwood bolt with both hands. The bolt was a length of sturdy, hewn post that ran through iron hasps on each side of the double grating. Slowly, flexing his shoulders, the dwarf eased the lock aside a few inches, then took new holds and eased it again. The wood made a slight, shuffling sound as it moved through its hasps, and the unseen dwarf beside Derkin whispered, "Shhh!"

Beyond the portal, someone snorted, coughed, and stirred. Derkin pulled back his hands, which were plainly visible beyond the edge of the unseen cloak. There was silence for a moment, then a chorus of snores came through the grating.

Derkin returned to the task of sliding the bar aside. As the heavy timber cleared its first hasp, it tilted, its free end falling toward the floor. But Derkin had expected that. As the bar moved he thrust his chisel through an opening, wedging the timber against the door. Beside him, Calan expelled a nervous breath and a spectral hand appeared, to wipe sweat from a ghostly face that seemed to float, unattached, in the shadows.

Derkin eased the free half of the gate open and stepped through, sensing the movement as old Calan slipped through after him. At the warders' table, a single candle guttered low in a rough holder, dimly lighting the forms of two large men asleep on the benches.

Carefully, and as soundlessly as possible, Derkin closed the gate, retrieved his chisel, and eased the bar back into its hasps. Then he turned as a snore turned to a rattling gasp. Beside the table, old Calan's head and hand seemed to float in midair. In the hand was a dagger, dripping blood. One guard lay dead, blood flowing from beneath his beard. Before Derkin could object, the old dwarf hurried around the table and cut the second guard's throat. The hand and dagger disappeared, and the old head turned, grinning. "Why did you lock the gate?" he whispered.

For a moment, Derkin merely stared at him. Then, slowly, he said, "I thought maybe nobody would notice that there's been an escape. I guess they'll notice now, though."

"What difference does it make, once we're gone?" Calan rasped.

Shaking his head, Derkin pointed toward the enclosed cell. Then, realizing that Calan couldn't see his hand, he lifted the robe and pointed again. "Because of them," he said. "They'll all be punished for this, you know. For the dead guards."

"I thought you didn't care about the rest," Calan muttered, relieving one of the dead guards of his club. "Come on, let's get out of here." He raised the cowl of his robe and disappeared from sight. "Follow me."

"How can I follow you if I can't see you?" Derkin hissed.

"Oh, rust! Here." Derkin felt a strong, cloaked hand grasp his wrist. "Here, put your hand on my shoulder, and don't lose me."

As the old dwarf led the way, Derkin pulled up his own cowl and followed. "There will be more guards up ahead," he whispered. "Do you plan to kill all of them, too?"

"Not unless I get the chance," Calan said casually.

"Reorx," Derkin muttered, still hot with anger. He couldn't think of any reason why the old dwarf should have killed those sleeping guards. The act was worse than unnecessary, it was stupid. Still, he had the impression that, whatever else Calan Silvertoe might be, he was not stupid.

The corridor turned, and ahead was its end, with the floor of the mine pit beyond. Several armed humans were at the entrance, three of them kneeling on a tattered blanket, playing bones, while others dozed or slept nearby.

"Keep your face covered," Calan whispered, slowing. On silent feet, they crept past the guards and out into the torchlit pit. The big hole was quieter than its normal daytime bedlam, but still there was activity. Ore carts still rolled from the various shafts, and small groups of slaves, watched over by human guards, worked at sorting heaps. Derkin gazed across at the steep ramp that was the only exit from the place and cursed quietly. Halfway up the ramp, a small fire had been built, and a dozen or more humans sat around it. The ramp was blocked.

"We'll never slip past that bunch," the Hylar whispered, pulling Calan to a halt. "There isn't enough room to pass."

"We're not going there," the old dwarf's voice came back. "I told you, I know a way out. A better way."

Clinging to Calan's invisible shoulder, Derkin found himself being led diagonally across the pit, toward a stone wall marked only by a hanging scrap basket beside an outcropping of rock. As they approached, though, a human guard sauntered past them, paused beside the basket, turned, and looked around, then yawned and leaned back against the outcrop.

Calan halted. "Rust!" he muttered.

"What?" Derkin asked.

"That man is in our way," the unseen voice said. "That's where we're going. There's a hole behind that thrust of stone." He paused, then said, "You wait here, Derkin. I'll draw the man away. As soon as he moves, you go to that hole and wait. I'll be right behind you." He pulled loose from Derkin's grip and was gone.

With nothing else to do, Derkin stood still, waiting. A minute passed, then another, and suddenly a howl of pain echoed around the pit. He turned in time to see a human pitch forward onto the ground, screaming. Then another fell a few feet away, and another, their screams joining the first as if in chorus. Other humans hurried toward them, and Derkin saw a wooden club materialize beside one man and lash out at him. The man fell, as the others had.

By the stone outcrop, the lounging guard stood erect, gawking at the melee out in the pit, then drew his club and hurried toward it. Keeping his invisible cloak tight around him, Derkin raced to the wall, found the shadowed hole behind the stone, and stepped into it, then stopped. "Hole?" he muttered. "There is no hole here. It's a dead end." He turned, started out of the shallow trap, and collided with something solid and invisible. Thrashing legs appeared as Calan fell backward, then disappeared again. "Watch where you're going!" his angry voice demanded. "I told you to wait here, didn't I?" A callused hand appeared and pushed Derkin back into the shadows.

"You said there was a hole here, a way to escape," Derkin rasped.

"There is!" Calan spat. "Just be quiet and hold on to my shoulder."

It was only two steps from the opening to the back of the concavity, but as they approached it, the rough stone receded, and the opening became a lengthening tunnel. "Magic!" Derkin rumbled.

"Of course it's magic," Calan said, ahead of him. "Shut up and come on. I don't like magic any more than you do."

"Then why are you using it?"

"Stop complaining. It's the only way. Come on."

The tunnel lengthened ahead of them, dim and curving, seeming totally dark, yet somehow lighted faintly by a slight, greenish glow that came from nowhere.

"I thought you weren't going to kill any more guards back there," Derkin snapped, still peeved at the seemingly senseless killings of the sleeping guards outside the cell.

"I didn't kill these," Calan snapped. "I just broke some kneecaps to make them yell. It worked. They yelled."

"How did you find this tunnel?"

"A friend showed it to me. Will you stop yammering and hurry? All this magic makes me nervous."

A few steps farther on, the tunnel widened, ending in a small cave deep within the mountain stone. The same slight, greenish glow provided just enough light to see. Calan stopped, shook free of Derkin's hand, and became visible from the feet up as he pulled off his unseen cloak. "We won't need these now," he said. "From here on there will be no one to see us."

Derkin pulled off his concealing garb and breathed deeply. As with most dwarves, the very presence of magic was offensive to him. He tossed the cloak aside, then immediately wished he had not. It might take an hour of crawling around to find the thing by touch, and, magic or not, such a thing might prove useful again.

As though reading his mind, the old Daewar rasped, "Forget about the cloaks. I told you, we won't need them anymore."

The only feature of the place was a shallow, dark bowl resting on the stone floor, and Calan approached it. Derkin followed Calan, stooping once to pick up the unseen cloak he had dropped. He could not see it, but his fingers found it. Quickly, he rolled it, thrust it under his tunic, and secured it beneath the chain wound around his waist.

The darkwood bowl contained an inch of milky liquid. Calan squatted beside it, staring into its silent, mysterious depths. Derkin glanced at the bowl, then went on past, to the back wall of the cave. With spread hands, he started exploring its surface, wondering where the next tunnel would appear.

Behind him, he heard Calan say, "Despaxas? We are here."

Derkin turned, but there was no one there except the old dwarf squatting beside the dark bowl. With a shrug, he turned back to the wall. "Where is the next tunnel?" he asked. "I can't find any . . ."

Abruptly, the stone seemed to swim before him. He felt dizzy, lightheaded, and disoriented. He closed his eyes, opened them again, blinked, and fell on his back. Overhead, stars glittered in a vast sky, and the light of a rising red moon silhouetted the branches of a tree. Not far away, precipitous slopes rose on both sides, great walls of stone climbing away toward the sky. He struggled upright, feeling slightly sick to his stomach. A few feet away, old Calan squatted on stony ground, bracing himself with his one arm and shaking his head. "Rust, but I hate that," he growled.

"What . . . what happened?" Derkin gasped. "Where are we?"

"Away from the mines," Calan said. "I told you I knew a way out." Still shaking his head, the old dwarf got to shaky feet and rubbed his belly with a gnarled hand. "What happened was a transport spell. Magicians use them sometimes."

"You're a magician?" Derkin glared at him.

"You mind your mouth," Calan snapped. "I certainly am not a magician! But Despaxas is."

"Who is Despaxas?"

Calan turned, pointing. "He is," he said.

From the shadows of a grove of conifers, a lean, cowled figure appeared. Derkin could see nothing of him but his stature and form as he strode forward. But one thing was clear: he was no dwarf.

The figure approached, lithe and graceful even in the muffling of his full robe, and Derkin squinted, trying to discern his features. Then the newcomer spoke, and his voice was rich and clear, musical as few human voices and no dwarven voices were. "Welcome to freedom, Derkin Winterseed," he said. "I am Despaxas."

"Where are we?" the Hylar demanded.

"About four miles from where you were," the hooded one said quietly. "This is Tharkas Pass. The mines of Klanath are back that way, to the north. And south of here, through the pass, lie the dwarven lands . . . or what used to be dwarven lands."

Derkin looked where the figure had pointed, then swung back. "What do you mean, 'used to be'?" he demanded.

"You think you were the only one captured by slavers in these past years?" Calan rasped. "Well, you weren't. The human emperor's soldiers hold the dwarven mines now, and the lands all the way to Sky's End. And all the miners who worked those mines are now slaves in them, just as you have been a slave in Klanath."

"I never made it that far," Derkin said grimly. "We were attacked on the road south of the Tharkas mines by human raiders. My escorts were all killed. Only one survived with me, and he died of his wounds before they got us to Klanath."

"Those were no raiders," the hooded one said. "Those were scouts for the assault force that invaded Kal-Thax and took over the Tharkas mines. Only a very few dwarves survived that assault, got away, and made it to Thorbardin."

"Then the alarm was spread?"

"It was," the cowled one said sadly. "But no one came. The tribes were at war again within Thorbardin, and no one thought it important to defend the mines outside the undermountain realm."

"Gods," Derkin whispered, realizing the enormity of what he had just heard. Since his capture, Kal-Thax had been invaded by humans. And now the humans ruled the northern ranges. "And what of Thorbardin now?" he asked.

"It stands," the figure assured him. "There are reports that some order has been restored, at least temporarily. But still there is no help for these northern realms."

Again Derkin squinted, peering into the shadows of the cowl. "Who are you?" he demanded. "What do you want of me, and how do you know all this?"

With an eloquent shrug, Despaxas reached up and pulled back his cowl, dropping it to his shoulders. Rising moonlight revealed a chiseled, serious face with long, lustrous hair and no beard. It was a faintly ironic face, but the smile on it was as innocent as a child's. It was a face almost—but not exactly—human.

"You're an elf!" Derkin said.

"Of course I am," Despaxas admitted. "My mother was a good friend of an ancestor of yours. She admired him, in a way. Look here." The elf knelt and brushed back gravel and dust with a graceful hand. Beneath was a glint of iron. "This is a claim spike, Derkin. A long time ago, it was driven here to mark the boundary of the dwarven lands.

My mother was here when that was done. The person who set the spike was named Cale Greeneye. His sister was your great-great . . . well, several greats, grandmother."

"And your mother was alive then?"

"Yes. She still is. Her name is Eloeth. It was her idea, frankly, that I should come and find you."

"Why?" Derkin frowned up at the innocent, ironic face. His frown became a startled stare as his eyes shifted. Behind the elf, only a few feet away, *something* was watching . . . something he could barely see. As he stared, the creature seemed to unwrap itself, unfurling wide, shadowy appendages that seemed to ripple in the shadows. Undulating gracefully, it rose silently, then turned and glided away, disappearing from sight.

Derkin stared after it. "What in the name of corrosion was that?" he hissed.

"I call him Zephyr," Despaxas said. "He's a verger."

"A what?"

"Verger," the elf repeated. "It means he doesn't exactly exist in this world, but he isn't exactly out of it, either."

"It's Despaxas's pet shadow," Calan Silvertoe rumbled. "It follows him around. Ugly, isn't it? I mean, what you can see of it."

"Zephyr doesn't see you any better than you see him, Calan," the elf said softly. "He probably doesn't see your body at all. What he does see, though, is your soul."

Derkin stared at the elf, then at the empty night where the almost-creature had gone. "That thing looks at souls?" he growled. "Why?"

"So he can tell me what he sees there," the elf said. "Zephyr is my friend."

Derkin shook his head in amazement. There was something he had meant to ask these odd people—something about his escape from the mines—but for the life of him he couldn't remember what it was.

3
The Reluctant Leader

From a high, cold pinnacle of stone, two dwarves and an elf looked down upon a scene of desolation, and Derkin Winterseed felt a hard, stubborn anger begin to grow within him. They were south of Tharkas Pass, and the steep ranges below—just now touched by morning sun—were the region of the Tharkas mines. Once a rich, productive cluster of hard-ore shafts, the mines had been carefully developed over a span of more than two centuries by the dwarves of Kal-Thax. Originally delved by Daergar experts from Thorbardin, the mines had proven immensely productive, yielding the highest grade of precious iron ore any of them had ever seen.

Once before, when he was very young, Derkin had seen the Tharkas mines, and he well recalled the busy, bustling slopes where hundreds of Neidar worked the shafts and the mills, the scours and the seines, preparing top-grade ore for transport to Thorbardin for processing in the great smelters deep within the mountain fortress. It had been a happy scene, as the Hylar remembered it. Everywhere he had looked there were hundreds of bustling dwarves laboring in relative harmony, doing what dwarves most enjoyed—working for their own purposes.

But the scene now was different. Where there had once been neat, orderly ore dumps and the methodical ring of hammers and drills, a sound as musical as dwarven drums echoing among the mountains, now there was an ugliness about the entire area. Everything seemed discordant. Slag flows ran here and there at random, the ore heaps were messy hills of ill-sorted stone, and the ring of hammers and drills had no rhythm to it, only the heedless clatter of slaves at labor. Even without the companies of armed humans that roved the area, it would have been obvious to any dwarf that these were no longer dwarven works. Everywhere, the thoughtless sloppiness of human mining methods was obvious.

Here was proof of what every dwarf knew—humans were poor miners at best, and even the skills of dwarven slaves could not improve their methods. Unlike dwarves, humans found no harmony with their enterprises. They didn't work their mines as dwarves did, cooperating with the stone to ease its riches from it. Instead, humans fought the mines, as one would fight an enemy. They fought the mines, fought the ores, and fought the very mountains that provided their riches. The human concept of mining, to most dwarves, was like the human concept of most things: take what you want any way you can, usually by brute force. The scene below the pinnacle seemed proof of that. The few cabins and sheds below the mines—three of the buildings were the remains of what had once been a pleasant Neidar village—now looked run-down and unused. It was obvious that the shelters now served only as sleeping quarters for the human conquerors. Even from the pinnacle, one could see the dejected weariness of the few dwarven women working around what had once been a handsome longhouse. Like the dwarves in the mines, the females too were slaves, kept by the humans to cook and clean for them.

The only other habitation visible, as far as they could see, was a small, distant campsite farther along the mountainside, beside a pretty lake that Derkin remembered from his childhood. The lake was a reservoir, built ages ago by dwarven craftsmen. A long, curving stone dam contained the flow of several mountain streams, channeling it slowly into a series of walled canals that wound along the slopes.

This system had once provided reliable water for the entire Tharkas region. But that had been in the golden times of Thorbardin, the days of the great Road of Passage, when people of all races and nations traveled between southern Ergoth and the northern lands, along a route maintained jointly by the dwarves of Kal-Thax and the knightly orders of human Ergoth.

Those times were gone now. The old road had fallen into disuse, and parts of it had been obliterated. And while the mountainside reservoir remained, its channels were choked with clutter and debris. The lake remained, but it no longer served dwarven villages and farms.

Squinting, Derkin tried to make out who was camping there now, and Calan said, "Those are humans over there. Nomads from the plains. See how they avoid the empire soldiers at the mines? They come and go, passing through, but most plains people have no use for the emperor."

Scowling, Derkin stared down again at the sad scene below and cursed beneath his breath. Then he turned to the hooded elf who had led him here. "Two years?" he demanded. "They have made this much ruin in just two years?"

"They would have done the same to Thorbardin itself," the elf replied, "but they couldn't get in. Lord Kane sent an assault force south to test Northgate. Zephyr observed them for me. The humans finally gave up and came back. They never got past Thorbardin's outer defenses. But they do hold the mines, and have been stockpiling ore for nearly a year to send through the pass to Klanath."

"But why hasn't Thorbardin sent troops to drive them out?"

"What troops?" old Calan Silvertoe rasped. "You have been in Thorbardin since I have, young Hylar. How long has it been since the thanes within stopped their feuding long enough to send a force outside?"

"My father restored order in Thorbardin!" Derkin snapped.

"Yes, of course," the old one sneered. "And the Hylar Peace lasted slightly longer than your father did. Then, as you know better than I, they started at it again, Theiwar against Daewar, Daergar fending off Klar, the Hylar holed up and pouting in their Life Tree. . . ."

"I know," Derkin rumbled. "That was why I left Thorbardin. But I didn't know they had turned their backs on the outside lands."

"Well, they did." Calan's frown was as fierce as Derkin's. "And without Thorbardin's troops, the world outside fell into the hands of . . . humans!" Disdainfully, the old dwarf pointed downward, his single hand a rigid arrow of accusation, pointing out shame.

"Rust and corruption," Derkin muttered.

Behind him, Calan whispered to the elf, "He reminds me of his father when he looks like that."

"He will need to be as strong as his father," Despaxas replied.

Derkin whirled on them, turning his back on the sad scene below. "It's high time somebody put a stop to that atrocity," he said. "Humans don't belong in Kal-Thax. This land is for dwarves."

"I couldn't agree more," the elf said sympathetically.

"One would need an army to reclaim this territory," Calan pointed out.

"Then I'll go to Thorbardin myself and bring back an army," Derkin snapped.

"What army?" Calan shook his head. "We've kept abreast of what's going on in Thorbardin. There is no army. Just a bunch of bickering clans barely kept in check by Jeron Redleather and Dunbarth Ironthumb, with every reliable follower they have working to police the undermountain. Nobody is coming from there to help. Not until the time comes when Thorbardin has a real leader again, like in the old days."

"There *is* an army," Despaxas said softly. "At least, there could be. But you won't find it in Thorbardin."

Derkin frowned at the elf, hard Hylar eyes seeming to pierce him. "Where, then?"

"Back there." The elf gestured northward. "Back where you just came from. The humans have a few hundred dwarves working these mines south of the pass, but there are nearly eight thousand dwarven slaves in all laboring in Klanath. They would make quite an army if they had the right leader."

"You're crazy," Derkin snapped. "I'm free of there. I'm not going back."

"That's too bad," Calan said. "You know, those pit slaves back there are going to pay dearly for the two guards who died so unfortunately when we . . ."

"You murdered those men yourself!" Derkin spat. "You cut their throats gleefully, and now you're worrying about who will be blamed?"

The elf pulled his cowl forward, hiding the slight smile

that pulled at his cheeks. "It was *your* escape, Derkin. Do you want to be responsible for the misery that will befall all those innocent dwarves?"

Derkin stood silent for a moment, looking from one to the other of his odd companions. Then his eyes narrowed. Glaring at Calan Silvertoe, he said, "I wondered why you killed those guards. It seemed a needless, senseless thing to do. But you had a reason, didn't you, Daewar? I should have known. A Daewar always has a reason."

"You're Hylar," Calan said, "and whatever else they might be, the Hylar do have strong notions of chivalry and honor."

"And a strong distaste for manipulation," Derkin snapped. "I see it now. You planned it all out, the two of you. You want something from me. What is it?"

"We want the same thing you want," Despaxas said softly. "We want to drive Lord Kane's human invaders out of Kal-Thax and reestablish the boundary in the pass. To do that will require an army. An army of dwarves. We want you to mold that army and lead it."

"Why me?"

"Because you can," the elf said. "Zephyr has read your soul, and we know your lineage. We know quite a lot about you, Derkin Winterseed. We have studied you for nearly a year."

Derkin glared at him. "Why?"

"Have you ever heard of an elf named Kith-Kanan?"

"Not that I remember. Why?"

"Kith-Kanan is a friend of my mother, Eloeth," Despaxas said. "Kith-Kanan has been concerned about the human emperor, Quivalin Soth, whose soul is the darkest Zephyr has ever seen. Kith-Kanan asked Eloeth for advice about Kal-Thax, because Klanath is so near to Kal-Thax and because Eloeth has dealt with dwarves. She, in turn, asked me to help, and I asked Calan, because he is my friend. He lost that arm saving my life nearly two hundred years ago."

"That's fine." Derkin glared at the elf. "But it doesn't answer my question. Why all the interest in me?"

"Because of what we have learned about you." Despaxas shrugged. "You are the direct descendant of Colin Stonetooth, who brought the dwarven thanes together when no one else could. You are also descended from Damon Omenborn, who was foretold to be the father of kings. You are kin of Cale Greeneye, and descendant of Willen Ironmaul, who led armies. You are the son of King Hal-Thwait of Thorbardin. . . ."

"His name was Harl Thrustweight, and he was never king!" Derkin said angrily. "Thorbardin has no king!"

"Oh, we know that," the elf assured him. "But it is a useful fiction for the outside world to believe. But you, Derkin Winterseed, you have the blood and the soul of mighty leaders, and those around you recognize that, whether they realize it or not. The slaves of Klanath will follow you. Some of them had decided to follow you already, even if you didn't want them to."

"This whole thing is preposterous!" Derkin growled. He glared at Calan Silvertoe. "You yourself told me that the slaves could not escape from the pits en masse. You said such a thing would never work."

"Not an escape from inside." The old dwarf shrugged. "But an assault from outside, that's another thing."

"An assault? By the three of us, I suppose? It would take hundreds of fighters just to get in, not to mention getting out again."

Calan shrugged again, stepped to the south ledge of the pinnacle, and pointed downward. "There are hundreds of dwarves down there, Derkin. And not nearly so many humans to contend with as across the pass at Klanath."

Again Derkin stared at the two of them, first one and then the other, the one-armed old Daewar and the lithe, hooded elf.

"First mold an army, then lead it," Despaxas coaxed. "There is a great deal of difference between a mob of unruly dwarves—escaped slaves or whatever—and a dwarven army. Your Hylar ancestors proved that very well, in a time my mother remembers."

Derkin stepped directly in front of the elf and reached up—the elf was nearly a foot taller than he was—to fling back the shadowing cowl. "What's in this for you?" he demanded. "Skip the part about Kith-Kanan and Eloeth. You're no dwarf, and neither are they. Why do elves care about the dwarven lands?"

Despaxas gazed at him with level eyes. "A fair question," he said. "Lord Kane and his mine claimers are your problem, not ours. But the emperor, whom Lord Kane serves, has vast ambitions. Already he is moving forces onto the plains east of here, and beyond those plains lie elven lands. There will be war between the humans of Ergoth and the elves of Silvanesti, Derkin. It cannot be avoided. It will come, very soon. And it will be a long, hard war."

"It isn't our war," Derkin pointed out.

"In a way, it is," the elf told him. "The emperor will use Klanath as a base to equip and reinforce his human hordes against the elves, and we may be conquered because of it. Then Lord Kane's reward from the human emperor will be the dwarven lands."

"I see," Derkin breathed. "So to disrupt the humans' supply lines, you plan a backfire here, using a dwarven army for your purposes."

"For *your* purposes," Despaxas said. "Which will serve ours as well."

"Devious," Derkin sneered. "Devious, but . . . well, maybe it makes sense, after a fashion."

"Thank you," the elf said. "My mother will be pleased that you approve."

"Approving is one thing," old Calan snorted. "Agreeing is something else. Do you agree to go along with this, Derkin?"

"I don't know," the Hylar said slowly. "What would I have to do first?"

"Get into the dwarven mines down there, organize the dwarves, get rid of the humans—there is only one foot company and a dozen or so slave tenders—then train the dwarves as an assault force and march on Klanath."

"Oh, is that all?" Derkin's chuckle was cold and ironic. "And exactly how do I do all that?"

"That's up to you," the old dwarf said. "You're the leader."

"And while all this is going on, what's happening at Klanath?"

Despaxas pulled up his cowl again, covering his head. "A diversion has been arranged there," he said emphatically. "It should keep everyone occupied for a time."

* * * * *

Dawn's light had not yet touched the soft-ore pits of Klanath when the husky, broad-shouldered slave named Tap Tolec came awake to the tug of a hand at his shoulder. It was nearly pitch-dark in the great, reeking cell, but he knew the whisper at his ear. It was the Daergar, Vin the Shadow. Tap groaned and turned his head, trying to see. "Vin?" he muttered. "Is that you? Let go. I'm awake. What's the matter?"

"Look at this," Vin whispered. He sounded urgent, excited.

"Look at what?" Tap grumped. "My eyes aren't like yours. I have to have a little light to see."

Impatiently, Vin grabbed the Theiwar's hand and thrust something into it. Even in the dark, Tap recognized the heft of a stout hammer. He sat up, exploring the tool with his fingers. "You got it!" he whispered. "How did you manage that?"

"I didn't manage," Vin said. "I just woke up and . . . well, see for yourself!"

Vin scuttled away from him, and Tap heard sounds like someone rummaging through a tool trove. Around them, other dwarves stirred and began to awaken. Nearby, someone—obviously another Daergar miner—muttered, "Wow! Look at that!"

"What?" someone else whispered. "What do you see?"

Then there was a quick series of rasping noises, accompanied by tiny flashes of dim light. Tinder glowed in a leathery palm, was breathed aflame, and those nearby saw Vin the Shadow raising a freshly lit candle. "There," he said. "Now you can see. Look!"

Tap stared, his eyes going wide. All around him, other dwarven slaves rubbed sleepy eyes and gawked at what Vin indicated. On the floor of the cell, in a random cluster as though someone had just dumped it there, was a large pile of implements, and more and more gasps sounded as more and more slaves realized what they were seeing. Hammers and axes were there, steel-tipped javelins and gleaming swords, maces and daggers, goblin-fashioned crossbows with bales of deadly bolts, even a few elven-style bows of lacquered lemonwood and sheaths of fletched arrows. The candle's light danced on myriad deadly shapes and surfaces.

Behind the piled weapons, shadowed by the stack, were bits of armor of numerous kinds and designs, shields and chest-plates, various kinds of helmets, leather-slung caplets and braces—it looked as though someone had foraged hurriedly through a used-armor bazaar and picked up a little of everything. And farther back in the shadowed recess were bales and kegs. Vin gazed at these, and his large eyes went narrow. "See the markings there," he said. "Those come from the mine master's stores."

Vin's attention was on something else, though. Just in

front of the pile of weapons, a small, shallow bowl of dark wood rested on the stone floor. He crept closer and looked into it. In the bowl was a bit of milky liquid that seemed to glow as he stared at it, a dim, greenish light. "What's . . ." he began, then flinched as a voice came from the bowl—a quiet, musical voice.

"Arm yourselves," the milky liquid said. "Barricade the grating and fortify the cell. Break your chains and defend your gate at all costs. Arm yourselves and hold the cell . . . hold the cell. . . ."

A thick-bearded dwarf peered into the bowl skeptically. He stirred the liquid, to no apparent effect. "That's crazy," he growled. "We can't hold out here, in this cell."

Nearby, a gnarled dwarf with deep scars on his back and only one eye hoisted a sword and picked up a shield. "To blazes with talking bowls," he rasped. "Let's get these chains off and go kill some slavers."

A low thunder of approval began, then subsided quickly as they realized that their voices could carry to the guards outside.

"First things first," a burly slave rasped quietly. "Some of us can watch the gate, while the rest get free of their chains. Then when we're ready, we can . . ."

"Hold the cell," the musical voice coming from the bowl repeated urgently. "Beyond the cell lies death. Hold the cell."

"Tarnish that," someone snorted, a bit surprised to be talking to a bowl of what seemed to be milk. "How long can we hole up in a cell with no way out? The humans wouldn't have to come in after us. They could just wait until we starve. Or bury us alive in here."

"Hold the cell," the voice repeated, flowing over them like music. "Help is on the way. One comes who will lead you out. Arm yourselves, barricade the gate, and hold the cell. . . ."

The greenish light dimmed, and the voice was gone. In

the cavern cell now was only momentary silence and the flickering light of Vin's candle outlining the faces of hundreds of dwarves, some of them suspicious, all of them grim.

Suddenly there was other light—dim, dancing beams from lanterns beyond the cell grating—and the unmistakable sounds of human guards in the corridor beyond. Within, hundreds of dwarves listened in breathless silence.

The silence lasted only a moment. In the corridor a human voice said, "Here, you two! Wake up! It's time for the . . . What's this?"

"They're dead," another human voice said. "Both of them. Their throats have been cut! Sound the alarm!"

Weapons rattled, a trumpet blared, and there was the sound of hurrying feet, distant but approaching.

As one, the dwarves in the cell crowded toward the gate. "What nitwit killed the night guards?" Vin the Shadow rasped. "Now they'll all be on us before we can gather our wits."

"Maybe it was whoever brought all this stuff in here," Tap Tolec suggested.

"Nobody 'brought' it here," Vin said. "It came by magic. That bowl proves that."

"I never saw magic," someone else said.

"I don't *trust* magic," another said.

Beyond the grated gate, a lamp was raised. Its light danced through the bars, a moving pattern on the solid mass of dwarves crowding forward. A human voice shouted, "Here, you dinks! Get back there. Get away from this gate!"

"Nobody in here killed the guards," Tap Tolec told Vin the Shadow. "See, the bar is in place. The gate is still locked."

Those in the fore continued to crowd toward the grating, curious and pressed by those behind them. Beyond the grate, the human shouted again, and a spear flicked through the bars, threatening the mob inside. But before its tip could reach anyone, a muscular hand grasped the shaft, and a short, stout arm lifted and pulled. The human beyond was jerked up against the grating, and froze there as a sword flashed through the bars, skewering him from belly to brisket. The man screamed, hung for a moment where he was, then dropped to the stone floor as the sword was withdrawn.

Within the cell, a dwarf—the one-eyed slave with the deep scars on his back—wiped his sword blade on his tunic and rasped, "That's one."

Then the corridor was full of armed humans and bright lamps, and the dwarves in the cell backed away from the gate.

"Quick!" Vin the Shadow barked. "Don't let them free that bar!"

Spears and narrow pikes licked through the grating of the portal, and human hands grasped the gate bar, starting to slide it aside. It moved only an inch before a hail of arrows and crossbow bolts from within the cell tore into the humans beyond. Men screamed, men fell, and men fled. Crazy shadows danced in the suddenly deserted corridor, where fallen lamps flickered on the floor.

"Well, that's that," Tap Tolec breathed. "But they'll be back. What do we do now?"

"Barricade the gate!" a dozen voices chimed.

"Break it down and attack the pits!" other voices shouted.

"Kill humans!" several suggested.

"Hold it!" someone roared. "Whatever we do, we'd better all do it together. Who's in charge here?"

"Not me," a dozen voices answered together.

"Well," a querulous voice came from the crowd, "somebody's got to take the lead. Who's it going to be?"

"Don't look at me," the one-eyed dwarf snapped at several others around him. "I can fight, but I'm no leader."

"The Hylar!" Tap Tolec said, with sudden inspiration. "Where's that Hylar? He can lead us!"

It took several minutes for all of them to realize that the Hylar, the one they knew only as Derkin, was no longer among them, and when that became clear, the cell was quieter than it had been. For a moment, every dwarf there had envisioned a grand victory—fighting dwarves cutting a path through masses of humans, winning their way to freedom. The way it might have been in the old, great days that the lore spoke of. Dwarven fury overwhelming, overcoming desperate odds . . . led by a Hylar chief.

But only for a moment had the vision lasted. Now there was only reality. They had—from where or what infernal magic no one knew—arms and some supplies. But they still were only a gang of slaves, trapped in a stone cell, and outside were the slave masters, backed by hundreds, or maybe thousands, of human warriors. They were trapped here like rats in a barrel, and the humans could come for them at their pleasure.

"I guess we'd better do what that bowl said," Vin the Shadow said bleakly. "Barricade the cell, hold the gate, and wait for reinforcements."

4
Assault in Small Force

Despaxas had gone off someplace. One minute he was there, the next he was gone, and when Derkin asked Calan Silvertoe where the elf was, the one-armed Daewar simply shrugged and waved a careless hand. "He comes and goes as he pleases," he said. "I don't try to keep up with him."

"That shadow thing is gone, too," Derkin noted.

"Zephyr?" Calan shuddered. "That thing is hardly ever around, but even now and then is too much."

"Is it dangerous?"

"Despaxas says it isn't," Calan said. "But I don't like it, anyway. I was with him the day he . . . called it up. He was fooling with little spells, just sort of practicing his magic, and all of a sudden there was that thing, right there with us. Despaxas says it wasn't really there. He says its actual body is in some other plane—whatever that means. He thinks one of his spells got tangled up with somebody else's spell in that other place, and Zephyr wound up stuck halfway between. So the elf made a pet of it . . . or of the part of it that's here. I guess it's harmless. I just don't like magic, and I don't like things that look like bat-fish shadows."

The two dwarves passed the hours of daylight in a small, deep cove high on a mountainside. There was a little, crystal-cold spring there, and game trails all around, but Derkin lay in wait beside the spring for more than an hour, festooned in shrubbery and pretending to be a bush, before anything edible showed up. Had he been armed with a sling, or even a throwing-axe or javelin, he would have hunted the trails for a deer, wild hog, or even a small bear. But all he had at hand was a stout stick, so he waited in ambush and settled for a brace of rabbits.

Calan had a little fire going in a deep glade, and while they cooked their dinner, the old Daewar told Derkin—in exquisite detail—of the habits and routines of the humans who ruled the Tharkas mines. The foot company of soldiers numbered eighteen, the slave masters and warders an even dozen, and only one shaft was being worked. It was worked through the daylight hours, by several hundred dwarves divided into small groups. The shaft entrance was guarded, and only a few dwarves were allowed out at any one time. These carried the best ores outside, for stocking.

Each night, the shaft was sealed with all the slaves inside, while the soldiers stood guard in three six-man shifts.

Derkin was astounded that the old dwarf, who had been a slave himself in a distant pit mine until the night before, could know so much detail about this place. But as with all subjects, Calan Silvertoe said just what he intended to say, explained what he intended to explain, and refused to comment on how he knew.

The longhouse was just what it seemed, Calan said. Once the central hall of a thriving dwarven community, now it served as kitchen and washhouse, and as quarters for the female dwarves who worked in it as slaves.

By the time the sun was sinking behind the western peaks, Derkin had a clear, detailed picture of the movements and habits of the humans below, and only one remaining question.

"How do they control the slaves inside the shaft?" he asked. "If only the mine masters enter there, and never the guards, what's to keep the dwarves below from simply ganging up on the slavers and killing them?"

"I'm not sure," Calan admitted. "Maybe it's the goblins."

"What goblins?"

"Well, when Lord Kane's troops first came here to take control, there was a company of goblins with them. When the area was secured, and the attack force left, the goblins weren't with them. And they haven't been seen since. So maybe they're in the mine shaft. Goblins are right at home underground. Maybe the humans hired them, and left them there as enforcers."

"Wonderful," Derkin rumbled, suppressing a shiver. If there was one thing most dwarves detested more than magic, it was goblins. "Goblins in the mine," he muttered. "As if things weren't complicated enough."

By last light of evening, Derkin lay concealed just above the mine camp, watching the closing of the shaft and the positioning of the guards. It was just as Calan had said. Food was brought from the longhouse, then six armed humans remained outside, taking up positions in a wide arc around the mine yards, while the rest retired to a pair of old dwarven cabins to sleep.

Those on guard made no fires, and Derkin realized that they would have light enough to see soon. Within an hour, at least one of Krynn's moons would be in the clear sky, and the humans felt no need of firelight.

The positioning of the guards indicated that the men did not expect trouble, and certainly not from beyond their perimeter. They had placed themselves to watch the mine and the buildings, not to watch the surrounding wilderness. A slight, cold smile tugged at the Hylar's whiskered cheeks.

"How you do this is up to you," the old Daewar had told him, shrugging as though he hadn't the slightest interest in what came next.

"Then how I do it is my way, and mine alone," he had snapped. He had left Calan dozing beside the little spring, and was glad that he had. He had no need of anyone as unpredictable as Calan Silvertoe.

His plan was a simple one—take out as many guards as he could, as quietly as he could, then open the mine shaft and somehow free the dwarves within. If there were also goblins in there . . . well, he didn't know where they were or what they might do, so there was nothing to be gained by worrying about them.

He carried one weapon at hand—a stout, hardwood stick four feet long, sharpened at both ends. It was as near to a delver's javelin as he could improvise. In Thorbardin, Derkin had once prided himself on his skill with the working javelin.

In deep dusk, he crept to the first of the guard positions and peered around. By last good light, he had seen a human guard seat himself beside a fallen tree, leaning back against the trunk. At that moment, he had selected this one as his first target.

Derkin came up behind the man, soundless feet sure on the mountain slope. He was almost within arm's reach when the human heard or sensed something. The man started to turn, started to rise, but it was too late. With a lunge, Derkin flung himself across the tree trunk, thrust his javelin over the man's head, and snapped it back, under his chin. Gripping the shaft with both hands, Derkin heaved back. The man gurgled; his feet drummed the ground. Then his neck snapped, and he lay limp.

Derkin relieved the man of a dagger, leaving his other weapons where they lay. The bow and arrows and the awkward, light-bladed human sword weren't worth carrying around.

The second guard was harder to get to. This man was in a narrow, upright cleft of rock, hidden from both sides. The dwarf could have charged in on him, and finished him with a thrust of his javelin, but the chance of a silent kill in that manner was nil. The man would have time to shout or scream before he died.

For a moment, Derkin puzzled over it, then he crept up beside the cleft, remaining just out of sight. When he was near enough to hear the human breathing, he drew his dagger and tossed it onto the sloping ground just outside the cleft. It landed with a little thud, and lay glinting in the starlight.

In the cleft, the human stirred, muttered something to himself, and stepped forward, squinting. Another step, and he was out of the cleft, bending over, reaching for the dagger. He never heard the quick whir of Derkin's javelin as it lashed downward, its stout staff colliding with the exposed base of his skull. The man staggered, pitched forward, and Derkin thrust one of the sharpened ends of the staff into his throat, cutting off a strangled scream before it began.

He retrieved his dagger, relieved the guard of what he had already decided he wanted—a bronze-headed belt mace—and went on. The third guard, he knew, wore no helmet.

Five of the guards lay dead, and Derkin was stalking

number six, when he froze in his tracks. Nearby, someone or something had moved, a slight rustling of brush. Motionless, he waited, and again heard the slightest of sounds. Just off to his left, someone else was creeping stealthily toward the position of the dozing guard.

A deep scowl lowered Derkin's brows as he mouthed silent curses. "Calan," he whispered to himself, "if you mess this up for me, I swear I'll brain you."

* * * * *

In the dark of evening, when the ore slopes were quiet and cool breezes drifted through the mountains, Helta Graywood slipped out of the dusty, suffocating grain loft, down the narrow ladder to the floor of the longhouse, and padded across on small, bare feet to the rear door, staying in shadows in case any human outside might happen to glance through the broken shutters of a window. Around the dimly lit main room, several dwarf women sat on benches or lay on makeshift cots, resting from the day's labors. Some of them glanced at Helta as she passed, and the nearest one—a gray-haired matron with deep creases around her eyes—said, "Stay close, Helta. There will be bright moonlight tonight."

The girl paused. "I'll be careful, Nadeen," she said. "But I do need some fresh air."

Nadeen nodded, understanding. The grain loft was never a pleasant place to work, even under the best of circumstances. Close and stifling, the little chamber above the kitchen was always dusty, always hot, and always reeked of the acrid odor of decaying grain. And now, with the redoubled supplies the human invaders had brought in, the place was nearly unbearable.

Helta Graywood was the youngest of the female slaves kept at the mining compound. She was hardly more than a girl, and strikingly featured, with a face that combined the soft, delicate lines of Daewar ancestry with the wide-set, slightly slanted eyes and dark, lustrous hair of a Hylar grandfather. Generally speaking, human males had little interest in dwarven women, finding them sometimes amusing but rarely attractive. It was the judgment of the women of the longhouse, though, that Helta Graywood might be an exception. And that being the case, it was best to keep her out of sight of the humans in the compound.

Thus it had become Helta's lot to be permanent warder of the grain loft, ever since the human invaders had come. It was the one place available to them that no human was likely to go.

Helta spent her days in the loft without complaint. But sometimes, after a day when the sun on the loft roof had made the space inside seem like an oven, it became just too much. Some evenings, she simply had to go outside for a time, just to feel the breezes and breathe the clean, scented mountain air.

Now the mine shaft had been sealed, the night guards were out on the perimeter, and all of the other humans had gone to their bunks. Helta peered out the back door, looked this way and that, listened carefully, then slipped out and closed the door behind her.

There would be an early moonrise, but right now it was dark outside, the only light a faint, frosty glow from the stars in the ebony sky. For a time, Helta simply stood and breathed, enjoying the cool, clean air. Then, as was her habit on these forays, she walked. The exercise felt good, and she had long since figured out the limits of the area hidden from the night guards' positions by the longhouse. Captive dwarves were not allowed outside after sundown, but as long as she remained hidden from view, she felt fairly safe.

As she walked, pacing back and forth the length of the building, she thought melancholy thoughts of the family she would never see again—her father dead at the hands of human invaders, her mother and sisters led away for sale at some slave market in the human lands. The humans had come through the pass in force, a surprise attack that was cruel and bloody.

For a time, armies of humans had swept the lands all around. All the able male dwarves had been taken into the main shaft or herded north toward the human mines at Klanath. The old and disabled among the captives had simply disappeared, and most of the women and children had been taken away. Then the armies had gone, but still there were the guards and the overseers.

Helta dreamed lonely fantasies about sneaking away, breaking free, and getting even. Every day and night for the past two years, she had dreamed such dreams. She dreamed of escape, but more often she dreamed of bashing human skulls, of poisoning human beverages, of somehow—through some elaborate combination of craft and luck—stampeding every human in the region over a cliff, or something equally satisfying.

The thoughts were only silly fancies, but they gave her something to think about besides the never-ending drudgery and fear of life in bondage.

And sometimes she dreamed of a hero, of someone who would come marching in and lay waste to the entire human population. She envisioned a sturdy young dwarf brandishing a sword or an axe or something equally lethal, who would challenge the humans, then take them all on at once and kill every last one of them in battle, without ever ruffling his beard. She even imagined how he would look. He would wear exquisite polished armor, his helmet would be studded with gems, and his eyes would glow with strength and courage.

He would look like those old paintings she had once seen at a Neidar fair, of the magnificent Hylar warriors of the old days—back when the dwarves ruled all of Kal-Thax, and legendary Thorbardin was in its golden era.

She had never seen Thorbardin. Nobody she knew ever had. But still there were the legends, of a time when the Hylar came from the east to unite the warring tribes into a great nation and to build a mighty fortress beneath a mountain summit.

Helta paced, waving her arms back and forth, getting the kinks out of her small, sturdy frame, and letting the cool breeze cleanse her lungs and caress her face. Near the longhouse was the shed where the human masters kept their equipment, and she was tempted to slip in there again—as she had in the past—to look for weapons. But moonrise was near, and she would risk being seen. Besides, she had never found anything useful in the shed, just big coils of rope and cable, racks of heavy planking, and a row of winches and braces.

A hint of moonrise was touching the sky above the eastern peaks when she decided it was time to go back inside. She turned toward the longhouse door, then paused, listening. It seemed to her that she had heard voices, somewhere near. She listened, then decided it must be some of the humans snoring in the two cabins they used as barracks. She reached for the latch and heard something else—very clearly. A gasp, scuffling sounds, and a thud. Then, again, low masculine voices as though in fierce but quiet argument.

Curious, she crept to the corner of the longhouse and looked beyond. There in the starlight, in plain sight of the guard posts, stood two shadowy figures—a dwarf and a tall man. And they were obviously arguing.

Though their voices were only hushed whispers and angry mutterings, their gestures were plain. The dwarf pointed an angry finger at the man and muttered something, and the man threw out his hands in a gesture of exasperation. Then the man pointed his finger at the dwarf, wagging it directly in his face—and abruptly flew off balance as the dwarf grabbed his hand, pivoted, and flung the man sprawling over his shoulder to land on his back with a thud. Before the man could move, the dwarf was on top of him, covering his mouth with one hand, thumping the side of his head with the other. The man stopped struggling, and the dwarf rose to stand over him, still muttering angrily.

At that moment the rim of the white moon appeared above the eastern peaks, and there was light. The dwarf was out in the open, in plain sight of the guard perimeter.

"Oh, mercy!" Helta breathed, and ran. On flying bare feet she sprinted the dozen yards to where the dwarf stood over the fallen human. The dwarf was just turning toward her when she dodged around him, grabbed his arm and pulled him as fast as she could, back into the shadows behind the longhouse. There he gaped at her, opened his mouth to speak, and she clamped a hand over it. "Sh!" she whispered urgently. "The guards will catch you." With sudden decision, she gripped his arm, braced her feet, and propelled him toward the door, opening it and pushing him through into the longhouse.

Most of the women were asleep, but Nadeen raised her head, glanced up, then sat bolt upright. "Helta!" she whispered, "What . . . ?"

"Sh!" Helta closed the door quietly, then half-dragged the bearded dwarf toward the ladder, again holding a hand over his mouth. "Here," she said. "Climb. I'll hide you in the loft."

Here in the candlelight, she could see him better. He wasn't anyone she knew, but he obviously needed help. His beard and hair were unkempt and filthy, his only garment was a stained, ill-fitting smock of some kind, and there was blood on his hands, on the dagger at his waist, and on the odd, sharpened stick he carried.

With eyes like saucers, Nadeen stared at him, then at Helta. "Who is this?" she whispered. "What in the name of . . ."

Abruptly the back door opened, and they turned toward it. The person who entered was a human, stooping to clear the low frame. He was carrying an armload of weapons of various kinds. He slipped through, closed the door behind him, and stared accusingly at the strange dwarf.

"You didn't need to give me a knot on the head," he growled. "A word of thanks would have sufficed." For a second he and the dwarf glared at each other, then the man laid his accumulated weapons on the plank table beside the ladder and turned, taking in the big room at a sweeping glance. Satisfied, he looked at Nadeen, then at Helta, and his harsh, cruel-looking human face lighted with a sincere smile. "Hello," he said. "I'm Tuft Broadland. I've been helping your friend here kill empiremen . . . though he has a strange way of showing his gratitude."

* * * * *

High on a mountainside in a moonlit glade, an elf and a one-armed dwarf knelt beside a shallow bowl, staring into the milky liquid it held.

"He's doing well," the elf said. "All of the night guards are disposed of, and not a trace of any alarm. The other guards and mine masters are sound asleep. But there are others with him, now. The females in the longhouse, and a man."

"A man?" Calan Silvertoe's eyes widened. "A human?"

"Don't be alarmed," Despaxas said softly. "The man isn't of the empire. I would guess he is one of those nomads from the lakeshore camp."

"Well, what's he doing there, with Derkin?"

"Arguing, apparently," the elf said.

Calan snorted. "Two cabins full of sleeping enemies and a mine shaft full of goblins to take care of, and he dawdles with women and takes time out for debate with a passing nomad? What does he think he's doing?"

"I don't know," Despaxas said. "But remember, you're the one who told our chosen 'leader of dwarven forces' to do things his own way."

5

The Leader

"No, I won't tell you about our mission," Tuft Broadland said for the third time, ignoring Derkin's ferocious frown. "Pass the bread, please."

Derkin broke a piece from the dark loaf on the table and handed the rest across. "You won't tell me what you and your friends are doing in these mountains, but still you expect me to let you wander around loose? You expect me to trust you?"

"After all," the man said, "I did save your life out there a while ago. That last guard would have killed you."

"He wouldn't have known I was there if it hadn't been for you crashing through the brush behind me," Derkin rumbled. "You're about as stealthy as a blind buffalo."

"I tripped," Tuft protested. "I'm not used to tilted places. Where I'm from the ground is flat, as the gods intended ground to be. But be that as it may, that last guard would have skewered you like a sausage on a stick if I hadn't put an arrow through his gullet." He glanced around, and said, "Leave the bow and arrows alone, ladies. They're mine. Help yourselves to the rest, though."

All around them dwarven women were tying up their skirts, braiding their hair, choosing weapons from the pile the man had brought in, and generally getting ready to do battle. A clatter erupted as someone dropped a sword on the hard floor, and Tuft Broadland jumped to his feet, narrowly missing banging his still sore head on a low rafter.

"Quiet, please!" he ordered. "Remember, there are still a lot of empiremen out there. If they wake up too soon, we'll have a problem." Tuft picked up the dropped sword, reversed it, and handed it to a scowling female. "Here, let me show you how to hold this," he offered.

At the table, Derkin finished his bread and washed it down with tepid water. Then he noticed that the pretty one, Helta somebody, was staring at him thoughtfully. As he met her eyes, she shook her head and shrugged. "You certainly don't look much like I expected," she explained.

"You expected me?"

"Well, not exactly," she admitted. "But I've been hoping that someone would come along and rescue us. Only, I had a somewhat different picture of who it would be. I expected someone handsome and charming and elegant, all dressed in shining armor and . . . and . . . well, what I mean is, you're kind of a mess. And if you have a charming side, I haven't noticed it yet."

With a growl, Derkin shoved himself away from the table and strode across to peer out through the broken shutters of a window. "Those two cabins out there," he said. "I saw men go into them. Are they all in there?"

"All but the six night guards," Helta said, crowding against him to point. "Those are the only two cabins with wood floors. I guess humans like wooden floors. The guardsmen sleep in that farther one—the largest—and the mine overseers sleep in the nearer one. What are we going to do about them?"

"Kill them," he said distractedly. "Be quiet. I'm trying to think." He rubbed his bearded chin, his brow wrinkling. "Be a lot easier if they were all in the same cabin."

"Well, they're not," Helta said. "They always use those two. . . ."

"I said, be quiet," he growled. Then, to himself, he said, "Twelve more armed guards, and a dozen slavers. And not a thing to work with but a handful of women."

"And a Cobar warrior," Tuft Broadland proudly reminded him, wandering past. The man was busily instructing dwarf women in the use of swords, spears, and daggers.

"And a blasted human," Derkin corrected himself. "We could charge the door, I guess, at one cabin. But two?"

A hand tapped his shoulder, and he looked around. It was the gray-haired woman, Nadeen. "She said to tell you to look in the shed," she told him. "She says you might find something useful there."

"She? Who?"

"Helta," Nadeen said. "She asked me to tell you that."

"The shed," he muttered. "All right, I'll look. What's in it?"

"She knows," Nadeen said. "She's been in there."

He glanced past her. A few feet away, Helta stood, pointedly looking in another direction. "Why didn't she tell me herself?" Derkin asked.

"You told her to shut up," Nadeen explained. "I think you hurt her feelings."

Derkin stepped past the woman. "Show me the shed," he said. Helta ignored him. "Oh, rust!" he muttered, then,

"I'm sorry I snapped at you. Please?"

"All right." She turned. "In the future, I'll just ignore your bad manners. Come on."

* * * * *

As the second moon added its light to the first, brightening the glade high on the slopes, Calan Silvertoe asked Despaxas, "What's he doing now? Can you see?"

"I can see," the elf said. "He has all the females out in the compound, unrolling metal cable. They're winding it around one of the buildings."

"What?" Calan snapped, leaning to peer into the milky bowl before he recalled that only the elf could see things in it. "Why are they doing that?"

"I haven't the vaguest idea," Despaxas said.

* * * * *

Both moons were high when the women of Tharkas Camp finished wrapping the guards' cabin. Silently and grimly, with Derkin directing the work by whisper and gesture, they had carried rolls of steel cable from the shed, straightened and spliced them, and wound the resulting length around and around the cabin. Planking covered the single door and the two windows, and the entire building now was wrapped with cable. Derkin completed the task, tightening and securing the lashing with a hand-winch. Then he stepped back, surveyed the result, and nodded. "Well, nobody is coming out of there," he muttered. He glanced at the smaller cabin nearby, wishing he could treat it the same way. But there was no more cable.

"All right," he told the women quietly. "Go get those jugs now, and bring torches."

They were back in moments, carrying a half dozen large clay vessels, a bundle of wrapped torches, and a shielded fire pot from the kitchen. Derkin pulled the cork from one jug and sniffed it. It was good dwarven lamp oil, probably looted by the humans from some Neidar village. With the women following him, he worked his way around the sealed cabin, emptying jug after jug of the oil, soaking the walls. The dry timbers absorbed the oil thirstily. With one jug left, Derkin backed away and turned. "Light the torches," he said. "It's wake-up time."

As torches flared alight, he raised the last jug of lamp oil and threw it high. The vessel landed on the cabin's sturdy roof and shattered, oil streaming from it. From inside the cabin, they heard the sounds of voices, then thumps and shouts as the awakening guards began to realize that they were trapped.

Derkin picked up a torch, but Helta was ahead of him. "Let me," she said. "I've *dreamed* about this." With fire-glow radiating her pretty face and glinting in fierce, happy eyes, the dwarf girl trotted around the secured building, igniting the soaked walls.

Derkin snapped his fingers, and Nadeen handed him an axe. He turned toward the human, Tuft Broadland, who had been standing back, watching. Tuft's craggy face was somber, his eyes wide with awe. "Gods," he whispered as the flames along the cabin walls spread, becoming a single, rising blaze.

"Well?" Derkin approached him. "If you haven't the stomach for this . . ."

"Gods," the man said again. "You people are thorough, aren't you?"

"Are you going to try to stop us? Those are humans in there, like you."

"Not like me," Tuft spat. "Those are empire soldiers. I'm a Cobar."

The cabin blazed, and the shouts inside turned to screams. At the second cabin a door crashed open, and men came rushing out, gaping at the blaze, shouting in confusion. The first two or three never saw the dwarven women waiting in the shadows, until the swords, axes, and clubs hit them. Others tried to fight, and some in the rear had picked up weapons. But it was over with in a minute. Taken completely by surprise, groggy with sleep and half-blinded by the glare of the burning cabin, the slavers had no chance against a dozen angry dwarven women swarming among them, cutting them down without mercy.

Thrown torches routed the last two slavers out of their shelter. One of them ducked aside, started to run, then saw Helta Graywood standing alone, gazing raptly at the blazing cabin. With a roar, the man charged toward her, raising a sword, then toppled as Derkin's axe buried itself in his chest. The last slaver was running for the wilderness when an arrow from Tuft Broadland's bow brought him down.

Derkin wrenched his axe from the dead slaver and snapped at Helta, "Pay attention! You could have been killed." Then he stalked around the grounds, counting dead humans. When he was satisfied that none had gotten away, he looked around for Tuft Broadland. At first there was no sign of him, then he appeared from the shadow of the longhouse. And behind him were other humans, following him in single file.

Just as Derkin saw them, some of the women spotted them as well. "There are some more!" Nadeen shouted. "Come on! Get them!"

"Wait!" Derkin roared.

All around him, women hesitated, then lowered their bloody weapons. Followed by his motley, blood-spattered female volunteers, Derkin approached the humans. Besides Tuft Broadland, there were six more, all wearing the soft buckskins and bright weaves of nomads.

"These are my companions from the lake," Tuft said. "They came when they saw the fire."

A tall, gray-bearded man nodded at the dwarves, then asked Tuft, "The empiremen . . . are they all dead?"

"Every last one," Tuft assured him.

"Good," the gray-bearded man said. "Then there will be no alarm across the pass at Klanath."

"No, but you had better go now if you want to slip through before morning." Tuft turned to Derkin. "This is Wing," he said. "He is chief of our mission."

Derkin glared at the gray-bearded man named Wing. "What do you people want?" he demanded.

Wing gazed at the dwarf. "You're Hylar," he said. "Do you come from King Hal-Thwait?"

"There is no such . . ." Derkin started, then changed his mind. "I've been sent by no one," he said. "Who or what do you seek?"

Wing nodded. "Tell him whatever he wants to know," he told Tuft. "He may be useful to us." With that the man turned, waved, and trotted away. The other five strangers followed him, running as silently as elves.

"Aren't you going with them?" Derkin asked Tuft.

"No, I'm staying with you for now," the man said. "Think of me as an observer. We're on the same side, you know."

"I don't *know* anything. You haven't told me anything. What same side are we on?"

"We're against the emperor of Daltigoth." Tuft shrugged. "Those were his people you roasted, you know."

"I don't know anything about human emperors," Derkin said. "I'm here to get an army. What do you have against the emperor?"

"I'm a Cobar," Tuft said. "The emperor's troops have invaded Cobar lands east of here. We're at war. So I'm sticking around. You might find me useful. By the way, where is this army of yours?"

"Up there," Derkin pointed. "They're locked in that

mine shaft. I'm here to free them."

"That sounds simple enough. Let's go get them."

"I think there's a company of goblins in there with them," Derkin added.

"Oh." The man gazed up the slope thoughtfully. "That complicates things, doesn't it? Have any ideas?"

"I do now," the dwarf said. "You said you could be useful. Now you can prove it."

* * * * *

At dawn, a grim-faced man wearing the garments and armament of a guardsman appeared at the closed entrance of the main Tharkas mine shaft. He lifted the heavy bolt from its hasps, then banged on the plank gate. From inside came the sounds of another bolt being withdrawn, then the gate opened slightly, and a sallow, bloated face peered out at him. "Time open mine?" the face asked.

For an instant, the man hesitated, his nose wrinkling. In all his life, Tuft Broadland had never seen a goblin. He had heard they were ugly things, but had never realized just how ugly they were. Large, dull-looking eyes stared at him from a face that was wider than it was long. A wide, lipless mouth revealed glimpses of dark, pointed teeth as it spoke. Below the mouth was almost no chin, just a fleshy wattle that tapered down to its bronze chestplate. It wore a flat-looking iron helmet and held a crossbow in one greenish hand.

And the draft that wafted through the gate it had just opened stank. For a second, Tuft felt as if he was going to be sick. But he tightened his shoulders, stood tall, and frowned fiercely at the creature. "Come on, open up!" he demanded. "The slaves are wanted down in the camp."

The goblin blinked at him. "All of 'em?"

"All of them," Tuft said. "Bring them out, now!"

The goblin opened the gate a few inches more and

stepped out. It was about as tall as a dwarf, but there the resemblance ended. Tuft felt as though he were looking at a pale, erect frog.

With a suspicious glance at the man, the goblin looked past him, shading its eyes against the morning light. It scrutinized the compound below, then pointed at the smoking ashes that were all that was left of the guard cabin. "Wha' happen?" it asked. "Have fire?"

"It isn't your concern," Tuft snapped. "Just do as you're told. Bring out the slaves. They're wanted in the compound."

The goblin gazed at him again, then stepped back through the door. He heard its guttural voice rasp, "Men want all th' dwarves brought out."

Another, similar voice asked, "Why?"

"Dunno," the first said. "Looks like there been trouble. Maybe they gonna kill some dwarves."

" 'Kay," the second voice said. "They say bring 'em out, we bring 'em out. Open th' gate."

Suppressing a sigh of relief, Tuft Broadland stepped back, putting a little distance between himself and the stench coming from the opening. He had heard about goblin-stink, but realized now that one had to actually smell it to really appreciate the foulness of it.

A chorus of shouts, curses, and commands echoed from the darkness of the mine shaft, then a squad of goblins filed out and formed a double line before the gate. All of them wore body armor, and each had a crossbow at its shoulder and a bronze sword in its hand.

More commands were shouted, and dwarves started coming out of the shaft. Tuft shook his head in sympathy as they appeared. Many of them had minor wounds, some of them had open sores, and all of them looked as though they had been systematically beaten and abused.

More and more dwarves appeared, prodded along by grinning goblins, until the entire staging area before the shaft was crowded with tattered, sullen dwarves, surrounded by armored goblins brandishing weapons.

Steeling himself, Tuft stepped forward, pointing as he singled out individual dwarves from the crowd. "You," he said pointing. "And you, and you. Step out here." As the selected dwarves moved forward, he picked out others. "You," he said. "You, and you, and you."

The twenty dwarves he singled out were those who looked the strongest and fittest. They were all young males, and all in fairly good shape, compared to their peers.

"I'll take these twenty first," he told the goblin who seemed to be in charge. "Hold the rest of them here until I come back."

"Better take some guards," the goblin said. "They might try to run."

"If they do, they'll meet arrows," Tuft said. Imperiously, he beckoned his selected group of dwarves. "Follow me," he commanded. After a few steps, one of the dwarves behind him said, "I haven't done anything. . . . Who—"

"Hush!" he rasped. "Just be quiet and follow me. I'm a friend."

Nearing the compound, first one and then others of the dwarves gasped, some of them breaking step as they gaped at the "slavers" coming and going in the open area. "Those are women," someone said. "Our women, wearing guard clothes."

"That's my mother over there," another exclaimed.

"Hush up and keep walking," Tuft commanded. "Those goblins up there are watching."

He led them to the longhouse, and, after ushering them inside, slumped on a bench. "Whew!" he breathed. "I never thought that would be so easy."

The mine slaves looked around in bewilderment at the few dwarven women sorting armor and weapons, and at the man who had led them from the mines. "Who are you?" one of them demanded. "What's going on here?"

"He's with me," Derkin Winterseed said, coming through the back door. "I came to free you."

The slaves stared at him, and one of them asked, "Why?"

"Because I need you," Derkin said. He picked up an axe and tossed it to the questioner, who caught it neatly. "Do you know how to use that?"

"Of course I do," the miner said. "Who am I to use it on?"

"Goblins," Derkin explained.

Within moments, all of the ex-slaves were armed and ready, and Derkin sent Tuft back up the hill.

When the man returned, followed by nearly two hundred dwarves and thirty armed goblins—the entire company—the compound was empty. The man strode to the front door of the longhouse, opened it, and jerked a thumb at the dwarves. "Inside," he said.

Sullen and silent, the prisoners filed through the door while grinning goblins prodded them from behind.

Thoroughly occupied with tormenting their charges, none of the goblins saw that both doors of the building were open, and as fast as the dwarves entered the front, they were hustled out the back, handed something that would serve as a weapon—prybars, hammers, table legs, saw blades, anything available—and led around to the far side of the equipment shed. Only when the last dwarf had entered the building did a few goblins look inside and notice there were only a dozen or so dwarves, and they were turning to attack.

One goblin actually got into the longhouse, impaling a dwarf on his bronze sword before another dwarf brained it with a stool. The rest were stopped at the door and pressed back, dwarves flailing away at them with anything that came to hand.

His sword singing like winter wind, Tuft Broadland

beheaded one goblin and cut the legs out from under another before the rest realized that he was attacking them. Then when they turned toward him, a howling, surging tide of armed dwarves came around the corner of the building, flooding through and over them. Dark, rancid goblin blood flowed like water.

Most of the goblins fell within moments, overwhelmed and outnumbered. A few broke and ran, but were quickly overtaken and killed. Derkin had made it clear that no enemy was to be allowed to escape, and the dwarves were thorough in their slaughter.

When it was over, four dwarves were counted dead and three others injured. At Derkin's direction, the victors collected every goblin corpse in the vicinity, as well as those of the dead slavers hidden in the other cabin, and threw all the bodies into an abandoned pit, which they then filled in. They kept all the fallen weapons and bits of human armor. The goblins' armor was buried with them. As Derkin explained to Tuft, no dwarf would ever wear anything that had been worn by a goblin. It was impossible to wash out the stench.

When all that was done, Derkin gathered his new army in the compound. "We'll rest here a few days," he told them. "You'll eat well, tend your wounds, and clean yourselves. Those fit to work can set up a forge and start making weapons. We'll need hammers, axes, swords, pikes . . . anything any of you know how to use. And I am going to drill you in orderly combat. I—"

A hand went up, and a dwarf said, "Excuse me . . ."

Derkin turned to him. "Yes?"

"That all sounds fine," the miner said. "But just who the blazes are you, anyway?"

"My name is Derkin," he said. "I'm your leader."

"Who says?"

"I do," he said flatly.

Nobody dared disagree.

Behind the longhouse, the dwarven women had fires going and great tubs of water heating, and were cutting soap into small bars. They had decided that the first thing to do was to get the "soldiers" fit to be around. Dwarves, clothes, tools, and weapons all were to be thoroughly scrubbed.

When they were ready, Helta went to Derkin and handed him a piece of soap, a comb, and a pair of shears. "You, too," she said. "If you're going to be a leader, then look like one."

6

The Chosen Ones

"I have to admit, I'm impressed," Calan Silvertoe told Derkin as they strolled across what had been—only days before—the central compound of a slave-run mine camp. All around them, dwarves in all sorts of dress and oddments of armor toiled, two by two, flailing away at each other with wooden swords, defending with shields made of everything from hardwood to stretched leather. Nearby, hammers rang on anvils, and a makeshift forge made the air above it dance with heat-shimmers. Dozens of crafters worked there, turning smelted iron into weapons. In the nearby shed, stacks of weapons of all sorts grew by the hour.

Among the combatants on the field, seeming to tower over them, Tuft Broadland stalked, shouting instructions and criticisms—mostly the latter. As Neidar dwarves, the miners—even the women—were naturally skilled with axes, hammers, slings, javelins, and spears. They had used such tools all their lives. And as miners, most of them were expert shield users. But few of them had ever held a sword, and Derkin had set the human to teach them how.

"We have no steel here," he had explained to them. "The weapons we can make readily will be rough iron. In battle, they will dull quickly, and some will break. We may have to outfit ourselves from what the enemy drops. The enemy will be mostly humans, and most humans prefer swords."

"Where are we going, Derkin?" some of them asked.

"Beyond Tharkas Pass, to Klanath," he said.

"Why?"

"To get the rest of our army."

It was answer enough for the freed slaves. They had accepted him as their leader, and in the manner of most dwarves, they were satisfied to let the leader worry about the details. So, for now, the kitchen turned out substantial meals morning and night, poultices and liniments did their work on sores and wounds, and every dwarf able to stand erect practiced swordplay and battle tactics every waking hour.

In a span of three days, Derkin converted a wretched gaggle of freed slaves into a formidable fighting force. The Chosen Ones, they called themselves. How the name originated was unclear, but every member of Derkin's little tribe seemed to have adopted it. It was a source of pride, and it gave them strength. But still, the passing of time chafed the Hylar. He was troubled and tense now as he walked with Calan Silvertoe, watching the sword drills.

For the first time in more than two years, Derkin Winterseed felt—and looked—like the Hylar he was. Soap and hot water had sloughed away the accumulated filth of the slave pens. Good food and sunlight had brought rich color to his cheeks, and a determined shearing by Helta and Nadeen had tamed his long hair and tangled beard. Now in leather kilt and soft-weave blouse, sturdy boots, studded gauntlets and flowing cloak, and wearing a lacquered steel breastplate and a horned helmet—where the women had found such things remained a mystery, except that the armor was very old indeed—Derkin looked every inch the Hylar warrior. His dark, backswept beard was trimmed short, his hair curled at his collar, and his cloak was of heavy red cloth, fresh from a newly rebuilt loom in the longhouse. He carried a small forearm shield, and a heavy hammer was slung at his shoulder.

He had been embarrassed at the elegant attire when the women first brought it. But he discovered quickly that his "army" followed him far more happily when he wore it. It was as Helta had said: to be a leader, look like one.

Helta had surveyed the results and given him a dazzling smile. "Now you look like him," she had said.

"Like who?" he wondered. But she had only smiled again, a secretive, satisfied smile, and ignored the question.

Now old Calan Silvertoe glanced at him and frowned. "You look worried," he said. "What's the matter?"

"The pit slaves, back at Klanath," he admitted. "Too much time is passing. They may all be dead or mutilated by now. If so, then this whole effort is wasted."

"They're all right," Calan assured him. "Despaxas and his pet shadow are keeping an eye on them."

"How can they be all right?" Derkin demanded. "The humans have had all these days to punish them."

"But they haven't," Calan said. "Your cell mates are holed up in their cell, with food and weapons, and no human has touched them."

"Where did they get food and weapons?"

"The elf has his ways." The old dwarf frowned. "As I understand it, he . . . uh . . . *transported* some things from the guards' quarters and the central larder. So they're barricaded in the pit cell, and for the time, nobody is bothering them."

"Why not?"

The old Daewar grinned wolfishly. "Do you remember the pit boss, a man called Shalit Mileen?"

"I remember him," Derkin growled. "He ordered the beatings I took . . . and the heavy chain."

"Well, it seems Shalit Mileen is keeping it a secret that his slaves have revolted. He was plotting against the Master of Mines, and Renus Sabad will blame him for everything. Now Shalit Mileen is plotting to try to keep his head, thanks to you. And to me, of course, and Despaxas."

"How does Despaxas know what's going on in the pit?"

"Don't ask me." Calan shrugged. "I don't understand his magics."

"But you trust him," Derkin said, stepping in front of the old dwarf to look into his eyes.

"As much as I've ever trusted anybody," Calan assured him. "He says I saved his life once, and I suppose that's true. It was a long time ago, when I was still a trader out of Thorbardin, and before Despaxas learned his spells. A wild ogre had him cornered, without his weapons, and I happened along. I killed the ogre, but not before it bit off my arm."

"But how do you know an elf can be trusted?"

"He could have left me there to die," Calan said. "But he didn't. He nursed me back to health." The old dwarf squinted, then turned and pointed across the training field. "How do you know you can trust that human?"

"I believe his interests are the same as mine," Derkin said.

"And so are the elf's."

"I don't like magicians."

"Nobody likes magicians," Calan agreed. "But you'll have to admit, a decent one can be useful now and then."

Directly behind Calan, the air shimmered, and suddenly Despaxas stood there, his smooth cheeks drawn in an ironic smile. "Thank you," he purred.

Calan spun around, almost tripping on his own feet. "I wish you'd stop doing that!" he snapped.

"Sorry," the elf said. "But I have disturbing news. Lord Kane has arrived at Klanath to prepare for the inspections. He has ordered a brigade through the pass to fortify this compound. He intends to open all the shafts over here and build a citadel. With a presence at both ends of Tharkas Pass, Lord Kane can claim all the lands from here to Thorbardin's north gate."

"Like blazes he can!" Derkin hissed. "This is dwarven land."

"A brigade!" Calan frowned. "When are the soldiers coming?"

"They are on the march now," Despaxas said. "Both cavalry and foot. By nightfall, they will be in the pass."

Tuft Broadland had arrived in time to hear the report. He swore, shook his head, and glared at the elf, then sighed. "Then you've lost before you begin," he told Derkin sadly. "We'll never get to Klanath now."

"We'll get there," Derkin growled. His cloak swirling, he turned and beckoned. Instantly, the burly dwarves who made up his personal guard, the Ten, hurried to him. "Let everyone prepare to travel," he told them. "We are going to Klanath."

"Aye," the First of the Ten said, saluting crisply. Followed by the others, he hurried away.

Tuft stared at Derkin and shook his head. "It's impossible," he said. "We'll never get past an entire brigade in that pass with barely two hundred fighters."

"We aren't going through the pass," Derkin snapped. "We're going over it."

The man blinked, then looked at the high, sheer walls of mountain climbing toward the sky. "No man could climb that," he muttered.

Beside him, Calan Silvertoe grinned. "We aren't men," he reminded the human. "We're dwarves."

* * * * *

First light of a new morning touched the mountaintops and reflected downward to light the lower slopes. Where Tharkas Camp had once stood, now there was nothing but the riven slopes, desolate ground, and feathers of smoke that rose from a place not only abandoned, but razed and leveled. Leaving Tharkas with his Chosen Ones, Derkin Winterseed left no one behind, and nothing that could benefit human intruders. Where once there had been mine shafts, now there were only tumbled slopes. The mines had been caved in and sealed. Where there had been a few buildings, now there were piles of ash. Everything that might be useful and could be carried, the Chosen Ones had taken with them. Everything that was left, they had methodically destroyed, scattered, hidden, or buried. Except for the diminishing smoke from the ashes and the scars left on the land by two years of human-directed mining, there might never have been a place called Tharkas Mines. A stranger viewing the scene on this morning would have seen no trace of life anywhere about—unless he looked upward.

There, a pair of miles away and half a mile above, a winding string of tiny dots moved on the sheer face of Tharkas Heights. In a place where no human could have gone, on a sheer, nearly vertical granite slope that no human could have scaled, Derkin Winterseed and the Chosen Ones crept upward, climbing toward the crest above the west side of Tharkas Pass. By rope and hammer, by spike and sling, by javelin and throw-line, by hand-and toehold, hoist, and piton, and by sheer, stubborn determination, the dwarves worked their way upward, doing the thing that was as much second nature to dwarves as was delving or metalcraft—climbing.

And those who could not climb—a few of the mine dwarves who were sick or injured, old Calan Silvertoe because he had only one arm, and Tuft Broadland because he was human—were hoisted, lifted, and carried in slings as baggage. For Tuft, it was an experience he would never forget. As they neared the top, he found himself swinging in space over a ledge, the nearest horizontal surface thousands of feet below him as he clung to a flimsy rope rising slowly to the tugs of a pair of burly dwarves perched precariously on an impossible slope above.

"If I ever get out of this," he swore over and over, "I hope I never see another mountain."

Just above and to his right, Calan Silvertoe lounged happily in a net sling, also being hoisted aloft. His voice rich with suppressed laughter, he said, "We've been trying for centuries to explain to you people, this land just isn't for humans. I guess now at least one of you agrees."

The journey to the crest above Tharkas Pass took most of a day. From the stony peak, the dwarves looked down into the shadowed depths of Tharkas Pass. More than half a mile below, seeming almost straight down, columns of soldiers moved, heading south. Lord Kane's expeditionary brigade was on its way into old Kal-Thax to take command of the dwarven realm.

"I'd like to drop rocks on the whole army down there," Calan Silvertoe growled.

"Leave them alone," Derkin ordered. "With them gone, we'll have fewer to contend with at Klanath." Turning away from the chasm, he got his shield and hammer from one of the baggage slings, donned his horned helmet and red cloak, and headed northwest, angling away from the deep pass. The slope on this side of the mountain wall was less precipitous, a long, rolling decline where wind-shaped trees dotted the rugged landscape, foretelling the forests that would begin lower down. It was easier travel than the long climb had been, but it was still twenty miles to Klanath, and he was anxious to be on his way. The Hylar had no illusions about how he had gotten into this venture. He had been manipulated by a magic-using elf and an old one-armed Daewar schemer. But with true dwarven stubbornness, Derkin Winterseed—once committed to a task—would pursue it with as much grim determination as if it had been his own idea all along.

Behind him, the Chosen Ones gathered up their packs, their supplies, and their weapons, and hurried to follow. Most of them had only the vaguest notion of what lay ahead, but the Hylar called Derkin had freed them from slavery, from imprisonment, and from goblins. He was their leader. He was their chieftain, and where he went they would go.

* * * * *

When Sakar Kane arrived at Klanath, with three brigades of the emperor's troops in addition to his usual retinue, the first thing he did was send one brigade south through Tharkas Pass. Rumors had come to his ears in Daltigoth that there were those among the secondary nobility who had designs on the former dwarven realm, now that the dwarves of Thorbardin seemed no longer to be a threat. Lord Kane had heard that at least two of his peers at court had plans of their own for the mountain lands and were gathering supporters.

By placing his own troops south of the pass, Lord Kane intended to stop any such venture before it began. The one who held Tharkas, he reasoned, would control access to the land the dwarves called—or had once called—Kal-Thax. Lord Kane had been assured that, in return for his services at Klanath, the emperor would grant the mountain lands to him to govern. He intended to have those lands thoroughly within his control when that occurred.

With the brigade on its way south, Lord Kane assigned the rest of his army to garrison and retired to the citadel that was being completed for him. He entered, followed by his servants, porters, personal guard, and attendants, and had the great gates closed. The dozen or so other nobles who had arrived with him, he left to find their own accommodations.

When he had dined and been entertained by musicians and dancers, he sent runners to find the Master of Klanath Mines, the chief of guards, and other local functionaries to command them to attend him. Then he retired to his private quarters.

Within the hour, every local notable in Klanath would be gathered in Lord Kane's great hall, awaiting his pleasure. He would let them all cool their heels for at least a day, pacing and fretting. It would remind them of who he was. Then, when he was ready, they would report to him individually. After that he would personally conduct the usual formal inspection of the mines. It was a tiresome routine, but the emperor commanded that it be done.

Lord Kane did not look forward to the inspection. The mines were dirty, stinking holes and did not interest him. But they were the public reason for Lord Kane's being here. The private—and primary—reason was to establish a base for a general invasion of the central plains to the east.

The assault had already begun, of course. It had been under way for nearly three years, but it had been a covert, scattered incursion so far. Small units of the armies had escorted hordes of "settlers" into various parts of the plains, driving out those already settled there and replacing them with people committed to the emperor's purposes. It was preparation for a full-scale invasion in force, that would carry the banner of the empire as far as the Khalkist realms and the elven forests.

The "quiet" invasion had gone very well, indeed. Vast areas east of the Kharolis mountains now were populated by the faithful. Only in two areas had there been real trouble. Those "settlers" entering the lands of the Cobar nomads had met fierce opposition. The Cobar tribes—barbarian horsemen mostly—had united against the intruders, and had literally driven them away, again and again. What should have been a simple taking of lands had turned into an all-out war, and it was still going on.

And far to the southeast, the emperor's subjects had come up against another kind of force. Elves from Silvanesti had come out of their beloved forests, and were scattered throughout the rolling lands of eastern Ergoth. And the elves neither welcomed nor honored the empire's presence. Led by an elf called Kith-Kanan, the western—or "Wildrunner"—elves had stopped the emperor's "settlers" far short of their goal.

Privately, Lord Kane doubted the empire's ability to win a war against the elves, if it came to that. But that would be someone else's problem, not his. He had his own assignments and his own plans.

He would conduct his inspection of the emperor's mines and prepare supply lines for the armies that would soon be coming through, heading east. Then he would set about securing his hold on Tharkas Pass and the mountain lands beyond.

* * * * *

For days, nothing much had happened in the vicinity of the big underground cell behind the first soft-ore pit. Within the cell, some two thousand dwarves ate, slept, stood guard on their fortified gate, and waited. There had been some fighting right at first—companies of guards slipping into the outer corridor to try to direct attacks on the cell—but the dwarves had turned the attacks with swarms of missiles hurled or fired through the grating. And then, the soldiers had withdrawn. Now there was a strong guard on the corridor itself, but no assaults on the cell. The dwarves could tell by the sounds echoing in from the great pit that work was proceeding there. Other slaves had been transferred from other pits, and the mining went on.

It was Tap Tolec who first realized what was going on. "The inspections," he said, with good Theiwar intuition. "Those trumpets we heard before, they meant the inspectors have arrived from Daltigoth. I think the deputy is trying to keep us secret until the nobles leave."

Vin the Shadow crouched beside him. "Why would he do that?" he asked.

"He has been plotting against the Master of Mines," Tap surmised. "That's why the rich ore was hoarded in the seventh and ninth shafts. Shalit Mileen planned to bring it out at inspection and disgrace the old man. But then we barricaded the cell, and the guards couldn't reach us. For that, the disgrace would fall on Shalit Mileen. I think he's hiding us and using the hoarded ore to make it seem that the pits are in full operation so no one will know that a fourth of his slaves are in revolt and barricaded in their cell."

"It could be." Vin nodded. "Such a thing would truly disgrace him if it were known."

"Probably cost him his head." Tap grinned. "Maybe we should get the word out that we're here. I'd like to see the pit boss beheaded."

"They'd behead us first," Vin pointed out.

"Well, yes, there is that," Tap agreed. "Of course, after the inspection, Shalit Mileen will have plenty of time to do with us as he will. My guess is, if we don't surrender then, he'll set delvers above and bury us alive."

"That bowl said help was on the way," the Daergar reminded.

"I know what the bowl said," Vin grumbled gloomily. "And I find myself wondering if we're all crazy, believing something a bowl told us."

Distantly, then, a trumpet sounded, followed by others. Around the dark cell, dwarves listened and glanced at one another. They had all heard that particular call before. It was evening call, but much more. It was inspection call, telling everyone in Klanath to prepare.

"Whatever that bowl has in mind," Tap said darkly, "it had better hurry. The inspection begins at first light tomorrow."

Vin the Shadow jumped to his feet. "Hush!" he said. "Listen!"

The distant blaring of trumpets had become a mighty chorus, with every caller in the city joining in. The blast of sound almost drowned out other, lesser noises . . . but not quite. Good dwarven ears heard something else, as well. Somewhere very near, weapons rang, and deep war cries —dwarven war cries—echoed the cries of frightened, surprised men.

7

Battle of the Pit

Arriving on the heights above the Klanath mines, Derkin Winter-seed waved his followers into cover and crept forward to survey the scene below. For a moment, the sight staggered him. He had never seen Klanath from above, and the sheer sprawl of the settlement shocked him. It was a fair-sized city, spread out on the flatlands and low hills below the mines. On a central knoll stood a grand stronghold—a palace rising among scaffolds, surrounded by walled courtyards. All around the central compound were clusters and rows of all kinds of buildings, many hundreds of them stretching downward and away toward the distant forests beyond.

At first glance, Derkin's impulse was to call the whole thing off. There were humans down there by the thousands, and among them armed patrols carrying the pennant of the empire. Even in evening shadow, as the sun of Krynn went to its rest beyond the western ranges, the task looked impossible. How were two hundred dwarves— more or less—ever going to slip unnoticed through such a place, to even reach the pit mines, much less free the dwarven slaves there?

Frowning and worried, he scanned the terrain below, memorizing it. And in memorizing it, he analyzed the patterns of it, and felt a bit more hopeful. City or not, the place was like any slave camp. Its defenses were designed to keep people in, not to keep people out.

Directly below him, and spreading out on both sides, were the ledges and ramps behind which were the shaft mines. Farther down the steep slope was a sprawl of ramshackle buildings, most of them no more than pole sheds. And just beyond those were the soft-ore pits—four deep, wide holes where lamps and torches moved. The nearest of the pits he recognized by its wide entry ramp. It was the first pit. And within it was the cell he had so recently occupied.

Everywhere in the city were patrols and guards, and on the distant northward road was a large encampment of empire soldiers. But the mining section had only perimeter guards, and those were mostly on the downward side. The various mines themselves had guards, of course, but mostly inside. There was no need for the Chosen Ones to make their way through the teeming sprawl of human Klanath. The city lay beyond the mines, below them. With a slight smile from a god or two, they could be in and out of the mines before forces from the city could react.

"Reorx," he muttered, making quick plans, "favor us now."

He signaled with his hand, and others crept forward to

crouch beside him. "There," he pointed, indicating a brushy draw that led down the slope, separating the ledges of the shaft mines into two sections. "There is our path in, and with some luck, our path out as well."

At dark of evening, Derkin began his assault. Leaving the women and the injured hidden on the high slope, he led the rest into the wide, brushy cut and downward. Passing between shaft mines where lanterns were being lighted, they crept silently down the slope. A hundred yards, and they paused, listening. Another hundred, and they gathered in brush shadows above the cluster of barns and sheds. In a hushed voice, Derkin selected two squads of a dozen dwarves each, and gave them their orders. The selected ones were all young, strong, and agile, and all had at least some Daergar blood. When they understood what they were to do, he signaled the rest and stepped out of cover, heading straight toward the ramp of pit one. From here to the pit there was no cover, but Derkin was counting on the dusk and surprise, and counting even more on human nature. The guards at the ramp, he assumed, were interested in two things—the pit below them, and the stone-paved road that wound its way upward from the city.

"Humans are creatures of habit," his father had told him once, a long time ago. "They are quick to see what they expect to see, but slow to notice what they do not expect."

Beyond the sheds were fifty yards of open ground, with nothing to hide their approach. Therefore, Derkin discarded stealth in favor of speed and silence.

One hundred seventy pairs of strong, short legs raced toward the top of the ramp, where four cloaked guardsmen leaned on their spears. Sand scuffed beneath one hundred seventy pairs of running feet, and one of the guards raised his head curiously. Then another, and another.

"Reorx," Derkin muttered, taking a good grip on his

hammer. And as he had barely dared to hope they would, all four guards became alert at the approaching sound . . . and all four turned their backs on the charging dwarves, turning instead toward the Klanath road.

Without warning or challenge, the dwarves hit them. One fell sprawling as Derkin's hammer thudded between his shoulders, smashing his spine. From the corners of his eyes, Derkin saw other guards fall, and he raced on, down the ramp. It seemed to him that their encounter had been noisy and clattering, but he realized instantly that the four guards at the foot of the ramp had not noticed it. It was always noisy in the pits, and the four were kneeling in a tight circle, playing bones. It was doubtful that any of them ever knew what hit them.

On the floor of the pit, slaves just completing their day's tasks gawked in astonishment as the armed dwarves streamed among them, heading for the cell corridor. One surprised slave dropped a loaded hod, and suddenly the mouth of the corridor was crowded with humans, gaping at the approaching attack, stumbling over one another as they grabbed up weapons.

Again without hesitation, Derkin led his Chosen Ones directly into the thick of the humans, slashing and battering with his hammer, his forearm shield dancing as blades rang against it.

There was no more silence now, nor any need for it. Derkin bellowed the only battle cry he had ever learned— an old Hylar war cry from distant times—and all around him other dwarves took it up, and the din of battle echoed with the chants that once had accompanied the beating of war drums.

The guard force at the corridor was a full company— fifty tall human males, armed with swords and maces, spears and daggers. The sheer force of the dwarven attack carried Derkin well into the cell corridor and halfway through the clot of men. Then he found himself in the midst of all-out fighting on all sides. Nearby, a hastily crafted axe splintered its edge against a human shield, and a dwarf went down, writhing, with a spearhead through his chest. Dwarves were falling, but men were falling, too, and every good steel weapon that was dropped was grabbed by a dwarven hand before it stopped ringing.

The former slaves fought with a ferocious energy, making up in zeal what they lacked in practice. In a glance, Derkin saw two howling dwarves leap onto a human guard, wrench his sword from his hand as they bowled him over, then slash him to death with it.

For what seemed like hours, the fighting raged. Then the fury of it diminished suddenly. More than half the guard company was down, their blood mixing with that of a dozen or more dwarves who had seen their last sunrise. The rest of the humans were in panic, trying to escape the fury of the dwarves. A few scampered away, past attackers and out into the open pit. Most, though, turned and ran along the corridor, toward the slave cell. Shouting, Derkin pursued them, his Chosen Ones following. The corridor veered, then straightened, and the barricaded grating of the cell gate lay just ahead. Beyond it, the corridor ended.

It was then that the panicked humans realized they had fled into a trap. They spun about in desperation. But even as they turned, raising bloody weapons, a hail of bronze bolts, sling-stones, and various other flung objects erupted through the grating to smash among them. Everywhere, men fell, but they were not alone. A heavy dart sang between two of the men, missed Derkin's face by an inch, and buried itself in the skull of a dwarf behind him. And as men pitched forward, dying, more missiles thudded among the dwarves.

"Hold!" Derkin roared. "You in the cell! We're on your side!"

The hail of missiles stopped abruptly, and a voice beyond the grating shouted, "Well, rust th' buckets! It's that Hylar! Come on, let's get out there and help!"

Barricades were tumbled aside, and the big gates lurched open, dwarves by the hundreds streaming through. Some had weapons and some did not. All were ragged, filthy, and disreputable-looking, but the fervor with which they fell upon the few remaining humans bordered on sheer, savage joy. Within seconds, the only living souls in the corridor were dwarves.

Pushing and cursing, Derkin shouldered his way through a thickening crowd. "Follow me!" he shouted, trying to be heard above their babble. "Let's get out of this place!"

Gradually, with a lot of help from his lieutenants and others, he got the crowd silenced and headed for the open pit. He found himself caught up in a stampede of dwarves. Strong hands on both sides of him clutched his shoulders and hurried him forward as a wedge of dwarves plowed through the moving crowd, clearing a path with fists and curses.

"Make way!" someone roared. "Make way for the leader! He can't lead from back here, for rust's sake!"

Abruptly, Derkin was at the head of the exodus, and the hands at his shoulders set him down. In dim torchlight, he recognized the Neidar slave called Tap, and the Daergar miner called Vin the Shadow.

"Glad you made it." Tap smiled at the Hylar, admiring his bright garb and glistening armor. "Though I'd never have recognized you if you hadn't opened your mouth back there."

"I'm here to get you people out," Derkin said.

"We know," Vin the Shadow rasped, a grin splitting his matted beard. "That bowl told us."

Derkin didn't have a chance to ask what bowl he was talking about. They were moving along the corridor at double time, and at that moment more dwarves met them, just inside the entrance. The first one stopped, gawked at the resplendent Hylar with the horde of fighters and slaves behind him, then turned and backed away. Behind them, a double file of ragged slaves had entered the tunnel, dragging the bleeding, mutilated corpses of several human guards.

"These tried to get away," one of the new dwarves explained, squinting. "We, ah . . . sort of guessed that you didn't want them to."

"They're pretty messed up," another said, as though apologizing. "Chains and hod-poles do that, you know."

"Thanks," Derkin said. "Now stand aside. We have to get out of here before—"

"Out?" a dwarf interrupted, frowning at him. "You don't have everybody yet. There are three more cells, in the other three pits."

"I didn't plan on . . ."

"We sent word through the tunnels," a slave assured him. "It shouldn't take long. Everyone will be ready to leave as soon as you free them. What are you going to do about our chains, though?"

Tap Tolec stepped past Derkin. "Get your friends out of their cells," he said. "We'll get their chains off of them."

Derkin glared at the slaves around him, and realized that—leader or not—he didn't have the deciding vote on this. He had come for two thousand slaves. He would leave with eight thousand, or not leave at all. "All right!" he snapped. "Chosen Ones, follow me! The rest of you, keep to cover and be ready to break chains. Reorx!" he added to himself. "By now every human in Klanath will have heard the fighting."

"Probably not," a slave said. "Couldn't hear much at all, out in the pit. I doubt if anybody above heard a thing."

* * * * *

Derkin had planned for not more than a quarter-hour in the pits. Strike hard, move fast, and get out quickly had been his strategy. But the campaign took on a life of its own, as campaigns do, and an hour had passed by the time the Chosen reached the fourth pit. There had been only a few sleepy guards in pits two and three, and the releases there had been quick and fairly silent.

There was a surprise, though, at pit four. Moving fast and silently, seasoned now by practice, the Chosen Ones stormed that pit's cell corridor, killed the entrance guards cleanly, and were on their way to the cell beyond when dozens of robed and armored humans appeared, coming around a turn in the tunnel. The man in the lead was the pit boss himself, Shalit Mileen.

The men stopped, gawked at the bloody weapons and hands and the fierce eyes of the advancing dwarves. Mileen's mouth dropped open, then he drew a broadsword from his shoulder sling, shouted "Kill them!" and charged. Derkin Winterseed, in the lead, deflected the burly man's first slash with his shield, but the impact of it bowled him over. He rolled to the side, broke the knee of a man going over him, and knocked the feet out from under another, then struggled upright. Furious combat filled the ringing tunnel, and more than a few dwarves fell as they bore down on the humans.

Abruptly, though, the clatter diminished, and only one man remained on his feet. It was Shalit Mileen. The man stormed and flailed about him, keeping dozens of dwarves at bay with his flashing broadsword.

Quickly, Derkin laid down his arms, removed his chest armor, and tugged his blouse from beneath the waist of his kilt. With hard hands, he unwrapped the length of heavy chain from around his waist, doubled it, and swung it in a circle over his head. "Back away!" he ordered the dwarves. "This one is mine."

Shalit Mileen whirled at the sound of his voice, and

cruel eyes brightened. "Ah," he said. "The red-cloak. What do you have there, dink? A chain?"

"You should know," Derkin rasped, his voice as deep and cold as mountain snow. "You gave it to me."

The man's eyes widened. "I gave it . . . Yes! I know you! Troublemaker!" With a roar of rage, he sprang at Derkin, his big sword flashing downward. The Hylar dodged aside, and the blade clanged on stone. Derkin lashed out with his doubled chain. The heavy links struck like a snake, coiling around the human's ankle, and Derkin set his feet and pulled. With a crash, Shalit Mileen went over backward. He rolled, trying to get to his knees, but Derkin was astride his back, pummeling his ribs with drumming heels. The chain slipped around the bull neck of the pit boss, and the dwarf's shoulders bulged as he looped it and pulled, tightening it like a garrotte.

Shalit Mileen thrashed and tumbled, rolled and struggled, but the dwarf clung to him like a shackle, never for an instant releasing the brutal pressure on the chain. The man's face went dark, his eyes bulged, and his tongue protruded. Flailing, he rolled onto his back, with the dwarf beneath him, still increasing the strangling pressure of the heavy chain.

For a moment more, the man struggled, his thrashings diminishing to twitches. Then he was still. Derkin clambered from beneath him, tossing aside the ends of the chain. He looked around, found his hammer, picked it up, and pointed it at the slave cell. "Open that gate," he said. "Let those people out."

"Look at this," a dwarf said nearby. Someone raised a lantern. Beyond the cell, where the gate was being opened, the light revealed another cavern—a large, newly delved place, half-filled with heaps of bright, rich metallic ores.

"He was hoarding the ore," a dwarf said, delivering a kick to the body of Shalit Mileen. "He thought he could become Master of Mines."

"He isn't master of anything, now," another freed slave said. "That hammerhand over there"—he pointed toward Derkin—"if anyone is master of the pits now, I'd say it's him."

Tap Tolec glanced around at the words, thoughtfully. "*Hammerhand*," he said, to no one in particular. "A good name, Hammerhand. Aye, Derkin Hammerhand is the true master of these pits. And I for one will help him become master of anywhere else he decides to go."

* * * * *

They would say in future times that Derkin Hammerhand was favored by the gods. They would say that when he called upon Reorx, that mightiest of all gods chose to assist him. The story would be told, and any who doubted would be reminded of the Night of Klanath, when Derkin Hammerhand—whose name up to then was Derkin Winterseed—had invaded the Klanath Mines with two hundred Chosen Ones and freed nearly eight thousand dwarves from slavery in the pits. The gods—at least Reorx and maybe others as well—must have favored Derkin, they would say, for not once in the entire invasion was the city of Klanath ever alerted. Not a human guard in the pits remained alive when the army of slaves made its way up the ramp and the mountainside beyond, and none among the emperor's subjects north of Tharkas were aware that anything was happening.

Only on the following morning, when Lord Kane and his contingent arrived to inspect the mines, did the humans discover that all their miners were gone—eight thousand dwarves vanished up a steep mountainside with the aid of rope slings stolen from the sheds, and all the other slaves of various races gone off in their own directions.

And not only among the dwarves would that story be

told. The Night of Klanath would become a legend also among the humans known as Cobar. In his later years, Tuft Broadland would never tire of telling the tale . . . and the tales of what came after.

"I can see them to this day," he would say. "We were up on the slopes, above the shafts, waiting. They took a lot longer than we had expected, and we were worried. That pretty little creature, Helta, had lost patience and was ready to go down there herself and do . . . whatever she had in mind to do. Then, suddenly, there they were, coming from past the sheds, starting up the slope. And so many of them! Can you picture eight thousand dwarves all coming up a mountainside at once? It looked like the entire mountain was alive.

"Maybe the gods favored Derkin, as they say, or maybe that elf, Despaxas, had something to do with it. In those days he often had that shadow thing with him—Zephyr—and maybe the creature helped somehow. But not an alarm was sounded. Even when those slaves climbed past the shaft mines, no guard saw or heard them.

"I asked Derkin where we were going next, and he just said, 'Past Tharkas, into the wilderness. I have an army to build. But you aren't going on this journey, human. It will be no place for your kind. Here is where we part.'

"Then he stopped suddenly and turned, and right behind him that Zephyr thing appeared in the air, just sort of floating, like a fish in water. It seemed to stare at Derkin, and he stared back. Then it was gone, and Derkin swore it had spoken to him. He said it told him to pay attention to his dreams, for in sleep he would learn the ways of the Calnar. I asked him who the Calnar were, and he said they were the people before the Hylar.

"The dwarves and I parted there . . . for a time. I made it out of those mountains, then found a horse and got back to my people. We were in an all-out war with the emperor's invaders by then. Within a year I was chief of

101

my tribe, though it was no happy ascension. I became chief because our old chief, Plume Plainswind, died with a Caergothian spear through his heart.

"The war stretched from months into years. We kept thinking it must end soon, and some of the Wildrunner elves we shared fires with thought so, too. But there were others whose predictions proved better than ours. Among the elves, they spoke of a leader called Kith-Kanan. And they spoke of Despaxas sometimes. They said Despaxas had sent Zephyr to look into the heart of the emperor's general, Giarna, across battle lines. They said the soul reader found neither weariness nor any regard for the cost in lives and suffering. And Despaxas had gone farther than that, they said. Somehow the elven mage had reached across half a continent to look into the heart of the emperor himself. He said it was like looking into a black pit that reeked of ambition and the need for power.

"And there was another story, among the elves. They said Despaxas believed that the emperor, Quivalin Soth, had the power to be two people—though the second of the two had no soul at all.

"The elves prophesied that Ullves's War would never end until the emperor controlled all of Ansalon . . . or until the emperor was dead.

"And the war did go on . . . and on and on. For a time, we heard strange tales of wild dwarves coming down from the mountains to make lightning raids along the empire's supply lines. They said the dwarves would strike caravans, take what they wanted, and disappear to the south. They took weapons, horses, food supplies . . . all kinds of things.

"There were rumors everywhere, that Thorbardin would open its gates and the dwarves would march into battle. But then the tales of dwarven raiders died down, and seasons passed without any word of them. It was as though all the dwarves in the Kharolis mountains had simply disappeared. Most who thought about them at all assumed that the wild dwarves had joined their mountain brothers in that fabled fortress of theirs, and simply shut themselves off from the world.

"I never really believed that, myself. I thought often of Derkin, and what he had said when we parted. He had an army to build, he said. And there was something in the way he said it. . . . I always had a hunch that I'd see him again one day. There was something about Derkin, something in his eyes, in the way he stood and the way he spoke. I had a feeling even then that the emperor's warlords had not heard the last of Derkin."

Part II:

Master of the Chosen

Century of Rain
Decade of Cherry,
Spring, Year of Tin

8
Out of The Wilderness

Guards at a winter outpost high on the west face of Sky's End Mountain were the first to spot the approach of the strangers. Up there, where the cold season's snowpack still gave teeth to the freshening winds, frost-bearded young volunteers kept watch in relays. For more than a century, the wardens of the great undermountain fortress had maintained these sentinel lairs on the icy crowns of the highest peaks around the mountain called Cloud-seeker, beneath which lay the stronghold of the mountain dwarves.

In good times and bad, through years of dissolution and strife, even in the days when the feuding among thanes in

Thorbardin had erupted into full-scale war, the Council of Chiefs and the Council of Wardens had maintained sentinel outposts to guard against intrusion. Thorbardin was impregnable, but not immune, and those within knew it. Even in the midst of fighting among themselves, the thanes paid common tariff to pay for outposts and sentinels, and volunteers were drawn from every tribe.

The volunteers served for one season at a time, and were paid according to the season. The hardiest among them sought the winter duties. A young dwarf tough enough to last out a winter in one of the Sky's End posts, or one of those atop the Thunder Peaks to the south, could earn a full year's easy living in Thorbardin, with coin left over for carousing among the dens and back ways of any of its several cities.

The west sentinel post on Sky's End was at an altitude of nearly twelve thousand feet, and its six lookouts—a Hylar, a Daewar, two Daergar, and two Theiwar—could see what seemed half the world on a clear day . . . or in the case of the Daergar, a clear night. Now, as the icy winds began to soften just a bit, and the valleys far below grew coats of green, they were all more than ready to go home. They had seen no one all winter—no little groups of migrating Neidar, no far-ranging elven patrols, no smoke of human campfires such as had been common in recent years since the fighting broke out on the eastern plains, not even so much as the occasional wandering ogre. All through the winter, an odd quiet had reigned in the mountain fastness, and the spotters were more than just tired of the ceaseless cold and the singing, mourning winds. They were thoroughly bored as well.

In recent weeks, their off-duty conversations had turned often to the comforts and pleasures of Thorbardin —mugs of heady ale before roaring fires in the countless ale shops of the cities, challenge matches in the pits, the smell of dark bread emanating from the bakeries, the pleasure of lifting fine metal from a cherry-red forge bed to craft upon an anvil, the joy of a leisurely game of bones, the excitement of wagering on worm-pulls . . . and the girls. Each of them had wonderful memories and exciting anticipations regarding some special female awaiting his return—or of two or three females or, in the case of the gold-bearded young Daewar, at least a dozen.

A camaraderie had grown among them during the long, cold season, and they shared their thoughts and their dreams as they would among close friends, ignoring the fact that, once returned to Thorbardin, they would likely be caught up in the clan feuds there as before, and soon be at one another's throats. Such harsh realities could fade from the mind in the course of a winter season on Sky's End.

Morning, evening, and night, by twos, they stood their watch on the cold mountainside and anticipated the bright coins they would receive beyond Northgate.

And then, one bright morning, their boredom ended.

The Daewar and one of the broad-shouldered Theiwar, on morning watch on the concealed ledge outside the sentinel cave, were the first to see the strangers, and they woke the others. Far in the distance, at least thirty miles to the west, there was movement on a ridgetop, the tiny, methodical "flowing" motion of a great many people—or some kind of creatures—on the move. For a time the six all stood on the ledge, bundled in the heavy bearskin robes that made them look like bearded badgers with bright helmets, as the distant movement continued. "There are a lot of them," a Theiwar observed. "Thousands, it looks like."

"And they are coming this way," the Hylar decided.

For an hour or more, the flow of distant movement continued, rank after rank of tiny specks appearing atop the faraway ridge, and moving down its visible slope, disappearing into some valley below.

"A herd of bison?" one of the Daergar suggested.

"Not likely." The Hylar shook his head. "They're moving in the wrong direction for bison in this season. I think those are people. Maybe a trade caravan?"

"From where?" the Daewar protested. "They're coming from the west. There's nothing out there but wilderness."

"There are Neidar settlements."

A Theiwar shook his head, frowning with intuition. "Those are people, all right, but they're not Neidar."

"The only dwarves outside Thorbardin in this season are Neidar." The Daewar frowned. "Do you suppose those are humans or something?"

"What would that many humans be doing out in the wilderness?" a Daergar puzzled. "And why would they be coming here?"

"Why do humans ever come here? To attack Thorbardin."

"They've been trying and failing for centuries. That last time—what was it, four or five years ago? Lord Kane or some such name? He brought a whole army all the way from Daltigoth. But they didn't get in. They just banged on Northgate for a while, then gave up and went away."

"But they came from the north. These people are coming from the west. Maybe they don't know that they can't get in. Or maybe they've forgotten. I hear humans are very forgetful."

The Hylar had brought out a far-seeing tube—a brass cylinder with glass lenses mounted in it—and they took turns peering through it. But the distant specks were too far away even for magnified vision. Then, after a time, there was nothing to look at. All of the moving specks had disappeared from view, hidden by intervening rises.

"I think we had better signal," the Hylar decided, turning toward the enclosed cave.

"Signal what?" a Daergar scoffed cynically. "Do we say something moved, and we saw it but we don't know what it was? I say we wait and get a better look."

The Hylar went on into the cave, and returned with a large vibrar and a pair of wooden mallets. But he set the drum aside and crouched on the ledge, waiting. "We'll take a better look when they're closer," he said. "But then, whatever or whoever is out there, we signal. Any time several thousand of anything approach Thorbardin, the gatekeepers ought to know about it."

"I agree." The Daergar who had spoken crouched beside the Hylar, his face hidden by the slitted iron mask his dark-sighted people favored in daylight. "But there's plenty of time. There are still a lot of miles out there, between us and whoever is coming to call."

The sun stood directly overhead when the strangers appeared again, topping another rise in the mountain terrain. Though still far away, they were closer now by several miles. And the direction of their line now was obvious. They were moving south of east, directly toward Thorbardin. The Hylar sentinel put the seeing-tube to his eye, peered through it, and grunted, "By Reorx! Those are dwarves!"

Beside him, the Daewar blinked in surprise. "Dwarves? What dwarves? Who are they?"

"I can't tell," the Hylar said, squinting into the seeing-tube. "Neidar, I suppose. All the other thanes are in Thorbardin. But so many? There are thousands of them! I've never seen more than a few dozen Neidar traveling together. Here, see for yourself."

The Daewar took the device and peered through it. Magnified, the distant horde was still tiny, barely identifiable, but there was no doubt: they were dwarves. He tried to estimate their number and gave up. It was as the Hylar had said. There were thousands of them. Several thousands. And they marched as an army marches—distinct companies in orderly ranks, maintaining their formations despite the rugged terrain.

In the lead and on both flanks rode mounted companies, brightly clad dwarven figures mounted on big horses, and among those afoot were hundreds of other large beasts, some pulling carts, some laden with packs.

Here and there among the strangers, the high sun glinted on bright armor—the familiar flash of metal helmets, shields, and body plating—but what was more striking were the bright colors of fine garments. Each group and company seemed to have its own combination of colors. In one unit, yellow and brown were prominent. In another, green and black dominated, and in still another, blue and tan. Only among those in the middle of the array—those walking with the carts and pack animals —did there seem no pattern of colors, though even there bright hues were plentiful.

"They dress colorfully," the Daewar noted, his gaze dropping to the very head of the moving band. At the point of the first mounted unit, whose preferred colors seemed to be red and gray, rode a figure whose helm and breastplate reflected the sunlight like a mirror. He wore a cloak of bright red, and the same red was used in the trappings of his horse. The sentinel peered, trying to see more detail, then handed the tube to another volunteer, one of the Theiwar. "What do you make of that one in the lead?" he asked. "I don't think he's a Neidar. For that matter, none of them look like Neidar to me."

The Theiwar gazed through the tube's lenses, then handed the device back to the Hylar. "You look," he said. "See if that's somebody you know."

The Hylar squinted, then shook his head. "I can't make out any features at this distance. Why did you think I might know him?"

"I don't know." The Theiwar shrugged. "There's just something about him that reminds me of Hylar."

"When you've seen one Hylar, you've seen them all," the Daewar chuckled. "Of course, that applies to Theiwar, too. You people have arms as long as your legs."

"You can keep your opinions to yourself, gold-molder," the Theiwar growled good-naturedly.

The Hylar sentinel took another look, then passed the seeing-tube along and picked up his vibrar, hitching its leather sling over his shoulder. "We've seen enough to signal the gate," he said, gripping his mallets.

A masked Daergar turned toward him. "What are you going to say is coming, a caravan or an army?"

"That mob could be either one," another sentinel said, squinting through the tube. "Or it could be a little of both. Reorx! Look at all that armor!"

Ignoring them, the Hylar stepped to the edge of the sentinel ledge, raised his mallets, and began a deep, thunderous tattoo on the big vibrar's taut head, using the elaborate drum-talk his ancestors had brought to these mountains centuries before. The mountainside resounded with the voice of the drum. About a minute later, another drum—around on the south face of Sky's End—took up the song, echoing and relaying it. Moments later another drum joined in, farther away, and then another, a growing chorus of deep, thrusting rhythms, a string of receding thunders relaying the message toward the north gate of Thorbardin, many miles away on the lower slopes of Cloudseeker Peak. Some minutes passed as the drums sang, then the Theiwar who was still watching the strangers through the seeing-tube said, "Those people out there have stopped. They must have heard the drums."

"What are they doing?" the Daewar asked.

"I can't tell. Something is going on in that lead unit, but I can't see what."

The Hylar sentinel continued his tattoo for a time, then lowered the drum and listened. From the south came a brief response, and he nodded. "Message received," he said. "Northgate is alerted."

He was heading into the shelter cave to put up his vibrar when the air rang again with distant thunder. He turned abruptly, listening. The sound was coming not from the south, not from Thorbardin, but from the west, and the message of it made his mouth drop open. "It's them!" he shouted, pointing. "The strangers—they are signaling with drums!"

For a moment, all six sentinels stared in wonder at the distant assemblage. It was incredible that strangers, coming from the western wilderness, should have such drums. It was even more incredible that they would know how to use them. Even among the thanes of Thorbardin, few dwarves other than the Hylar ever mastered the vibrar signal-song.

The sentinels stared across the miles, listening, then the Daewar turned to the Hylar. "Well, what do they say?"

"They speak to Thorbardin," the Hylar said slowly. "They say greetings from Hammerhand, to the chieftains and the Council of Thanes. They say Hammerhand comes to trade. They say Hammerhand will make camp below Northgate, and invites the trade wardens out to inspect his goods. He also says that he will meet with the Council of Thanes."

"Who is Hammerhand?" the Daewar puzzled. "I've never heard the name. Have you?"

None of them had. "Whoever he is, he's arrogant," a Theiwar said. "An outsider, requesting audience with the Council of Thanes!"

"He isn't requesting," the Hylar said, still listening to the drums, interpreting their song. "He doesn't ask for a meeting. He demands it."

Throughout that day, and all of the next, sentinels on Sky's End and sentries on Cloudseeker watched as the throng of strangers approached, moving at the leisurely pace of the pack beasts among them. By the end of the second day, they had cleared the final ridges, with Cloudseeker's north slopes directly ahead of them. The encampment they made there, along an icy little stream, was no more than three miles from the stepped slopes where the big mountain began.

By then, hundreds of seeing-tubes were trained on them, from the sentinel posts and from the walled ledge at the top of the great ramps that led to Northgate. The great oval gate was open, its impregnable plug retracted into the shadows behind its steel sheath, and a growing crowd of dwarves was gathered on the ledge, watching the intruders.

The strange drums were silent now. The strangers went about their chores, making camp for the night, and seemed to pointedly ignore all those on the mountain ahead who were gaping at them. Several times, drummers had come out of Thorbardin to signal, asking the strangers to identify themselves, asking where they were from and what they had that they wanted to trade, asking who was this Hammerhand who demanded access to the Council of Thanes. But there had been no response. It was as though the strangers had said all they had to say and were not interested in answering questions.

About sundown, Hylar guards appeared on the ledge, using their shields to clear a path through the crowd there. Behind them, two dwarves stepped from the great open portal, and walked to the wall to look down. If anyone could be said to be "in charge" of Thorbardin in these troubled times, it was these two. Both were mature dwarves, in their middle years, and both were hardened by the burden they carried. Of all the various chieftains, wardens, bosses, and gang leaders who came and went throughout the vast, subterranean realm of the mountain dwarves, it had fallen to Dunbarth Ironthumb and Jeron Redleather to keep Thorbardin functioning despite the explosive feuds and myriad hostilities within.

Jeron Redleather, chieftain of Thane Daewar and senior

member of the Council of Thanes, was a burly, bright-eyed dwarf. The elaborate gold inlays of his helmet and breastplate reflected the gold of his flowing hair and full beard, and both the exquisite faceted stone set in his helm, just above his bushy brows, and the rich blue of his flowing cloak reflected the color of his eyes. Ruddy cheeks and a round pug nose gave him the appearance of constant, secret laughter, and the rich gaudiness of his attire might have seemed to indicate a strutting vanity. Like most Daewar, Jeron Redleather enjoyed bright color and rich attire to the point of seeming—to dwarves of other thanes—pompous and a bit preposterous, but was actually nothing of the sort. Jeron Redleather could be jovial on occasion, and might strut a bit now and then, but those who knew him—friend and foe alike—were well aware he could be as tough and rigid as the very stone of Thorbardin.

His companion, Dunbarth Ironthumb, was every inch the Hylar chieftain, though he had refused for years to be chieftain of his thane. To be chieftain, he felt, would oblige him to take part in the various feuds that kept erupting in Thorbardin, and he had no interest in feuds. Of all the tribes, or thanes, only the Hylar had managed over the years to avoid the constant conflicts under the mountain, though even Harl Thrustweight, the last Hylar chieftain, had been hard pressed to remain aloof when all about him were at one another's throats.

Harl Thrustweight was a legendary name among the Hylar. He had maintained and enforced the "Hylar Peace" among the thanes until his untimely death in a mysterious rockfall near the Theiwar city of Theibardin. Although nothing was ever proven, it was suspected that the rockfall was no accident, and a band of Theiwar led by the schemer Than-Kar had left Thorbardin soon after, never to return.

Harl Thrustweight had been the last chieftain of the

Hylar, because Dunbarth Ironthumb refused to take the job, and his stubborn people refused to choose someone else. Thus the Hylar now had no chieftain. Dunbarth Ironthumb did, though, represent Thane Hylar on the Council of Thanes. And with the passing of time he had become its strongest member in many ways.

Between them, with or without the support of the rest of the council, the Daewar and the Hylar exercised enough wisdom and influence to keep Thorbardin functioning as a realm, and to keep the still simmering grudges and feuds among the thanes from erupting into any further outright civil wars.

Dour and thoughtful, the Hylar's dark eyes, dark hair, and short, backswept beard gave him an air of aloofness which was as misleading as the Daewar's appearance of careless joviality. Attired in his usual muted colors—leather kilt, dark leather boots, gray-brown jerkin, and gray cloak, his body armor, shield, and helm almost devoid of ornamentation—Dunbarth Ironthumb might have appeared cold and remote, uncaring of the tumults and turmoils of the dwarven realm he so influenced. Those who knew him, though, knew better. Not in all of Thorbardin, most agreed, was there anyone more dedicated to the welfare and perpetuity of the undermountain realm than Dunbarth Ironthumb.

Now the two leaders, the Daewar and the Hylar, looked out across the valley below the slopes, puzzled and worried. They had never heard of a dwarf called Hammerhand, nor of any such formidable array of dwarves as was now spread along the little stream.

The leader had been described to them by sentinels who said he looked to be of Hylar origin, but no one recognized him or knew his name. And now, with the horde encamped a few hours' march from the ramps of Northgate, he was nowhere in sight. None of the hundreds of watchers had seen him since the night before, when the strangers were still fifteen or more miles away.

"Any ideas?" Dunbarth asked now, shielding his eyes against the last rays of sunset.

"They say they come to trade," Jeron Redleather said. "And those carts and pack beasts seem to carry goods. I think we should—" He stopped abruptly, turning half around, then shrugged. "Odd," he muttered. "I thought someone brushed against me just then."

"You were saying?" Dunbarth reminded.

"Oh, yes." The Daewar turned again to the low wall. "I think we should send traders to meet them tomorrow. If they have goods to trade, why not welcome them?"

"But the rest of it? That demand for a meeting with the council?"

"Oh, we won't do that, of course," Jeron said. "And we certainly won't let any of them inside Thorbardin. Not until we know a good deal more about them at any rate."

"Then after the traders go out tomorrow, we'll close the gate and keep it closed," Dunbarth concluded.

They gave orders to the guards nearby, then walked back through Northgate, through the gatehouse with its huge screw and driving mechanisms, through the old delves of Gatekeep and out along the catwalk that led from one end of Anvil's Echo to the other. All around them, alert eyes watched from murder holes, but they had no concern. The eyes were those of Dunbarth's elite home guard. Across Anvil's Echo and a few steps into the great tunnel that was the northern road to the central cities of Thorbardin, Dunbarth Ironthumb stopped suddenly and turned. A dozen yards back, his guard company halted, weapons at the ready.

For a moment, the Hylar leader looked around, then resumed his walk, striding alongside Jeron Redleather,

"What's the matter?" the Daewar asked. "Why did you stop just then?"

"I don't know," Dunbarth said. "I had the feeling, for just a moment, that someone was following us. It seemed as though there was somebody walking right behind us."

9

Balladine

At break of dawn, the fresh west wind whispering in the valleys and up the slopes of Cloudseeker had a smell of spring about it. Northgate of Thorbardin had been closed through the night, but now its great screw turned again and the huge, steel-clad stone plug that was the gate receded slowly into the gatehouse, letting the breeze and the morning light enter. Guards stepped out through the great portal, took up positions on the ledge and the ramps, and gazed curiously out across the valley below.

Cookfire smoke rose above the big encampment there, and there was movement everywhere as the strangers from the west had their breakfasts, tended their livestock, and began taking down their travel tents. They were preparing for a march, and the dwarves above, at Northgate, watched curiously as the pace of activity increased its tempo.

From such a distance, the tiny figures by the stream seemed to all be moving in unison, going about their various morning chores, but with a visible rhythm, as though there were music there, and they were all listening to it.

Then the wind shifted a bit, wafting up the slope, and the guards on the ledge heard it, too. The faint sound was that of a single drum, beating softly and steadily, a deep, throbbing rhythm that seemed to touch the dwarven soul. In fascination, the guards on the mountain watched and listened, then snapped to quick attention as a platoon of the elite guard stepped through the open gate into the dawn light.

The new arrivals spread out, looking up the slope above Northgate, down the slope below the wall, and down both climbing ramps. When their surveillance was complete, they spread apart and saluted. Jeron Redleather stepped out into the morning, followed by Dunbarth Ironthumb and old Swing Basto, chieftain of the Theiwar.

Like the guards, the three leaders gazed curiously out across the westward valley, where the strangers were packing their animals and rolling their tents. The smoke that had floated above the encampment was gone, the cookfires extinguished. Obviously, the strangers were ready to move out.

"Is there any sign yet of their leader?" Jeron asked one of the guards, who held a seeing-tube.

"Haven't seen him," the dwarf answered. "At least we haven't seen that red cloak and bright armor. Maybe he changed his clothes."

"If he did, he could be anywhere over there, and we wouldn't spot him," another guard said. "Nobody has had a good look at him yet."

Dunbarth Ironthumb had wandered to the wall, and stood there now, listening intently. "That drum," he muttered. "There is something about that drum. . . ."

"What is it?" Jeron asked. "Is the drum talking?"

"No, it's just singing. But there is something about that rhythm. It's like something I should remember, something I should understand. But I'm sure I've never heard it before."

"Maybe your ancestors heard something like it," Jeron suggested. "You Hylar have always been drum people."

"Yes, possibly," the Hylar agreed. Still, though, he listened, feeling as if the faint, haunting beat were talking to him personally. Among the guards, some of the other Hylar had similar expressions of puzzlement.

Even without the seeing-tubes, they could see the people out in the valley scurrying into formation, bright cloaks swirling, bright armor flashing as they made ready to cross the stream. The long line of carts and pack animals was brought forward, and on the flanks, dwarves in bright costume climbed aboard their saddled mounts and wheeled into position. The red-and-gray company assembled, mounted, and rode across the stream, bright water splashing under the hooves of their horses. There was, though, no sign of the red-cloaked figure who had led them when they were first seen.

When they were across, all the rest began to move, crossing rank by rank and group by group to take up their march positions. It looked as though a whole city were on the march.

"There certainly are a lot of them," Jeron noted as the strangers spread and advanced, heading toward Thorbardin. "Thousands of them."

"My guards estimate at least nine thousand," Dunbarth told him. "Maybe more than that. I can't imagine where they came from. I don't recall there being anything west of here larger than an occasional Neidar village. But by

Reorx, there are as many people down there as there are in all of Hybardin."

"Speaking of Hybardin," Jeron said, "do you know whether any of your people might have been prowling my shore last night? The guards didn't see anyone, but there was a Hylar boat at the dock this morning, and nobody around to account for it."

"You, too?" Swing Basto asked. "I've had a dozen reports of prowlers wandering around Theibardin during the night. And one of my water-pipers swears he turned around and saw the face of Harl Thrustweight looking at him."

"Too much ale." Jeron grinned. "Or too much imagination. Harl Thrustweight, you say?"

"No, not Harl Thrustweight. Just his face. There wasn't any body attached to it."

"Definitely ale," Jeron repeated. "Ale, and possibly a troubled conscience. That would account for seeing ghosts."

"That water-piper had nothing to do with the Hylar chief's accident," the old Theiwar blustered. "And even if anybody in my thane did, they're all long gone now."

"Hush!" Dunbarth raised a commanding hand. "Listen!"

Out in the valley, the entire caravan of strangers was now across the little stream and approaching at a stately, steady pace. The soft drum still throbbed its haunting rhythm, but it was louder now, as though mufflings had been removed. And another drum had joined its voice, adding a stirring counterpoint to the beat. As they listened, another drum joined in, and another, each adding a new tone and dimension to the growing sound.

"What is that?" Jeron rasped. "Are they saying something? Is it a signal?"

Before Dunbarth could answer, a gray-haired old Hylar hurried onto the ledge, glanced about, then pulled a sheet of rough paper and a graphite stick from his robe. Those around him were a bit surprised to see old Chane Lowen out and about at such an early hour, though as lore-keeper of Thorbardin, he generally came and went as he pleased. Listening intently, the old dwarf began making quick, strange marks on his paper, in time with the drumbeats. Jeron Redleather glanced over the newcomer's shoulder and scowled. He had never been able to decipher either the signals that the Hylar vibrars sent, or the odd, curled runes by which they were recorded.

"If they're talking," Dunbarth answered Jeron's question, "it's no drum language I recognize." He turned to the signal-master. "Chane, do you . . . ?"

"Hush!" Chane rasped, frowning and scribbling.

For long minutes, the chant of the drums grew on the wind, while Chane Lowen scribbled its tones, rhythms, and nuances. Then he pulled an old, yellowed scroll from his robe and unrolled it. For a moment he held both papers before him, comparing them. Then he looked up, his old eyes bright with awe and excitement. "It is!" he said. "It truly is!"

"It is what?" Dunbarth prodded.

"Here, look at this!" Chane thrust the ancient scroll at him. "This has been handed down for centuries. It was among the scrolls of Mistral Thrax. It is from the old times, from the first Hylar. Or before. It is . . ." He cocked his head, listening. "I've studied this, but never heard it before. It has never been played in these mountains. But this scroll is what those drums are singing. Listen! It is truly beautiful."

"I agree." Dunbarth nodded. "It's pretty. But what is it?"

"A drum-song from long ago, from a place very far away. It was the song of summer solstice, there."

"Summer solstice?" Jeron Redleather cocked a bushy, golden brow. "But it is barely spring."

"The song was used to call assembly," the old Hylar

continued. "It was the song of festivals and trading time. It was the Call to Balladine."

"Legends of ancient Thorin," Dunbarth mused. "Maybe there really was such a place."

"A trading call," Jeron studied the throng in the valley suspiciously. "Maybe they truly are here to trade. We'll see."

"Traders who march like an army?" Swing Basto growled. "And why would traders demand to meet with the Council of Thanes? It's obvious, those people intend to invade Thorbardin."

"In that case," Jeron assured him, "we'll do what we always do. We'll close the gates until they go away."

"Do what we always do," Dunbarth muttered. "Sometimes I wonder . . ." He didn't complete the thought, and Jeron Redleather only glanced at him and shrugged. Dunbarth could be moody sometimes, like all Hylar, and Jeron had heard him complain many times that the people of Thorbardin had lived within a shell so long that they were no better than turtles. In a way, Jeron agreed with him, but there wasn't much that could be done about it. The entire purpose of Thorbardin was its impregnability. The undermountain fortress was created to give the dwarven thanes a secure, unassailable place where they could live safe from intrusion. In Thorbardin, the dwarves were safe from the outside world. Many of them had come, over the centuries, to feel that Thorbardin *was* the world, and that nothing outside mattered.

Like the Hylar leader, Jeron Redleather often regretted that it was so. People less secure and less secluded, he thought, might find other interests beyond simply eating, sleeping, squabbling, and holding grudges against one another.

Jeron felt a slight touch, as though someone's cloak had brushed him, and turned, but there was no one there. A moment later one of the guards on the west ramp hissed, started to draw his sword, then looked around in confusion. Dunbarth Ironthumb turned at the sound and called, "What's the matter over there?"

"Nothing, I guess," the guard said sheepishly. "I thought I saw something, but I guess I didn't."

"Well, what did you think you saw?"

"A face. Right in front of me, looking at me. But then it was gone."

"Ghosts," Jeron Redleather muttered.

Within an hour, the approaching throng of strangers was less than a mile away, and well into the meadowed valley between the slopes of Cloudseeker and Sky's End peaks. A growing crowd had gathered on the Northgate ledge, watching the strangers curiously and listening to the haunting music of the drums. The sun was high now, intensifying the bright colors of the panoply below, and the watchers could see things they had not seen before. Among the mounted units, only one dwarf in three or four wore metal armor, and the armor—though bright and well kept—was a motley assortment of types and designs, as though gathered from bazaars or collected on battlefields.

All of the strange dwarves, even the women and children among them, carried weapons. But some of their weapons were crudely crafted, as though made in haste, and many looked to be of human or elven design. "They have rough iron, but not much good steel," Jeron Redleather noted. "Wherever they come from, their weavers and tanners have had materials to work with, but their metalworkers have had to settle for what they could find." He turned to the warden of trade. "Take note, Agate. Many of those pack animals carry bales of fine furs, and I'd wager those carts have some excellent fabrics in them."

"They've been scavenging, by the look of some of their metals," Dunbarth Ironthumb added. "A lot of them carry human blades."

Still, with their fine horses and bright cloaks, the strange dwarves had a formidable look about them, purposeful and determined.

As the assembly came even nearer, one of the riders in the first unit—the red-and-grays—spurred his mount and galloped ahead, leading a spare saddled horse. The second animal was finely outfitted, with a fine dwarven saddle, silver-accented leathers and headstall, and a skirt of fine steel chain, all embellished by patterns of bright red fabric.

"That's the horse their leader was riding when we first saw them," a guard said.

"But where is their leader?" Dunbarth muttered.

Then, at the ledge wall, someone said, "Look!" and eyes turned downward and to the left. At the foot of the west ramp was a scarlet-cloaked dwarf whose dark hair glinted in the sunlight as he strode down the slope.

The lone rider sped toward him, but reined in when he raised his hand. Without looking back, the red-cloak stepped to the riderless horse, took its reins, and climbed up on its back, rolling up the sling-ladder behind him and snugging it to his saddle. Loosing thongs on the pommel, he released a slung shield, helmet, and hammer, and donned them. With the other rider following, he rode out into the meadow, turned his mount full around, and raised his arm again. Instantly, in the approaching throng, the drums ceased their song, and a single drum beat a brief, complex tattoo.

"They say they will be ready to receive our traders by noon," Chane Lowen translated so all those on the ledge could hear. "They also say the Council of Thanes is to be assembled tomorrow."

"Like rust!" Swing Basto spat. "Dunbarth, let your drummers tell them that the Council of Thanes meets only in the Great Hall of Thorbardin, not outside."

At a nod from Dunbarth, two drummers stepped forward and sent the message. A moment later, the strange drums responded. "Hammerhand would have it no other way," they said.

"Arrogance!" the Theiwar chieftain snapped when the signal was translated. "I say we close the gate, and to corruption with these intruders!"

Before anyone could answer, one of the guards on the ramp shouted, "That's him! That's the face I saw before me!" The guard had found a seeing-tube and was peering through it at the scarlet-cloaked rider down in the meadow.

Dunbarth Ironthumb took a tube from his nearest guard and looked through it. The face of the newcomer below turned toward him, and he squinted. Strong, blunt features framed a pair of dark, brooding eyes that seemed to be looking directly at him. Dark, wavy hair fell below a finely crafted helmet, and a trimmed, backswept beard parted to reveal strong, white teeth in a wide, resolute mouth.

Dunbarth swore aloud, and pressed the tube to his eye. In some ways, the face below resembled the long-dead chieftain of the Hylar, Harl Thrustweight. The set of the high cheekbones, the level gaze of those commanding eyes. "I feel I should know him!" Dunbarth rasped, handing the seeing-tube to Jeron Redleather. "Look! Who do you see?"

The Daewar peered, then turned, frowning. "Who else but a son could so resemble a father?" he said thoughtfully.

"Are you suggesting that is Harl's son, Derkin?" Dunbarth demanded.

The Daewar peered again, muttering. "I don't know," he conceded. "There is a resemblance. And yet . . . that is surely not the Derkin I remember."

Without ceremony, old Chane Lowen pushed forward, elbowing chieftains aside, and wrested the seeing-tube from Jeron's hand. Leaning against the ledge wall, he sighted through the tube, then turned to the rest of them. "I have seen that face," he said slowly. "There is an old painting in the deepest archives in Hybardin. The painting is as old as Thorbardin itself. And the face in the painting is that face down there."

"Are you saying that isn't Harl Thrustweight's lost son?" Dunbarth demanded.

"I vaguely recall Derkin Winterseed," the old lore-keeper said. "He was a reclusive youth, quiet and given to moods."

"Moods?" Jeron Redleather rasped. "As I heard it, Derkin had only two ways of associating with people—either ignore them, or insult them. It was a wonder somebody didn't brain him. I don't think even his father liked him very much. Personally, though, I don't think I ever met him."

"He wasn't around much," Chane Lowen said, searching his memory. "Derkin was an odd one. He never seemed a Neidar, but he was always going off to outside places. He didn't like Thorbardin and made that clear. Then, the last time he left—many years ago—he just never came back." Chane half-turned, pointing toward the meadow. "If that person down there was ever Derkin Winterseed, he isn't anymore. See his movements. That person commands and leads. Derkin would never have led anyone."

"The old painting in the archives," Dunbarth pressed. "Whose face is in it?"

"Colin Stonetooth," Chane said. "The first chieftain of the Hylar. The dwarf who united the thanes to build Thorbardin. In the painting, he is much older, but I swear, that is his face down there."

On the meadow below Northgate, a vast encampment grew. Banners fluttered above brightly colored pavilions, surrounded by stalls and displays of wares. Wagons and carts disgorged bolts of bright fabric, big coils of hemp rope, and oiled leather weaves; intricately patterned carpets, arrays of fine, hand-carved furniture and wooden fixtures; bits of sculpture, tapestries, and paintings done in many styles and fashions; bundles of herbs, spices, and pots of exotic oils; dyes and essences; casks of prized white salt, dried fruits, and wild grains; myriad bits of elven-ware; bales of cured pelts and tanned hides—a wealth of goods such as Jeron Redleather's Daewar traders had not seen since the wars in Ergoth had disrupted so many of the trade routes.

"He certainly knows his goods," a trader commented, watching from above as the red-cloaked figure called Hammerhand directed the placement of wares and displays on the valley floor.

"He knows what is prized in Thorbardin," another agreed. "He knows what is hard to get here. Look at those western timbers! And the furs! Half of Thorbardin will be trying to outbid the other half for those."

"When we get them," the first trader pointed out.

"Oh, we'll get them, all right. The only question is, what will we have to give in trade?"

At midday, the drums sang again, and dozens of Daewar traders, followed by several hundred merchants from the various cities within Thorbardin, made their way down the ramps, accompanied by a squad of armed guards.

The guards were for display only, of course, and everyone knew it. With thousands of armed strangers awaiting the contingent below, the traders and their followers would have no chance at all if hostilities broke out. But such was always the life of traders and merchants. To acquire goods, they must go to where the goods were, barter for them, and take the risk. Further, there was something in the song of the drums, muted now but still beating, that was reassuring. This is an occasion to trade, they seemed to say, a time to haggle, but not to quarrel . . . a time to do business, not to do violence.

Throughout the afternoon, hundreds of dwarves from Thorbardin wandered about the valley camp, inspecting goods and setting prices, making lists and copious notes. At evening, as the sun of Krynn sat upon the western ranges, they gathered with their guards and returned up the ramps to Northgate to disappear inside. Guards saw them safely in, then wheeled to follow them, and the great plug of Northgate closed as the last rays of sunlight crept up the high peaks.

Inside, the merchants wandered off toward their cities and their shops, each accompanied by his band of hired armsmen. No street, way, or tunnel in Thorbardin could be considered entirely safe. Ambushers often lurked in shadows, waiting for a chance to attack some feud-enemy or anyone else of that enemy's clan.

The appointed traders hurried to where Jeron Redleather awaited their reports. A delved chamber near Northgate that usually served as a storage barn had been hastily refurnished the night before as a situational headquarters.

The Daewar leader generally was in charge of all matters involving commerce, just as the Hylar leader was conceded to be the person in charge of policing and defense. Surprisingly, though, the traders found almost the entire Council of Thanes awaiting them. Dunbarth Ironthumb of the Hylar was there, as were Swing Basto of the Theiwar, Trom Thule of the Klar, and even Crag Shade-eye of the Daergar. The only missing member of the Council was Grimble I, Highbulp of Clan Aghar, but that was no surprise. Not for a long time had anyone seen the gully dwarf leader or, for that matter, any of his tribe. During unsettled times, the Aghar tended to disappear.

The traders presented their lists and reports to the assembled leaders. The wares brought by the strangers were indeed valuable and would greatly benefit Thorbardin. And what the strangers demanded in trade was steel.

"Steel?" Swing Basto rasped. "Just . . . steel?"

"Forged steel," the warden of trade noted, poring over

notes and enscrollments. "They cite some types of tools and utensils that they will accept, but mostly they ask for armor and weapons. Hammers, axes, swords, knives, darts, javelin-points, shields, helms, a wide assortment of armor—"

"As we suspected," Jeron Redleather interrupted. "Those people have not had access to smelters or to the fine forges and metalshops we have here."

"But they certainly know about us," Dunbarth pointed out. "They seem to know exactly what goods we most need and exactly what we can best produce for trade. They are very familiar with Thorbardin."

"Their leader is." Jeron nodded. "That *must* be your old chieftain's son, the one who disappeared. Derkin. Who else could it be?"

"One of our people heard the name Derkin mentioned," a trader offered. "But the name that is most commonly used for their leader is Hammerhand."

"Tell us the rest," Jeron said, leaning forward, bright-eyed. In addition to being crafty merchants, his corps of traders were among the best spies in the dwarven realm, or maybe in the world.

The answer disappointed him though. "That's about all there is." The chief trader shrugged. "They showed us what they offer, told us what they want, and named their leader. Hammerhand. By observation, we learned that there are at least nine thousand in their party, and many carry healed battle wounds. They have seen combat. Also, some carry brands—the way humans sometimes mark slaves—and the marks of whips. Most of them speak with a Neidar accent, though the accents vary. They seem to be from all over."

"Nomadic dwarves?" Trom Thule muttered.

"They aren't nomads." The trader corrected him. "They carry no looms, anvils, or hearth-irons. That—and the grain, leathers, and woodcrafts they bring—indicates that they have a permanent base somewhere. There are women among them, as well, but we saw very few children.

"They have choice leathers, fine fabrics, and excellent wooden instruments, but the metal goods of their own crafting are of crude iron, copper, bronze, and brass. Everything we saw made of steel was obviously of human crafting, modified to suit dwarves.

"With one exception," another trader reminded him.

"Oh, yes. One exception. Their leader's armor—Hammerhand's—is of dwarven craft, and of the finest quality . . . though its design is very old." The chief trader paused, then shrugged. "We weren't able to get much information beyond that. I've never seen such close-mouthed people in my life."

A runner from the gatehouse appeared at the door of the chamber, looked inside, then entered. "The drums," he said, "those drums in the valley, they said bring the message here."

"Here?" Dunbarth frowned. "To this chamber?"

"Aye." The runner nodded. "Those drums said to come to this chamber, and tell the Council of Thanes to assemble tomorrow in the Great Hall, to meet with Hammerhand."

"Rust!" Jeron Redleather scowled. "Now how would those people out there know exactly where we would be, right now?"

"The drums said to say," the runner said, "that Hammerhand will speak with you tomorrow."

The assembled chiefs exchanged glances. "Let a signal be returned then," Dunbarth said. "Say that Hammerhand may enter Thorbardin at dawn."

"But only with ceremonial escort," Swing Basto grumped. "We don't want a lot of strangers running loose in Thorbardin."

"I shall assign the best guards to them," Dunbarth agreed, annoyed as usual by the Theiwar's sullen manner. "Jeron, your son's company is available. I'll assign them."

10
Thorbardin

Drums thundered at first dawn, and the dwarf called Hammerhand strode up the west ramp of Northgate with his "ceremonial" escort—ten burly, battle-hardened veterans in red-and-gray draped armor, all carrying sturdy shields and good swords that bore the nicks and scratches of enthusiastic use, and all with axes slung at their shoulders. The twelfth member of the group was an old, one-armed dwarf in leathers and linens. A reed basket slung from his shoulder bulged with rolled scrolls, and dagger hilts were visible at his belted kilt, the tops of both his boots, and the collar of his gray cape.

With the others following closely, the scarlet-cloaked

Hammerhand strode along the gateway's wide, walled ledge to the very center of the massive, steel-clad gate. The great plug, a solid wall of stone sheathed in time-darkened steel, was patterned all over its surface with the small dents, scratches, and tool marks of those who, over the centuries, had tried in vain to get through it. Like its twin on the south face of the mountain, many miles away, Northgate was a monument to the stubborn refusal of the mountain dwarves to be troubled by outsiders.

The one-armed old dwarf peered closely at the mute steel of the gate and pursed his lips, an expression that made his beard stand out before his face. "I haven't seen this gate in eighty years," he noted, "but it hasn't changed. Its face reads like a testament to the futility of invasion."

"More like a monument to the stone-headed stubbornness of those within," Hammerhand growled. Loosing his hammer-loop from a powerful shoulder, he paused, glancing at the eastern sky. "Has that dratted girl been found yet, Calan?"

"Not yet." The graybeard shook his head. "Nobody's seen her since yesterday, right after you came back from your scouting." He lowered his voice, stepping close. "You realize she saw you put away that invisibility cloak, don't you? She watches you every minute, it seems. It's a wonder you have any secrets from her at all."

"I'm not sure I do," Hammerhand growled. "Well, she's probably hiding somewhere, pouting. Maybe I should have been a bit gentler yesterday when I told her she couldn't come with us this morning."

"She certainly has a mind of her own," Calan agreed. As the younger dwarf had done before, he glanced at the eastern sky. Patterns of dawn light painted the distant clouds. The sun would be up soon. "It's full dawn," he noted. "Time to go calling."

Hammerhand nodded. Raising his hammer, he delivered a single, imperious blow to the time-darkened surface of the huge gate, then stepped back. Several seconds passed, then the gate grated in its frame and slid slowly inward, backing away from those waiting on the ledge. It cleared several feet of steel framing, then receded a few inches farther and stopped. From both sides, eyes peered through the crack. A suspicious voice called, "Identify yourself!"

Without looking aside, the red-cloak stepped forward and struck the stopped gate another ringing blow. "I'm Hammerhand!" he stated, his voice deep, commanding, and loud enough to be heard by anyone in the gatehouse beyond. "I come to meet with the Council of Thanes. Open up!"

"How do we know you're him?" the same voice queried, sounding argumentative.

The old, one-armed dwarf stepped up beside Hammerhand to growl, "Open this gate or we'll make a new gate of our own! We're coming in."

From the crack at the other side of the gate, another voice—a voice of authority—commanded, "Open the berusted gate, you imbeciles! We've got our orders, and that's the one we're supposed to let in."

"The rest of 'em, too?" the first voice asked suspiciously.

"Stop arguing and open the gate! It's all right!"

There was muttering from the cracks, then the huge gate began moving again, receding into its shadowed gatehouse. The dwarves on the ledge waited in stony silence until it was fully open, withdrawn twenty feet into its housing. Then the one with the scarlet cloak put away his hammer, growled an ironic "Thank you," and stepped forward, followed by his escorts.

Within the gatehouse, they filed around the massive gate, some of them pausing momentarily to gape at the sheer size of the steel-sheathed stone plug and the huge, milled auger behind it. But the one called Hammerhand

and the old one-arm barely glanced at the huge mechanics of the gatehouse and strode on, while the rest hurried to follow. Gatekeepers and surly-looking guards stepped back as they passed, and a gold-bearded young Daewar with the insignia of a Home Guards officer fell into step beside Hammerhand. "I'm Luster," he said amiably. "Luster Redleather. I'll show you the way to the Great Hall."

"I know the way," Hammerhand rasped, then eased his tone slightly as he glanced at the Daewar. "Luster Redleather? Are you Jeron Redleather's son?"

"You know my father?" The Daewar brightened.

"They call me Hammerhand," the red-cloak said, ignoring the question. Indicating the old dwarf with the reed basket, he added, "This is Calan Silvertoe."

Luster nodded at Calan and glanced around at the ten heavily armed warriors flanking and following them. "And these?"

"The Ten," Hammerhand said. "The one with the crested helm is Tap Tolec. He's First of the Ten. Are you the only escort they sent? One alone, to keep all of us out of mischief?"

"Hardly." Luster chuckled. "I have a full hundred waiting just beyond Anvil's Echo. For your protection, of course. We have a long walk ahead, and the ways can be, ah . . . hazardous at times. My father wouldn't want anything to happen to you . . . at least until he satisfies his curiosity about you."

"What's he curious about?"

"Just about everything," the Daewar said. "Who you are, where you came from, what your purposes are."

"He knows that," Hammerhand rasped. "We came to trade goods for steel."

"Of course." The young Daewar nodded. "Steel armor, steel weapons . . ."

"The best smelters and forges in the world are in Thorbardin," the red-cloak said. "Where else would we go?"

"But after you have your, ah . . . steel goods," Luster pressed, "what then? You must have a specific use in mind for all those weapons."

"And curiosity must run in your family," Hammerhand noted.

They passed between long rows of closed passages, lining both sides of the big, sky-lighted tunnel. Broad delvings beyond had once been a construction camp for Northgate and were now used as warehouses. Abruptly the tunnel opened out in all directions, and the path became a suspended bridge—a catwalk leading from end to end of a great cavern lined above and on both sides with small, dark openings.

Neither Hammerhand nor Calan Silvertoe more than glanced at the murderous ports and the vertiginous path as they strode out into the opening, but Luster heard whispers among the ten who followed: "So this is Anvil's Echo. I've heard about it." "I guess you have to see this to really believe it." "Look at those murder-holes! Do you suppose we're being watched from those things?"

On impulse, Luster said, over his shoulder, "There are probably a hundred watchers at those ports right now, maybe more. But don't worry. They're all Dunbarth Ironthumb's people. Nobody gets into the defense lairs without his approval."

"It's a shame the rest of Thorbardin doesn't have the discipline of its defenses," Hammerhand muttered.

"The Hylar would agree with you on that score." Luster grinned. "You look like a Hylar, yourself. Are you?"

"I'm Hammerhand," the red-cloak rumbled. "That's all I am, at least for now."

Unabashed, the young Daewar said, "Chane Lowen says you look like Colin Stonetooth."

"He probably does," Calan Silvertoe rasped, then went silent at a glance from his leader.

The catwalk ended, the sun-tunnel-lighted way began

again, and the party marched between the waiting ranks
of a hundred dwarven soldiers, standing at attention. As
they passed, the guards fell in around and behind them,
ringing them closely. With a suspicious glare at the soldiers, Tap Tolec muttered orders, and the Ten closed ranks
around their leader and the two walking with him. Their
frowns made it clear to the guards that they were to keep
their distance from Hammerhand. Responding to their
glares, some of the Thorbardin guards pressed closer,
tauntingly. Then one of them yelped and backed off,
stooping to rub his ankle.

"What happened?" one of his companions asked.

"One of these outsiders kicked me on the shin," the
injured one snapped.

Hammerhand swung around, stopping the procession.
He glanced at Tap Tolec, then from face to face of his other
nine bodyguards. All of them shook their heads. "Nobody
kicked your soldier," Hammerhand told Luster. "If any of
them had, he'd be more than just bruised." Imperiously,
he turned again and strode on, the double ring of escorts
reforming around him.

Luster Redleather's eyes twinkled with amusement.
"Your people look after you," he noted.

Hammerhand didn't respond, but Calan Silvertoe said,
"The Ten are the chosen of the Chosen Ones. Your soldiers
would be well advised to treat them with respect."

"My soldiers—a hundred of Thorbardin's best?" Luster
asked, grinning.

"If they're your best, then you don't want to lose them,"
Hammerhand said quietly. "If they crowd my people,
what happens to them is their fault. The Ten don't like
being crowded."

With a wave of his hand, Luster Redleather signaled his
hundred, who eased away from the compact group of
warriors, giving them respect and a bit more room. From
somewhere on the left flank came an angry whisper: "One

of them *did* kick me! I don't know who, but *somebody* did."

After a half-hour's walk, the big tunnel they were following—called the Second Road—bent sharply to the left, and carved runes in the stone wall said that Theibardin—first of the Theiwar cities—lay ahead. The Thorbardin guards had now formed a complete circle around the visitors, and marched with eyes alert and shields high. A hundred yards past the turn, several dozen shadowy figures suddenly darted from a side-delve, shouting a babble of taunts and insults. Several of them hurled stones at the approaching company. The leading Thorbardin guards deflected the stones casually with their shields and drew hand weapons. With more taunts and insults, the mob of attackers turned and ran, disappearing around a bend in the distance.

"Somebody doesn't like us here," Calan Silvertoe drawled.

"It isn't you," Luster Redleather assured his guests. "It's us. A lot of people here don't like the Home Guards. We've doubled the patrols since the last riots and spoiled a lot of people's fun."

"This is a riot zone?" Calan asked.

"Sometimes I think all of Thorbardin is a riot zone," Luster told him sadly. "Every city in the cavern has had trouble of one kind or another during the past few decades . . . except maybe the Hylar city. The Hylar don't usually get involved in the feuds. But everywhere else, there's always somebody ready to lead a gang against somebody else."

"What do they fight about?" one of the Ten asked.

"Anything and everything." Luster shrugged. "Who knows? My father says the darkest quality of dwarven nature is that we never forget a slight or forgive a grudge. And, of course, in Thorbardin we've had a lot of generations to accumulate grudges."

"And nothing better to do than feud?" Calan asked.

"For some among us, no. There isn't enough real work to keep everybody busy."

"There should be," Hammerhand muttered. "There would be, if Thorbardin hadn't forgotten why it's here."

Luster glanced at him, curious about the smoldering anger in the stranger's voice, an anger that seemed to deepen with every step into the cavern realm. "What does that mean?"

"That's what I came to talk to the council about," the red-cloak said, his brow furrowed and stormy beneath his polished helm.

The delves of Theibardin spread around them then, and they turned at a wide road that led to the central cavern of Thorbardin. Everywhere, dwarves by the hundreds turned out to watch them pass. Most of the dwarves here were Theiwar, identifiable by their smoke-brown hair and beards, and the wide shoulders and long arms that were characteristic of their clan. But many among them were obviously of mixed blood, with features that came from Daewar, Daergar, Hylar, or Klar lineage.

Generations of intermarriage among the thanes had in many ways strengthened the dwarves of Thorbardin. But it also had started its share of feuds.

Most of the people they passed seemed to harbor no hostility, only curiosity. But here and there they heard taunts and catcalls, and a few stones clanged off the shields of the Home Guards. Then a fist-sized stone from aside and above flew over the raised shield of a guard, straight at Hammerhand.

As casually as the Thorbardin guards had, he deflected the stone with his shield. But even as the missile clattered away, he sensed furious movement directly behind him and heard the unmistakable hum of a sling. He spun around in time to see a small hand dart out of the group, expertly unleashing a woven sling. Its stone whistled through the air, entered a shadowed, open second-level doorway, and a distinct thud was heard. A second later a dwarf staggered into sight there, clung to the doorway for an instant, blood flowing down his face, then toppled forward and fell to the pavement below.

With an oath, Hammerhand lunged and grabbed the small hand with the sling. The hand seemed to be connected to nothing, but as he grabbed it a pretty face appeared, turning toward him.

Swearing beneath his breath, Hammerhand gripped empty-seeming air beside the face and pulled away the emptiness. All around, Thorbardin guards gasped as a complete person was revealed—a startlingly pretty dwarf girl, who returned the red-cloak's angry glare with stubborn eyes and a set, determined chin. "You see?" she snapped at him. "It's a good thing I came along. That person tried to stone you."

Nearby, one of the guards knelt beside the fallen dwarf, then stood and shrugged. "He's dead," he called. "His head's cracked open."

"Well, well, well," Luster Redleather declared with open admiration, staring at the girl who was still glaring at Hammerhand. "And who have we here?"

"Her name is Helta Graywood," Hammerhand growled. "Among other things, she is a nuisance."

Tearing his fascinated eyes from the girl, Luster peered at the red-cloak's dangling hand. It seemed to contain nothing, but some of the fingers had disappeared. "Magic!" the Daewar muttered. "What is it? A cloak of some kind?"

"An elf made it," Calan Silvertoe admitted.

"I see," Luster said, his blue eyes alight. "Ah, yes. That accounts for the rumors from the other night. We were reconnoitered, it seems. And by Hammerhand himself."

"I've been away from Thorbardin for years," Hammerhand replied. "I decided to have a look around, privately."

"You've been away—" Luster started, then grinned and

planted his fists on his hips. "My father is right, then. You *are* Derkin Winterseed!"

"I was," Hammerhand admitted. "But my people gave me a new name."

"Derkin Hammerhand," Luster said. "It's a good name. But why all the mystery? As Harl Thrustweight's son, you could just have walked in openly. You're a citizen."

"I don't care to be a citizen of Thorbardin," Derkin rasped.

"Why not?"

"That's what I will speak to the council about. If we can proceed to the council hall without further interruption."

"The dead Theiwar is one of the local troublemakers," one of the Home Guards reported. "If she hadn't brained him, someone else would have, sooner or later."

"Then there are no claims or challenges?" Luster asked.

The guard shook his head. "None stated."

"In that case, let's get going." Luster swept his arm in a courtly gesture, bowing slightly to Helta Graywood. "The rest of the walk will be far more pleasant, with such attractive—such *visibly* attractive—company."

A bright smile lit the girl's face. "Thank you," she said, curtsying. Then the smile was replaced by a frown as Derkin Hammerhand strode away.

11
The Kal-Thax Mandate

The Great Hall of Audience of Thorbardin, located in the southern reaches of the fortress complex, was packed to capacity when Derkin Hammerhand arrived there. Word had spread quickly of the impending meeting of the Council of Thanes—a meeting demanded by the strangers from the wilderness—and it looked as though half the dwarves in Thorbardin had decided to attend. Tens of thousands of people packed the rising tiers of cut stone seats that ringed the big, circular cavern, and it sounded as though they were all talking at once. The echoes of their voices could be heard a quarter-mile away in the wide concourse of the Ninth Road tunnel.

But when Luster Redleather and his Home Guards escorted their charges into the great chamber, the place went almost silent.

Only a few in Thorbardin had actually gone to Northgate to see the army of strangers now camped in the meadows beyond, but everybody had heard about them—about the music of their drums, the goods they brought to trade, and about the mysterious leader of the outsiders who resembled an ancient Hylar chieftain and wore the armor of a long-ago time. Speculation was rampant as to whether the strangers beyond Northgate were here just to trade, or also to invade.

Now the one called Hammerhand was here, in Thorbardin, and most of the dwarves in the undermountain realm waited curiously to hear what he had to say.

Runners had preceded them into the Great Hall, and Derkin Hammerhand assumed that those waiting—at least the thane leaders and officials gathered on the raised dais in the center of the cavern—now knew everything that Luster Redleather knew about him, including his full name. The suspicion was confirmed by whispers that reached his ears as he led his group down a sloping aisle, between packed rows of waiting dwarves. "Derkin," someone whispered. "He is Derkin, the son of Harl Thrustweight."

Followed by Helta Graywood and Calan Silvertoe, and flanked by the Ten, Derkin strode to the dais and stepped up on it, then scanned the crowd waiting there with thoughtful eyes. Vaguely, he recalled Dunbarth Ironthumb of the Hylar, who had once been Captain of Guards under old Harl. The rest he had never seen, but he knew who they were. The shrewd-eyed, middle-aged Daewar with the trade wardens behind him obviously was Jeron Redleather. The suspicious-looking old Theiwar scowling at him from his council seat would be Swing Basto. Crag Shade-eye of the Daergar removed his face mask as a courtesy, letting the stranger see his features, then donned it again, squinting in the light of the chamber's overhead sun-tunnel and reflectors.

The bushy, unruly hair and beard of the next chief identified him as Klar, the chieftain Trom Thule. The sixth and seventh seats were vacant. Nobody knew where to find the bumbling little Grimble I, Highbulp of Thane Aghar, and many years had passed since any Neidar had met with the council.

Derkin studied them one by one, then nodded and stepped to the center of the dais. "I am called Hammerhand," he told them. "My people call themselves the Chosen Ones."

Jeron Redleather bowed slightly, welcoming the newcomer, then glanced at those with him. He had already heard—from his son's guards—of the beauty of the dwarf girl with Hammerhand, but his eyes widened when he looked at the old one-arm with the reed basket. "I know you," he said. "You are Calan. You left Thorbardin long ago, some said to live among elves."

"Your memory is excellent, Sire." Calan Silvertoe grinned. "That was at least eighty years ago."

"And now you return, with another who preferred outside ways to our own." Jeron shifted his gaze back to the red-cloaked warrior. "My son tells me that you are indeed Derkin Winterseed, the son of a Hylar chieftain."

"I am called Derkin Hammerhand now," Derkin said. "The name pleases me. My people chose it."

"And who are your people?" Dunbarth Ironthumb asked. "Where do they come from?"

"They call themselves the Chosen Ones," Derkin repeated.

Frowning, Swing Basto rumbled, "Chosen ones? Who chose them?"

"I did," Derkin said. "And as to where we are from, we are from Kal-Thax."

146

"Kal-Thax is here," the Klar chieftain pointed out. "Kal-Thax is our land."

"It used to be," Derkin said. "Until Thorbardin abandoned it. Most of my people have been Neidar. Many of them come now from the same cells and slave pens as I come from—slave quarters owned by the human invaders that you people have not troubled yourselves to drive away."

Angry voices were raised in the vast audience, and others joined them. The babble became a roar that died slowly as Jeron Redleather raised a commanding hand. All over the great chamber, companies of Home Guards spread and positioned themselves, ready to enforce order if necessary.

"This person is our guest!" the Daewar chieftain announced, his voice carrying through the Great Hall. "As he is our guest at this assembly of the thanes, it is our right to question him, but it is also his right to speak freely and be heard."

"So question him!" a voice called from somewhere in the crowd. "Why is he here? What does he want?"

"Those are fair questions," Jeron conceded, nodding at Derkin.

"We are here for two reasons," Derkin continued. "The first is to trade. Your traders," he indicated the trade wardens standing behind Jeron, "have inspected our goods and heard what we want in exchange."

"Mostly steel implements," Jeron said.

"Implements?" Derkin raised an eyebrow, his eyes piercing the Daewar chieftain. "Call them what they are. We want weapons. Good weapons crafted from good dwarven steel."

"Weapons, then," Jeron conceded.

"Provided you have the steel to make them," Derkin added. "I saw no smelter glows at the Shaft of Reorx."

"We have steel," Dunbarth Ironthumb growled. "We

have excellent stockpiles of steel."

"Good for you," Derkin drawled ironically. "Then we will make trade?"

"What do you want the weapons for?" Swing Basto demanded.

"To wage war against the human legions who have invaded our land."

A murmur spread through the crowd.

"You said you came for two reasons," Dunbarth said. "What is the second?"

Derkin planted his fists on his hips. "I also want Thorbardin troops to help me in my war."

The murmuring doubled in volume. There were scattered shouts and cheers.

"Why should we help you?" Swing Basto growled. "Your war is not our concern."

"The land I intend to retake is the land of the dwarves." Derkin glared at the Theiwar. "It is the land of Kal-Thax."

"It is outside!" Swing snapped. "Our concern is Thorbardin. Let those outside do their own fighting."

"Klar don't have time to go off to war," Trom Thule said. "Plenty to do right here."

"If we were to send troops," Dunbarth Ironthumb asked, "who would lead them?"

"I will lead," Derkin told him. "My people and I. We know the land, and we know the enemy. We will conduct the war against the human Lord Kane. I ask you to join us in this cause."

Jeron Redleather stood. "Those are your requests, then? That we trade you weapons, and that we send an army to join you?"

Derkin nodded. "Those are my requests."

The voices in the crowd had died down. All were silent, waiting for the council's answer.

"Then the council will deliberate the matter. Do you intend to stay and listen? Derkin Winterseed and Calan

Silvertoe have the right, as citizens, to observe council action."

"But not the rest of these who are with me." Derkin shook his head. "No, I will wait with them in the concourse. We will return to hear your decisions." Turning, he strode from the dais, followed closely by Helta Graywood and the Ten. Calan Silvertoe walked to the nearest audience row and sat down, bustling several dwarves aside to make room for himself. "I'll stay," he muttered. "It's been eighty years since I last heard thane leaders bicker."

Derkin and his party left the hall through wide plank doors. Luster Redleather and about half of his company followed them out, and the doors closed behind them.

"I'm not supposed to let you out of my sight," the young Daewar told Derkin.

"How do you think it will go?" Derkin asked.

Luster shrugged. "Who knows? My father might favor your proposal, and maybe Dunbarth Ironthumb. They both regret the way Thorbardin has gone. But the others? Who knows?"

* * * * *

Hours had passed, and the sun-tunnels were dimming when the Great Hall's doors opened again and a guard signaled. Followed by Helta and the Ten, Derkin walked again to the dais. As he passed Calan Silvertoe, the old dwarf frowned and shook his head. "These idiots haven't changed a bit," he whispered.

The conclusions of the Council of Thanes, read to Derkin by Jeron Redleather in a level voice that told few details of what had occurred in the privacy of the packed hall, confirmed Calan's whisper. Thorbardin would produce the weapons and armaments demanded by Hammerhand and would trade them for the goods offered by the Chosen Ones. But Thorbardin would raise no army and would not join in Hammerhand's war.

Aside, Dunbarth Ironthumb whispered, "I'm sorry, Derkin. The vote was three to two."

From beyond the dais, Calan Silvertoe's old voice rasped, "Can you guess what argument carried the decision, Derkin? It was that, if Thorbardin sent an army outside, there wouldn't be enough reliable guards left inside to keep the peace."

"To keep the peace?" Derkin muttered. Then, to the chieftains, "You have made your decisions. We of Kal-Thax are on our own. You will trade us weapons, but you will not help us fight. You, Jeron Redleather, said earlier that I have the right to speak. Have I that right still?"

"This council is still in session." The Daewar nodded.

"Very well." Derkin turned, addressing the entire assembly, his voice cold and clear.

"Your ancestors once put aside their grudges and their feuds," he said slowly, "to form a nation in these mountains. Now there is no nation here. Even within this fortress, where you all breathe the same air, drink the same water, eat from the same fields and stores, and hide behind the same gates, there is no real nation. You tell yourselves that Thorbardin lives! Because the vents still bring you fresh winds, and the water troughs still flow, and the warrens still yield food, you tell yourselves that all is well.

"I say Thorbardin does not live! I say Thorbardin is asleep, and if it does not awaken soon, it will truly die!"

A rumble of voices erupted in the crowd, and Derkin turned to glare at the rows of dwarves, his eyes as dark as storm clouds. Gradually, the clamor subsided.

"Once the gates of Thorbardin were funnels of life," Derkin growled, his deep voice filling the great chamber. "Once Southgate thronged with the traffic of the mines—ores coming in from the Daergar mines around the Thunder Peaks and from Theiwar digs all over the Promontory. Once there were Thorbardin patrols and scouts roaming as far as Sheercliff and the Anviltops, seeking rich new areas to mine. Once Northgate stood open every day, and Neidar from all of Kal-Thax came there to trade the produce of the forests and the fields for the produce of Thorbardin's mighty forges. Now the gates stand closed except by decree, and Thorbardin is an elaborate prison.

"Once the Shaft of Reorx fed smelters that operated night and day, fed by the ores from Daergar shafts and Theiwar veins. Now the smelters are silent, and the forges are still.

"Once the people of all the thanes labored side by side to give themselves a home like no other home on this world and to forge a mighty destiny for themselves. Now Thorbardin is not a home, but just an arena for petty bickering and useless feuds. And that great destiny forged by your ancestors is as forgotten as the reason it was forged."

"What great destiny?" a dwarf in the audience shouted sarcastically, then went silent as Derkin's eyes fixed on him.

"The Covenant of the Thanes," Hammerhand said. "That great covenant made long ago to preserve the dwarven lands. That is what has been forgotten! The Covenant has not been repealed. It has simply been ignored! Your ancestors fought to defend Kal-Thax against human invasion and built Thorbardin for that purpose. But you have turned your backs on Kal-Thax! Where were Thorbardin's mighty armies when humans marched across Kal-Thax and looted Neidar villages? Where was Thorbardin when the Emperor of Ergoth sent his slavers through Tharkas to capture dwarven slaves for his mines? And where is Thorbardin now, when Lord Sakar Kane and his regiments occupy the passes south of Tharkas and develop more mines there—mines stolen from dwarven people—to feed the human emperor's wars in the east?

"Thorbardin was created for one purpose—so that Kal-Thax would always be protected against invasion. Thorbardin was to be the sinew and the beating heart of a nation! The dwarven nation of Kal-Thax!

"But Thorbardin has withdrawn into itself, and Kal-Thax lies invaded, conquered, and occupied! And when I come here seeking Thorbardin's assistance—so that I can do the task that is Thorbardin's task—what do I find? Do I find armies ready to march, to defend the land of the dwarves? No, I find only Home Guard companies, marching between closed gates to keep down riots and hold troublemakers at bay. Do I find the hard-working, stubborn people who built this great fortress and made it powerful and rich? No, I find sullen, sniveling crowds with nothing better to do than vandalize their neighbors and throw rocks at one another in the streets."

Here and there in the Great Hall, clamors of outrage erupted, but were quickly stilled by the guards.

When he could be heard again, Derkin continued, "When I left Thorbardin years ago, when I chose the life outside over the life within, it was not because I preferred Neidar ways. I was a person of the hammer, not of the axe. But I was sick of watching my home—the home of my father and of his father and their fathers before them—turn from steel to rust. I was ashamed. I was *sick* with shame!

"And now I return, and I am still ashamed! Jeron Redleather has called me a citizen. By right of birth, I am a citizen. Hybardin, the Life Tree of the Hylar, was my cradle, and Thorbardin was my home.

"But no more! When I leave Thorbardin this time, I leave my citizenship behind. I renounce it. Prepare the weapons you have agreed to trade and submit them to Calan Silvertoe. He will remain here until the weapons are ready to his satisfaction. When they are, you will send them—and him—to my camp below Northgate. We will trade, and when the trading is done my people and I will leave. We will go from here to Tharkas, and we will make war on behalf of Kal-Thax. Reorx willing, we will find a way to drive Lord Kane from Kal-Thax once and for all."

Again voices rang in the Great Hall, shouts and questions mingling with comments of grudging agreement, and again the guards restored order while Derkin waited.

"We will win, or we will die," the red-cloak said when the hall was quiet again. "But if we succeed, then Kal-Thax is ours! It hasn't been yours for a long time. Thorbardin abandoned it, so you will have no claim to it."

He paused thoughtfully for a moment, then continued, "It may be that, when the goods we brought have been used up, you of Thorbardin will want to trade again. But next time, the Chosen Ones will not come to you. You will have to come to us. Somewhere west of here, in the wilderness, we will build a new town—a place of trade. Its name will be Barter, and your traders—*anyone's* traders—will be welcome there, far away from Thorbardin. This is Hammerhand's gift to you. It will do some of you people good, to have to go outside to get what you want."

Softly, behind him, he heard hands clapping. He turned. Jeron Redleather and Dunbarth Ironthumb both were standing, applauding his words and ignoring the glares of the other thane leaders.

With a curt nod, Derkin Hammerhand stepped down and headed for the door. Beside him, Helta Graywood's lovely eyes glowed with a fierce fire.

In the concourse, Luster Redleather halted them, waiting for his company to reform. "You certainly make your opinions known." He chuckled, grinning at Derkin. "I think I'll miss you when you've gone. But I guess you won't be coming back, huh?"

"I don't know," Derkin said thoughtfully. "I might."

"But you said you were renouncing your citizenship in Thorbardin!"

"If I come back to Thorbardin," Hammerhand said slowly, "it won't be as a citizen."

Beaming with fierce pride, Helta Graywood stepped up beside Derkin and took his hand in hers. "Me, too," she said.

* * * * *

Far to the north of Thorbardin, long lines of human soldiers moved eastward along a winding mountain road. Above them, on the right, stood the impassable, snow-capped heights of the Skywall Range. Below and distant on the left were the vast, misty forests, and ahead lay the stronghold of Klanath, at the mouth of Tharkas Pass.

The snows of winter were gone now on the lower slopes, and the emperor's forces were on the move. The eastern expansion campaign, which many had begun to call Ullves's War, would soon be entering its fourth year, and the emperor's "boy general," Giarna, had been in the field for three years. In that time, the war of conquest had grown and spread. Strong elven forces from Silvanesti, led by the elf prince Kith-Kanan and the Wildrunners, had moved out onto the plains of eastern Ergoth to counter the humans' assaults. And increasingly strong units of elves —often reinforced by human nomads from the plains— ranged as far as the forests northwest of Kal-Thax, to harass the humans moving eastward from Daltigoth and Caergoth.

What had once been foreseen as a quick, simple campaign to extend the empire of Quivalin Soth V—or Ullves —entirely across southern Ansalon, now had become protracted war as the human invaders met stubborn resistance far beyond their anticipation. Not only had the elves proved to be masters of strategy and tactic, and truly formidable fighters, but they were increasingly reinforced by the free tribes of humans on the central plains. Under the leadership of the fierce, implacable Cobar tribes, hordes of nomadic Sackmen and Baruk warriors, stealthy Phaerots, and men of a dozen other tribes had joined forces to counter the empire's aims.

Often, in recent seasons, empire units had found themselves fighting desperately against consolidated armies of humans and elves, all with one common goal: to keep their people and their lands free of the yoke of the empire.

But still the armies came, marching out of Daltigoth, reinforced at Caergoth, and provisioned at Klanath as they streamed eastward, season after season, to fight and die at the pleasure of the Emperor Quivalin Soth V.

And though the emperor's commanding general, Giarna, led each campaign, there was often another with him—the dark, enigmatic man known only as Dreyus. It was whispered that where Dreyus went, no enemies survived the battles.

Each winter brought a lessening of hostilities, simply because travel was difficult in the cold season. But now it was spring again, and the armies of the empire were again on the march. By regiment and brigade, by company and platoon, the empire's units advanceed eastward, toward the lesser ranges and the plains beyond, to press again for conquest.

A key to the assault strategy was the fortress of Lord Kane at Klanath. Located at the mouth of Tharkas Pass, the fortress not only stockpiled supplies and provisions for the final marches into the plains, it also provided a safe zone, a midway place where travel-weary soldiers could rest and regain their strength for the assaults ahead. Lord Kane's forces held a wide perimeter here, with regular patrols along the fringes of the enchanted forest where elven rangers and guerrilla units lurked, and into the mountains south of Tharkas, to guard against any attack from that side.

For a time, after the slave revolt at Klanath Mines,

dwarven raiding parties had harassed and tormented the empire's armies and supply trains. In a span of months, there had been hundreds of scattered attacks, always sudden, always unexpected, and almost always successful. Small, deadly parties of armed dwarves had seemed to come out of nowhere, slashing and killing, looting and pillaging, then vanished as quickly as they had come.

The horses, weapons, supplies, and equipment they had taken in these raids would have outfitted and fed a sizable army.

But then the raids had stopped. For almost two years now, Lord Kane's scouts and patrols had not seen so much as a single dwarf. It seemed as though the dwarves had tired of their raids and withdrawn completely from this part of Ansalon. Many of Lord Kane's advisors assumed that the wild dwarves had retreated into the vast mountain wilderness of the distant Anviltop Range, far south and west of Tharkas. Others suspected that they had withdrawn southward, to that mysterious and impregnable subterranean fortress that they called Thorbardin. A few even suggested that the dwarven raiders had migrated into the frozen lands.

But wherever they had gone, they had disappeared. And though the human patrols still had to range far into the mountains of old Kal-Thax, the lord's task of holding Klanath was easier now that they no longer had to deal with the short, fierce people whose mountains these had once been.

Part III:

Master of Tharkas

12

A Cobar Outing

Had Sakar Kane been a lesser man, the disgrace he had suffered some years earlier—when thousands of dwarven mine slaves had revolted, murdered their overseers, and escaped into the mountains beyond Tharkas—would have ruined him. The Emperor of Ergoth was not a forgiving man, nor one who tolerated failure. The Wall of Skulls in Daltigoth was evidence of that.

The Wall was seven feet thick and higher than a tall man could reach. It surrounded three sides of the formal garden abutting the east wing of the emperor's palace. And it was built entirely of the bleached skulls of those who had displeased Quivalin Soth V and his imperial ancestors.

Another man in Lord Kane's situation—having lost most of his best slaves, thus compromising the production of the emperor's mines—would have suffered recall to Daltigoth, inquisition by the emperor himself, subsequent prolonged tortures, and death. And his skull would have become part of the Wall of Skulls.

But Sakar Kane was no ordinary subject of the empire. Without waiting for recall to court, Lord Kane had acted. He immediately sent armed patrols to find and arrest all of his subordinates and bring them to the inner hall of his Klanath fortress. When they were all gathered there—everyone from old Renus Sabad, the Master of Mines, down to his deputies, chief warders, and even his accounting clerks, most of them still in their sleeping gowns—Sakar Kane gave orders to fifty of his most trusted field troops. On that morning, the only people who left the inner hall alive were those fifty blood-soaked men.

Then, with the brigades at his command, Sakar Kane swept eastward through Redrock Cleft, the final mountain portal to the vast plains, and launched a lightning sweep northward, striking camp after camp, village after village of the barbarians who roamed the arid plains beyond the Cobar steppes. With the several thousand slaves taken in this raid, Lord Kane had the mines in operation again long before the emperor's spies reached Daltigoth. And with the additional slaves he was able to purchase at Xak Tsaroth—nearly depleting his personal coffers—he had actually expanded production by the time the emperor's wardens reached Klanath.

He had a stroke of luck, as well. In one of the pit mines, his guards found a large stockpile of fine, already mined ores, obviously hoarded by some overseer for his own purposes.

Lord Kane was recalled to Daltigoth, escorted by the emperor's wardens. He went not in chains, but riding proudly at the head of the procession, followed by the empire inspectors who had just seen the bustling mines and rich ores. And he returned some months later, not in disgrace, but as Prince of Klanath. Quivalin Soth V was a cruel man, and a ruthless one, but he was not stupid. He understood both what had happened at Klanath—the successful revolt of dwarven slaves—and what Sakar Kane had done so expeditiously to regain favor.

Such a man would serve him well, the emperor knew, as long as he could serve himself in the process. In making Lord Kane Prince of Klanath, the emperor gave him a free hand as concerned the old dwarven lands south of there . . . and an excellent reason to do all in his power to build and sustain a mighty empire presence at the mouth of Tharkas Pass.

In the years since, Klanath had become a powerful seat of the empire. Not only was the fortress strengthened, but wide perimeter walls had been erected around it, and the sprawling, ungainly mining camp of before had become a walled city—a city that served and defended the southern road of the empire, where marched the armies, reinforcements, and supplies required by General Giarna in his eastern campaigns.

For a time, both the outlying areas of Klanath and the road approaching it were plagued by those wild dwarven raiders, striking swiftly and fiercely from the dizzy heights south of the road. Many hundreds of horses had been stolen by raiders from herds being driven eastward. Supply trains had been attacked—often in the dark of night—and large quantities of supplies, consigned to Klanath's stores, had disappeared. Countless weapons had been taken, and the number of drovers, drivers, handlers, and guards killed by rampaging dwarves had risen into the hundreds over a few seasons.

Lord Kane issued orders to all of his units to take prisoners when possible. It proved difficult. Even when a trap was sprung, and a party of raiders surrounded, the dwarves refused to lay down their weapons, preferring to fight to the death. Finally, though, a mounted guard company did bring in five dwarf captives. The guard captain reported that they were all that remained of a group of fourteen, decoyed and trapped on the supply road, and that it had cost him eighteen men to collect them.

Two of the prisoners were females, and all five of them bore the marks of slaves. One of the males had worked in the Klanath mines. The other two, and the females, had been slaves at Tharkas.

Lord Kane had the five taken through the pass, deep into the mountains to the south, and tortured to death on a ridgetop where their bodies would be found, to serve as a warning to the wild dwarves. Through it all, even in dying, only one of the dwarves made a sound. That one, a female, spat at the men who broke her legs and said, "Hammerhand will deal with you, when he is ready."

There was only one more raid following that incident. Early one morning, five of Lord Kane's household guards were found dead on the very doorstep of his Klanath fortress. They had been bound and gagged, then tortured to death. After that, the dwarven raids had ceased, and the dwarves simply disappeared.

Lord Kane kept one of his brigades in residence south of the great pass as a permanent outpost and center for roving patrols. But the dwarven threat was only part of the reason for that. In Klanath, Lord Kane kept a staff of mapmakers and planners who received regular reports from the roving patrols. It was Lord Kane's plan—once General Giarna's campaigns were concluded—to populate the once dwarven lands with people of his own choosing. The dwarves' revolt had emptied Kane's coffers. One day the lands taken from dwarves would amply refill them.

* * * * *

Tuft Broadland came out of sleep in the manner of a Cobar warrior. In one instant he was asleep, in the next he was awake, crouching beside his sleeping mat with his naked sword in hand, his eyes searching the gloom around him, his ears aware of every minute sound.

For a moment, he sensed no presence but his own. A summer breeze fluttered the fabric of his small tent, and from beyond came the muted night sounds of a guarded camp—the reassuring night-bird calls of sentries, the faint stampings and shufflings of horses' hooves in the nearby rope corral, and the quiet voices of people talking at some fireside.

He knew it was not these sounds that had awakened him. It was something else. As chief of the Tekar, one of the seven Cobar tribes, he had his own tent and on this night had not shared it. But now he sensed that he was not alone. Then, in the shadows a few feet away, something moved, and a quiet voice said, "Hold your sword, human. I mean you no harm."

Tuft squinted, still tensed to strike, and the voice said, "Don't you remember me, Tuft? It has not been so long."

Now he recognized the voice and let the point of his sword angle downward. "You!" he muttered. Without turning, he reached to the edge of his mat and drew out a little soft leather pouch. Opening it with one hand, still holding the sword in the other, he withdrew a small metallic object, a palm-sized container with a hinged lid which opened at the press of his thumb. Within the lid, under his thumb, was a small serrated wheel of tempered steel resting against a shard of flint. He flicked the wheel, and sparks flared, igniting a cotton wick soaked with distilled mineral spirits.

The flame was small, but it was enough to see by. In the far corner of the little tent, a hooded figure squatted comfortably on soft-booted heels. "I see you still carry the toy I gave you," the intruder said, his voice low, musical, and not quite human. "Flint, steel, and kindling all in one small package. One of my mother's more practical ideas, I think. Eloeth has no taste for magic, but she does enjoy conveniences."

"Despaxas," Tuft said, laying his sword aside. "You could have made a less dramatic entrance, elf. You almost made my heart stop."

"There is nothing wrong with your heart," the newcomer said, throwing back his hood to reveal a tapered, ageless face with wide-set, amused eyes and no beard. The delicate tips of pointed ears were almost hidden by his long, flowing hair. "There's nothing wrong with your reflexes, either, I might add. One slight whisper, and you were awake and ready to fight."

The Cobar drew a candle from his pouch, lit its wick from his flame, then closed the flint-and-steel tool and put it away. "What are you doing here?" he asked. "I thought you had gone back to your forests years ago."

"I did." The elf nodded. "But now I've returned. A seed you helped plant back then has grown well and is ready to bear fruit. I thought you might enjoy participating in the harvest."

"A seed . . ." Tuft paused, his eyes brightening. "The dwarves? Has Derkin molded his army?"

"He has prepared himself," Despaxas said. "A season ago, he encamped below the dwarven fortress with his 'chosen' people, all of them willing to fight at his command, even without proper arms. Now the season has turned, and they are on the march toward the pass at Tharkas. They carry the finest weapons dwarven skills can produce."

"He plans to attack the soldiers at the pass? With a mob of dwarves?"

"With an army," the elf corrected. "Maybe a fine army. Would you like to observe the campaign?"

"Of course I would," Tuft snorted. "But I know you,

Despaxas. You have something more in mind than just to allow me to watch while Derkin tests his forces against Lord Kane's stronghold."

"Naturally." The elf smiled. "Nothing is ever quite that simple." He waved an eloquent hand toward the tent's closed flap. "You have a strong tribe here, Tuft. I estimate at least three hundred warriors in this camp."

"Three hundred and eighty-one," the man admitted. "And that many more women and children."

"A hundred will be enough for what I have in mind," Despaxas said. "A hundred of your best cavalry."

"They're all my best!" the man snapped. "They're Cobar warriors. They're the finest cavalry in the world."

"Fine. Then any hundred will do. We'll leave at first light. We should be able to reach Redrock Cleft in two days, shouldn't we?"

"If the weather holds fair," Tuft replied. "But my men and I aren't going anywhere without a reason."

"Of course not." Despaxas shrugged. "Is a chance to ambush a column of empire footmen reason enough?"

"It might be." Tuft's eyes narrowed. "Are they on their way to Cobar territory?"

"I could tell you that they are," the elf said. "But, no, they aren't. They're on their way to the southern plains, to reinforce General Giarna's forces there. The path they follow will miss your steppes by many miles."

"Then they're the elves' problem," Tuft observed. "Why have you come to me about this? Why aren't you talking to Kith-Kanan? His Wildrunners are as adept at ambush as we are."

"As you suggested," the elf said, "there is more to it than meets the eye. If the empire's reinforcements are hit by elves, Lord Kane is unlikely to come out of Klanath to retaliate. He knows the elves, and would know that his chance of pursuing and overtaking Wildrunners isn't very good. He might have to follow them all the way to General Giarna's cordon. Lord Kane has his own interests in mind and wouldn't expend that kind of resources."

"But he might if Cobar attacked. Is that it? He might send his horse companies, because he knows we don't have that far to retreat." Tuft frowned. "What are you suggesting, elf? That we go out and sting the bear, then lead it back to our house?"

"Not lead them home," Despaxas said. "Just let your warriors draw out Lord Kane's horsemen and keep them amused for a time. Lead them in circles or something for a few days. How difficult can that be . . . for the world's finest cavalry?"

"I don't mind putting arrows into some empire soldiers," the man admitted. "Nor do I mind leading Lord Kane's clanking churls on a merry chase. But I don't commit my warriors without knowing why. You were talking about dwarves a few minutes ago. Does this have to do with them?"

"Of course it does." Despaxas's level-eyed smile was as innocent as a baby's, but Tuft had long since learned that the elf's look of smooth-faced innocence was most pronounced when he was at his most devious and calculating. "Derkin's Chosen Ones are tough and well armed, but they are still dwarves. They've done well harassing humans in the past, but only as small raiding parties. To launch and sustain a major assault, dwarves must have a secure base. Let Derkin's dwarves entrench themselves in Tharkas Pass, and you know what will happen next."

"Sure." The Cobar nodded. "All blazes will break loose there. Tharkas Pass is right in Klanath's lap. Lord Kane can't tolerate a hostile base so near his headquarters. He'll have to drive them out."

"He'll have to try," Despaxas said. "And when he tries, Derkin will counterattack."

"You don't really believe a bunch of dwarves can take Klanath, do you?"

"I don't know." Despaxas shrugged. "Our Derkin has changed since you saw him last, and you haven't seen his army. The point is that Giarna isn't likely to run his troops and supply lines through a battlefield. He isn't interested in those dwarven mountains, or in Sakar Kane's ambitions."

"But if they don't cross the mountains there . . ."

"Exactly. The only other supply route from Caergoth to the southern plains is nearly a hundred miles north. They will have to go all the way around our forests. Even Giarna's best don't care to face the Wildrunners on their own ground. If the dwarves break General Giarna's supply lines at Tharkas, it will add weeks—maybe even months—to the time it takes supplies and reinforcements to reach the invasion forces."

"And give us that much more open country to—as you say—amuse them in," the Cobar noted, a fierce grin ruffling his beard.

"Is that reason enough?" the elf asked quietly.

Tuft rose to his feet, crouching slightly to avoid the low braces of his tent. He turned, opened the flap, stepped outside, and stopped, his eyes narrowing. Directly in front of him, something floated in midair—something that might have resembled a lazily swimming bat-fish if it had not been so hard to see. The Cobar whirled and stepped back into his tent, glaring at the elf. "Why did you bring that thing here?" he demanded. "You know my people don't like it."

"Zephyr won't hurt your people." Despaxas shrugged. "And I needed him. It has been a long time since we last met, Tuft. Humans sometimes change."

"So you had your pet shadow read me?" The Cobar's frown deepened. "And what does he say now?"

"He says that your soul is as strong as your heart," the elf said. "Just like before."

When Tuft stepped out again, Zephyr was nowhere to

be seen. With a shudder, the Cobar took a deep breath. He knew that the verge-swimmer meant him no harm. He had accepted Despaxas's assurance of that long ago. Still, there was something about the idea of a magical creature that could be seen only in shadow, and that had the body of a manta ray and teeth like scorpion stingers—a thing that appeared and disappeared at will, and that could read a man's soul as easily as a man might read a scroll—that revolted him.

Tuft whistled—a call that any but a Cobar might have mistaken for a night bird's shrill. Immediately, all around him, the quiet camp began to teem with activity.

Tuft stepped back into the tent and picked up his boots. "We'll leave at first light," he told the waiting elf.

* * * * *

Less than five miles to the east of Klanath, the wall of soaring peaks that framed Tharkas Pass turned and divided, ranges of peaks extending north and south, separating the mountain fastness of old Kal-Thax from the foothills and plains that rolled away to the east. And it was here, where the giant range turned, that the road from Caergoth entered a narrow, winding valley called Redrock Cleft. The valley was a natural pass leading to the eastern slopes beyond. From it, the empire road wound downward in a series of serpentine arcs and switchbacks, to become many roads on the plains below.

It was through this cleft that the original armies of conquest had gone, heading for the southern plains and the elven forests beyond. And it was through this cleft that supply trains and reinforcements now moved, refreshed by a midway rest at Klanath.

Three days after the visit of Despaxas to Tuft Broadland's camp, a long line of men issued from the cleft. Nearly eight hundred in all, with pack animals among them, they bore the banners of the empire and marched at the steady pace of men who have come a long way and still have a long way to go. There were three companies, assigned to join General Giarna's forces in southern Ergoth.

An hour after clearing Redrock Cleft, the rank was snaking down the slopes with the gentler foothills ahead. Another hour passed, and the road became gentler and straighter. In the rough lands above, many of the soldiers had marched with shields on their arms and swords in their hands in case of ambush. But now, as the land grew flatter, most of them slung their shields and put away their blades. They could see for miles out here, and there wasn't anyone in sight except themselves.

Then, abruptly, there was. With shrill battle cries and thundering hooves, a hundred mounted barbarians charged over the rim of a little draw that hadn't seemed deep enough to hide a rabbit. Like messengers of death, the riders came, bows drawn full and the slanting sunlight brilliant on beaded buckskins and featherwork headgear.

Within a heart's beat of the first battle cry, the galloping attackers were thundering down upon the panicked line of soldiers. Arrows pinged and thudded among the footmen, aimed with deadly accuracy and driven by stout bows. Dozens of soldiers fell, and more dozens broke and ran in blind panic. Behind the barrage of arrows came the howling riders, bows slung now, and gleaming swords flashing as they charged through the ranks of soldiers, wheeled around, and charged again, laying about them with swift blades that ran red in the sunlight.

Then, as quickly as they had come, the riders were gone. Disappearing through their own dust, into that same eye-fooling draw they had come from, they reappeared on the far side, loping away casually toward the north. Behind them, the ground was littered with dead and injured empire soldiers. Officers ran here and there, calling back their troops, trying to restore order.

"Cobar," a senior officer muttered, looking after the retreating horsemen. "What are Cobar doing this close to Klanath?" Turning, he raised an arm, signaling others to him. "Send runners with signal mirrors back up to the cleft, on the double," he commanded. "There is still good light. From there, signal Klanath what has occurred. Tell Lord Kane that if his men move at once, they can catch those Cobar and make an example of them."

"Catch Cobar?" a junior officer questioned. "Sir, those people are . . ."

"Are you blind?" his senior snapped. He pointed. "You see where the barbarians are going? Look beyond them. That smoke in the distance must be their camp. They think we won't follow them, because we are not mounted. They are as stupid as they are arrogant. Do they honestly believe that a mounted battalion can't find them?"

13
First Blood

From the tower of his fortress, Sakar Kane watched his Third
Horse Battalion fan out along the road toward Redrock
Cleft, as dawn flagged the sky ahead of them. It had taken
all night to reach the battalion and recall them from their
outpost stronghold south of Tharkas Pass, and Lord Kane
was not pleased that he had to do so. Still, the signal from
Redrock had been clear and authoritative. Wild tribesmen
had ambushed the emperor's reinforcement column in
the foothills beyond the cleft, then had withdrawn to their
camp.

Only a few miles north, the signals said. Mounted
troops could overtake them there, surely within a day or

two. The Prince of Klanath had hesitated only a moment. The Third Battalion was growing restive and sullen after long seasons of fruitless patrol in the brutal mountains south of Tharkas. A bit of action now would be good for them. Besides, if he caught and punished the wild tribesmen, General Giarna would owe him a favor. Sakar Kane had no love for the so-called "boy general," but it was well known that Giarna was a favorite of the emperor. Even the sinister Dreyus, the man they said was Quivalin Soth's closest advisor, seemed to find no fault with Giarna. It would be a good thing, Sakar Kane knew, to have Giarna indebted to him.

The eastern sky was bright by the time the trailing elements of the Third Battalion disappeared into the cleft, tiny in the distance. Lord Kane turned away to enter his chambers, then stopped and tipped his head. What was that noise he had heard? Something faint and far away, just a touch of sound on the morning breeze coming down from the mountains.

He listened, and it came again, vague and fitful, as erratic as the cool breeze that carried it. He stepped to the parapet and looked downward. Below was the inner court of the fortress, and beyond it the walled battlements that faced the bustling little city. On the battlements—and on the more distant city wall—guards patrolled in pairs. He could tell by their casual pacing that, unlike him, they had heard nothing unusual.

Then he heard the distant sound again and shook his head in irritation. Thunder, he thought. Echoes of distant thunder, far away in the mountains. Somewhere beyond Tharkas Pass.

Oddly, though, there were no storm clouds in the clear morning sky—at least none that he could see from his tower.

* * * * *

The old mining camp of Tharkas lay shadowed and almost silent as dawn light appeared above the tall peaks around it. Once destroyed by dwarves, at the time of the slaves' revolt, the camp had been rebuilt as an outpost of Klanath. Though austere, it was amply equipped and fortified to serve as the headquarters of Lord Kane's mounted battalion, the Third. But now most of the battalion was gone, recalled through the great pass for maneuvers of some kind. Only cooks, servants, orderlies, and two companies of footmen remained, and most of them were asleep. They had been awake most of the night, helping the mounted forces saddle their beasts, don their armor, prepare their weapons, and pack their gear. It had been past midnight when the battalion trotted away, entering the pass by the light of twin moons.

A single cookfire was beginning to blaze in the compound, and sleepy perimeter guards were making their dawn rounds, stifling yawns, when thunder erupted around them—an intricate, rhythmic, pulsing thunder that seemed to come from everywhere and sent chills into the bones of those who heard it.

At the cookfire, men jumped to their feet, turning this way and that, trying to see where the sound came from. Then one of them shouted, "Look!" and pointed. On the nearest slope, where the old mine shafts stood boarded and blind, hundreds of short, armored figures were on the move. Quick and surefooted on the steep slope, which would have been almost impassable for humans, the horde of figures raced downward, shields and weapons flashing in the dawn.

The men at the fire gawked, then scrambled for their shields as a perimeter guard shouted, "Dwarves! Those are dwarves! We're under attack! To arms!"

As the men spotted them, the dwarves shouted war cries, deep voices rising in bloodcurdling chants, blending with the rhythm of the drums above.

The sleepy camp came abruptly awake as humans struggled into armor and officers dashed about, trying to assemble a defense. The attack was aimed at the northwest wall of the compound, and armed units headed in that direction, then hesitated as their officers shouted contradictory orders. With unbelievable speed, the dwarves had descended the vertiginous slope and raced across the outer clearing. Now they were at the wall and coming over it—a flowing tide of short, burly figures in bright armor. There were hundreds of them, and more coming behind.

A perimeter guard flung his pike at them in terror, then turned and tried to run, but the dwarves were already all around him. One dodged beneath the guard's sword and lashed out with his own, a whirling, roundhouse swing. The guard screamed and fell, his feet cut out from under him. Another dwarf paused to raise a warhammer and strike downward with it, then ran on.

"Spread and retreat!" a human officer shouted. "Back to the far wall!"

As one, the packed human troops spread out, sword-arm's reach apart, in defense mode. In the field, the tactic was sound. It gave each man room to use his blade and shield, and presented a broader front against the enemy. Within seconds, the human soldiers were spread in a thin double line across the camp compound, retreating slowly as the tide of dwarves bore down on them.

Fighters clashed all along the line. Steel rang against steel. For a few seconds the charge of the dwarves was slowed, but then their deep-voiced chanting rose again, and they pressed forward, shields high, heavy weapons lashing out like snakes' tongues. Blood gushed and flowed in the growing dawn light, and the nearest men could hear the syllables of the roaring chant. "Hammer-hand!" they were saying. "Hammer-hand! Hammer-hand! Hammer-hand!"

Overpowered by the ferocity of the charge, the human line swayed, then broke. "Retreat!" an officer wailed. "Retreat to the wall!"

The human rush to the far wall was barely a retreat. It was more like a scramble, and everywhere around and behind them, fighting dwarves struck and struck again.

"Over the wall!" an officer barked. "This is a trap in here! Get outside! We'll fight them there!"

Of the more than three hundred men in Tharkas Camp that dawning, less than two hundred made it to the south wall of the compound, and still fewer made it to the top of the wall. And those who did stopped there in terror and confusion, some toppling the eight feet to the hard ground as those coming up behind shoved them aside.

There was no refuge outside the wall. At its foot, several guards lay dead. And beyond them were dwarves—long ranks of stubby fighters waiting with raised blades. And beyond these were mounted companies, dwarves perched on short-stirruped saddles atop armored warhorses. For every dwarf within the compound, there looked to be ten or twenty more outside the wall. It was as though the entire dwarven race had come to Tharkas—and come to kill.

As the bleeding, terrified human mob packed the narrow walkway on top of the wall, a dwarven rider stepped his horse ahead of his company. His armor gleamed mirror-bright in the morning light, and a bright, blood-red cloak flowed from his burly shoulders.

Without hesitation, he unslung a great hammer from his shoulder and raised it high over his head. The drums began to sing again, as though speaking the language of that hammer. With a fierce frown, the dwarf swept his arm downward, pointing his hammer at the humans on the wall. Along the front rank of the dwarven army, dozens of dwarves paced forward by twos. Three steps, then they stopped in unison. In each pair, one dwarf knelt and aimed a crossbow. The second set a stone in a webbed sling and began its spin. The drums crescendoed, then went silent. Slings hummed and spat. Crossbows twanged. Fist-sized stones and bronze bolts with steel tips whistled through the air, slammed into flesh, and where there had been many human soldiers jostling one another atop a stone wall, now there were only a few.

With a roar that echoed from the peaks all around, the dwarven ranks surged forward.

* * * * *

As the sun of Krynn rose above the eastern peaks, Derkin Hammerhand and the Ten walked their horses along a line of bright-eyed dwarves and human captives. Fifty-four men of the empire had lived through the assault on Tharkas, fifty-four out of more than three hundred who had been there when it began. None had escaped. Those who tried had been run down and killed by dwarven horsemen.

At the middle of the inspection rank, where the huddled humans stood stripped of their gear and surrounded by armed Daergar warriors in steel masks, Derkin reined in as Calan Silvertoe strode forward to meet him. "Prisoners," the old one-arm growled, indicating the little crowd of humans. "What do you want to do with them?"

"I don't want any prisoners," Derkin said. "Why are they still alive?"

"This bunch wouldn't fight it out," Calan said. "They all threw down their weapons and refused to pick them up again."

"So?"

"Well, when Vin's Daergar moved in on them, they all fell to the ground and started babbling and bawling. They refused to defend themselves."

"So?" Derkin repeated impatiently.

From the dwarves guarding the humans, a sturdy masked figure strode forward. He didn't raise his mask, but Derkin recognized Vin the Shadow. "We didn't know what to do about them," the Daergar said. "I just . . . well, it isn't much fun to kill people who are groveling at your feet. Even humans. So we waited for you to decide."

"I didn't want any prisoners," Derkin growled.

"No problem." Old Calan Silvertoe grinned. With his one remaining hand he drew a razor-sharp dagger from his boot. "We'll just cut their throats." He turned, happily, and headed for the humans.

"Hold!" Derkin barked. "As long as we have them, let's make some use of them. They can clean up the mess in this compound and bury the dead."

"Oh, all right," Calan agreed. He put away his dagger and turned to face Derkin. "*Then* can we cut their throats?"

"When everything is cleaned up here, take them up to the main shaft and lock them in," Derkin commanded. "I may think of another use for them later."

"That old shaft?" one of the Ten snorted. "It'll still stink of goblins. Goblin-stench never goes away."

With Tharkas Camp secured, Derkin prowled around for a time, making assignments, detailing guard and patrol plans, and generally putting people to work. And thinking. During his visit to Thorbardin, and in the months afterward while the Chosen Ones camped outside Northgate, trading wares and arming themselves, he had done a lot of thinking . . . about the ways of the world, and mostly about the ways of his people. Aside from their families and their comforts, he realized now, there were two things that every dwarf loved more than anything else: working and fighting, in that order.

It was their nature . . . his own and every other dwarf's. Given the chance, a dwarf would work. He would delve caverns, build roads, erect mighty structures, or dig tunnels. He would construct beautiful furniture, forge tools, carve toys, string beads, paint pictures, or carry things to the tops of mountains. He would raise crops, tend herds, and harvest forests. He would hammer and saw, pound and temper, shape and reshape objects. He would taste a stone, then carve it into a pillar, a statue, or a trinket. He would taste metal, then make something useful out of it. He would build monuments or fortresses, or make whistles from reeds. Whatever the work, any typical dwarf would dive into it with energy and enthusiasm . . . as long as he was doing it because he wanted to.

But dwarves without work turned quickly to their second love. They bickered and argued, and when the arguments became feuds they fought. Thorbardin was evidence of that. The mightiest fortress in the world had become a hotbed of petty bickering and useless feuds, because it had closed itself off from the outside world and gradually diminished its resources to the point that there was not enough ore coming in to keep the smelters running, not enough timber coming in to keep the woodshops busy, not enough trade with the outside world to have any reason to produce much of anything.

And as the work diminished, the fighting grew.

It had been a revelation to some of those in the undermountain fortress, he suspected, that as the forges were fired up to produce the goods the Chosen Ones requested, the feuding and street fighting in Thorbardin's cities had diminished by half. Those months of summer, he thought, with his people camped outside and the forges going inside, were probably the best months Thorbardin had seen in a century or more.

But now he put Thorbardin out of his mind and thought of his own people, the Chosen Ones. They called themselves that, they said, because Hammerhand had chosen them. Actually, Derkin knew as well as they did that it was the other way around. He had not chosen them, he had merely freed them. They had followed him, and others along the way had joined. It was they who had chosen him, as their leader.

Just as Tap Tolec and Vin the Shadow had chosen him so long ago, in the slave cell at Klanath Mines, so these thousands of others had chosen him. They chose to follow him, to do his bidding, because—like working and fighting—it was their nature to follow a leader, as long as he was a leader they had chosen, and as long as they were following because they wanted to.

Working and fighting. It was the nature of these people . . . of *his* people. Working or fighting, choosing and following, living and deserving to live in their own land, by their own design, free of intrusion and invasion by the Lord Kanes and the Emperor Quivalin Soths—by all the alien forces that made war, it seemed, throughout every land they touched.

"These are my people, and they deserve to live as they choose!" he muttered, then turned, slightly embarrassed, as a small hand closed on his own. Lost in his thoughts, he had wandered away from the old mine camp with its human-ordered wall. Now he found himself standing on a crested ridge on the mountainside, looking out over the pretty lake that had once served dwarven miners on dwarven soil, but now served no one at all.

Tap Tolec and the rest of the Ten were nearby, of course. They always followed him closely wherever he went. And standing beside him, looking up at him with concerned eyes, was Helta Graywood. Derkin had no idea how long she had been standing there with him, or following along after him.

Still holding his hand, she reached up and brushed his cheek with gentle fingers. "You're worrying about your people, aren't you?" she asked. "You're thinking that none of us might survive tomorrow, or next week, or next year. That we might go back to being slaves, or maybe just all die."

"I wasn't thinking any such thing," he growled, shaking his head stubbornly. "I was thinking that I'd better see that everybody has a job to do. Otherwise we'll never get that pass barricaded."

The girl's eyes held his, unwavering. "If you were just thinking about jobs and barricades," she asked quietly, "then why was there a tear on your cheek just now?"

"There was no tear!" he snapped. From the corner of his eye, he saw Tap Tolec and some others of the Ten look away quickly, as though embarrassed.

Helta nodded. "They saw it, too," she said.

With a sniff and an angry cough, Derkin drew himself up harshly. "Well, you won't see another one there," he promised. "Kal-Thax requires sweat, and sometimes it demands blood. But it has no use for tears."

Back at the compound, Derkin found Calan Silvertoe waiting for him. "We'll have at least a week," the old Daewar said. "But not more than two. Those horse soldiers who left here last night are out chasing barbarians. Despaxas promises that they'll be . . ."

"Despaxas?" Derkin stared at him. "Your elf? Is he here?"

"He's not my elf!" Calan snapped. "And he's not here. But sometimes he . . . ah, sort of talks to me inside my head. I don't know how he does that, but he does."

"I believe it." Derkin nodded. "And what does he say?"

"He says the Cobar will keep the human soldiers occupied for at least a week, and maybe more than that. But he says we'd better hurry, because even if they keep those troops out there longer, Lord Kane's post patrols still use the pass, and the next one will be coming through in about two weeks."

"Then let's get work parties organized," Derkin said. "Break out trowels and prybars, splitting mauls and winches. I'll take the red-and-grays and scout the pass. You get some foresters up on those slopes for timber.

Tomorrow we build stone-boats."

"Aye," Calan agreed. "And where do we go for good stone, then? There isn't time to quarry and cut it."

"We have enough to start with right here." Derkin turned, pointing at the big eight-foot wall encircling Lord Kane's outpost compound. He extended the gesture, pointing at one and then another of the big stone barracks within the area. "We'll begin with these stones," he said. "The humans won't have need of them anymore."

At one end of the compound, human prisoners sweated in the sun, digging a pit to bury the hundreds of dead soldiers stacked there like cordwood. All around them were armed dwarves, watching and guarding. No human from Tharkas Camp had gotten away to carry an alarm to Klanath, and none was going to. At the far end, outside the compound, some dwarves also were digging, burying their own. They would not permit the humans to even touch, much less bury, a fallen comrade. In the background, drummers maintained a soft, mournful tattoo on muffled vibrars.

Derkin gave orders for the red-and-grays to assemble, then strolled to where the dwarven graves were being dug. For a moment he stood watching, his helmet in his hand. First blood, he thought. We have sworn to retake Kal-Thax, with or without anybody's help, and now we have made a beginning.

There weren't many dead dwarves to bury, but there would be more.

Kal-Thax, he thought. Land of the dwarves. Land of my people. Kal-Thax needs sweat . . . and sometimes it demands blood.

14

The Reclamation

It was after sundown when Lord Kane's Third Horse Battalion came within sight of the barbarians' camp. The wide plains here, below the Kharolis foothills, could fool the eye. What had appeared to be campfire smoke four or five miles away had proven to be campfire smoke nearly fifteen miles away. But now they were within a mile, and in the mountain-shadowed light of evening, the soldiers could see the fires beneath the smoke.

"About a hundred savages," a lieutenant remarked, riding beside the battalion's leader, Commander Tulien Gart. "That's what the footmen back there estimated. I see nine or ten separate fires, and that's about right for a camp of that size. What do we do with them when we have them?"

"We shall have to kill some of them, I suppose," the commander said, his austere features showing his distaste. As a proud soldier and descendant of knights, Gart found no honor in harassing simple barbarians. "They'll fight when we fall upon them, but we shall take as many prisoners as possible." Privately, he wondered if sparing any of their lives was a kindness. As prisoners, they would become the property of Lord Sakar Kane. The prince would likely use them as examples—a message to any other savages who might think of attacking an empire march.

"These plainsmen have fast horses," the lieutenant noted. "If they see us coming, they'll run."

"We'll wait until just dark, to attack," Gart decided. "I want no talking, no clattering armor, no sound at all from this point. We proceed in silence, by hand signal only. Pass the word to all units. Silent approach, then at my signal spread, form, and charge."

The lieutenant grinned and saluted, reining his mount around. "The savages will never know what hit them," he said.

As darkness fell across the rolling plains, the members of the Third Battalion walked their mounts up a grassy swell. They paused there, spreading and wheeling into a long line, facing the peaceful camp three hundred yards away. Signals were relayed from the center by platoon officers, and each soldier carefully removed the mufflings and strappings from his armor and the armor of his horse. Such muffling was necessary for a silent approach by an armored unit, but would only get in the way in a charge.

With shields and lances at the ready, the line of horsemen waited, squinting, peering at the little camp. It looked as though no alarm had been given. The fires were burning low, and a few recumbent figures sprawled near some of the fires or sat in the entrances of the three or four little shelters that were visible in the firelight. No sentries were visible, and no one seemed to be doing anything beyond just sitting around, enjoying the evening breeze.

"Poor, ignorant savages," Commander Gart muttered, raising his arm. "This won't take any effort at all." All along the line, lieutenants raised their arms, ready to relay his signal.

"And to think we get paid for this," a soldier whispered somewhere.

The evening had darkened, and the time was as good as any. With a sigh of anticipation, Tulien Gart brought his arm down and forward, and put spurs to his startled mount. The big horse gathered its haunches and surged forward in a fast trot that became a belly-down run. To the right and left, the entire line moved in unison with the commander, and the quiet of evening erupted into a thunder of hooves and a rattling of mail.

In nine seconds, the thundering line had gone a hundred yards. In seven more seconds it covered the second hundred, and six seconds later it smashed into the little camp, a wide, sweeping juggernaut of armored men and armored horses, bristling with leveled lances. Fires were scattered by flailing hooves and smothered by rising clouds of dust. Tents and lean-tos collapsed and were trampled into the soil. Lances pierced the reclining figures, vaguely seen in the turmoil, and voices were raised in surprise. "What is this, anyway?" a soldier shouted. "This isn't a man! It's nothing but a straw dummy!"

"Same over here!" another responded. "Where are they?"

"Dismount and search!" Tulien Gart ordered. "Find them! Find their tracks!"

"They can't have gone very far," a lieutenant noted. "These fires have been tended within the past hour."

For a time, the entire Third Battalion was afoot, torches held high and swords in gauntleted hands, searching.

Tulien Gart stood in the center of the ruined dummy camp, shouting commands as the search widened, then widened again. But when an hour passed with nothing found, he sighed and called them all back in. "We'll camp here tonight," he decided. "It's too dark to move. In the morning, we'll find their trail."

The battalion was just building its fires when an ashen-faced brace of lieutenants hurried up to Tulien Gart and saluted. "We're missing some horses, sir," one of them said.

"And we know where the savages have gone," the other added.

Gart stared at them. "Missing . . . horses? How many horses, and what became of them?"

"About twenty, it looks like." A lieutenant shrugged. "We're still counting."

"Why are we missing twenty horses?" Gart snapped.

"They were stolen, sir," a lieutenant said, scuffling his steel-shod feet. "While we were searching around the camp, it looks as though some of the plainsmen just walked in and led them away. There was a lot of confusion and . . ."

"Gods!" Gart stormed. "I'll want the name of every horse handler on duty during that search." He cursed for several seconds, a stream of carefully chosen invectives that was an education to some of his younger personnel. Then he turned again to the pair of lieutenants. "You said you know where the savages are?"

"Yes, sir," one of them replied.

"Well, where?"

The soldier turned and pointed eastward. "Over there, sir," he said.

Gart looked, and began swearing again. There, out on the prairie, were the lights of fresh fires, a night camp being prepared. In the prairie distance, the little camp might have been only a mile or so away. Or it might have been fifteen or twenty miles.

* * * * *

"Well, that was entertaining," Tuft Broadland said to Despaxas as they sipped hot ale beside a fresh fire. "And we picked up twenty-three horses in the bargain."

"Will they follow?" the elf asked.

"Of course they will. They can see us as well as we can see them, and those Ergothians have no eye for distance. They'll wait for morning, then they'll come clanking and crashing after us. I think tomorrow it might be nice if a few of them happen to fall into a pit or something, just to keep them interested. And maybe we'll put a few more of them afoot. Gods, it must be uncomfortable, walking in cavalry armor, carrying those horseback shields and heavy lances! But of course they won't discard as much as a gauntlet or brace. That would be disgraceful!" He grinned wolfishly.

"Can your people take it from here?" the elf asked. "I mean, without your presence, can your warriors keep those soldiers occupied for a week or so?"

"Of course," Tuft assured him. "One thing about empire troops, you can count on them. In a close chase, it will be several days before they'll admit to themselves that they're being dawdled. And by that time, they'll be at least a week's travel from where they came from. But why do you ask?"

"I promised you a chance to observe Derkin's army," Despaxas said. "If you'd like, we can go now."

"To Tharkas?" Tuft inquired. "Yes, I'd like to see what that sourpuss dwarf is up to. We can be there in a couple of days."

"No, I said 'now,' " the elf corrected. "Zephyr is close by. In his own plane, he is a great wizard. As a verger, he can lift us from one place to another in a moment by wrapping us in his wings."

"Absolutely not!" the Cobar snapped. "I'll be hanged if

I'll let myself be wrapped in fish wings."

"Then I'll transport us myself." Despaxas shrugged. "Transport is a simple enough spell."

The man glared at him across the fire. "I know about your transport spells," he reminded the elf. "They make people dizzy."

"It only lasts a moment," Despaxas said.

"I'm not going anywhere without a horse under me!" the Cobar growled. "Being afoot is for Sackmen and Ergothians."

Despaxas smiled—an innocent, disarming smile. "Then get your horse," he said.

* * * * *

In the span of a single day, the floor of Tharkas Pass had become a beehive of activity. Thousands of bustling, busy dwarves worked in the shadows of the great, precipitous walls of the pass, barely four miles from Lord Kane's stronghold at Klanath.

At the place where a dwarf named Cale Greeneye had driven a metal spike centuries earlier, marking the boundary of the dwarven land of Kal-Thax, the Chosen Ones worked at building a massive stone wall. By the hundreds, dwarven workmen disassembled the stone walls three miles south at Tharkas Camp, while hundreds of others loaded the great stones onto stone-boats. With teams of oxen, bison, and even a few elk, dwarven teamsters hauled the stones into Tharkas Pass.

Within the pass, at the site Derkin Hammerhand had selected, stonemasons recut, sized, and drilled the great blocks of solid rock, hoisted them with winches and slings, and set them in place while hundreds more scurried about, fitting each joint with "pegs" of iron bar to secure them. Every stone weighed at least a thousand pounds, and some weighed a ton. With blocks of such size, human builders would have settled for mortared joints and relied on the weight of the materials to make the wall secure. But these were not humans. These were dwarves, and they held to the dwarven philosophy of construction: if you can't build it right, don't build it at all.

Nothing short of an earthquake would ever move this wall so much as an inch, once it was completed.

The pass at this point was only sixty feet wide at the bottom, and the growing wall extended from one side to the other, completely closing it off except for a reinforced gap in the center where a narrow gate would be hung. Within the space of a day, the wall was two tiers high—shoulder-high to its builders—and Derkin's masons estimated that it would be at least twenty feet high before they ran out of prequarried stone. Twenty feet was not as high as Derkin envisioned the great wall, but it would be a start. Within a week or a little more, Tharkas Pass would be closed to casual travel. The single gate, made of steel-reinforced timbers, would be four feet wide and nine feet tall. Once the wall was up, and the gate closed and guarded, nothing less than an all-out siege would open northern Kal-Thax to outsiders again. The wall would not be impenetrable—not as Thorbardin was—but it would be a formidable obstacle to any who tried to enter uninvited.

Throughout the day, the dwarves had worked. Now as evening shadows darkened the pass, they changed shifts. Those of Daewar, Theiwar, and Klar ancestry were replaced by dwarves of Daergar ancestry, whose eyes were sensitive in daylight but excellent at night. In this way, the work would continue without stop until the task was finished. Torches were lighted for the day's last caravan of stone-boats, and these were being hauled into place for unloading when, abruptly, chaos broke out in the pass just a few paces south of the rising wall.

Where there had been only empty ground just moments ago, between groves of mountain spruce, suddenly there was a bucking, pitching horse with a man clinging to its light saddle. Dwarves by the hundreds turned to stare at the unexpected sight as the horse spun and danced, rearing and bucking enthusiastically. The man on its back clung grimly, shouting curses and threats as he tried to bring it under control. Dozens of dwarves had grabbed weapons and begun closing in on the spectacle when a second figure appeared out of nowhere—a cloaked, hooded figure that was obviously not a dwarf. The second apparition gazed at the bucking horse and its clinging, swearing rider for a moment, then turned and raised a hand toward the surrounding dwarves.

In the crowd, blades flashed and slings began to hum. Then Derkin Hammerhand strode forward, turned full around, and commanded, "Hold your weapons! These are not enemies!"

"Hello, Derkin," the cloaked figure said. "It has been a long time."

"Despaxas." Derkin nodded. "Calan said he thought you might come." He pointed at the still-pitching horse and its angry rider. "What's going on here?"

"Horses don't like transport spells." The elf shrugged. "They usually act up a bit upon arrival."

It took more than a minute for the man to bring his horse under control, and when he was once again in charge he swung down from his saddle and pointed an angry finger at Despaxas. "You knew that would happen," he snarled. "Why didn't you warn me?"

Despaxas shrugged eloquently. "You said you wouldn't go anywhere without a horse under you," he purred. "And far be it from me to try to tell a Cobar anything about horses."

For a moment, the man glared as though he were contemplating murder. Then he shook his head. "Crazy elf," he muttered. He turned, his eyes roving the crowds of dwarves all around, then turning upward toward the shadowy stone that climbed skyward on both sides. "Where are we?" he asked.

"In Tharkas Pass," Despaxas said. "At the place where a dwarf once marked the border of his homeland."

"And where is . . ." His eyes lit on the sturdy, red-cloaked figure of the dwarven leader and blinked. "Derkin? Is that you?"

"Hello, Tuft Broadland," the dwarf said.

"Well! You certainly have changed, these past years. I hardly knew you."

"We all change," Derkin said, then glanced at the elf. "Well, most of us do anyway. Come with me. Our main camp is just at the south end of the pass, where there's water. You two can tell me all the latest news. I understand the war on the plains is still going on?"

"And on, and on," Tuft said bleakly.

"Well, we'll eat, and you can tell me about it. Tomorrow I'll show you what we're doing here."

In the busy, crowded dwarven camp, people stared at the human and the elf with surly suspicion until Derkin made it clear to everyone that they were his guests. Then it seemed the dwarves couldn't do enough for them. They crowded around with platters of roast meat, freshly baked dark bread, and tankards of ale. Tuft marveled at the sumptuous feast that seemed to be ordinary fare for these people. "How do you do it?" he asked Derkin. "I mean, I see an army here, but where does the food come from?"

"You only see about a third of us here," Derkin told him. "We have farms and granaries all over southwest of here and herds in every valley. Armies must have food and provisions, so the Chosen Ones are more than an army. They have become an entire people. The first year after we freed ourselves from the empire's mines—the last time you saw us—we devoted our efforts and time mostly to gathering those Neidar who wanted to go with us and to scouting new trails and territories. The Neidar have been a scattered people, which is why so many of them wound up as slaves in the human mines . . . that, and the fact that Thorbardin didn't protect them as it was supposed to. But they aren't scattered now. And they aren't slaves, either."

Helta Graywood came from a shelter, carrying blankets for them to sit on while they ate. Tuft grinned at the girl and bowed slightly. "I remember you," he said.

"Everybody always remembers Helta," Derkin said softly.

"But she wears no token," the Cobar noted. "Haven't you married her yet?"

"No, he hasn't," Helta said. "I've told him a dozen times to marry me, but he puts me off. He says he won't commit to anything except reclaiming Kal-Thax. He's stubborn, among other things."

And stupid, too, Tuft thought, but kept the notion to himself. Most of the dwarven women he had seen were far from beautiful, at least to his human eyes. But Helta Graywood was a striking exception.

Old Calan Silvertoe joined them, then, and they spread their blankets beside a fresh fire. Finishing off a roasted haunch of some delicious meat, Tuft said to Derkin, "I'd like to see your settlement in the wilderness. You people must be doing wonders there."

"No human has seen what we are doing out there," the dwarf said levelly, "and none will. But if you people ever get through with your stupid war, you'll see the results. We intend to open trade routes and trading centers—east, west, and north."

"That's after you reclaim Kal-Thax, of course," the Cobar said bluntly.

"Of course. That's what we're doing now. That's why we're building a wall."

"The land you're claiming—or reclaiming—is territory that Lord Kane considers his own," Despaxas said. "The

Emperor Ullves granted it to him."

"Then the Emperor Ullves lied to him," Derkin said. "This land is ours. It was never his to grant, and never will be."

"You think a wall is going to stop Lord Kane from trying to take back what he considers his?" Tuft asked.

"Maybe not." Derkin shrugged. "Walls are like fences. They are built primarily to keep neighbors out. But they don't mean much to enemies."

"Then what's the purpose of it?"

"It will slow him down, at least," the dwarf said.

"You'll have to fight him," the elf said quietly.

Derkin studied them both with shrewd, dark eyes that were far more experienced than the same eyes had been just a few seasons before. His scrutiny also fell on Calan Silvertoe. "I expect to," he said. "And I'm beginning to understand why each of you was so anxious to help me before . . . and why you want to encourage me now."

"What you are doing here will help us in our war against the invaders," Despaxas said. "There's no secret about that."

"But I wonder if you—any of you—understand that I want no part of your war," Derkin growled.

"You didn't want to be anybody's leader either," Calan Silvertoe reminded him. "Sometimes there isn't much choice about things like that."

Derkin turned away, yawning, ignoring him. But he caught the glance that passed between Despaxas and Calan Silvertoe and felt a sudden coldness in his bones. They knew. The old, one-armed dwarf and the ageless elf, they knew what Derkin knew but didn't want to admit, even to himself. The human lord of Klanath would see Derkin's wall not as a boundary, but as a challenge. He almost certainly would not choose to turn away and leave Kal-Thax alone.

In the deepening night, muffled drums sang their songs

through the mountains. Drums that Hylar crafters had taught Derkin to build and use as a boy—as his Hylar ancestors had always built and used them—and that Despaxas the elf had taught him a new song for, somewhere in the wilderness. The song of Balladine.

Now the drums were signaling, as they always signaled. Derkin's people—and the far-ranging Neidar who had joined them—now numbered some twenty thousand. The nine thousand here at Tharkas were the Chosen Ones, the fighting core of what had become a new and widespread clan. Most of the rest were in the wilderness, near a place called Sheercliff, though some were still farther west, staking out territory for a future trade center to be called Barter.

They were far separated in miles, but not in mind, and the drums carried their messages back and forth through the mountains.

15
Master of the Pass

For eleven days the dwarves worked on their wall, laboring night and day while the sole human among them, Tuft Broadland, watched with amazement. Except for his brief adventure in this place, years before, when he had helped the former Derkin Winterseed free dwarven slaves from the goblins in the Tharkas mine shaft, then watched as those slaves freed thousands more from the mines of Klanath, Tuft had never associated with dwarves.

He was amazed now at their energy, their stubborn intensity in the face of a task, and at their sheer physical strength. He knew, of course, that a mature dwarf a foot shorter than himself would weigh as much as he did, and he had heard that the massive little people were stronger, pound for pound, than humans. But as he watched their craftsmen handle and set huge stones day after day, the Cobar was awed. Time after time he watched a half-dozen dwarves—or sometimes as few as four—roll a ton of square-cut stone from side to side, working its surface with ringing tools, punching reinforcement holes in it with hammer drills, then wrestle the stone onto a sling board for other dwarves to lift from above.

They used winches and wedges, levers and slings, and all manner of other tools, in ways he had never seen such things used. And while some among them were more skilled than others at the cutting or drilling or setting of stone, he had the impression that any one of them at random could have done the job of any other.

"They work as though they were born with tools in their hands," he remarked to Despaxas as the Tharkas Wall towered overhead, growing tier by tier.

"They almost were," the elf said casually. "It is the manner of dwarves. It is said that a dwarf can climb before he can walk, hew stone before he can talk, and delve before he's out of his swaddling."

"They're an amazing people," Tuft allowed. "But can they use their weapons?"

"You will see soon enough," the elf answered. "To a dwarf, a weapon is just another tool. The only difference is in its application."

Now, on the eleventh day of the project, as the last of the stones salvaged from Lord Kane's outpost were hauled upward to be set into place, Tuft stood back to look at the huge construct. The wall was butted into solid stone on each side of the pass, completely filling it from side to side. Stout battlements of carved stone lined its top, protecting a bastion that could be reached by ramps on the south face. The north face of the wall, facing toward Klanath, was solid, almost seamless stone. And low in its center was a single, small opening, tall and narrow, sealed by a gate that looked as solid and massive as the wall itself.

Not an impassable obstacle, the Cobar decided as he studied the wall. Determined men equipped with grapples and lines could scale its north face and get across. But with a good defense on that bastion top, the price of such an attack would be fearsome.

And it had been built in eleven days! Such a project would have taken human craftsmen half a year to complete.

With the wall in place, most of the Chosen Ones moved their camp into the pass, just behind their barricade. And now Tuft saw the builders of the wall become soldiers of Kal-Thax. Putting away their stoneworking tools, the dwarves donned exquisite steel armor and clothing of a variety of bright colors. Fine, dwarven steel weapons were unwrapped, brought out, and buckled or strapped into place. Within a day after the completion of the stone wall, the Cobar found himself surrounded by thousands of stubby, helmed warriors, most of whom looked as fierce and formidable as Derkin Hammerhand himself.

Another thing he noted then, about the dwarves. A hundred pounds or so of steel plate, helmet, slung shield, and weaponry was no burden to a sturdy dwarf. In full battle attire, each dwarf appeared as comfortable and as nimble as though he were clothed only in kilt and smock. Afoot or on horseback, the short, sturdy warriors seemed as at home in armor as though it were part of them.

Tuft was admiring the throngs around him when a cold, deep voice asked, "What are you grinning at, human? Do you find my people funny?"

Derkin was beside him, hands on his hips, and there was no humor in his wide-set, thoughtful eyes.

"Not at all," Tuft hastened to reply. "Quite the opposite. I was thinking how fierce your people seem, and how colorful."

"Then what were you grinning about?"

The Cobar paused, then pointed at a group of two or three dozen armored dwarves strolling past. "Even fully armored, your dwarves make no racket. My people have fought the emperor's armies for years now, and our ears are an advantage. When those churls put on armor, they clank so that one can hear them a quarter mile away."

"If you find that amusing, you'll have plenty of entertainment soon," Derkin said, turning away. "The drums spoke this morning. That human battalion that left Tharkas to chase your raiders has returned to Klanath. They'll be on their way here shortly." As though in afterthought, he glanced back at the man, and now he was grinning, too. "They're short a few men, by my sentinels' count. And they're short a lot of horses."

It was the following morning when soldiers of the empire appeared in Tharkas Pass. Remounted and reprovisioned—and thoroughly chastened by Lord Kane himself—Commander Tulien Gart led his Third Battalion out of Klanath, heading for the outpost they had left nearly two weeks before. Above them on the peaks, muted thunders rolled, then died away, and soldiers in the ranks craned their necks, looking upward. But there was nothing there to see.

Entering the pass, the battalion strung itself out, riding at an easy pace, expecting no surprises. Two miles into the gap, though, an outrider swung his mount around and galloped back to salute his commander. "There's something in the pass, sir. I can't tell what it is," he reported.

Within a quarter-mile they could all see the something, and they paused, peering. "What is that?" Tulien Gart demanded. "First platoon, go forward and see what that thing is!"

About thirty riders spurred their mounts and trotted away up the pass. For long minutes the rest of the battalion waited, then a rider came toward them, moving fast.

Almost losing his seat as he skidded his horse to a haunch-down halt, he snapped a quick, wide-eyed salute and said, "That thing is a wall, sir! A great big stone wall. It blocks the whole pass, and someone on top of it told us to go away and never come back."

"Who told you that?" the commander rasped. "Who was it on that wall?"

"I don't know, sir." The soldier shook his head. "The rest of the platoon went ahead for a better look, but the lieutenant sent me to report."

"A wall!" Tulien Gart muttered. "Now what?" Impatiently, he signaled and spurred his mount, and the entire battalion trotted forward behind him.

It was indeed a wall—a high, wide wall of solid stone, with battlements at its crest and a single, narrow door that was firmly closed. Just below the wall, the first platoon was spread out, still mounted, with shields and swords at hand. As he neared the wall, Gart could hear his lieutenant shouting, ". . . can't put a blasted wall in this pass without Lord Kane's orders! Who do you people think you are?"

"We know exactly who we are!" a deep, resonant voice answered from above. "And we know who you are, too! Now go away!"

With an oath, Tulien Gart reined his mount in beside the lieutenant's and demanded, "Who is that up there?" When the lieutenant shrugged, Gart straightened himself in his saddle and cupped his hands. "You on the wall!" he demanded. "Identify yourselves at once! Who are you?"

A silhouette moved above, a polished helmet glinted in the light, and a deep voice called back, "Who's asking?"

"I am Tulien Gart!" Gart shouted. "In command of this battalion, in service to the Lord Sakar Kane, Prince of Klanath by order of Our Illustrious Emperor Quivalin Soth the Fifth! Now, who are you, and why are you here?"

"I'm called Hammerhand!" the deep voice responded, sounding unimpressed. "I'm here because I choose to be! This is the border of Kal-Thax, and as of now the border is closed! So go away!"

"Border of what?" Gart shouted. "This land is the fief of Lord Kane! He owns it!"

"No, he doesn't," the deep voice assured him casually. "It's ours."

From the rear of the battalion column came a muttering that traveled forward. A lieutenant turned, listened, and wheeled toward his commander. "Sir," he said, "the men farther back can see better. They say those are dwarves up there."

"That's right," the voice from above called. "We're dwarves. This wall marks the boundary of Kal-Thax. Kal-thax is dwarven land. It has always been ours, and it always will be. It begins right here, at this wall. Now, for the last time, turn around and go away!"

Muttering a curse, Tulien Gart shaded his eyes against the bright sky. Now there were many helmed heads visible between the stone battlements above, and he could see the bristle of weapons. Turning in his saddle, he called, "Archers forward!"

Immediately, a company of mounted bowmen advanced at his bidding. Above, the deep voice rang out, cold and deadly. "Be careful, Commander Gart! You are about to make a serious mistake!"

Ignoring the dwarf above, Gart commanded, "Archers! Clear that wall!"

In unison, a hundred bows were raised, drawn, and released, and a hundred deadly arrows hurtled upward. But where the silhouettes of heads had been, there were now bright shields. Arrows clattered, shattered, and caromed away. Then the shields dropped from sight, and in their place were pairs of dwarves, drawing aim on those below. Slings whirred and spat, crossbows thudded, and panic erupted among the archers. Dozens fell from their saddles, pierced or brained, and the rest became a melee of stamping, wheeling, bucking horses and men, shouldering one another in their haste to back away. More men and several horses went down under trampling hooves.

Through it all, Tulien Gart held his reins and his ground, his angry eyes locked on the figure above, the one who called himself Hammerhand. That one, he noticed, had not moved either. But now the deep, cold voice came again, and Gart felt the impact of shadowed eyes beneath a glistening helm—eyes that he knew were locked on his own. "Hear the words of Hammerhand, human!" the voice thundered. "Hear me well, and tell your master what I have said! At this point, Kal-Thax begins! From this day, Kal-Thax is closed to you and your kind! Kal-Thax belongs to dwarves, not humans!

"If you leave us alone, we will leave you alone! But if you attack—as you have just learned—we will respond! Now go away! Go, and don't come back!"

Reluctantly, Tulien Gart turned his mount and led a retreat, but only for a few hundred yards. Once beyond the range of slings and crossbows, he halted the battalion and dismounted. A few minutes passed, then two squads of humans approached the wall again, this time on foot and carrying no bows. Instead, they carried stretchers. Almost timidly, expecting death at any minute, the men neared the wall and began collecting their wounded and dead. But the dwarves above launched no volleys. They only watched.

On the ramp behind the wall, Tuft Broadland also watched, then turned to Derkin Hammerhand. "You'd better tell them to take their fallen mounts, too. They're just leaving them."

"We'll keep the dead horses," Derkin declared. "There's enough meat there for two or three days."

The blood drained from the Cobar's face as he stared at

the dwarf, shocked and astonished. "You . . . you people eat horses?"

"Meat's meat," Derkin said, casually. "We can eat anything that doesn't eat us first. We've learned that in the slave mines and in the wilderness."

The humans collected their dead and wounded, and returned down the pass to where the battalion waited. But instead of mounting up and moving away, the soldiers seemed to be settling in.

"They aren't leaving," Calan Silvertoe noted.

"I didn't think they would, yet," Hammerhand said. "That commander can't just take my word for it that they aren't welcome here. He has to try a few more tricks."

Throughout the morning and early afternoon, the dwarves on the wall could see furious activity down the pass, men hurrying here and there, doing things. At first, it was hard to tell what they were doing, then sharp eyes aloft spotted a heavy, freshly hewn log being dragged up the pass from a grove beyond.

"They're making a ram!" old Calan snorted. "They intend to test our gate."

"Can the gate withstand a ram?" worried Tuft Broadland.

"Making a ram is one thing," Derkin responded. "Getting it here is another."

Several hundred yards away, men lined up beside the heavy log, two men on a side. Squatting, they slipped harnesses over their shoulders, then stood, lifting the ram with them. At the wave of Tulien Gart's hand, they started toward the wall at a trot.

The dwarves let them approach to within fifty yards, then all along the battlements, dwarves with slings and crossbows appeared. The ram bearers saw them there and faltered, slowing to a stop. Tulien Gart saw them, too, and shook his head. "Call them back," he told a trumpeter. "They'll never make it."

At the sound of the trumpet, the relieved rammers turned, sighing visibly, and trotted back the way they had come, carrying their log.

"Next he'll try a shielded ram," Derkin said.

An hour passed before the rammers tried it again, and this time they came under a cover of shields—dozens of shields laced together to form a solid roof over the men and their ram. From above, the men could not even be seen as they trotted forward toward the gate.

"Now what do you do?" Tuft asked Derkin.

"Just watch," the dwarf said.

As the ram bearers gathered speed, aiming their juggernaut at the gate, a foot-high hinged panel opened in the bottom of the portal, with crossbows massed behind it. The men under the shields, seeing sudden death only yards away, pointing up at them, faltered. One stumbled, three fell, then they all went down, dragged to the ground by their log ram while lashed shields clattered down atop them. From the deadly portal, a voice called, "Just get up and back away if you want to live. Leave the log where it is. You won't need it anymore."

With no choice at all, the men under the fallen shields slipped out of their shoulder straps and struggled to their feet. On the wall above them, a voice said, "Leave the shields, too. They're fair trade for the bolts we've expended."

The men hobbled away, bruised and shaken, one being supported by two of the others, apparently the victim of a broken leg. Behind them, Derkin called, "Tell your commander that the reason you're still alive is that no one here has been hurt!"

The gate opened then, and hordes of dwarves spilled through under cover of the weapons on the wall. By the time the rammers had returned to their commander, all of the shields and dead horses had been dragged to the south side of the wall, and the log ram was disappearing through the portal, which slammed shut when it was clear.

In the evening, as shadows deepened in the pass, arrows began to reach the top of the wall. Soldiers had crept along the brushy sides of the pass and taken shelter in a grove of conifers in bow range of the wall.

Crouching behind battlements, Derkin and his defenders studied the grove and waited. Darkness came quickly in the deep pass, and the archers' light was failing. Their arrows had done no damage.

At full dark, the dwarves heard scurrying sounds as the attackers withdrew for the night, and Derkin went down the ramp to find Vin the Shadow. "You know what to do," he told the Daergar.

"We could do more than that," Vin suggested, but Derkin shook his head. "No," he said, "you heard what I told the commander. Those arrows haven't hurt anybody yet."

With a curt nod, Vin rounded up a dozen more Daergar. They removed their iron masks, revealing the large eyes and foxlike features of their clan. Quickly they gathered torches, tinder, and vials of oil, and filed out through the gate. They were back within minutes, and behind them fires blazed. By morning, the grove of trees that could hide archers would be nothing but smoldering ashes.

For two more days, the standoff in Tharkas Pass continued. Tulien Gart tried everything he could think of to get past the dwarves' wall, but nothing succeeded. Climbers sent in the dark of night, with grapples and rope, were easy targets for dark-seeing Daergar on the wall. An unmanned ram consisting of two whip-stung horses with a log slung between them went afoul when dwarves above dropped flaming straw in their path. The damage the ram horses did to Gart's camp as they fled through it was truly awful.

On the morning when Lord Kane's post patrol showed up in the pass, Gart decided it was time to return to

Klanath and report to Lord Kane. Maybe the prince could root out dwarves from Tharkas Pass, but Gart accepted that the Third Battalion, alone, could not.

Before leaving, though, Gart mounted his horse and rode alone to the dwarves' wall. Sitting his saddle straight-backed and haughty, he looked upward. "Hammerhand!" he called.

Above, the same bright-helmed silhouette appeared. "I'm here, Commander," the deep, resonant voice responded.

"I'm leaving to return to Klanath," Gart said. "I will give your message to Lord Kane, though they may be the last words I ever utter. But just for my own curiosity, who the blazes are you, anyway?"

"That's pretty obvious," the voice above said. "I am Master of Tharkas."

As the commander rode away, the wall's gate opened and a small crowd of dirty, disheveled humans scurried through it. They were the survivors of the Tharkas outpost who had been held in the mine shaft. Derkin had no further use for them, so he was sending them home. On the wall, dozens of dwarves burst into laughter when the ragged crowd caught up with their commander, who promptly turned his head and backed his horse away from them. Those poor wretches would smell like goblins for weeks, no matter how they scrubbed themselves.

Derkin Hammerhand turned to the Cobar standing beside him. "That commander is a fair soldier," he said. "He's more than just a 'clanking churl.' "

"I agree." Tuft Broadland nodded. "Tulien Gart is a true soldier. I could admire a man like that, if it weren't for the colors he carries. He's in the right line of work, but he's in the wrong employ."

Part IV:

Master of Kal-Thax

16

The Turning of War

Sakar Kane stormed and raged at the incredible tale brought to him by the commander of his Third Battalion. A stone wall across Tharkas Pass, the man reported. And dwarves! Dwarves forbidding entry into *his* lands, by *his* own troops.

"You're telling me that you—with a full battalion—could not overcome a bunch of stupid, cowering dwarves hiding behind a simple wall?" the Prince of Klanath hissed, his eyes burning into those of his commander.

Tulien Gart accepted the tone and the angry glare. Standing parade-erect, holding his plumed helm in the crook of his arm, the commander seemed resigned to the consequences of his words. Streaks of gray at his temples and the dark lines beneath his eyes made him look tired. Tired, but not defeated. He held his lord's gaze and neither blinked nor looked away. "Yes, Sire," he confirmed. "I tried everything I knew to try, short of a suicide rush which would have cost Your Highness most of the battalion. With all respect, Sire, the wall they have built is more than a 'simple wall.' It is a bastion. And in my opinion, the people defending it are neither cowering nor stupid. They are well armed, quite disciplined, and—from what I could make out—more than willing to do whatever they must to hold their ground."

"It is not *their* ground!" Kane snapped. "It is mine!" With a snort of disgust he paced half the width of the pillared chamber which was his seat of power, for the moment ignoring the veteran soldier still standing at stiff attention. Then he whirled and pointed an accusing finger at the man. "Tell me again what that . . . that dwarf said," he ordered.

"Yes, Sire. He said he is called Hammerhand. He said Kal-Thax begins at the point where the wall stands, and . . ."

"What is Kal-Thax?"

"According to my clerk, Sire, it is a dwarven term, taken from some ancient language of theirs. Literally, it means 'cold forge,' but its meaning in practice is 'land of the dwarves.' "

"Continue," Lord Kane commanded.

"Hammerhand said the wall is the border of Kal-Thax, and that from this time on, Kal-Thax is closed except to dwarves. He said if the dwarves are left alone, they will leave us alone, but if they are attacked, they will respond."

"And you tested the dwarf's words?"

"I lost forty-nine men in the process, Sire. Thirty-five dead, fourteen wounded. To the best of my knowledge, though, Hammerhand lost none."

"Who does that dwarf think he is?" the prince thundered.

"I asked him that, Sire. He said only that he is the master of Tharkas."

Still pacing, Lord Kane stopped abruptly before his commander, leaning close to glare directly into his eyes. "You speak almost as though you admire that dwarf," he hissed. "Are you a traitor, Tulien Gart?"

Gart's sun-dark face blanched at the insult, but he held his expression tightly in check as he said, "No, Sire, I am not. I have done all in my power to serve Your Highness honorably and well."

"*Honorably* be hanged!" the prince snapped. "I want those dwarves cleared from that pass. I want them run down and killed or put in chains. I want that blasted wall torn down, my outpost restored . . . and I want this Hammerhand's head brought to me on the point of a lance. This is my desire. Will you obey such an order, if I command it, Tulien Gart?"

"I will attempt to do as my liege orders," Gart said. "But with only a battalion at my command, it cannot be done."

"And why not?"

"It will require a legion, Sire, with provisions for an all-out siege."

There was a rap at the closed door of the chamber, and Lord Kane turned as the portal opened and a liveried messenger stepped inside. "If this interruption is less than an emergency, I'll have you gutted on the spot!" the prince roared at the newcomer, who was hardly more than a boy.

The messenger's eyes went wide with fear, and his knees began to shake. "I . . . ." he gulped and tried again. "I . . . ah . . ."

"Out with it!" Kane ordered.

"Y–Your Highness, there is a—an emissary at the gate,

demanding immediate audience. He is f–from . . ."

The door opened wider and a burly, dark-cloaked figure strode in, pushing past the boy. "I'll deliver my own demand," he announced, throwing back his riding cowl.

Lord Kane stared at the man. "Dreyus!" he whispered.

"Aye, Your Highness." The big man's curt bow was arrogant and ironic, almost a challenge. His presence seemed to fill the room, as though the air within suddenly held an aura of power and cruelty. "I have ridden twelve days to reach this place, and have killed four horses. I do not care to wait on an audience."

Lord Kane stared at the emperor's emissary for a moment, then sighed. Like almost everyone else in Ergoth, Sakar Kane was a bit afraid of the man who stood before him now. Even the emperor, it was whispered, might well be careful not to offend the man called Dreyus —although it was rumored that no one in Daltigoth had ever actually seen the two together. Though not proclaimed as a wizard, Dreyus had certain strange powers. He was seldom present in the imperial halls in Daltigoth, but seemed always to know of each intrigue and whisper there. And though he had no official title or discernible status in Ergoth, he often represented the emperor in matters of import.

No one seemed to know where he had come from. Neither the clerical orders nor even the Orders of High Sorcery seemed to have any control over him, any more than did the marshals of the empire's armies, or even—it seemed—the emperor himself.

With a nod that became a slight bow, the Prince of Klanath waved Dreyus toward a secluded niche at one side of the Great Hall, where stood an amber-topped table and chairs of carved ivory. "Of course the eminent Dreyus is welcome here," Kane said. "You surprise me, though. I had heard that you were with General Giarna, in his elven campaign in the east."

Dreyus shook his head. "The general's elven campaign is failed, and Giarna is . . ." He paused, glancing aside at Tulien Gart, who still stood nearby at rigid attention. "Who is this?"

"No one, Eminence," Lord Kane said, as though he had completely forgotten the commander's presence. "One of my officers." To Gart he said, "You are dismissed for now, Commander. You are to confine yourself to quarters and await my pleasure."

"Yes, Sire." Gart saluted smartly, turning away. As he approached the door, it opened for him. There were palace guards there, and he knew without seeing Lord Kane's signal that the guards were for him. Lord Kane had not finished with him, and until he did, Gart was a prisoner. Undoubtedly his entire battalion had already been isolated and put under guard. Looking straight ahead, the commander stepped through, and the guards pulled the portal closed behind him. But just as it closed, he heard the voice of the man called Dreyus, saying, "Giarna has lost his campaign. Our legions were routed at Sithelbec, and I am . . ." The door closed, and he heard no more.

Was the war over? The words he had overheard amazed Gart. If the "boy general" was, indeed, defeated, and his campaign routed, did it mean an end to the emperor's dream of expansion into the eastern plains and Silvanesti?

For a moment, the commander felt a sense of relief. But only for a moment. No, his intuition said, Quivalin Soth V would not abandon his ambitions because one effort had failed. Things would change, but they would remain the same. In some form or other, the war of expansion would continue.

Outside the palace, Gart looked upward in surprise. When he had entered, the day had been clear and sunny. Now, though, the skies were dark with heavy, sullen clouds.

* * * * *

"Giarna waged a fierce campaign," Dreyus told Lord Kane. "But in the end he was stupid. He failed to reckon on the tenacity of the elves, or to realize that not all of the elves are forest recluses. The western elves—the Wildrunners—fight as plainsmen when they must. They can be full of surprises. They even control griffons, it seems. And the general allowed himself to be betrayed by a woman. His own doxy, Suzine."

"Suzine des Quivalin?" Lord Kane's eyes widened. "A relative of His Majesty . . . ?"

"Enough!" Dreyus's voice went low and cold. "The woman is never to be referred to by family name, or by lineage. She is not related to *anyone* in Ergoth, not even the lowest tradesman or serf. Is that understood?"

"Perfectly." Kane nodded. "But the campaign in the east, is it . . . ?"

"It continues," Dreyus said. "Giarna failed, but the empire has not. The war will continue. Even now, the scattered forces of Giarna's army are being gathered on the plains to await my return from Daltigoth. And that brings me to my reason for stopping here in Klanath on my way to Ullves's palace. We shall require certain, ah, augmented services from you, *Prince* Kane. Klanath was important to the previous campaign, as you know. It will be far more important to the coming campaign."

"I shall do my best to serve," Kane said smoothly. "As you doubtless know, I have managed to keep the road open and the mines in full production, despite some small problems."

"Some small problems," Dreyus drawled with heavy irony. "Yes, I know about those. First you lost several thousand slaves, then for two years or more you allowed empire caravans to be plagued by raiders and thieves."

"I have accounted for all of that," Kane snapped. "The

empire's coffers suffered no loss from the slave revolt. And as to those isolated raids . . ."

Dreyus raised a hand. "Enough," he said. "I know all about it, and am not here to take you to task. You have proven to be a capable subject of the empire, Lord Kane. Or perhaps only an incredibly lucky one, but that doesn't matter. What matters now is how well you serve my conquest of the eastern territories."

"*Your* conquest?"

"When I return from Daltigoth, I shall lead the forces that will finally put an end to the resistance of barbarian tribes and frontier elves," Dreyus said bluntly. "I . . . *we* shall no longer entrust such matters to mere generals."

"I see." Kane clapped his hands, and a servant slipped through a sliding wall panel to fill two goblets, then hastened away. "And my duties, Eminence?"

"Klanath will be my base for the duration of the campaign," Dreyus said. "You shall be privileged to serve as host to my headquarters, my supply stores, and certain of my troops. Another of Giarna's several mistakes, you see, was to use Klanath only as a depot and rest stop for reinforcements. He should have realized from the outset that the sheer distance between Daltigoth—or even Caergoth—and the barbarian plains gave an undue advantage to his enemies. I shall give them no such advantage."

Dreyus picked up his goblet and downed its contents. Although the vessel held the most precious of spiced wines, cooled by chips of clear ice from the lofty peaks above Klanath, the big man drank it as though it were no more than vulgar ale. Then he tossed the goblet aside and continued, "Starting shortly after my arrival in Daltigoth, my lord, you may expect caravans carrying all the things that I shall need for my campaign. These goods will be delivered into your care, to hold for me until I return here. I will expect to find them intact and undamaged when I arrive."

Lord Kane simply nodded, saying nothing.

"Also," Dreyus said imperiously, "you will close your mines for the present."

"Close the mines?" Kane rasped, frowning.

"Close the mines," Dreyus repeated. "For the present, you will have other work for your slaves. They shall be set to quarrying stone, immediately. Upon my return, I shall require suitable quarters for myself, my staff, and my servants. You will have these quarters built to specifications that will arrive with the first supply caravan." He gazed at Kane with eyes that shone with power and determination. "I trust you have no objection."

"It will be as you command, Eminence." Kane nodded. "And when will you return?"

"In the spring, possibly. Or in the summer. I shall return when I am ready to return. And you, Prince of Klanath, will be ready to welcome me when I do."

"As you say," Kane conceded.

"For the duration of my campaign in the east," Dreyus went on, "my command will be in residence at Klanath. You shall govern Klanath, of course, but until Ullves's empire extends to Silvanost itself, you shall govern for my convenience. Is that clear?"

Lord Kane's jaws were tight with anger, but he kept his voice steady. All he had heard about Dreyus, he realized, was true. Being face-to-face with the big man was like being face-to-face with Quivalin himself. The two bore no resemblance in physical features, but in force of presence, they might have been the same person. "Quite clear," Kane said.

"I—*we*, His Imperial Majesty and myself—will hold you personally responsible," Dreyus said. His business attended to, the big man leaned back, relaxing slightly. "We will not make the mistakes that Giarna made," he added casually. "We will not be plagued by delayed supplies, traitors in our own beds, unexpected storms, unexpected griffons, unexpected dwarves. . . ."

"Dwarves?" Lord Kane's ears twitched.

"A legion of dwarves took part in the battle at Sithel-bec," Dreyus noted. "On the side of the elves and their allies. It was just one more of the things Giarna failed to anticipate."

When Dreyus had gone, Lord Kane paced alone in his great hall, shaken and angry. Close the mines, the man ordered! Without the mines, much of Kane's wealth would be gone. Still, there was no choice in the matter. A man who has once survived the emperor's displeasure could not hope for forgiveness a second time. What the emperor demanded, the emperor must receive, fully and immediately. And he had no doubt that, when Dreyus spoke, it was with the emperor's voice. The feeling of presence was uncanny. In some way, it was as though Dreyus *was* Quivalin Soth V.

But what had shaken him most was Dreyus's demand that Klanath and the Klanath region—the granted fief of Lord Kane—be guaranteed under control and trouble-free.

Dwarves had fought at Sithelbec. And now, if Tulien Gart could be believed, an army of dwarves was en-camped behind a stone wall just four miles from Klanath. Such a thing was aggravating, at the least. But now—in light of Dreyus's plans—it was intolerable. Something would have to be done, and quickly.

He was very glad that he had confined the Third Battalion to quarters. It would not do for Dreyus to learn about the problem in Tharkas Pass. That was something that Lord Kane would have to deal with himself.

* * * * *

In a quiet glade on the perimeter of the Chosen Ones' encampment, Despaxas and Calan Silvertoe sat together, the old dwarf watching the elf while the elf gazed into a shallow bowl partly filled with milky liquid.

Long minutes had passed this way, and Calan was growing impatient. "Come on," he rasped. "What does it say?"

Despaxas looked up innocently. "It doesn't 'say' anything, my friend. That isn't how it works."

"I don't care how it works," Calan said. "I just want to know what you've learned."

"Well, I've learned that Kith-Kanan and his allies were victorious at Sithelbec."

"I already know that," Calan grunted. "You told me that a week ago. What's the news this time?"

"General Giarna is disgraced," the elf said.

Calan grinned. "Good," he said. "Couldn't have happened to a more deserving person. Does that mean the war is over?"

"No." Despaxas shrugged. "The human emperor will start again, with new command. That's what puzzles me. The command has already been decided, but I don't know who it will be. There is someone . . . a presence . . . but I'm not sure there's really anyone there. It's as though he—the presence—is somewhere else entirely."

"That doesn't make any sense," Calan snapped.

"It might." Despaxas frowned. "Three years ago I was with Kith-Kanan on the Singing Plains, where the Wild-runners were fortifying a village. Giarna was only forty miles away, with his army, and I went to have a look at him. Zephyr was with me. We reconnoitered the human army, but there was something puzzling about it. There was a man there, with Giarna . . . an emissary of the emperor's, named Dreyus. I saw him, but Zephyr couldn't. To Zephyr, there was no one there."

"Magic," Calan growled.

"Magic, yes," Despaxas said. "But not a magic I have been able to understand. I'm wondering now if the new commander of forces might be that same Dreyus." The elf gazed into his bowl thoughtfully. Then, with a quick twist of his hand, he turned the bowl over, spilling its contents onto the stony ground. The wet spot lasted only seconds, then was gone. The elf stood, slipping the bowl into his robe. "I'll be needed now, where Kith-Kanan is." With a quick nod, he strode away from Calan, who sprinted after him.

With his one hand, the old dwarf grabbed the elf's cloak and halted him. "Here, now!" he demanded. "You mean you're leaving again, just like that?"

"Of course." Despaxas smiled. "I'm not needed here now. This situation is in good hands." He glanced at the stump of Calan's arm and corrected himself. "Well, in good *hand*." He reached out, clasped the old dwarf's burly shoulder for a moment, and just for an instant Calan thought he saw a deep sadness in the elf's eyes. It was as though Despaxas were saying a final farewell to his old friend. But then the look was gone, and the elf turned again and walked away.

Halfway across the encampment, Despaxas found Tuft Broadland. "Get your horse, human," he said. "It's time for me to leave, and your people will be missing your leadership by now . . . if they've noticed yet that you're gone."

"Crazy elf," Tuft said sourly. "Shouldn't we say good-bye to Derkin before we go?"

"Why? He'll know we've gone."

"I'd like to bid him well," Tuft said. "And you should, too. He has done a remarkable thing here."

"Derkin's task—or his ordeal—has only begun," Despaxas said quietly. "We leave now, human. I have seen a glimpse of what is to come. But I cannot help Derkin Hammerhand. Destiny is upon him."

"If you know something of use to him, he deserves to be told," the Cobar said with a scowl.

Again, there was a flicker of sadness in Despaxas's expression, quickly replaced by a cold determination. "Trust me, Tuft Broadland. We must leave here now."

Confused, as he often was by Despaxas, the Cobar hesitated. Still, he had trusted this strange elf in the past, and had never regretted it. "All right," he said finally. "I'll get my horse, and you can say your spell. But I'll be hanged if I'll be in the saddle when you do."

17

Lord Kane's Revenge

Weeks had passed since the defense of Derkin's Wall against the attacks of the Third Battalion. And during those weeks, not a single soldier had been seen in Tharkas Pass.

Derkin's lookouts, hidden in shallow, camouflaged delves high on the peaks above Klanath, reported strange, unexplained activities in and around Lord Kane's stronghold. The great mines outside the city lay silent now, and it appeared that all of their slaves had been relocated. Some of them had been taken to bustling new stone quarries nearby, others into the city itself. And now, building stones by the hundreds were being hauled into the city, and there was construction going on in a large enclave just east of the palace. Timber crews moved back and forth between Klanath and the forests to the north, bringing back hundreds of logs.

It looked, the drums said, as though the humans were building a new fortress within the city.

Derkin Hammerhand admitted to those close to him that he was puzzled. What the humans were doing in Klanath was their own business, but he was surprised that there had been no further attempts to clear Tharkas Pass. He had been sure that Lord Kane would launch at least one attack in full force. It was not like the man to simply accept an ultimatum such as the dwarves had sent. Kane was not a passive person, nor one to accept a loss. He considered the lands south of the pass as his own. Would he lose them without a fight?

The Chosen Ones were becoming restless, too, and that added to Derkin's worries. With the wall in place, and no plans for permanent delves at the pass, they had little to do. Quarrels, brawls, and fistfights had become common in recent days, and Derkin knew it was the result of sheer boredom. Without work to do, his people turned to fighting, and there was no one here to fight except themselves.

He longed to leave the wall, to somehow know that Tharkas Pass was safe from invasion so that he could take his people back into the mountains. There, they could join their ten thousand peers in the work of hunting and herding, of planting and harvesting, of building and delving and living their lives.

The wall, like the little metal stake on which it was built, was really nothing more than a symbol. It was a signal to those beyond that the lands south of it were not theirs for the taking. It had needed to be built, and they had built it. It had been a certainty that the humans would test it, and the dwarves welcomed the test.

But Derkin had not intended to spend months or years here in Tharkas Pass. There were other places to be, and other things to do. Just as a great nation of dwarves had been carved out of the mountain wilderness so many centuries ago, now that nation must be renewed, and securing Tharkas Pass was only the first step.

In his dreams, Derkin saw a time when the Neidar of Kal-Thax could live securely, where and how they chose, knowing that they had champions to come to their aid if they were threatened. The Chosen Ones would be those champions. They would be the army of Kal-Thax. They would serve the dwarven nation as the Holgar—the people of Thorbardin—had once promised to.

He had little hope that Thorbardin would ever reverse itself, ever again become the vital, central fortress of Kal-Thax. Not enough of the people now living in the subterranean fortress had the spirit their ancestors had once had. There were a few Dunbarth Ironthumbs and people like the Daewar leader Jeron Redleather and his son Luster, but only a few, it seemed.

If Kal-Thax was to be restored as a realm, it would be up to the Chosen Ones to do it.

But this silence was unnerving. Not only had Lord Kane not come with his armies to test the walled border in force . . . he hadn't done anything at all.

Each evening's breezes, coming through the great pass, were cooler than those the evening before. Each morning now, there was frost. Winter came quickly in these mountains, and it would come soon. Derkin Hammerhand chafed at the silence, and at the waiting.

And then, four weeks to the day after the defense of the wall, the drums told of people coming. A small party, riding toward the border.

When they came into sight, Derkin went to the battlements. The people coming were human soldiers, wearing the colors of the empire and carrying the banners of Klanath. But there were only a dozen of them. As they neared, Derkin recognized the one in the lead. It was the officer he had given his message to, the one named Tulien Gart. With sudden decision, Derkin hurried down the ramp, opened the gate, and went out to meet him. The Ten, as always, went with him, but he ordered everyone else to stay.

Tulien Gart saw the dwarves come out from the gate and halted his escort. Then, holding a hand up, palm out, he rode forward alone. Six paces from the group of dwarves, he drew rein. "I am Tulien Gart," he said. "I have words for Hammerhand."

The dwarf in the lead stepped forward a single pace. Gart recognized the polished helm and the scarlet cape, and now he could see the face that went with them—a wide, stern dwarven face with dark, backswept beard and eyes that seemed to look right through him.

"I know you, Tulien Gart," the dwarf said, in the deep voice the man remembered. "I am Hammerhand."

"I carried your words to my prince, Lord Kane," Gart said. "He has sent me with his response. Lord Kane directs me to say that he does not recognize your claim to the lands bestowed upon him by His Imperial Majesty, but neither does he wish to expend his forces and his energies in needless combat. He therefore suggests a truce."

"A truce?" Hammerhand scowled, and Gart noticed that the Ten behind him raised their shields slightly, as though preparing to draw their weapons. But Hammerhand eased them with a gesture. "What sort of truce does Lord Kane suggest?"

"Lord Kane asks your word of honor that you and all your people will remain south of your . . . ah . . . border, and make no move against Klanath, until such time as Lord Kane and Hammerhand can negotiate their respective claims and possibly arrive at a peaceful solution."

"I will gladly speak with Lord Kane," Hammerhand said. "The ownership of Kal-Thax is not open to negotiation, but there may be agreements by which Lord Kane can be compensated—through trade, for instance, or an alliance."

"May I tell Lord Kane that he has your word of honor that you and your people will not come beyond your border, pending negotiations?"

"What does Lord Kane offer in return for such a pledge?"

"He makes the same promise," Gart said. "His Highness offers you his pledge, upon his honor, that no force will be brought against you, pending negotiations."

"And when will such negotiations take place?"

"Unfortunately," Gart replied with a shrug, "not until spring. Lord Kane has received orders from His Imperial Majesty that will keep him occupied through the winter."

"Orders to build a new fortress in Klanath?"

Gart blinked, then smiled slightly. "Ah, you know about that, do you? Yes, that is part of his task. I can tell you no more."

"It's none of our concern," Hammerhand noted.

"But for you to know of it, you must have spies watching the city. And to see the city, they must be north of here. Lord Kane's request is that your people no longer come north of the border . . . which you yourself have designated."

"I will stand by my pledge," Hammerhand said, "as long as he stands by his." Hammerhand waved the Ten back and strode toward the mounted man. When he was only a few feet from him, he looked up into his face, studying him carefully. "Can I trust your Lord Kane in this, Commander Gart? Do you trust him?"

Gart hesitated. He felt as though the dwarf were seeing right into his head. For an instant, he suspected magic. But he had never heard of a dwarf using magic.

"I'll ask my question another way, Commander," Hammerhand said. "Do you believe that Lord Kane means to stand by his pledge to me?"

"Yes," the man answered. "I believe he does. He said he would."

Hammerhand nodded. "Thank you," he said. "I think you do not truly trust the man you work for. But I believe that you expect him to keep his pledge, for whatever reason. It is enough. Tell Lord Kane that he has the pledge of Hammerhand, and that I have his. We will negotiate in the spring. Oh, and I will withdraw my observers from the peaks. It really is none of our concern what you people do over there, as long as you don't bother us."

The dwarf turned and walked away, not looking back. For a moment, Tulien Gart watched him, wondering what sort of mind could seem so perceptive, yet so readily trust one who hated him, as he must know Lord Kane did. Would Hammerhand really pull his spies back, away from Klanath? If I were him, Gart wondered, would I?

The commander sincerely hoped that Lord Kane would keep his promise. Yet the dwarf was right. Sakar Kane was not a man he himself would trust. As Hammerhand approached his waiting guards, Gart turned his mount and rode away, back to his escort. By the time the dwarves had disappeared behind their wall, the emissaries were filing northward, down the pass.

Calan Silvertoe was aghast when he heard of the pledge Derkin had given. "You aren't really going to call in the sentinels," he demanded. "You'll leave us blind."

"It was a fair request," Derkin said. "By our own declaration, our watchers are four miles beyond our boundary. They are trespassing." He turned to his nearest drummer. "Recall the sentinels," he ordered.

The drums began to speak, but still Calan ranted. "You're making a mistake!" he shouted, his nose inches from Derkin's. "You can't trust humans!"

"If I expect Lord Kane to keep his pledge, then I must keep mine," the Hylar said flatly. "Besides, there's no reason for him to betray us. Winter is coming. This pass would be of no use to him until spring, even if he held it."

With the old one-arm and the Ten trailing after him, the Master of Tharkas Pass strode through his encampment. Everywhere were sullen, irritable dwarves. Thousands of them, and everywhere Derkin looked he saw the signs of their discontent. There were broken noses, blackened eyes, bandaged knuckles, and various, assorted bruises. For a few weeks they had been idle, and they looked as though they had been in a pitched battle.

"Boredom," Derkin muttered. "Our worst enemy is simple boredom. It is our nature." Turning to his escorts, he ordered, "Get the Chosen Ones packed and ready to travel. I want this pass cleared as soon as all the sentinels are in."

"Where are we going?" Calan asked, bewildered.

"Home," Derkin rasped. "Home to Stoneforge, where there is work to do. If we remain here much longer, we'll be killing one another."

"And leave the pass unguarded?" Calan Silvertoe and Tap Tolec asked in unison.

"I'll remain here, with the Red-and-Grays," Derkin decided. "We'll stay until first snow. After that, the pass will guard itself until spring. Send for Vin the Shadow. He can take command for the trek to Stoneforge. I'll catch up along the way."

"You're being foolish, Derkin," Calan told him.

"I'm doing what I must," Derkin growled, gazing around at his people, with their accumulated boredom scars. "A few more days of doing nothing, and the Chosen Ones will be no better than those idiots in Thorbardin!"

* * * * *

Even before Tulien Gart had returned from Tharkas Pass, watchers on Lord Kane's battlements spotted movement high on the peaks above Klanath. With dwarven-crafted far-seeing tubes, they saw dwarves in the heights emerging from hiding, clambering away along impossible slopes.

"My message has done its work," Sakar Kane gloated when he heard the report. "The dwarves have had spies watching us, but now they are being pulled away." He strode across his great room and slammed the door open. "Captain of the guard!" he shouted.

When the captain of his household guard appeared, Kane said, "Ready the engines, Morden. We move on Tharkas Pass."

"It worked then?" Morden's scarred face split in a toothy grin. "The dwarves believed in the truce?"

"I knew they would," Kane said with a sneer. "I knew it when that fool Gart described their leader to me. A Hylar dwarf, he said. It is well known that many of the Hylar are inflicted with those idiotic principles of chivalry and honor that our own Orders of Knighthood hold so dear. That is why I chose Tulien Gart to carry my message. He himself is something of a fool where chivalry is concerned . . . and he truly believes that I mean to keep my pledge to those dinks."

"Commander Gart is going to have a fit when he sees our siege engines rolling into the pass." Morden grinned.

"I seem to recall that the scar on your cheek came from Gart's blade," Kane said. "Does it ever pain you?"

"Its memory does," Morden answered. "One day I may repay the favor."

"As you please," Kane said. "Tulien Gart is of no further use to me."

* * * * *

Only six hundred dwarves remained in Tharkas Pass when great, lashed-timber siege engines rolled out of morning mist and were hauled into line a hundred yards from Derkin's Wall. Hammerhand had sent the Chosen Ones southward, toward Stoneforge. All that remained were Derkin himself, the Ten, the Red and Gray Company, and roughly fifty others who had volunteered to stay.

Now three full battalions of human soldiers and a thousand footmen drafted from the streets of Klanath emerged from the mists, towing tall engines of death, and methodically arranged themselves in siege-and-attack formation as dwarves crowded onto the wall in fury and disbelief.

"I told you so!" Calan Silvertoe shouted at Derkin Hammerhand. "I told you not to trust the humans!"

"I believed that man spoke the truth," Derkin said bleakly.

"He may have, but his prince didn't," Tap Tolec observed.

The sound of sledges rang in the pass as a dozen tall catapults were anchored into the stone, while ox-drawn carts came carrying the stones to feed them. Atop the dwarven wall, slings began to hum, and crossbows thudded. Here and there among the humans, men fell, but only a few. The range was too great for either sling-balls or bolts.

Without preamble, the first catapult was loaded, aligned, and released. Two hundred pounds of stone whistled through the air and crashed into the wall's battlements. Where it hit, stone shards flew and a dozen dwarves fell.

"Clear the wall!" Derkin roared. "Everyone down! Use the wall for shelter!"

Dwarves scurried past Derkin and the Ten, streaming down the ramps as those in the pass behind closed in, massing themselves behind the wall. Another catapult stone smashed into the wall, just below the battlements, and broke into a dozen pieces. Where it had struck was only a shallow dent, and Derkin thanked the gods for his people's habit of building sturdy structures. The catapults could punish the reinforced wall, but they would not tear it down.

Archers had positioned themselves between the siege engines, and now arrows flew around the few dwarves remaining atop the wall. Most flew past harmlessly, and some shattered against the stone, but several had to be deflected with shields. "Get down!" Tap Tolec begged Derkin. "It's you they're aiming at!"

"To rust with them," Derkin snapped. "Look, there beyond that second engine. It's Lord Kane himself!" Grabbing a crossbow from one of the Ten, he drew it, fitted a metal bolt into its slot, aimed carefully, and fired. A horseman directly behind the Prince of Klanath fell, pierced through the throat.

"I missed," Derkin rasped. "Give me another . . ."

"Hammerhand!" Tap Tolec roared. "Look out!" But it was too late. A huge stone, propelled by a catapult, whined over the wall, directly into the little cluster of dwarves there. The last thing Derkin Hammerhand saw was a flash of hurtling stone, and then only darkness.

Among the attackers, Sakar Kane raised his fist. "There," he shouted. "Their leader is dead! Now kill the rest!"

Captain Morden squinted at the wall, then turned. "They are protected, Sire," he said. "Our stones bounce off that structure."

"Then raise your line of fire!" Kane snapped. "Aim for the sky, above the wall. Let the stones fly high and fall on those behind."

"Aye, Sire," Morden grinned. "That should do it."

"When we've dropped enough rocks on them," the Prince of Klanath added, "send footmen with grapples. I don't want a living dwarf left when we're finished here."

* * * * *

Cold winds sang through the valleys, low clouds hid the rising peaks, and spitting snow had begun to dust the marchers on the Stoneforge trail when those in the rear of the great caravan heard running hoofbeats overtaking them. A single rider came into sight around a precipitous bend, and those who had turned to look saw the colors of Hammerhand's personal guard, the Ten.

Within a moment Tap Tolec was among them, almost falling as he dropped from the saddle of an exhausted horse. A crude sling held his right arm close against his armored breast, and the right side of his face was crusted with dried blood.

"Where's Vin?" he demanded. "Send word ahead to Vin the Shadow!" As drums spoke and runners hurried forward, the First of the Ten staggered and sat down on the hard ground.

A few minutes later Vin was beside him, mask pushed up and large eyes bright with concern. "Tap," he said. "What is it? What's happened?"

"The truce was a trick," Tap told him, his voice thin with anger. "You hadn't been gone half a day when Lord Kane attacked with his entire garrison. They used siege engines . . . catapults. We didn't have a chance."

"And Derkin? Is Derkin . . . ?"

"Turn your column," Tap rasped. "We're going back."

18

A Time For Reprisal

In a snow-dusted mountain glade nine miles south of Tharkas, fourteen dwarves huddled around a little fire, sharing blankets from the day packs of three horses that stood head-low and exhausted a few yards away. Some of the dwarves had wounds, which others worked to bind the wounds with bits of torn fabric, snippets of leather, and tree bark.

Helta Graywood, her left cheek covered with a plaster of moss and mud, sat on a stone beside the fire, bathing Derkin Hammerhand's brow and right temple with a moist rag. His head rested on her lap. Nearby lay his polished helm, its right template scarred and dented. Grazed by a two-hundred-pound stone from a catapult, the old helmet—of long-ago Hylar craftsmanship—had saved his life, though he had only recently regained consciousness after several hours of nothingness. Now, as Helta bathed the crusted blood from his head, Talon Oakbeard—Third of the Ten—knelt beside him, talking in a low, tired voice.

"It was Helta who saved you," Talon said. "Most of us were knocked off the wall by that stone. We were all stunned, I guess. I think I was crawling around trying to see who else was alive and trying to remember what had happened. And there were people everywhere, all packed together, close behind the wall. Then I heard somebody say that you were dead, and all of a sudden Helta was there, with another woman. They were pushing people aside, and I saw your red cloak. Tap Tolec came and helped them. I started toward you, too, but just then a catapult stone fell from the sky. It brushed Tap, knocked him aside, and fell right on top of the woman with Helta."

Pain slitting his eyes, Derkin looked up at the girl's face. A huge tear welled from her eye, disappearing into the mud poultice on her cheek. "Nadeen," she said. "The stone fell and crushed her."

"Then more stones fell," Talon muttered. "The humans must have lofted their shots nearly straight up. Those stones began falling like rain, and there was no protection from them. I remember . . ." He sniffed, his voice breaking, then cleared his throat and went on. "Everybody was trying to hug the wall, climbing over one another. I was helping Tap get to his feet when I looked around, and there you were, fifty yards up the pass. Helta had you by one arm. She was dragging you, pulling you away from the raining stones. It was . . ." His voice broke again. "We went after you, Tap and I, and Brass Darkwood. Brass didn't make it. A few others followed, and some of us got saddles onto a few horses. We all climbed on . . . we could hear the stones still falling behind us. All those people . . . but there was nothing we could do. Nothing but try to get away."

"How many got away?" Derkin asked, his voice a harsh rasp.

"Those you see here," Talon said, stifling a sob of anger. "Just us, and Tap. We bound his arm, then he took one of the horses and went to catch up with Vin and the rest. He's probably found them by now."

"Just these?" Derkin whispered, looking around. "Only these escaped?"

"No one else." Talon shook his head miserably. "We were just beyond the cedars when I heard the stoning let up. I hung back for a minute to see. Those . . . those *men* came over that wall like a flood. Then they drew swords and began killing everyone who was still moving."

Derkin looked around the little camp again, his eyes stricken with grief. "Only these," he whispered. "All the Red-and-Grays . . . and Nadeen and . . . and Calan Silvertoe? What of Calan?"

"A stone," Helta said. "I saw it hit him."

"And you . . . ?" Derkin looked up at her, then reached up and eased back the mud poultice with gentle fingers. He winced and eased it back into place. Something, maybe a shard of stone—had left its mark on Helta Graywood. The prettiest girl Derkin had ever seen would never again be beautiful. The hideous, torn wound across her little cheek would leave an ugly scar for the rest of her life.

"Lord Kane," Derkin whispered. "Lord Kane betrayed his pledge."

Sounds came on the wind then—the sounds of thousands of marching dwarves. A few minutes later Vin the Shadow and Tap Tolec were kneeling beside Derkin, deep concern in their eyes.

"Hammerhand will be all right," Helta Graywood said. "His helmet saved him."

"His helmet and his woman," Talon Oakbeard murmured.

Wincing at the ache in his head, Derkin sat upright, then struggled to his feet. For a moment he staggered drunkenly. But then he steadied himself and planted his hands on his hips.

"Lord Kane pledged a truce," he rasped. "Lord Kane has broken his pledge." For long moments, Derkin stood, deep in thought, as more and more of his people gathered around him. Then he raised his head, and his voice. "Let there be these laws among the Chosen Ones," he said. "Three laws for ourselves, and one for our enemies. Let no dwarf of the Chosen speak falsely to any other of the Chosen. Let no dwarf of the Chosen act unjustly toward any other of the Chosen. Let no dwarf of the Chosen take from any other of the Chosen anything that is not willingly given."

"Let it be so," dozens of voices around him responded, while others farther away echoed them.

"Those are our three laws then," Tap Tolec asserted. "Good laws. Don't lie, don't cheat, don't steal. And the fourth law, Hammerhand? The one for our enemies?

"Let our enemies know, from this time forward," Derkin proclaimed, "that we will retaliate. For betrayal, for murder, for trespass . . . When the people of Kal-Thax are wronged, we shall *always* retaliate."

"And how are our enemies to know that?" someone asked.

"By example," Derkin said. "We will give them an example."

Hammerhand left two thousand people in the mountain glade—the injured, the frail and infirm, all of the women and children, and enough warriors to guard and care for them. With the rest of his army, he headed north under leaden skies that veiled the mountain terrain with winter's first flurries. Gone now were the brilliant colors of the regiments, the bright fabrics, the burnished armor. With resins and ash, with mineral spirits and crushed firestone, they had concocted dyes and paints. Now the entire army was garbed in blacks, browns, and grays—the colors of anger, of determination, and of mourning.

At Tharkas Pass they found no one living—only the mutilated, frozen bodies of the dwarves who had fallen there. Working in stone-faced silence, the dwarves buried their dead. Under a sheer stone cliff a short distance south of the still-standing wall, they laid the corpses out in dignified rows and ranks and removed their helms while Derkin called upon Reorx—and any other gods worthy of the name—to accept these honored dead with the respect they deserved.

When the brief ceremony was done, expert stonecutters and delvers clambered up the cliff's face. Fifty feet above the floor of the pass, they broke and shattered the stone so that it fell in a rain of rubble, covering and burying the bodies below.

Then Derkin replaced his helm, straightened his armor, and mounted his horse. It took three hours for the entire army to pass through the narrow gate in the wall. Daylight was beginning to fade, the clouds were dark and low, and each gust of wind whining in the pass carried fitful flurries of snow. When they were all through the gate, they closed it and headed north.

Derkin was not surprised that the humans had left the pass, and left the wall standing. Winter was coming on, and humans feared the mountain winters. Undoubtedly Lord Kane felt he had rid himself of dwarves and could wait for spring to open the pass.

All along the way, Derkin conferred with his unit leaders and with those who had served as sentinels above Klanath. Just at full dusk, they came out of the pass on a wide, sloping shelf overlooking the city directly ahead. Usually, this shelf below the pass was a busy place. Here stood Klanath's slaughtering pens, butcher stalls and tanneries, and the mills that ground the grain of those in the city. But now, as the dwarves had anticipated, the slope was deserted. It was nightfall, of a blustery winter day, and all who could would be behind closed doors, staying close to their hearths.

The usual perimeter guards would be in place, of course, and the strong guard forces of Lord Kane's compound. But out here on Slaughterhouse Shelf, there was nothing worth guarding on such a night.

Looking down on the snow-misted city, lying like a soiled crazy quilt beneath the low clouds and its own smoke, many of Derkin's army felt a twinge of doubt. Wedge Stonecut, a young dwarf who found himself now a member of the Ten, muttered, "It's so big . . . and all spread out. How does one attack a thing like that?"

"The way one attacks anything too big to wrestle," Talon Oakbeard said ironically. "Ignore its body and go straight for the head."

Hushed commands rippled through the massed units, and a company of nearly a thousand Daergar moved forward, led by Vin the Shadow. Most of these Daergar had been slaves in Klanath's mines years earlier, and none of them had forgotten the treatment given them by their human overlords. Now, grim and determined, they ranked themselves before Derkin Hammerhand and raised dark-steel blades in salute. All of them had their boots bound in fabric to still their footfalls, and all of them had removed their metal masks. Large, wide-set eyes glittered in shadowy, feral faces as they looked toward the waiting city.

Derkin returned their salute and nodded to his right, where several dwarves were pouring sand into a tin funnel set on a little platform of withes. "One hour's sand," he said to Vin the Shadow. "Then we will follow."

"An hour is enough," the Daergar said. "With Reorx's aid, or even without it, we can clear a fine passage in an hour."

"For Kal-Thax," Derkin said.

"For Kal-Thax."

Like silent shadows in the gloom, the Daergar slipped away toward the outskirts of Klanath.

"I wouldn't like to be a human guard in a dark place on this night," Wedge Stonecut breathed. "They say a Daergar can see when there is no light at all."

"Did you notice the blades they carried?" Talon asked. "Those curved, dark-steel swords . . . where did they get them?"

A few feet away, Derkin Hammerhand turned. "They've always had them, wrapped and hidden away. They've taken them out now, in honor of Lord Kane."

"They honor the human?" Talon asked, puzzled.

"In their way. It was the custom of Daergar long ago to carry such blades. They are as light as daggers, very swift and very sharp. And once drawn, they were never sheathed again until they had tasted blood."

"I wouldn't want to be a guard in that city tonight," Wedge Stonecut muttered, repeating himself.

As the sands flowed through the little funnel, Klanath dozed below Slaughterhouse Shelf. No outcries came from there, no trumpets or bells sounded, no slightest alarm. Except for having seen them go, the waiting army would have had no hint that a thousand dark-seeing Daergar now roamed those ways, doing their bloody work.

The funnel emptied itself, and Derkin climbed aboard his horse, looking around judiciously as other dark forms mounted behind him. Then he waved his footmen forward. No battle cries came from the thousands streaming down the slope now. Hammerhand had ordered silence, and the Chosen Ones complied.

Derkin waited until his foot legions were at the outskirts of the city, entering the dozen dingy streets that led toward Lord Kane's compound, then he and his horse companies moved out. For the first two hundred yards, they walked their mounts. Then at the bottom of the slope Derkin urged his horse to a trot, and all around him rose the muted thunder of hundreds of horses stepping up their pace. At the outskirts of the sprawling city, a few doors and shutters opened as the sound carried to them. Human faces peered out, then shutters were slammed and bolts were dropped into place. Most of the residents of Klanath probably had no idea what they had seen, but they wanted no part of it.

Along three narrow streets the mounted dwarves trotted, as long minutes passed. At a torchlit intersection Derkin saw a pair of Klanath guards lying in their own blood, and just beyond them at least a dozen more. No steam rose from the gaping, slitted throats of the men. The bodies were already beginning to cool. The Daergar had wasted no time opening a path for Hammerhand.

Sooty snow flurried and gusted along the streets, and the shacks and sheds became more densely clustered. Here they found more bodies—some in guard uniform and some not. And just ahead, there was the ring of steel on steel. The first footmen had reached the compound gates. But the sounds of combat were brief. A few clashes of steel, then a few more, and a series of muffled shrieks. Then the riders heard the distinct creaking sounds of great weighted gates being opened.

"At the gallop!" Hammerhand roared, and spurred his mount. The great horse, and all those behind it, bunched powerful haunches and leapt forward at a run. For a hundred feet, the three horse companies charged along parallel streets, then the streets converged, and the compound's wall lay just ahead. A pair of wide gates stood open, with thousands of armed dwarves pouring through. As the reunited horse battalion thundered toward them, the footmen spread to each side. Hundreds of charging horses thundered through, each rider shifting to one side of his saddle as a running footman swung aboard and clambered up the other side.

Within the compound, human soldiers were pouring from every barracks and redoubt, many of them only partially dressed, but all wielding shields and swords. But their resistance was puny against the overwhelming might of the dwarven forces. Faster than sleepy human companies could get themselves organized, solid ranks of dwarves swept through them, hacking and slicing. Somewhere a trumpet blared, then another and another, and torches came alive on the battlements of Lord Kane's palace fortress in the middle of the compound.

Leaving the panicked soldiers to the mercies of his footmen, Derkin led his horse company at full charge directly toward the open gateway of the main palace, where torches flared and chains began to rattle as surprised gatekeepers bent to their winches—far too late. The entire horse battalion thundered past the portcullis and into the inner courtyard, sending human guards and gate tenders flying in all directions.

The household guard, the most elite of all Lord Kane's forces, was just issuing from its halls when the courtyard abruptly filled with horses and dwarves. Better trained than the outside companies, these soldiers—led by a man with a scarred face—mounted a fierce defense. For long minutes, the battle swept this way and that through the courtyard, guards grouping and regrouping, fighting desperately while the dwarves thundered about, ranks and disciplined lines of hoofed fury, armored horses with death clinging to each side of their saddles.

Derkin had ridden halfway around the courtyard, shouting commands and wielding shield and hammer, when a human guard appeared from a niche, thrusting a deadly pike. Derkin heard the weapon strike the footman opposite him and felt the saddle shift as the dwarf fell away. With a kick, Derkin swung himself up into the saddle and struck downward. The pikeman didn't even have time to blink before a heavy hammer crushed his helmet and the skull beneath it.

Wheeling his horse, Derkin swung this way and that, searching. Then he saw what he was looking for. Below the tallest corner tower, a clot of humans was retreating slowly toward a stone gate, while dwarven riders hacked away at them. With a shout, Derkin reined toward that place, dropping from his saddle as he neared it. Behind him, the Ten did likewise, landing catlike on sturdy legs as their tall mounts clattered away. "The door!" Derkin shouted. "Secure that door!"

Afoot, Hammerhand and his newly reformed guard, the Ten, raced toward the archway. The soldiers there, concentrating on the pressing riders, weren't aware of the eleven afoot until they were among them, cutting a gory path through their formation. With shield and sword, hammer and axe, propelled by their own momentum, Hammerhand and the Ten plowed completely through the rank of defenders as the oaken door within the archway closed in their faces . . . but not quite. From somewhere just behind Derkin, a short, sturdy form hurtled forward, throwing itself into the narrowing gap. Stone and oak timbers closed on armor plate and stopped. Through the gap, Derkin saw a blade lash out and downward, and blood spurted.

He had no chance to see who had stopped the door. At full speed, he and the others with him hit the portal, massive shoulders flinging it back. The dwarves burst through into a large, brightly lit hall where men were scurrying about. Most of the men were unarmed, dressed as clerks or servants, and several of them shrieked and dived for cover as the door slammed open. Among them were soldiers, though, and these drew their weapons.

Derkin glanced from face to face, searching. He had seen Sakar Kane only a few times, and always from a distance, but he would know the face of the tyrant if he saw him. But all the faces he saw were strange to him. Backing away a step, Hammerhand knelt quickly at the doorway and looked down at the dead dwarf lying there, still in the portal. It was Wedge Stonecut, the young volunteer who had been so proud to become one of the Ten. Standing, Derkin pulled the body in through the doorway, then turned and closed the door. It muffled the clamor of battle in the courtyard beyond. Its heavy bar, as he dropped it into place, had a hollow, ominous sound.

Holding his shield and hammer, Derkin Hammerhand strode forward. Fourteen household guards, unnerved at his calm, grim appearance, hesitated and backed away a step. He took another long look around the Great Hall, then demanded, "Where is Sakar Kane?"

No one answered him. The guards were edging forward now, raising their weapons. "Which of you killed Wedge Stonecut?" Derkin demanded.

Again there was no answer, but he needed none. Among the guards was one whose blade still dripped with dwarven blood. For only an instant Derkin gazed at the man, then he spun full around, and his arm lashed out. The hammer flew from his hand, made one quick flip in the air, and smashed into the man's face. As the guard sprawled backward, dead, Derkin drew his sword. Flanked by the Nine, he charged the remaining guards.

19

The Smoke of Klanath

Sakar Kane was nowhere to be found.

By morning, the palace and its walled compound were
secure. The attack had been a complete surprise to the
humans of Klanath, catching the soldiers off guard,
unprepared, and without their leader to rally them. On
top of that, the prince's forces were outnumbered by
nearly ten to one. Within hours of the first sortie by night-
eyed Daergar, Derkin and his forces were all within the
fortress and had barred its gates. Many of the soldiers
were dead, many more disarmed and locked away in the
palace dungeons. The rest of Kane's household—forty or
fifty women, clerks, porters, cooks, and warders—were

locked into secure quarters high in one of the towers.

With the dawn, Derkin ordered a complete search of the facility. Hundreds of dwarves swarmed everywhere in the fortress, searching every room, every hall, and every stairwell. It was fruitless. The man Hammerhand had come to find was not in Klanath.

A quivering human clerk, brought before Derkin by blood-spattered dwarven warriors, told him that His Highness had returned from his expedition into Tharkas Pass to find a messenger awaiting him with a sealed scroll from the man called Dreyus. Kane had stayed only long enough to promote the captain of the home guards and put him in command of the Third Battalion. Then the prince rode out again, the clerk said.

Derkin perched in Kane's chair of state, his feet dangling six inches above the floor, his dark cloak and dark-painted armor encrusted with the blood of humans. He listened quietly to the clerk, then pierced the man with that cold-eyed gaze which people so often found disconcerting. "Where did he go?" he demanded.

"I don't know," the clerk said, his chin quivering. "As far as I know, he didn't tell any of the staff of his plans."

"He must have told someone!" Derkin snapped.

The clerk looked as though he might faint. "He . . . he might have told Captain . . . er, *Commander* Morden," he suggested. "His Highness left the commander in charge. I suppose he might have mentioned to him, ah . . . where he was going."

"Morden?" Derkin frowned. "Who is Morden?"

"He is the officer His Highness promoted just before he left," the clerk explained. "He was captain of the household guard and master of catapults. Now he is commander of internal forces and commander of the Third Battalion, as well."

"Why?"

"His Highness honored him." The clerk shrugged. "He

said Capt . . . er, *Commander* Morden did fine service in the . . . ah . . . campaign in Tharkas . . . against the . . . the dwarves." When Derkin made no response, the man added, lamely, "Besides, the Third Battalion was leaderless since Commander Gart's disappearance."

"Gart?" Derkin prodded. "Commander Tulien Gart?"

"Yes," the clerk said. "He just . . . disappeared. He never returned from Tharkas."

"Describe Commander Morden," Derkin said.

"The . . . the commander is a slim man," the clerk said. "Not as tall as some, but very strong. And he has a stitched scar across his face"—with a trembling finger, he traced a line from his own left cheekbone downward, across his mouth to the right side of his chin—"like that."

"The man who directed the catapults," Derkin muttered. "The one who lofted the stones."

"I saw a man like that," Talon Oakbeard said. "An officer. He was in the compound when we attacked."

"Is he dead?"

"Either dead or in the dungeons."

With a wave of his hand, Derkin said, "Take the clerk away, then find this Morden. If he isn't dead, bring him to me." He got down from Sakar Kane's throne and strode to a barred window at one side of the Great Hall. Beyond, little flurries of snow still fell, carried on gusting winds below a gloomy sky. Outside in the compound, companies and platoons of dark-garbed dwarves were everywhere.

"I want Sakar Kane," Derkin Hammerhand muttered to no one in particular. "I want to teach him the law of Kal-Thax."

After a time, a company of dwarves filed into the hall and saluted. "Sire, there is no Morden here," their leader said. "Some of us who saw him have searched. He isn't among the dead, and he isn't in the dungeons."

"And all of the living fighters are in the dungeons?"

"All of them," the searcher said. "We went to each of our units who were assigned to the perimeters last night, and to Vin's Daergar, who were stationed outside. From the moment we attacked this place last night, no one left."

Beyond the compound portal, voices were raised, and a young dwarven soldier poked his head in. "There's a man at the compound gate, Hammerhand," he announced. "He's been wounded, but he approached on his own two feet. He demands to see you."

"What man?" Derkin growled.

"A soldier, Sire. Calls himself Gart."

"Bring him in," Derkin ordered.

The man who came into the room, surrounded by surly dwarves, wore only partial armor and had no weapons. Linen bandages and plasters covered his upper torso. He was pale, and looked severely weakened, but Derkin knew him. He was Tulien Gart.

Without preamble, Gart saluted the dwarven leader and said, "I surrender myself to you, Hammerhand. Do with me as you will, but I ask a boon of you."

"First things first," Derkin said. "Do you know where Sakar Kane has gone?"

"Isn't he here?"

"His clerk says he left right after his return from the betrayal of his pledge . . . the pledge you brought to me."

"Betrayal," Gart murmured then strengthened his voice. "Yes, it was a betrayal. A thing without honor. Had I known what he intended, I would have resigned my commission rather than be party to it."

"So when you found out, you just disappeared?"

"It might have seemed so. I have been in a house in the town, a place where they dressed the knife wounds in my back . . . for a price. Wounds delivered by an assassin just this side of Tharkas Pass. The man thought me dead and left me. Then I crawled to where I could find help."

"And who was it who tried to murder you?"

"Another officer," Gart said. "The captain of His Highness's household guard."

"Morden?" Derkin asked.

"You know him, then? Is he still alive?"

"We haven't found him yet."

"The boon I ask is the opportunity to settle my score with Morden."

"You don't look like you could settle with anyone right now," Derkin pointed out. "You can hardly stand on your feet."

"I can deal with Morden," Gart assured him. "The man is a coward. It would take a weakness greater than my loss of blood from dagger cuts for him to defeat me."

Derkin turned again to the dwarven search party. "You've looked everywhere?"

"Everywhere a soldier might be."

"But not everywhere a coward might be," Derkin muttered. He turned to Talon Oakbeard and walked across the hall with him while he gave orders in a low voice. While Talon relayed the orders to several others, Derkin returned to the throne and parted its drapings. From beneath the throne he pulled a large stone and dragged it around behind. The wide wings of Sakar Kane's ostentatious chair of state hid the stone from view.

"You can rest here in safety," he told Tulien Gart. "Just stay out of sight."

A half-hour passed before one of the tower doors opened and armed dwarves entered the hall escorting several dozen humans—women, clerks, porters, and servants. At sight of them, Derkin Hammerhand climbed onto Lord Kane's throne and called, "Bring the civilians to me."

The dwarves herded their human charges forward, and Hammerhand's eyes scanned them, then fixed on the clerk he had questioned before. "You people are of no use to me," he said. "You are civilians, and noncombatants.

Therefore, you are free to leave this place. You will be escorted to the outer gate and set free. All I ask of each of you is your pledge that you will leave Klanath and never return, and that you will never take up arms against any dwarf. Do you so pledge?"

The clerk nodded ecstatically. "I most certainly do," he assured the dwarf. "On my father's name. Can I go now?"

"I want the same pledge from each of you," Hammerhand said to all of them. "Line up and address me, one by one."

Reluctantly, the humans formed a line and stepped toward the throne. A porter at the head of the line knelt when he was near and bowed his head. "I give my pledge," he said.

"Stand up," Hammerhand growled. "I'm no gut-bound human prince."

The porter stood and repeated the pledge. Derkin waved him aside. The next human was a woman, veiled as all the women were. "I so—" she started.

"Remove your veil," Hammerhand interrupted.

"Y–Yes, your . . . ah . . . your . . ." She released her veil and let it fall from her face.

"Don't worry about titles," Derkin said. "Just speak your pledge."

"I so pledge," she said.

Derkin waved her away and raised his voice. "No veils," he said, so all could hear. "I want to see your faces when I hear your promises."

The next human, a male in hostler's livery, was just stepping forward when there was a commotion in the line. A veiled woman near the middle suddenly caught up her skirts and sprinted for the open door to the compound. But Talon Oakbeard had been waiting. With a rush, he caught her around the knees and tackled her neatly, throwing her facedown on the stone floor. Then, with efficient unconcern, he twisted her arms behind her and sat on her.

"Next," Hammerhand said, as though nothing had happened.

One by one, the remaining humans made their vows and were waved aside. When the last one was done, Hammerhand stood upright on the resplendent throne and planted his fists on his hips.

"You have each given your word to Hammerhand," he announced. "I suggest that all of you be more honorable in such matters than Lord Sakar Kane. Also, as you go through that town out there, tell the people to pack what they can carry and leave. Now, get out."

Escorted by armed dwarves, the humans filed out of the hall toward the outer gate. Only when they were gone, and the door closed, did Hammerhand signal to Talon Oakbeard, who got off the back of the sprawled, kicking woman and backed away. "Stand up," he said. "And quit grumbling. You aren't hurt."

When the human was upright, several dwarves led her to the foot of the dais and pulled away her veil. "Well, well," Hammerhand said quietly. "Not a woman at all. I understand your name is Morden."

The dark, stitched scar across the man's face seemed even darker as the color blanched from his cheeks. "Let me leave," he gasped. "Let me just . . . go with those other people. I won't bother you, I promise. You'll never see me again."

Hammerhand ignored the plea. "You commanded the catapults in Tharkas Pass," he said. "You sent the stones that killed my people."

"Please!" Morden dropped to his knees. "Please, I was only following my prince's orders. He told me to loft the stones. He told me to!"

"I brought one of your stones back to Klanath," Hammerhand said. "I brought it for you, to drop on you from a high place."

"Please!" Morden sobbed. "Please, I . . ."

"But before I do that, I want an answer from you. Where is Sakar Kane? Where did he go?"

"H–His Highness only told me that he was summoned by Dreyus. He was to . . ." Morden's voice trailed away, his mouth hanging open, his eyes bulging as he stared past the dwarf.

"I told you he was a coward," Tulien Gart said, standing beside the throne.

"You're dead!" Morden shrieked. Abruptly he rose to his feet, whirled, and grabbed a javelin from the hand of a nearby dwarf. With a shrill cry, he raised the weapon, aiming it toward the dais . . . then faltered and seemed to dance as a dozen dwarven blades slashed into him from every side. More blades hit him as he fell to the floor.

Gazing at the butchered assassin, Tulien Gart said, "I wonder whether he meant that for you or for me."

"It doesn't matter now," Hammerhand growled. "I just wish you'd stayed out of sight until he answered my question."

"I'm sorry," the soldier said. "As to Lord Kane, though, if he was summoned by Dreyus, then he probably has gone to Daltigoth. Dreyus speaks for the emperor." With curious eyes, he studied the fierce dwarf still standing on the throne. "Did you really bring back a catapult stone to drop on him?"

"You've been sitting on it," Hammerhand said.

* * * * *

In the days following the taking of Klanath, squadrons of dwarves fanned out from the compound. Street by street and house by house, they went through the surrounding town. Most of the people had already fled, but wherever the dwarves found humans they cleared them out—sometimes courteously, sometimes not, but always firmly. And behind the evictors came teams of incendiaries with lamp oil and torches. Every structure built of stone, they tore down. And everything that would burn, they burned. For long days, thick smoke rose above Klanath to darken the threatening clouds overhead. Through long nights, the flames spread, outward and outward, until there was nothing more to burn.

As the fires died, Derkin had the human prisoners led up from the dungeons and herded out of the compound. Disarmed and cowed, without shelter, without employment, and without a cause, the men would wander away, most of them never to return. Some of them, perhaps many, might even join the emperor's enemies in the war on the central plains—a war that should have ended with the defeat of the emperor's general, Giarna, but which seemed destined just to go on and on.

When the sloping plain around Lord Kane's fortress was nothing but a wasteland of ash and rubble, Hammerhand gathered his lieutenants and issued new orders. "Bury that mess out there," he said. "I want it all plowed under, all the rubble and all the ash, before the ground freezes. Then, when that's done, we'll go to work on the Klanath mines."

"You want us to work those mines?" Vin the Shadow protested. "I still remember too clearly being a slave there."

"We won't mine them," Hammerhand said. "We are going to close them off, fill them in, and bury them. This place is too close to Kal-Thax for humans to have mines here."

"That will take all winter," Talon Oakbeard mused. "It might be fun, though." He turned, gazing around at the sumptuous, ornate fortress that Sakar Kane had built for himself. "What about this place?" he asked. "And those new fortifications the humans were building? Are we going to leave them standing?"

"We will leave nothing standing," Derkin decided. "When we leave, there will be no Klanath. It will be as though Sakar Kane had never come here at all . . . as though no human ever had."

"This *will* be fun!" Talon Oakbeard exclaimed.

"And keep us all busy for a while," Vin the Shadow muttered. Then the large eyes behind his iron mask crinkled in a hidden smile. Hammerhand was right, he decided. We're at our best when we have work to do . . . and choose to do it."

"I'd like to see Sakar Kane's face if ever the Prince of Klanath comes back here and finds he has nothing to be prince of," Talon chuckled. Then, more seriously, he asked Derkin, "Do you think Lord Kane will come back here?"

"I don't know." Derkin shrugged. "If not, maybe one day I'll go and find him, wherever he is." He strode across the compound, the others following him. From the wall, he looked across scorched ruins to the rising slope where Tharkas Pass began. "We will leave one thing standing here," he said. "A single stone . . . a monument, right out there where the city ended. Four miles from that point, Kal-Thax begins. We will inscribe that stone with the fourth law of Kal-Thax: 'If we are wronged, we will retaliate. We will *always* retaliate.' "

"I have a new name for our Derkin," Vin the Shadow told Talon Oakbeard. "He gives the law—*our* law—to our enemies, in ways they will understand. I have followed Derkin Winterseed, and I have followed Derkin Hammerhand. Now I follow Derkin Lawgiver, and proudly."

20

The Winter of Demolition

By the time the heavy snows began on the slopes north of Tharkas, there was almost no trace of the sprawling city that once had stood there. Every useable stone and timber had been carried away, and the remaining ashes and rubble were plowed into the ground. In the spring, new grass and seedlings would sprout there. Within a few seasons, no trace would be left of the human settlement that had dominated the northern Kharolis Mountains.

Among the thousands of dwarves involved in the project, the work became known simply as "The Tidying," because Derkin the Lawgiver had referred to it so.

The task of burying the Klanath mines was a larger

project, but the dwarves tackled it with enthusiasm. Many of them, like their leader, had once been slaves in these mines, and found great satisfaction in obliterating them. The shaft mines, high on the slopes, were caved in and sealed with stone. Then hundreds of delvers with climbing-slings and stone-drills went aloft above the pits. Working in conditions that would have been unthinkable for humans, the hardy mountain people began a series of "punches" in the stone face of the great peak. Master delvers went first, to "reckon" the stone—testing it, tasting it, marking its contours and slants, its seams and cracks, and noting the natural flaws in the granite. They patterned a half-mile's length of mountain with their scratches and marks, their chips and gouges, all the directional runes of delving.

Drillers followed, in teams of two, working on precarious platforms all along the length of the reckoning. From below, the platforms with their two dwarves each looked like a hundred tiny dots, high on the sheer stone. But when they began to punch—heavy sledges ringing on steel drills—the echoes of their efforts were a chorus that could be heard for miles around.

And joining the chorus was the ring of axes, as Neidar foresters worked in the nearby forests to the north. Day after day, they selected, cut, and hauled the timbers from which dwarven woodsmiths and binders were fashioning a fleet of sturdy sleds to be used as stone-boats. The dismantling of the palace compound, and of the partially constructed new fortress which Lord Kane's slaves had been building when the dwarves attacked, had taken only three weeks. Now, with several inches of good snow on the ground, the building stones were being hauled away into Tharkas Pass. As full winter closed on the lands north of Tharkas, the only structure still erect there was Lord Kane's palace. The tall structure served now as headquarters for Derkin's army and for the dismantling of Klanath.

With hundreds of horses, oxen, bison, and elk harnessed to the new sleds, dwarven teamsters were now busily transferring everything except the palace itself to the border of Kal-Thax, four miles away.

The work of hauling the stone was enhanced, the teamsters were forced to admit, by a bargain that Derkin had made—a bargain that most of the dwarves still could hardly believe. Among the countless hundreds of slaves they had found in Klanath there were no dwarves, but there were some of just about every other race the dwarves had ever heard of. Most of the slaves were humans, some were goblins, a few were elves, and two were ogres. On Derkin's orders, all of the slaves—even the goblins and ogres—had been freed and told to go away. But at the last moment, Derkin had called the ogres back. Then, while the Ten hovered near with drawn weapons and hundreds of other dwarves looked on with awe and disbelief, the Lawgiver had calmly invited the hulking pair into his chambers in the palace for a talk.

Their names were Goath and Ganat. Now they worked happily alongside the dwarven teamsters, hauling building stones into Tharkas Pass.

Only Derkin, the ogres, and the Ten knew exactly what had been discussed in that private meeting of the Master of Kal-Thax and two of his people's oldest ancestral enemies. But it was widely rumored among the Chosen that Derkin had made them a deal—fifty milk cows and a good bull from Lord Kane's herds in return for a winter's work.

It was known that the Lawgiver had given the ogres one law by which to govern themselves during their service. Derkin had told Goath and Ganat that if they so much as laid hands on any dwarf, other than to assist him, Derkin would personally tear their hearts out.

The ogres themselves verified that last condition of their employment, and there was no doubt that they truly believed that Derkin would do exactly what he said. The fact that each of them was more than twice as tall as Derkin seemed to matter not at all to them. From the time they came out of Derkin's chambers, it was clear that Goath and Ganat respected—and were somewhat afraid of—their employer.

At first, many of the dwarves were horrified at the idea of working alongside ogres. Dwarves and ogres had always been enemies. Ogres were dangerous, and never to be trusted. But as the weeks passed, the Chosen Ones realized that Derkin had made a good bargain. Each of the huge creatures could move as much stone in a day as two or three of the sled teams driven by dwarves.

The Lawgiver's only comment about the matter—a comment repeated throughout the encampment—was, "Ogres aren't necessarily bad. Dull, of course, but not bad. And they don't stink like goblins."

Goath and Ganat were still shunned by most of the dwarves. At night, the ogres made their own little fire at some distance from the dwarven shelters and ate and slept in isolation. Only Derkin approached them freely, though two or three times, when the ovens had been fired, Helta Graywood had led a party of women out to the ogres' fire, delivering fresh bread to go with their meat.

Now as midwinter approached, Derkin Lawgiver—he had accepted the name, since everyone suddenly seemed determined to call him that—climbed to the top of the highest tower of the palace and took a long look around at the work that had been done here and the work that remained. His gaze lingered on a distant group of dwarves working with picks and levers on the wide, stone slope just below the entrance to Tharkas Pass. The monument stone was complete—a ten-foot-high, rectangular obelisk of black quartz with the "fourth law of Kal-Thax" etched deeply into each of its faces. The workers out there had dug a hole in the stone of the slope, a socket into which the base of the law stone would be set.

"We will finish here in the spring," Derkin said. "Then we return to Kal-Thax."

"Back to Stoneforge?" Tap Tolec asked. With his broken arm healed, the broad-shouldered warrior had returned to his position as First of the Ten.

Derkin shook his head. "Some of us, but not to stay. Not for a while. We still have work to do at the border."

Tap glanced at the Hylar, wondering what Derkin Lawgiver had in mind now. But he didn't ask. Instead, he listened to the distant chorus of stone-drills high on the peak, to the sounds of axes in the nearby forest, the sounds of hooves and sled runners on the hard-packed snow below, and to the constant, never-ending chorus of voices—the voices of thousands of dwarves—boisterous, cheerful, and thoroughly at work. "You're right about our people," he said. "We don't idle well."

"It's our nature." Derkin nodded.

"I remember how Thorbardin sounded when we went there to try to get their help," Tap said, frowning. "The voices there—most of them, anyway—sounded sullen. The whole place reeked of anger and suspicion. It was an unhappy place. I didn't like it much, though I've thought that I might like to live there someday."

Derkin turned, gazing at his friend with unreadable, curious eyes. "Why?" he asked.

"I don't know," Tap confessed. "I've never lived beneath stone. I know some of my ancestors were Theiwar, but my people have always been Neidar, never Holgar. We have lived under the sun, not the stone. And yet, sometimes I feel a need to be . . . enclosed. As though maybe I really am Holgar at heart."

"I often have the same feeling," Derkin confided. "Some of my ancestors have been Neidar, but most were Holgar. I was born in Thorbardin. I left because I didn't like what Thorbardin had become, but there are times when I feel I would go back . . . if I could change things there."

"Change things?" Tap growled. "Those people are so set in their ways, you couldn't budge them with a prybar. How many angry fights did we see, just in the time we were there?"

"Dozens." Derkin shrugged. "They have nothing better to do. They have made it that way. But our people were contentious, too, when there was nothing to do except watch that wall in Tharkas. That's why I tried to send most of them home."

"They're not contentious now." Tap gestured, indicating the thousands of busy dwarves, everywhere one might look. "They're happy. I'm happy, too, except that sometimes I dream of having good stone over my head. Maybe I *am* Holgar, at heart . . . like you, Derkin."

Derkin dismissed the conversation with a shrug and headed down the spiral stairs of the tower. He had his own work to do—a thousand details of command, a thousand things to think about, to decide. Ever since his days of slavery in the Klanath pits, people had thrust leadership at him, forced it upon him, conspired to make him be their leader. At first, the idea had been repugnant. But now, he found that he enjoyed the challenges of leadership: to command an army, to plan a settlement like Stoneforge, to negotiate a treaty, to orchestrate the building of a wall—or the demolition of a human city—to think a thing through, to decide a course of action and then lead his people in doing what he had decided. In many ways, it was the hardest work imaginable, to lead. The responsibility he carried was heavier than any stone his workers were wrestling onto sleds. But somehow it had become a comfortable weight.

He recalled a thing he had found in some old scroll, a bit of advice from some forgotten Hylar scribe of long ago: "To live is to find the thing that one does best, and then to do it thoroughly, and always. To do less than this is to never live at all."

Tap's comments about Thorbardin had brought back old memories and old feelings. For a moment, it had seemed as though the Theiwar-Neidar was speaking his own thoughts. He didn't like Thorbardin. He was disgusted with the ways of Thorbardin life. He had left Thorbardin, never to return. And yet, in his heart, Derkin Winterseed . . . Derkin Hammerhand . . . Derkin Lawgiver was as much a part of Thorbardin as the undermountain fortress was of him.

More often than he would admit, Derkin knew the feelings Tap had described. Tap Tolec had always been Neidar, but at heart he was Holgar. Derkin had tried to be Neidar, but at heart he remained Holgar. Sometimes he longed to return to Thorbardin, to live again within the living stone.

If only the people there would live as dwarves should live. If only they would live!

At the foot of the tower stairs Helta Graywood waited for him, bringing his midday meal. She fell into step beside him as he walked toward the Great Hall. On impulse, Derkin said, "You've been inside Thorbardin, Helta. Could you live there?"

"I can live anywhere you live," she said matter-of-factly. "When are you going to marry me?"

"But Thorbardin is a sullen, idle place," he pointed out, ignoring her question.

"It wouldn't be," she said, "if you were in command there."

With a snort, Derkin crossed to Lord Kane's throne and sat down. The chair of state was the only item of human furniture that remained in the palace now, and even it was changed. Derkin had taken a saw to the thing, cutting its base down to a height more comfortable for a dwarf. Helta handed him his platter of meat and bread, then perched on a bench beside him with her own.

Derkin ate some of his food, then looked at her. The bandage was gone from her cheek now, and the scar there was as evident as he had known it would be. But, oddly, it did not make her ugly. If anything, it distinguished her. She was still the prettiest girl he had ever seen. Tearing his eyes from her, he went back to his dinner. "That's enough talk about Thorbardin," he said gruffly. "Thorbardin doesn't have a single commander. It never has had a single leader."

"Maybe that's what's wrong with it," the girl said. "Maybe it needs a king."

"Well, I'm not a king," Derkin snapped. "And I don't want to talk about Thorbardin anymore."

"You brought it up, not me," she reminded him. She said no more about Thorbardin, but a sly smile played at her lips when he looked away, a smile that seemed to say, "You aren't my husband, Derkin Whatever, but one day you will be. And who's to say what else you might one day be?"

When all of the stone from the two compounds had been removed to the border of Kal-Thax—huge, neat stacks of cut stone now stood in Tharkas Pass, completely hiding Derkin's Wall—the Lawgiver set his demolishers to work on the palace itself. Through the final weeks of winter, the towers came down. The entire palace seemed to shrink day by day. As sleeping quarters disappeared, temporary shelters were erected outside. And through all the activity, the distant ring of stone-drilling continued to echo from the peak above.

Then, abruptly and oddly, the weather changed. On a day that had begun clear and sunny, with a northerly breeze carrying promise of spring, it changed. Dark, heavy-looking clouds appeared in the west, and the wind changed to the same direction. By midday, the dark clouds were overhead, blocking the sunlight, turning the day to twilight. Then the wind died to stillness. The dense cover of clouds seemed to settle atop the high peaks, creeping lower and lower as the hours passed. After a time, the ring of stone-drills was stilled, and the delvers came down from above.

"The fog is dense up there," the chief of delvers told Derkin. "We can't see to work."

By the last murky light of evening, the dark clouds floated just overhead, low enough that a sling-stone, flung by a curious dwarf, could reach them. The stone disappeared into murk, then reappeared as it fell. The air was still, and heavy with chill vapors.

Hour by hour, the strange clouds lowered. Beyond the flickering illumination of the dwarves' fires, the night was as dark as any night anyone could remember.

By midnight, the cloud cover had settled to the ground, and dense mist was all around. Even the Daergar were blind in such conditions.

Derkin was awakened from brief sleep by Tap Tolec and the rest of the Ten. They carried hooded candles, but the mists outside had crept inside, and the candlelight was muted and eerie.

"We don't like this weather," Tap said when Derkin was awake. "There's something wrong about it."

Rubbing sleep from his eyes, Derkin glared at his friend. "You woke me up to talk about the weather? I can't do anything about the weather. What do you want?"

"It isn't right," Tap insisted. "We've all seen spring storms in these climes, but this isn't one of them."

"Then maybe it's a late winter storm."

"It isn't that, either," Tap insisted. "Put your boots on and come outside. Something's wrong."

"You and your Theiwar intuition," Derkin growled. But he pulled on his boots, wrapped his cloak around him, picked up his hammer, and followed Tap along one of the last hallways in the shrinking palace. Like his sleeping cubicle, the hall was murky with chill vapors. Tap pushed a door open and stepped outside, Derkin and the others following. It was very dark, and very still. The fitful light of the hooded candles carried no more than a few feet.

"It's dark and foggy." Derkin shrugged. "So what?"

"Just wait a minute," Tap said. "Wait and watch."

A minute passed, and then another, and suddenly there was flickering light around them. It was gone in an instant. Tap said, "There. That's what's worrying us."

"Lightning?" Derkin puzzled. "Since when are you afraid of—"

"Sh!" Tap hushed him. "Listen."

Patiently, Derkin stood and listened. The others did likewise.

After a full minute, Tap Tolec said, "That's what I mean."

"What?" Derkin demanded. "I didn't hear anything."

"Neither did we," the First explained. "It's been like this for an hour now. Lightning, but no thunder."

Again there was brief, flaring light in the fog, and again it was followed by only silence. Derkin had a sudden intuition of his own and shuddered. "Magic," he muttered. "It's some kind of magic."

"That's what we think, too," Talon Oakbeard said. "But who's doing it? And what's it for?"

"Find a drummer," Derkin ordered. "Alert everyone. It will be morning soon. Maybe this fog will lift then. When it does, I want everyone ready . . . for whatever is going on out there. Armor, gear, and weapons. And perimeter defense positions, as soon as we can see well enough to move around. If magic is being worked, there's usually a reason." Taking one of the candles, he strode back to his quarters and got dressed.

The candle's muted glow gleamed on the polished breastplate he strapped on, and glistened on his mirror-like horned helm. The kilt he wore was of studded leather, and his cloak was once again bright scarlet. For the taking of Klanath, dark tones had seemed appropriate to the Chosen Ones. But after the city had been taken, they soon reverted to their bright colors. The somber shades then had become depressing.

"It's our nature," Derkin mused to himself, slinging his shield and hammer at his shoulders. "Dwarven nature. We express ourselves with color, the way elves do with their songs."

The fog did not lift with the coming of morning. It simply rolled back as though it had never been there. One moment, the world was a gray, closed-in place. The next moment there was a final, flickering flash of that strange lightning, and the mist began to recede, rolling away on all sides, opening an ever-wider field of vision. Under cold, high clouds in a leaden sky, dwarves scurried everywhere, hurrying from their sleeping shelters and night posts to their assigned places on the perimeters of what had been Klanath.

And as the fogs rolled into the distance all around, Derkin Lawgiver and everyone else could see what the mist had been sent to cover. All around the dwarven encampment were ranks and legions of human soldiers. There were thousands of them, horse battalions and footmen, pikemen and lancers, companies of archers and boltmen—a full, mighty army in position to attack from all sides. And above each unit were the banners of Daltigoth, of the Empire of Ergoth, of the troops of the Emperor Quivalin Soth V.

Derkin turned full around, trying to count an enemy beyond counting, looking for escape routes that were not there. "Rust!" he muttered. "We're outnumbered. And we're surrounded!"

Part V:

Master of the Mountains

21

The Emperor's Road

For long moments the two forces—the Chosen Ones and the emperor's army—simply stared at one another. Then trumpets sounded, and a small group of human horsemen separated from the massed line below the peak. Carrying a banner on a tall staff, they rode forward at a walk until they were halfway across the space between their regiment and the nearest company of dwarves. There they stopped and sat waiting.

Derkin Lawgiver studied them for a moment, then turned to Tap Tolec. "My horse," he said.

Mounted, and flanked by the Ten on their own mounts, Derkin pranced his horse through his line, and rode out to where the humans waited. When he came near, the man in the lead raised his visor and held up one hand. "Are you the leader of these dwarves?" he demanded.

"So they tell me," Derkin responded. "Who are you, and what do you want?"

"My name is Coffell," the man intoned. "Sergeant-Major in the service of His Imperial Majesty's mounted lancers. On behalf of His Imperial Majesty, I offer you the clemency of the empire, provided all your people lay down their arms and surrender immediately."

"What does this clemency amount to?" Derkin asked.

The man raised his head slightly, sneering. "If you surrender without a fight, you will not be killed," he said. "Instead, it shall be your privilege to serve His Imperial Majesty in appropriate labors."

"You mean as slaves." Derkin returned the sneer. "Most of us have already tried that. We didn't like it. Did Sakar Kane send you people? Is he with you?"

For a moment the man hesitated, then he leaned aside to whisper to the man beside him. This second rider wheeled his horse and trotted back to his own line. Watching carefully, Derkin saw him approach a large, dark-cloaked man on a powerful-looking black horse. A moment later, the messenger raced back, to whisper something to Coffell.

The sergeant-major turned to Derkin again. "I am empowered to tell you that the man called Sakar Kane is no longer in either the service or the good graces of His Imperial Majesty," he said. "He has disappeared."

"Then who is in charge here?" Derkin demanded.

"You may deliver your decision to me," Coffell said. "Will you lay down your arms?"

"I don't want to talk to you." The dwarf glared at him. Then he pointed. "I want to talk to him."

Coffell turned, saw where Derkin was pointing, and frowned. "You are in no position to be arrogant," he chided.

Derkin signaled casually, and the Ten pulled crossbows from their saddle hooks. Efficiently and in unison, they drew the bows, set bolts in them, and raised them. "And you, human, are in no position to return alive to your friends," Derkin rumbled. "Now quit arguing. I want to talk to the man in charge."

Pale and angry, the sergeant-major whispered again, and again the messenger headed back to his own lines, this time at a gallop. After a moment, the dark-cloaked man stepped his horse forward and followed the messenger out to the conference. Ignoring the drawn crossbows, the newcomer gazed at Derkin with eyes that held a palpable force—eyes that resembled small, dark mirrors in a strong, brutal face. "I am Dreyus," he said. "And you must be the dwarf they call Derkin. All through the winter, wanderers have arrived in Daltigoth to tell of your attack on Klanath. They said you burned the city. Now I see that you've done much more than that. You've been busy little people, haven't you?"

"What do you want here?" Derkin asked.

"I am on the emperor's business, and this is the emperor's road," Dreyus purred. "What I want is for everything to be put in order, as I will direct. You can begin as soon as you have surrendered. You may do that now."

"I'll see you roast on coals first," Derkin explained.

"Ah," Dreyus hissed. "You are as they have said. Very well, you won't see me at all. Or anything else." He pointed a finger at the dwarf and muttered something in a language that was no language.

Remembering something he had found in an old Hylar scroll, Damon ducked his head and closed his eyes. The blinding light that leapt from the man's finger was like silent lightning. But instead of striking Derkin's eyes, it struck his mirror-bright helmet and rebounded. Coffell screeched and clapped his hands to his eyes, then fell over backward as his horse reared, neighing wildly. In an instant, blinded men and blinded horses were bouncing, pitching, falling, and staggering off in various directions. Of all the humans in the little group, only Dreyus still sat his saddle, ignoring the pandemonium.

"Don't do that again," Derkin suggested. "Next time, these people with me will make a porcupine of you."

"I assume you do not surrender?" Dreyus growled.

"Of course not," Derkin said. "We are free dwarves, and we will remain free or die. Furthermore, Klanath will not be put back, as you put it. It is too near Kal-Thax. We don't want human settlements this close. Also, this is not the 'emperor's road,' because there is no road here. If you and your emperor want to keep pestering those people east of here, you'll have to find another path. This one is closed."

"Closed?" Dreyus sneered. "You dwarves can't keep us from using Redrock Cleft."

"We don't have to." Derkin grinned. "There is no Redrock Cleft. My delvers caved it in a month ago. You might climb through it afoot, but you'll never get a horse across it."

The big man's eyes seemed to blaze, and his face went dark with fury. "You've lost your chance to live," he hissed.

"By the way," Derkin asked casually, "can you tell me where Sakar Kane is? I still have business with him. If there is one thing we won't stand for, it's a liar."

Dreyus glared at the dwarf. "You're insane," he said. Without a further word, he reined the black horse around and trotted away.

"Why don't we put a few bolts in him?" Tap asked. "He's still in range."

Derkin shook his head. "He hasn't attacked us, yet," the Lawgiver said. Unmoving, he watched as the big man returned to his troops. A moment later, a pair of riders withdrew from the line there and headed eastward at a gallop. "He doesn't believe me about Redrock Cleft," Derkin said. He turned his horse and headed back to his own lines. "Maybe when he finds out that it really is closed, he'll just turn around and go away."

"If he doesn't, we're likely all going to die here," Talon Oakbeard pointed out. "Those soldiers are all around us. We have no fortifications, and we're outnumbered two to one."

"Maybe we will die, then," Derkin agreed. With sad, angry eyes he scanned his encampment. Two hundred yards across in all directions, the barren center of what had once been Klanath was a tapestry of dwarven ranks, deployed for defense. All around the encampment was a solid ring of sturdy, armored forms. A pair of javelins stood above each dwarf, and a shield at each shoulder. On every second back was a slung crossbow, and those without crossbows had webbed slings. And each dwarf had a sword, axe, or hammer.

Within the circle, grim assault companies waited—hundreds of mounted, armed dwarves and many more hundreds of footmen. Even here, surrounded on a barren, open plain, without fortification except for the shrunken skeleton of the old palace where some of the women tended the infirm, Derkin's army was formidable. "They may kill us," the Lawgiver agreed, "but it will cost them dearly if they do."

* * * * *

It was midday when spotters on the palace ruins saw Dreyus's scouts returning from the east. Drums sang, and Derkin gathered his group commanders around him for a final time. "The human knows now," he said. "He has confirmed that Redrock Cleft is no longer passable. Now he will either leave or attack." He turned to the only human in his camp, Tulien Gart. "Which do you think he will do?"

Tulien Gart shook his head. "Any ordinary officer would leave," he said. "Oh, he might bluster around a bit, maybe curse you and send a few arrows your way, but he would see the futility of an all-out battle here, even a victorious one. He would withdraw and go in search of another route eastward. But that is no ordinary officer out there, Derkin. That is Dreyus. Dreyus does not like to be thwarted."

"You are free to leave," Derkin told the human. "They would pass you through their lines."

"No, they wouldn't," Gart said bleakly. "Dreyus would know that I have been here by my own choice. And he would know where you learned the field tactics of empire soldiers. If I must die, I'd rather it be here, quickly and with honor, than at the mercy of the emperor's torturers."

Derkin shrugged. "Arm yourself, then. And find a horse that suits you." He turned to his unit commanders. "Are we ready?"

Each commander nodded, and one said, "As ready as we'll ever be." They turned and headed for their units.

Tap Tolec nudged the Lawgiver and pointed. A short distance away, Helta Graywood had appeared outside the ruined palace. She was wearing oddments of armor and a helmet, all too big for her, and carrying a sword and shield. She was heading for the perimeter line.

"Do you want us to put her back in the shelter?" Tap asked.

"It wouldn't do any good," Derkin said. "She's decided to fight. Just bring her here, so I can keep her with me."

Trumpets sounded all around, and the human cordon began to close in on the dwarves. Dreyus had made his decision. Foot companies led the approach, with archers among them. When they were within seventy yards, the footmen halted and the archers paced ahead of them and spread, standing and kneeling in double ranks.

"First come the arrows," Derkin muttered, as though reciting from a manual of arms. "Drums!"

The drums sang, and shields were raised throughout the encampment. From the perimeter inward, the dwarven ranks became a wall of steel.

In unison, the human archers released their bows, and the sky came alive with arrows. But even as the arrows left their strings, small groups of dwarves charged through their perimeter at a dozen points, racing forward as fast as stubby legs could drive them. The arrows went over their heads to fall in the ranks behind them, and before the archers could recover or retreat, there were dwarves among them, slashing furiously this way and that.

Wide-eyed, bewildered bowmen, armed only with their bows and their daggers, fell by the dozens before the foot companies behind them could react. And when the better-armed soldiers did charge forward, hampered by retreating archers and the bodies of the fallen, they saw only the backs of the dwarven assault groups, scampering toward the safety of their shielded lines.

Among the dwarves, few had been hit by arrows. Most of the shafts had found only shields in their path. Others had hit nothing but the hard ground. Here and there, though, a few dwarves lay fallen, some dead and others injured.

"Bolts and slings," Derkin ordered. Drums beat a tattoo, and on the perimeter line every second dwarf knelt and raised his crossbow. Those between the boltmen whirled their slings, filling the field for an instant with a sound like big, angry bees. Then the crossbows twanged, the stones flew, and all around the dwarves, human soldiers screamed and fell.

"First assault, first reprisal," Derkin muttered. Clambering onto his war-horse, he pulled Helta Graywood up behind him. Around them, the Ten mounted and formed close guard. Drums tattooed, and all around the encampment, companies of dwarven riders climbed into their saddles. "He'll put his footmen forward one more time now," Derkin told himself. "Javelins!"

As though responding to Derkin's thoughts, trumpets echoed his drums, and human pikemen and macemen advanced at a trot from all sides. The dwarves on the perimeters knelt behind their shields, motionless, as the trot became a headlong charge. The humans closed to forty yards, then thirty, then twenty.

"Throw and rush!" Derkin ordered, the drums taking his message.

As one, the entire dwarven perimeter stood, aimed, flung their javelins, then followed instantly with a second throw. While the first wave of needle-sharp missiles was hitting the humans, and the second was on the way, every second dwarf in the outer ring raised shield and blade and charged forward, roaring their battle cries.

It was not a human strategy. It was a tactic the Chosen Ones had invented, and its effect was murderous. Still moving forward, confronted by javelins that tore through their ranks, stumbling over their impaled companions, the human pikemen and macers were taken completely off guard as a thousand or more dwarves hit their advance, cutting them down right and left. Edged pikes thrust and slashed, and usually went over the heads of the dwarves. Dwarven blades ran with human blood. Dwarven hammers and dwarven shields smashed human knees and jaws.

Then, as before, the dwarves wheeled and withdrew, hurrying back to their own lines. As they returned, those lines backed away, tightening and withdrawing toward the center, compacting their defense. Not all of the dwarves who had countercharged came back. Many lay now where they had fallen—their blood flowing, mingling with the blood of their enemies. But most returned, and the perimeter tightened inward to compensate for the losses.

All around the compact dwarven force, stunned confusion ran through the human ranks. At Dreyus's command, his officers had launched a standard field assault against a surrounded enemy. First an archery barrage, then pikes and maces to overrun the perimeter, with horse companies in reserve to mop up afterward.

It was a classical tactic, and it should have worked. But the dwarves had not played their part. Instead of cowering and fleeing from the arrows, they had come out under the barrage and decimated the archers. Instead of regrouping for defense against footmen, they had unleashed a deadly barrage of their own. And instead of falling before the pikes and maces, they had countercharged, and now the forward foot companies were in turmoil.

Trumpets sounded, and all around, human soldiers turned and retreated toward their original lines, some running as fast as they could.

Derkin walked his horse across to where Tulien Gart stood beside a human-saddled mount. "Thank you," the dwarf said. "You taught me well, about human strategy."

Gart looked up at him bleakly. "It isn't over," he said. "That was only the first assault. They'll come again."

"Why?" Derkin asked. "They've lost hundreds of men. Isn't it enough?"

"It might be, for a regular officer," the man said. "But you've humiliated Dreyus now. He can't let you get away with that."

Behind Derkin, Helta Graywood leaned to look around him. "Who is this Dreyus, anyway?" she asked.

"I don't really know." Gart shrugged. "No one knows much about him, except that what he does is the emperor's doing, and when he speaks it is the emperor speaking. Some suspect that he may actually *be* Quivalin

Soth, in some other form . . . in a second body, somehow. Two separate men, but with one mind. But even the wizards I've met don't know how that could be done."

"What will the soldiers do next?" Derkin asked the man.

"Probably try the horse-charge approach," Gart said. "With their lancers leading, and footmen behind them. It is a time-honored tactic in circumstances like this, when a first assault has been repelled. Quivalin Soth has never been a soldier, and Dreyus probably isn't either. So he'll let his officers advise him one more time."

"The horse-charge," Derkin said thoughtfully. "Yes, we've planned for such. And if that tactic fails, then what?"

"Beyond that I can't predict," Gart told him. "Were his officers to fail again, I think Dreyus would take full command. There's no telling what he would try."

With the humans withdrawn, dwarves scampered through their lines to retrieve their dead—those they could reach without an arrow finding them. Dragging them back into the besieged encampment, they laid them out honorably and stood over them for a moment, willing their spirits to the mercy of Reorx. There was no time for burial now. That would have to wait until they, under Derkin Lawgiver's leadership, had chased the humans away.

Spotters atop the ruined palace signaled, and the drums spoke. All around the beleaguered dwarves, the mighty human army was regrouping. Horse companies were moving into the fore now, mounted lancers followed by great tides of foot soldiers.

22
The Last Day

By last light of evening, the lancers came, a unified attack aimed at three separate points in the dwarven defense. From the south, northwest, and northeast they charged—armored men on armored horses, lowering their lances as they closed on the stolid ranks of dwarven shields. As the gap narrowed between lancers and dwarves, trumpets blared, and long lines of foot soldiers poured across the frozen ground, following where the horses went.

The dwarves at the assault points stood as though rooted in the rocky soil as the lancers bore down on them. Steel tips with the momentum of charging steeds behind them aligned on steel shields held only by dwarves. Then, at the last possible instant, the shields fell away. Each dwarven defender at those points fell backward, flat on the ground with his shield on top of him.

The lance tips met only cold air in passing, and thundering hooves clattered and faltered as wild-eyed horses tried to avoid the strange footing of horizontal shields. Here and there a shield was battered downward by hooves, but far more horses pivoted and spun, or launched themselves into ill-timed jumps to clear the frightening footing. A few lancers were thrown from their saddles, and some found themselves charging back the way they had come, directly into their own footmen. Most, though, passed over the fallen dwarves and into the encampment itself. Behind them, dwarves rolled and rose, got their feet beneath them and their shields up, and drew their blades.

Several hundred human lancers now milled and wheeled inside the dwarven line, as the line closed behind them. A few found targets for their lances, but the sport lasted only seconds. With a thunder of hooves, the lancers were hit—from all sides, it seemed, by charging dwarven cavalry. Each horse carried a dwarf on each side. Each dwarf wielded a weapon and a fighting shield. With deadly efficiency, the dwarven war-horses tore through the disarrayed lancers, wheeling to charge again and again.

Armored by plate and chain of dwarven steel and protected by the same shields that protected their riders, each horse was a thundering juggernaut among the lightly armored lancers. Men and their mounts fell right and left as dwarven blades and hammers lashed out from both sides of each war-horse, slashing and crushing whatever they could reach.

None of the lancers who had breached the dwarven perimeter returned to his ranks. Some, in their final moments, might have thrown down their weapons and surrendered, given the chance. But dwarves had died in the lancers' charge, and Derkin's signal when the trap was sprung was a down-turned thumb. No mercy, and no quarter. It was Derkin's fourth law, pure and simple: if dwarves were attacked, dwarves would retaliate. If dwarves died, their attackers would also die.

Throughout the slaughter of the lancers, Derkin had held back, simply sitting his mount with Helta behind him, watching the combat and hearing the singing of the drums. Now, as the last lancer fell, he looked at the dark sky and tasted the raw, cold wind that came with evening. He knew what he must do next. Hundreds of his people were dead and more were wounded. Through sheer, stubborn courage and wily tactics, they had accounted for three humans for every fallen dwarf, but were still surrounded and badly outnumbered. If the humans pressed their attack again tomorrow, the Chosen Ones would perish. It was inevitable.

"The enemy is withdrawing for the night," Derkin told Tap Tolec. "All this day we have defended. Now we must attack. Bring me our master delvers, and ask Vin the Shadow to attend me."

Tulien Gart drew near, leading a tired horse. The man was battered and bloody, his thigh gouged by a lance tip, but he stood with dignity before the dwarven leader. "I didn't think you could turn that charge," he admitted. "Humans could never have done it. Humans wouldn't have had the courage to fall under those horses, as your people did."

"They might have," Derkin said, "if they had ever been slaves." He climbed down from his horse and helped Helta down. "Take Commander Gart to shelter," he told her. "Bind his wounds and make a place for him at the fire. There is a cold wind tonight."

When the delvers were assembled along with Vin the Shadow and several of his Daergar companions, Derkin gathered them around him. "Is the stone-drilling complete up on the peak?" he asked the chief of delvers.

"It is ready, Lawgiver." The dwarf nodded, his blond beard bobbing in the firelight. "It needs only to be pried."

Derkin turned to Vin. "We have prepared the face of that peak above the Klanath Pits," he said, "to fill the pits with an avalanche. That was to have completed our work here, after the last cut stones were hauled away. But now I need that avalanche to occur tonight. Most of the delvers are of Daewar descent. They cannot climb such slopes at night. Do you have people who can?"

Vin had removed his mask, and his large eyes glowed in the firelight as his foxlike face twisted into a tight grin. "There's plenty of light for us," he said. "Just explain what has to be done."

"The delvers have drilled pry-holes all along a fault high on that peak." Derkin pointed. "They can tell you what to look for, and how to break out the stone. And they can give you their climbing slings and prybars."

"Will an avalanche help us get back to Kal-Thax?" Vin asked.

"It might." Derkin shrugged. "The wind is cold tonight. Our spotters say that some of the humans have made their fires down in the pits, out of the wind. It is possible that their leader, Dreyus, is there. Without him, the rest might decide to turn around and go away, rather than lose more men tomorrow for no reason."

"Then let's hope Dreyus is warming himself out of the wind," Vin replied, still grinning. "If he is, we'll bury him there."

"Reorx protect you, Vin the Shadow," Derkin said. "When you have done your task, take your climbers on up, over the peak. If we survive tomorrow, we will see you at Stoneforge. If we don't come, tell our people there of the four laws." He clapped the Daergar roughly on the shoulder, then turned and strode away, the Ten following.

"Do you really think Dreyus will be in the pits?" Tap Tolec asked doubtfully as they toured the perimeter, gazing at the hundreds of human fires encircling them.

"Who knows?" Derkin shrugged. "If Tulien Gart is right, Dreyus may not even feel the wind's chill. But we did set out to bury the Klanath pits, and I wouldn't want to leave that task undone. Besides, it is a matter of law. All this day we have been attacked. Whatever happens tomorrow, we must retaliate tonight. And I know of no better way."

As evening dragged into the middle hours of night, Derkin's scouts and foragers roamed the field between the dwarven encampment and the surrounding army, searching for weak points, for possible avenues of escape. They found none, and their reports only verified what Derkin already knew. If the humans continued their attack tomorrow, his entire army was doomed. They could not escape, and they could not hold out through another day on this barren, defenseless flat.

Near midnight, the Lawgiver entered the ruined palace one last time. He found Helta Graywood and sat with her for a few moments beside a dwindling fire.

"We would have been married when we returned to Kal-Thax," he said. "It is what I was waiting for. I wanted to marry you on dwarven ground, in a land secured for dwarves."

"Are we going to die tomorrow, Derkin?" she asked quietly.

"There is a chance—just a slight chance—that the humans might withdraw," he said. "But if they don't . . ."

He let his voice trail off, not wanting to finish the statement.

Helta took his hand in both of hers. "As of this moment, you are my husband," she said. "I wish us long life, if that can be. But if it cannot, at least we will end life as one."

Suddenly the ground seemed to shake, and a rolling

thunder sounded through the walls. Still hand in hand, they hurried outside. The cold night wind had shredded the clouds overhead, and there was starlight. Beyond the human encampments to the south, and high above them, an entire mountain slope was in gigantic motion. Down and down, gathering momentum with each foot, millions of tons of shattered stone poured down the steep slope, flattening and burying everything in a half-mile-wide path of utter destruction. Within seconds, the avalanche rolled onto the lower slope, a huge wall of moving, churning stone racing toward the firelit pits of Klanath. Even above the thunder, the dwarves could hear humans screaming.

The bounding stones hit the mine pits, filled and covered them, and rolled on for another hundred yards, tearing through rank after rank of human encampments. And as the thunder died, great clouds of dust arose, riding on the wind.

Vin the Shadow had done his work. He and another fifty or sixty Daergar miners had completed the task the delvers had begun. The pits of Klanath were no more.

But even as he watched the dust clouds rise, Derkin Lawgiver knew that Dreyus had survived. Somehow he sensed that the strange, evil man—who might be another embodiment of the emperor Quivalin Soth V—had not been in the path of the avalanche. Dreyus was still alive, and tomorrow his army would finish what it had begun today.

With eyes as bleak and cold as the night wind, Derkin turned to Tap Tolec. "Awaken the camp," he said. "We move at once."

"But there's no way out," Talon Oakbeard muttered. "We're still surrounded."

"We go there." Derkin pointed at the still-billowing dust. "There, with our backs to the mountain, we can make them pay more dearly for each of us they kill."

* * * * *

Darkness and speed now were the dwarves' final allies. Before the soldiers east and west of the landslide's fan could close in, Derkin's entire camp had been moved. Leaving the barren clearing around the ruined palace behind them, they transferred themselves and everything they could ride, herd, or carry into the field of tumble-stone beneath the steep, sheared peak.

But as his people dug in there, in the final hour of darkness, Derkin remembered a debt of honor. At the edge of the avalanche fan, Tulien Gart was struggling with a balky horse, trying to follow the dwarves into the maze of scattered stone. Ordering the Ten to stay and organize their defenses, Derkin hurried down the slope toward the man. As he approached, he held out his hand. "You have done all you can for us, human," he said. "Dreyus lives, and if you stay here you will die. Get on that horse and follow the dust cloud. In the darkness and confusion, one rider might get through."

For an instant, Gart hesitated. Then he nodded. He could do no more here. The dwarf was repaying a debt of gratitude. Derkin was offering him his life. Pulling his horse away from the rocks, Tulien Gart bowed, a bow of true respect. "Farewell, Derkin Lawgiver," he said. "May whatever gods you choose protect you." He mounted then and rode away in the starlit darkness, heading east, following the drifting cloud of dust.

Derkin turned and hesitated. He sensed that he was not alone, but saw no one. Then a starlit face appeared from nothingness, and he sighed. Helta had followed him. "You still have that elf's invisible cloak," he rasped. "I thought I told you to . . ."

Running feet scuffed the ground, and excited whispers reached his ears. "It's the leader! Get him!"

"Derkin!" Helta shouted. "Watch out!"

But it was too late. Something heavy crashed against the temple of his helm, and the world went dark as the ground rose to meet him.

Stunned, unable to move or even gasp, Derkin saw torchlight flare, and there were humans all around. A patrol of soldiers, searching the field. A sling hummed and spat, a soldier screeched, and the torch fell and went out. In the darkness, Derkin felt something being spread over him. Then the voices came again—guttural, human voices. "Why, it's only a dwarf girl!" one said. "This is no 'leader,' Cooby."

"I swear he was here," another said. "At least, I *thought* I saw him."

"Well, there's no one here now except her. Whoop! Catch her! Don't let her get away!"

"It's all right. I have her. Ow! Give me a hand here! She's as strong as an ox!"

His mind screaming silently, Derkin could only listen as the humans carried Helta away. Seconds passed, and he felt himself beginning to recover, but already the sounds were fading into distance, and there was nothing he could do.

But then the fading footsteps halted, and a man's voice shouted, "Oh, gods, no!"

Other voices drowned his, shouting and screaming. There were several distinct thuds, and various crashing, clattering noises. With a thrust of iron will, Derkin forced his fingers to move, then his hands, arms, and legs. He rolled over, staggered upright, and the invisible cloak fell away from him. The world seemed to pitch and sway around him, but he forced his vision to steady itself as he saw movement. He squinted in the starlight, then gaped.

Helta Graywood came to him out of the starlit darkness, chattering and caressing. "You're alive!" she said. "Oh, I was so afraid."

He stared past her at the two towering, lurching creatures behind her.

Helta glanced around. "Goath and Ganat were watching," she said. "They saved me."

"Pretty one Derkin's mate," one of the ogres rumbled, sounding almost apologetic. "Nice little dwarf. Humans act bad to her."

"Won't bother her anymore, though," the other added. "We bashed 'em."

* * * * *

First light of dawn brought moments of confusion to Dreyus's forces. The dwarven encampment out on the flats was gone, but it didn't take long to find where they had gone. In the night, a huge avalanche had crashed down on the central section of the army's southern cordon. Where there had been great mine pits, now there was only a sloping field of rubble. And at least one battalion of soldiers camped there was gone as though it had never existed. But the dwarves were found. They had taken shelter among the fallen stones.

Just out of range of crossbows, javelins, and slings, Dreyus and his commanders assembled on the flats, looking up at the remaining dwarves.

"Sire, we have lost nearly two thousand men in a day and a night in this place," one of the senior commanders noted. "These dwarves cannot win, of course. They are trapped where they are, with that cliff at their backs and our units all around. But there are still thousands of dwarves here, and they fight fiercely. We will lose more men today. With the road closed beyond repair, is this place worth such a price to His Imperial Majesty?"

"My voice is the emperor's voice," Dreyus rasped. "Those dwarves have tampered with the destiny of the empire. They must die. No quarter, and no prisoners. We will put an end to them here."

Up on the rockfall slope, several dwarves appeared atop a wedge of stone, barely sixty yards from Dreyus and his officers. Dreyus recognized Derkin and snarled. The dwarf stood in plain view, fists on his hips, looking this way and that as though counting the human army . . . as though gloating at the obvious losses they had sustained.

"I want them all to die, here and now," Dreyus hissed. "And I want that one's head, to send back to Daltigoth."

"Yes, Sire." The senior commander saluted. "We will regroup, then. Their new position requires some changes in tactic."

"A delay?" Dreyus glared at the man. "How long?"

"Not past noon, Sire," the officer said. "A few hours to realign our troops. Then we can move on the dwarves."

"I want an end to this today!" Dreyus declared.

The officer conferred with his lieutenants for a moment, then saluted Dreyus again. "It shall be as you order, Sire."

Off to the humans' left, just beyond the east slope of the rockfall, a clamor broke out. For long minutes, the peak's sheared face echoed the sounds of furious combat, then a company of lancers and several hundred footmen came racing around the fan, shouting and pointing back. "Dwarves!" a leader shouted. "A thousand or more of them! They hit us from behind!"

The Chosen Ones, up in the rocks, had heard the clamor, too, and tried to see what was happening. A hundred or more of them crept to observation points looking eastward, just as a large party of dwarves piled into the rocks from that point. They were strangers, but where they had been, the rocky ground was littered with fallen humans.

Without ceremony, the newcomers scurried into the stonefall, and one of them, a stocky, gold-bearded young dwarf, shouted, "Where is Hammerhand?"

Derkin and the Ten hurried around a pile of stone. "I'm here," he answered. "Who are you?" He stopped, and blinked. "Luster? By Reorx's rosy red rear! It's Luster Red-leather!"

"Of course it is." The Daewar grinned. "And these are friends of mine." He indicated a burly, dark-bearded young Hylar beside him. "This is Culom Vand. He's Dunbarth Ironthumb's son. He and I sort of take turns leading this crowd. We've been looking for you since last fall. Then, a week ago, Culom had an odd dream."

"I dreamed of drumcall," the young Hylar said. "And there was a voice that said we should go to Tharkas Pass."

"So we did," Luster said. "Do you know that whole pass is full of cut stone? There's enough to build a city. Anyway, we came through the pass, and here you are."

"Why were you looking for me?" Derkin frowned. "Has the Council of Thorbardin changed its mind? If so, they're a little late."

"Well, not exactly. But the chieftains have had some second thoughts, after that business at Sithelbec."

"Sithelbec?"

"Oh, I guess you don't know about that. There was a great battle there, between the empire's forces and the elves. We went there, with Dunbarth, to help the elves. Afterward, Dunbarth and my father had some tough conversation with old Swing Basto."

Derkin glance curiously at the Daewar. "Basto? The Theiwar chieftain at Thorbardin?"

"The same," Luster confirmed. "It turns out those renegade Theiwar he was always defending had been up to their ears in that war over there, aiding the empire. Basto claims he knew nothing about it, but my father doesn't believe him. And speaking of war, you have a nice one going on here. May we join you?"

"You already have," Derkin pointed out. "But you may wish you hadn't. We don't have much chance of surviving the day."

Culom Vand had climbed to a high place. He was shading his eyes, surveying the massive human army spread out before the stonefall. "I see what you mean," he said. "Who are those people?"

"The emperor's army," Derkin said.

"The whole army?" Luster Redleather muttered, then pursed his lips in a low whistle. "Wow! We did barge into something, didn't we?" He raised his sword, looking critically at its wide blade. "Well, Hammerhand, since we're here, I guess we've just joined your army."

"*Lawgiver*," Tap Tolec growled. "His name is Derkin Lawgiver. Hammerhand was before, in Kal-Thax."

Throughout a bleak morning, the Chosen Ones and their unexpected reinforcements dug in among the fresh-fallen rubble and watched the movements of the emperor's legions out on the flat. Every dwarf in Derkin's army knew that this place would be their last stand, and that there was no hope for them. Even with the arrival of eight hundred warriors from Thorbardin, they could not win. But still they watched in fascination as the panorama of one of the world's greatest armies, positioning itself for a final, deadly assault, was played out before them.

"There will be no more horse charges," Derkin told those around him. "You see, the horse companies are being moved to the rear and the sides. They can't use horses in a field of boulders, any more than we can. But they've closed any possible retreat for us."

"I wish now we'd kept Lord Kane's catapults," Tap said. "We could use them here."

When the sun was high, the vast shifting of legions and battalions was at an end. Great combined companies of footmen in heavy armor now formed the front ranks of the human formation. There were thousands of them, row upon row and rank upon rank. Derkin didn't need Tulien Gart to tell him what the humans intended. They would come afoot, protected somewhat by their armor. Some would fall, but for each one down there would be ten more behind. Wave after wave of them would come up into the rocks, and they would keep coming. Nothing the dwarves could do would stop them now.

Trumpets sounded, and the first wave of the attack began. The thousands of armored footmen started for the avalanche fan. Marching shoulder to armored shoulder, they seemed to be in no great hurry. There was no charge, no rush. The footmen simply began walking, heading into the tumblestone field. Above them, dwarves waited, their weapons at the ready.

"Make them pay for this day," Derkin Lawgiver ordered his people. "Make them remember the dwarves of Kal-Thax . . . and of Thorbardin."

23
Day of Reckoning

The first armored footmen entering the tumblestone wilderness met javelins, hurled with deadly accuracy. Derkin's best delvers and some of the Thorbardin dwarves had gathered all of the remaining javelins and placed themselves in forward positions, where they could spring from cover, throw their weapons, then fall back.

The final lesson that many of the humans learned that day, about dwarves or anything else, was that pinpoint accuracy with a javelin was second nature to the short people—and especially to the delvers. For ages, the javelin had been a basic tool of most dwarven cultures. It had been used in climbing, in delving, in mining, and in the traversing of chasms long before it was ever used as a weapon. A capable climber or delver could virtually thread a needle with a javelin. At fifty feet, a delver could sink a javelin into a crevice an inch wide, with enough force that it would hold climbing lines securely.

Now, as the first ranks of men entered the rockfall, the dwarves found targets among them. Visor slits, unprotected throats, gaps between breastplates and shoulder mail, loosely fitted knee plates—any chink in the humans' armor large enough to admit a slim, steel-pointed shaft—all felt the sting of dwarven javelins. Nearly eighty soldiers fell, pierced by the slim spears, before the forward dwarves ran out of javelins to throw. And another fifty fell to bronze crossbow bolts and whining sling-stones, before any of them got far enough into the stones to use their blades.

But the tide of the assault was overwhelming. Dwarves fought the clanking humans on the lower slope of the fan, then fell back and turned to fight again, higher up in the rubble. Slowly, inexorably, the dwarves were sought out, pushed back, and compacted by the sheer weight of numbers.

Men died and dwarves died as the uncaring cliffs above echoed the clatter and clash of furious combat.

Derkin and the Ten were everywhere, reinforcing a defense here, defending a withdrawal there, setting up impromptu ambushes and counterattacks. Once into the maze of fallen rock, the humans were sometimes out of contact with their officers, and dozens of small, scattered bands of them wandered here and there, sometimes going the wrong way . . . and paying for their confusion with their lives. But the dwarven drums were singing constantly, orchestrating the strategies and movements of Derkin's disciplined dwarves. For an hour, and then another, it seemed the dwarves might hold their position among the rocks. Yet even as Derkin realized that they were holding, his drums told him of another wave of attackers entering the landslide fan.

As the sun of Krynn quartered in the western sky, the stonefall beneath the peaks was a bedlam of frantic, hand-to-hand fighting. Everywhere the dwarves turned, there were armored soldiers, pressing them, pushing them, cutting them down by the dozens. Derkin found himself in a narrow cleft between boulders, fighting for his life against three humans. Beyond the cleft, the Ten—or what was left of them—were standing off a dozen more. But five wandering soldiers had entered from somewhere else, and Derkin found himself and one other, fighting back to back against impossible odds. Hammer and shield against shields, armor, and slashing swords, Derkin Lawgiver admitted to himself that it was only moments before he would die. "For the Chosen Ones," he chanted. "For Kal-Thax."

Directly behind him a deep voice responded, "For Thorbardin. Everbardin, be open to this one." Hearing the voice, Derkin knew who was fighting behind him. It was the Hylar, Culom Vand, the son of Dunbarth Ironthumb.

Derkin deflected a vicious, two-handed slash with his shield and returned the blow. His hammer left a deep dent in the breastplate of a human and staggered him backward, but his foes kept up their attack. Behind him, the Lawgiver heard a gasp and the sound of pierced lungs. But then steel rang on steel again, and he knew that Culom Vand was still there, and that it was an attacker who had fallen.

Two blades came at him together, one high and one low. He ducked, caught the lower one on his shield, and braced himself for the overhead blow. But it didn't fall, and he saw the shadow of Culom's shield above him.

He recovered, thrust, and said hoarsely, "Thanks."

Behind him, Culom said, "My father really does want to talk to you . . . preferably alive."

Then, abruptly, above the din, the drums echoed a new call. A soldier glanced away for an instant, and Derkin's hammer crushed the man's helmet into his skull.

Behind him, Culom said, "That's the song I heard in my dream, before we came to the pass. What does it mean?"

Derkin ducked under a sword slash, braced his feet, and butted his nearest foe with his shield. The man doubled over the shield, and Derkin straightened, lifted the soldier, and flung him backward against the second one. Both of them fell, and Derkin raised his head, listening. Then his eyes widened. "It means reinforcements!" he shouted. "Let's get out of this place!"

"I'm with you," Culom rasped, pushing his own adversary back a step. Then, as armored men rushed the pair from both sides, the dwarves dropped to the ground, slashing at human ankles. With a resounding clatter, three soldiers collided above them, and sprawled against the stones. "Climb," Derkin ordered. Making a stirrup of his hands, he hoisted Culom to the top of the nearest standing stone, and the Hylar pulled him up an instant later. Beneath them, dazed soldiers were just getting to their hands and knees as Tap Tolec and Talon Oakbeard rushed into the crevice to methodically brain them.

The drums were beating a wild tattoo, and trumpets blared in the distance. Atop the standing stone, Derkin Lawgiver stared, openmouthed. Out on the barrens, beyond the landslide, there was melee everywhere. Human horse units wheeled and circled frantically, footmen scrambled in all directions, and a half-hundred pitched battles were underway.

And beyond, coming up from the forest, were elves. By the hundreds and thousands, they streamed onto the wasteland slopes, leaping and bounding, their deadly arrows flying ahead of them like swarms of angry wasps. Moon-blond hair flowing in the wind, beardless faces serene and intent, the elves had fallen on Dreyus's army from behind, and were methodically cutting it to pieces. And among them, riding and slashing like lithe, feral beasts with bright feathers in their hair, were hundreds of mounted Cobar warriors.

Scampering to the highest place he could find, Derkin raised his hammer high above his head, then swept it downward toward the open slopes. "Attack!" he roared.

Before the scattered, surprised soldiers of the emperor could reform to respond to the elves' attack, they found themselves hit from behind by thousands of howling, chanting dwarves pouring out of the landslide fan. Some of the soldiers responded bravely; some heard a confusion of orders and ran in circles. Some simply ran.

There were no strategies now, no planned assaults and defenses. This was open combat, with many pitched battles going on while horsemen wheeled and clashed among them. Derkin and the Ten—who were only the Six now—waded in, chopping and slashing at anything wearing the colors of Daltigoth. Behind them came the Chosen Ones, a solid wall of stubby, deadly rage, chanting to the rhythm of the drums. And on their flanks ran several hundred Hylar and Daewar, joining the chants. A milling legion of empiremen melted away before them, and Derkin found himself face-to-face with a hooded elf. "Hail, Lawgiver," Despaxas said, tossing back his cowl. "The Wildrunners and the rangers are here."

"I already noticed," Derkin growled. "You might have come a little earlier, though."

"We'd have been here two days ago if Redrock Cleft had still been open for our Cobar friends." The elf smiled, a smile that was childlike in its slyness. "But they had to go around."

"That's what you always wanted, wasn't it?" Derkin glared at him. "From the very first, you've used me—and my people—to block the emperor's path to the east."

"We all use one another." Despaxas shrugged. "To use

and be used, by choice, is the way of friendship. It's the stuff of alliances. The alternative is domination by emperors, and slavery."

A random arrow, with the markings of Daltigoth, whisked toward Derkin. Without seeming to take his eyes off Despaxas, the dwarf deflected the quarrel with his shield. Just beyond Despaxas, a buckskin-clad Wildrunner drew his bow and shot, returning the human fire.

All around them, the pitched battle raged.

Talon Oakbeard came then, mounted on his favorite horse and leading other mounts. Derkin's was there, its saddle already occupied. Helta Graywood eased back to make space for Derkin in the saddle, and he climbed aboard.

Derkin looked down, but Despaxas was gone. The elf had said all he had to say, apparently.

Other dwarven horse companies were mounted now, and sweeping here and there through human ranks, dwarves slashing fiercely from both sides of each saddle. Derkin picked out a promising fight and joined in.

Within an hour, the fighting had thinned and scattered. The sun was low, sinking behind distant peaks, and Derkin noticed an odd, dark cloud forming above the place where the old human compounds had stood. He worked his mount in that direction, swerving here and there to get in a hammer-blow at a scurrying soldier, then reined in abruptly. Just ahead, a big man sat silently on a black horse, staring at the dwarf with eyes that burned with hatred.

"Dreyus," Derkin muttered. With Helta clinging behind him, and the survivors of the Ten following, he spurred his mount toward the man. But the strange, dark cloud above swirled and lowered, a dipping funnel of darkness that reached downward to engulf Dreyus. It paused only an instant, then lifted, and Dreyus was gone. It was as though he had never been there.

Yet, just at the instant of the cloud's lifting, a shadow seemed to join it—a wide-winged bat-fish shadow that seemed more to swim in the air than to fly.

"Magic," Derkin muttered, turning away.

Then Despaxas was there again, beside him. With wide, wise eyes, the elf was staring at the place where the cloud had been. "Yes, magic," he said. "Of a strange kind, but Zephyr understood it."

"Zephyr?" Derkin cocked his head. "Your pet shadow? Did he help do that?"

"No, Dreyus did it, but Zephyr used it to escape the verge. He has gone back to his plane."

"I'm sorry," Derkin said, realizing that it was true.

"Be glad for him," Despaxas said. "For a long time, Zephyr has sought the path back to his world. I couldn't help him, but he found one who could. It's odd, the one who freed him from the verge was the only person I've ever known of that Zephyr couldn't even see."

Derkin was ready to fight some more, but it seemed there was no one to fight. All around, soldiers were throwing aside their banners and their heavy armor to flee in panic, while elves, dwarves and Cobar harried them on their way. Among the Cobar, Derkin thought he recognized Tuft Broadland, but the tall warrior was far off, and he couldn't tell for sure. He did see another human he recognized, though. Riding with the Cobar was the former officer of the empire, Tulien Gart.

Tap Tolec reined in beside Derkin. "We've run out of soldiers," he said. "What do we do now?"

"Have the drums sound assembly," Derkin said. "We're going home. There's still enough daylight left to see us back to the border of Kal-Thax."

By last light, the Chosen Ones and the Thorbardin volunteers made their way among great stacks of building blocks, to file through the almost hidden gate of Derkin's Wall. The war north of Tharkas Pass was at an end, and

Derkin Lawgiver left the elves and their allies to clean up the field. It was their land, not his.

The dwarves had gathered up all of their dead and carried them the four miles to the ancient place that a long-ago dwarf named Cale Greeneye had marked as the boundary of the dwarven lands. Tomorrow, the honored dead would be buried in their own land. For now, though, it was enough to simply build a few fires, tend wounds, and rest.

Derkin looked around him at the proud, battered people who had made him their leader and felt humble. For nearly a mile southward from their wall, they filled Tharkas Pass with their little fires, their clusters of bedding, their low, tired voices, and their snores. But they were far fewer than the bold army that had marched from this pass seasons earlier to depose Sakar Kane. For every three dwarves who had gone to war, only two had returned. Derkin found himself wondering if anything—even the fierce pride of a nation—was worth such a price.

As though reading his mood and his thoughts, Helta Graywood appeared beside him and gripped his hand with strong, warm little fingers. "If you decide to turn around this minute and do it all again," she said, "they will follow you. These people are your people, Derkin Lawgiver. They love you."

"I've never understood why," he rumbled.

"And I suppose you never will," she said. "But I understand."

Near midnight, guards came from the wall to awaken the Lawgiver. "There are people at the gate," they said. "They ask to speak with you."

"What people?" Derkin hissed, trying to rub the sleep from his eyes. It was the first time in nearly a week that he had slept, and now his nap had been interrupted.

"Not dwarves," a guard said. "One of them is that elf, the one who was with us before. There are others with him."

By the light of a single rising moon, Derkin made his way to the narrow gate, yawning and surly, more asleep than awake. The timber door stood open, but several dwarves were blocking it, denying entrance to those beyond. They stepped aside as Derkin approached, and two of them kindled torches. Despaxas stood just beyond the portal, with other lithe, silent figures behind him. They were all elves.

Peeved and grumpy from being awakened, Derkin glared at the elven mage. "What do you want?" he demanded.

"We have what we wanted," Despaxas said. "The mountain road between the human empire and the central plains is closed. It is likely that Quivalin Soth will continue his insane attempts at conquest, but he can no longer strike swiftly or sustain a siege. For that we thank you, Derkin Lawgiver."

"Fine," Derkin growled. "Then you won't mind going away and letting me sleep."

"When your great-uncle established this boundary," Despaxas continued, ignoring the surly dismissal, "the agreement was between him and my mother, Eloeth. Between a dwarf and an elf."

"So?"

"So, know that from this day forward, the land north of here is elven land. It will be called Qualinesti."

"Fine," Derkin growled. "So you want me to get my building blocks off of your property, is that it?"

"I suggest you use them as building blocks should be used," Despaxas said. "Build a city. Here, where you have your boundary wall, in Tharkas Pass. My leader, Kith-Kanan, suggests that your people and mine consider a treaty to formalize the boundary between our lands. And if the boundary were to be a city, perhaps we could build it together."

"Together?" Derkin gaped at him. "You mean . . .

dwarves and elves, *together*? Such a thing has never been done." He yawned. "Look, could we talk about this tomorrow? I'm tired."

"There is nothing more to talk about," Despaxas said. "I have presented thanks, and a suggestion. You have heard it."

"Fine," Derkin said. "I'll sleep on it."

With an innocent smile, Despaxas raised his hand and muttered something that Derkin could not understand. But suddenly the dwarf felt restored and content . . . and, somehow, very wise. "What have you done?" he asked.

"I have given you two gifts," the elf said. "One is from my mother. The second is on behalf of the people of Qualinesti. It is long life—if you don't get yourself killed first—and a touch more of that special talent which you have been acquiring over the past few years. You have the gift or the curse of leadership, Derkin. You will find now that you have it even more."

"Magic." The dwarf shrugged. "I don't like . . . Oh, well, thank you, I suppose."

With a nod—and another twitch of that innocent, cat-like smile—Despaxas turned away, the other elves following him. Derkin watched them go for a moment, then called. "Wait a minute! You said there were two gifts! What's the first one?"

"If ever you need to know, you will," Despaxas called back. "Farewell, Derkin Winterseed-Hammerhand-Lawgiver. You have been interesting to know."

"Aren't you coming back?"

"Who knows the future?" the elf called, and turned away again.

"*Who knows the future?*" Derkin muttered, irritated. "If anyone does, it's you, elf." Closing the gate between Kal-Thax and Qualinesti, the dwarf suddenly felt an odd loneliness—a sense of loss, as though a true friend had just gone away.

Helta was waiting for him beside his fire, but as he approached she backed away a step, her eyes widening. "Derkin," she said, pointing over his head, "what *is* that?"

"What's what?" He glanced up, saw nothing, and peered at her.

"Uh . . . nothing, now," she said. "But just for a moment, there was something above your head."

"There's nothing there," he insisted, looking again. "What did you think it was?"

"It looked like a crown," Helta replied in awe. "Like a crown of gold, with stones in settings."

24

A Place of two Nations

What had taken the Chosen Ones a winter's work to collect—
every usable timber and building stone in the now-van-
ished human city of Klanath—would take years to recut,
bore, and reuse. In ordering the dismantling of Klanath,
the Lawgiver had thought little about what to do with the
architectural materials which now filled half of Tharkas
Pass. His immediate concerns had been to make certain
that the human city could not be rebuilt, and to give his
people a season or two of enjoyable labor. Privately, he
had hoped that Lord Sakar Kane might show up if they
waited for a time on the slopes north of Tharkas. But Kane
had disappeared. No one—not even the far-ranging elves

—seemed to know what had become of him.

As a new season greened the pastures south of Tharkas, Derkin sent a crew of dwarves north one last time to complete "The Tidying" there. But they found nothing left to do. What the dwarves had begun, the elves who now claimed that land beyond the pass had completed. Except for the black quartz monument to dwarven law, there was not a trace or a hint that there had ever been a settlement of any kind there. The last vestiges of the old palace were gone, all traces of the mines were gone, all sign of the great battle that had been fought there had been removed, and the stony flats were green with grasses and clover.

The dwarves, reporting back, said that the forest seemed closer now, as though it were already advancing toward the mountains to hide the barren slopes in deep foliage. Only an enchanted forest could reclaim its grounds so quickly, they told their peers. They reported seeing a small band of elves, who waved at them from a distance. And two among them swore that they had seen a unicorn, just within the edge of the advancing forest.

But the elves had not touched Derkin's law stone. It stood where it had been, dark and austere among the wildflowers around it, with its stern warning: ". . . We will always retaliate."

Derkin had intended to take his people back to Stoneforge—their sprawling, bustling Neidar settlement in the western mountains near Sheercliff—but as the weeks became months, he delayed. The dwarves were hard at work here, building and hauling, climbing and hoisting, adding tier after tier to the wall they had built across the pass. And as the work progressed, the wall became two walls, with compartments and chambers between . . . then three walls.

"Give a dwarf work that satisfies him," Derkin mused to Helta Graywood one day, "and he'll work at it as long as there's breath in his lungs and life in his heart. It's the nature of our people."

"They'll leave here when you decide to go," Helta said. "If you tell them to return to Stoneforge, they'll go. They are your people, Derkin Lawgiver."

"They don't want to go back, though," he pointed out. "Most of them would rather stay right here and build walls than go to Stoneforge. You know that as well as I do."

"But whatever you want . . ." she started.

"Stoneforge is complete," Derkin said. "It has its fields to farm, its foundries and its shops, its herds to tend. It is a Neidar settlement, no different from any other Neidar settlement except that it is bigger. The people we left there are mostly Neidar and are content with Stoneforge. But these people—my Chosen Ones—they're different, Helta. Most of them have been slaves, and all of them have been warriors. Now they've found something to do that they enjoy doing, and that joy can last them through many generations."

"Building walls?" she asked, frowning.

"More than walls," he corrected. "Those walls, if they continue, will become the foundations of a great city as proud and fine as anything in this world. And more than a city. If I don't interrupt them, these people of ours might just construct a new way for dwarves to live."

"The city the elf called Pax Tharkas," she said.

"Pax Tharkas," he confirmed, nodding. "Right now, only dwarves are building here. Which is for the best, because what elves know about stonemasonry and the rodding of joints could be set down in three runes, with two of them used only for emphasis. But later, when our people have made the underpinnings of this place solid and sturdy, the elves will come. Then there will have to be a treaty between us, of course. A thousand understandings will have to be reached, and accords agreed to. When it is done, the Treaty of Pax Tharkas must signify once and

for all the sheathing of swords between two races. It won't
be easy, and I can't imagine it, truly—dwarves and elves
sharing the same city—but most of our people believe in
their hearts that such a thing can be done. Somehow, I
believe it, too."

As he said it, Derkin seemed so sure, so confident, that
Helta could almost share the vision with him. Still, there
was something that troubled her. Despite Derkin's seeming enthusiasm for the idea of expanding his border wall
into a great city, Helta sensed that his heart was else-
where.

Often, she had noted, it was Talon Oakbeard who
presided at planning sessions for new parts of the construction. The idea of Pax Tharkas, which Derkin had
come to espouse so openly, had found its true roots in the
former Neidar's heart. For Talon, the great undertaking
had become an obsession—a work of true love.

As the months passed, and the great cleft of Tharkas
rang with the pleasant pandemonium of thousands of
dwarves cheerfully building the first solid layers of a
great city, stone by stone, Derkin and Talon were everywhere among them. They counseled with stonecutters,
they drew diagrams and argued about them with the
masons, they suggested a tower base here and demanded
a shoring brace there.

In the concept of building a citadel, Talon Oakbeard
had discovered his true talent. Derkin, on the other hand,
had a different talent—the ability to lead. Yet now, the
people he led had chosen their own path, and it was not
the path he might have chosen for himself.

A dozen times, Helta found herself wishing that Derkin
would delegate the whole project to Talon and stop worrying about it. But spring became summer, and summer
became fall, and still Derkin lingered at Tharkas.

Most of the dwarves from Thorbardin were still with
them. With typical Hylar directness, Culom Vand had told

Derkin that he would not return to Thorbardin until Derkin agreed to go back with him. "Thorbardin needs your skill," he had confided. "I promised my father and Jeron Redleather that I would find you and bring you back, so that's what I intend to do. If you won't go now, then I'll stay until you do."

Having stated that, Culom Vand said no more about it. With typical Hylar dignity, he simply waited. In the meantime, he and most of the Hylar with him had found something to do. The beautiful old lake beyond Tharkas Camp, which had once served a great dwarven mining settlement but had been allowed to deteriorate during human habitation, was a challenge to the efficient-minded Hylar. They had taken it upon themselves to clear and reshape its channels and to build pump stages. "Thorbardin's glaziers could fit these lifts with lenses to make steam," Culom told Derkin. "And our foundries could produce steam-driven wheels to lift the water to your new citadel of Pax Tharkas."

Derkin's response had been only, "It isn't my citadel. It's theirs . . . the Chosen Ones."

Unlike the reserved, patient Hylar, Luster Redleather and the hundred other gold-bearded Daewar in the group had become enthusiastically involved in the construction of walls and foundations, and the dream of a great citadel that one day would rise to the very summits of Tharkas Pass to serve two nations.

"Think of the trade possibilities!" Luster exulted one autumn evening after a feast of roast boar, dark bread, and ale. His blue eyes alight with the Daewar love of commerce, Luster paced this way and that, his hands sometimes clasped behind him and sometimes waving happily over his head. "Elvencraft, here at the very gateways of Thorbardin! Elven wines and spices, elven fabrics and flosses . . . There are fortunes to be made here! We'll provide steel and glass for the elves, and we'll stockpile elvenwares at Thorbardin for trade with the world!"

"How are you going to trade through closed gates?" Derkin asked him morosely.

"Just the way you said." Luster grinned. "We'll build commerce towns at all of our borders. Places open to anybody who has something to trade."

"Did I say that?" Derkin frowned.

"You said you would build a place called Barter," the Daewar reminded him. "I'm just expanding on the idea."

"That idea is for Kal-Thax," Derkin snapped. "Not for Thorbardin."

"Kal-Thax is Thorbardin," Luster countered.

"Not while those gates are closed," Derkin said. "I told your Council of Thanes that."

Throughout the exchange, Culom Vand sat quietly to one side, simply listening. But now he said, "If you come back to Thorbardin, Derkin, maybe you can open the gates."

Derkin gazed at him with level, cynical eyes. "By a vote of three to two?"

"By decree," Culom said, "if you were king."

"There are no kings in . . ."

"Maybe it's time to change that." Luster interrupted him. "The Covenant of the Forge is only a document, after all. It can be amended."

Helta Graywood set down a tray and stood beside Derkin, ruffling his hair with her fingers. "That's what I've been trying to tell this stubborn oaf," she told the Daewar, "for ages."

Shaking his head, Derkin growled, stood, and strode away into the dusk. When Tap Tolec and some of the Ten rose to follow him, Helta waved them down. "Leave him alone this time," she said. "He needs to think."

Late that night, Derkin stood alone atop a craggy summit, gazing up at the living sky where autumn clouds rode the high winds, forming shifting, flowing patterns in the light of two moons.

"I want to go home," he muttered to himself. "Helta knows that, and Tap knows it, too. Maybe they all know it. But if I take my people away from here, they will lose their finest dream. Most of them now are neither Neidar nor Holgar. It is as Tap said, these people have become a new breed of dwarf. Maybe Pax Tharkas is their destiny. But is it mine?"

Troubled and confused, Derkin the Lawgiver raised his hands toward the flowing sky. "Gods!" he whispered. "Reorx . . . and any others who care . . . give me a sign!"

The clouds swirled slowly in the high winds above, shifting from pattern to pattern. Then, for a moment, one bit of cloud broke away from the rest and stood alone. And just for an instant, as the winds molded it, it seemed to take the shape of a wedge—or an arrowhead—pointing south.

Derkin lowered his arms and sighed. "Maybe it is a sign," he told himself. In the distance, dappled moonlight played on the massive construct that now filled the lower one-third of Tharkas Pass. Where "Derkin's Wall" had once stood, twenty feet of stone defending a mountain pass, now rose the beginnings of a city—a city that would one day bridge the gap between two alien worlds, the ancient land of the dwarves and the new land of the western elves.

Above the pass, flowing clouds shifted in the wind, and it seemed that there was a face there—a wide, bearded dwarven face that molded and remolded itself in its features as the breeze in the pass whispered long-forgotten names, a litany of generations of Hylar leaders. "Colin Stonetooth . . ." the breezes murmured. "Willen Ironmaul . . . Damon Omenborn . . . Cort Fireblend . . ." Fascinated, Derkin stood gazing upward as the breezes whispered names to him—the names of his own ancestors. And with each name, the flowing cloud-face became another face. "Harl Thrustweight . . ." the breezes whispered, and the face Derkin saw was that of his own father. And now the breeze shifted and the whispering was a voice like his father's voice. "Thorbardin," it murmured. "Thorbardin has never been ruled . . . but it must be governed. That is your destiny, my son."

The breeze died away, and the clouds above were again only clouds, but in Derkin's mind was the echo of a whisper. He knew now what his course must be, and he felt oddly at peace with it. "Destiny," he muttered.

Only one regret remained in his mind. He had failed to keep his pledge—to himself and his people—to bring Sakar Kane to the justice the man deserved. Sakar Kane had simply disappeared. "If only I knew," Derkin said aloud. "If only I could be sure that he is gone."

As though in answer, a voice spoke. He knew he was alone. There was no one else within half a mile of where he stood, yet the voice spoke clearly, as though at his side. It was a low, musical voice, the voice of Despaxas, and it said one word: "*Chapak.*"

Instantly, Derkin found himself deep within a dark, reeking place, a place where mildew grew on ancient stone walls, moist and glistening in the light of a single candle. On one wall hung the skeletal remains of a man—a man who had been dead for a long time—and Derkin knew exactly where he was and what he was seeing. With absolute certainty, he realized that he was looking at a deep cell in a dungeon beneath the palace of the human emperor of Daltigoth. And he knew that the shackled body hanging there was that of Lord Sakar Kane, the Prince of Klanath.

The single candle lighting the scene was held by a man who seemed to be two men. Each time the flame flickered, the man's appearance changed. At one moment he seemed a squat, bulky human with a braided beard and elegant robes, at the next a tall, burly man in dark robe and dusty boots.

Derkin knew one of the faces. It was the man called Dreyus. And he knew the other as well, though he had never seen him. The man with the braided beard was Quivalin Soth V, Emperor of Daltigoth and Ergoth.

Again the candle flickered, and Derkin found himself where he had been, standing on a craggy knoll in a mountain pass, half a mile south of the place that would be Pax Tharkas. Beside him, where no one stood, Despaxas's musical voice whispered, "This is the gift my mother wished for you, Derkin. To know that you did not fail."

His eyes wide with wonder, Derkin the Lawgiver turned full around, then shook his head. "Magic," he muttered. "A latent spell."

With one last glance at the sky above—which was once again only an autumn sky—Derkin headed back toward his quarters. On the way he stopped at the fire of Culom Vand, then at several other places in the camp. By the time he opened the door of his own quarters and stepped in, a crowd was following him.

Helta Graywood and the Ten were waiting for him, alert and concerned as he had known they would be. It was rare that any of them ever let Derkin out of their sight. Derkin stood before them, his fists on his hips, firelight gleaming on the polished luster of his armor, as other dwarves entered behind him. He looked from one to another of those gathered around his hearth, then let his somber gaze linger on Helta. "Do you still say you can live anywhere with me?" he asked.

"Anywhere," she asserted.

"Then live with me in Thorbardin," he said. His gaze turned to Tap Tolec. "Do you still dream of being a Holgar?"

Tap raised one eyebrow. The ironic expression, combined with his broad shoulders and long arms, made him look more Theiwar than most who were full-blood. "As always," he said. "Maybe as much as you do."

"Could you be the leader of a thane?"

Tap blinked, surprised at the question. "There is a legend among my family," he said, "that an ancestor of mine was a chieftain, a very long time ago. His name was Slide Tolec. They say he led the Theiwar when Thorbardin was in its glory."

Derkin nodded and turned. "And you, Talon Oakbeard? Could you be a leader of people?"

"I have no thane." Talon shrugged. "My people were always Einar or Neidar. What people would I lead?"

"The Chosen Ones," Derkin said. "They are your thane. If I pronounce you their chieftain tomorrow, do you pledge to lead them well?"

Talon stared at the Lawgiver for a full minute, hardly believing what he had heard. "I'd do my best," he said finally.

* * * * *

It would be spring before the one called Lawgiver could undertake the journey southward to Thorbardin. There were conferences to be held and plans to be made. There were messages to be sent and pledges to be given and received.

Some of the Chosen Ones would choose to go with Derkin, and some, like Tap Tolec who would replace Swing Basto as chieftain of Thane Theiwar of Thorbardin, would need time to adjust to what Derkin had in mind for them.

There was a great deal to be done and much to be decided before Derkin Winterseed-Hammerhand—Derkin the Lawgiver—could return to Thorbardin to find the rest of his destiny.

Epilogue
The First and Always King

In the spring of the Year of Nickel, the final year of both the Decade of Cherry and the Century of Rain, frost-bearded guards at a hidden outpost high on Sky's End Mountain looked up from a winter-long game of bones to see movement in the distance—a large caravan approaching from the north. Drums relayed the news to Northgate of Thorbardin, and runners carried the message from there to all of the thanes. It was the day those in the undermountain fortress had been waiting for ever since the message came from Culom Vand months earlier. Derkin the Lawgiver, Master of the Mountains, was coming home to Thorbardin. And this time he was coming to stay—not as a citizen but as regent of all thanes.

Five years had passed since the first visit of Derkin's army, when thousands of dwarves had set up trade pavilions below Northgate, and Thorbardin had rediscovered the value of trade.

This time, there were fewer in the caravan. Only those who chose to live as Holgar—about twelve hundred—had followed Derkin from Tharkas. And this time, they made no camp on the slopes below Northgate. Instead, their drums conveyed their greetings, and the great plug of Northgate opened to receive them.

Escorted by respectful Home Guards, the Lawgiver's party stopped first in Theibardin. They spent two days there, at the end of which time old Swing Basto dourly announced his retirement as chieftain of Thane Theiwar, and Tap Tolec was resoundingly accepted by the Theiwar as their new leader. His first act as chieftain was to grant amnesty to Swing Basto and his followers, forgiving them their past intrigues and pardoning them for their ill-considered involvement in the Wilderness Wars. His second act was a solemn pledge that if any Theiwar ever again embarrassed the dwarven nation by getting privately involved with human emperors and generals, Tap would personally feed the culprit to tractor worms.

From Theibardin, Derkin's party went to Daebardin, where Jeron Redleather pledged the support of the Daewar to Derkin's regency. Another two days were passed there, with Jeron and his councilors, working out details for trade agreements with the elves of Qualinesti.

From Daebardin, the new arrivals went to the unnamed Klar cities, where Derkin received the pledge of Trom Thule, then to Daerbardin, where Vin the Shadow spent hours with the chieftain of Thane Daergar, Crag Shade-eye, relating the nature of the stone and the richness of the ores to be mined at Tharkas, and where Crag Shade-eye pledged his allegiance to Derkin Lawgiver, then promptly began organizing a mining expedition.

As a matter of protocol, Derkin also paused for a few minutes at the rubble pits below Daerbardin, where the little tribe known as Thane Aghar lived—when they could find the place. There Derkin introduced himself to the gully dwarf leader, Grimble I, who wasn't quite sure why he was being accosted until Vin the Shadow took him by the shoulder and pointed at Derkin. "This is the new boss around here," the Daergar explained.

Grimble thought it over, then shrugged. "Fine by me," he said. With the matter concluded, the great leader of all Aghar in Thorbardin turned and wandered away.

Grinning and shaking his head, Vin told Derkin, "That's as near to a pledge as you'll get here."

At Hybardin, the Hylar city delved within the living stone of the stalactite called Life Tree, Derkin met with Dunbarth Ironthumb. "As your son told you," he said, "I have set conditions for accepting regency here. One of them is that you let the Hylar name you as their chief."

"I've never wanted to be chief," Dunbarth said.

"And I never wanted to be regent," Derkin responded, frowning. "But I will, providing that I have a Hylar leader I can trust. I trust you, Dunbarth Ironthumb."

Ironthumb spread his hands in acceptance. "It has already been done," he said. "I have accepted the title of chieftain because you demanded it."

"And I have your oath of allegiance?"

"You have it." The Hylar nodded. "I welcome you home to your kingdom, Derkin Lawgiver."

"I have not accepted a crown," Derkin snapped. "Only a regency . . . or, as an ancestor of mine once put it, I've agreed to be chief of chiefs."

"Why not be king?" Dunbarth gazed at him, puzzled. "All of Thorbardin is ready to bend the knee to you."

"I will not be king of a divided nation," Derkin said. "I will govern, but not rule, until I know that Thorbardin and Kal-Thax are truly united . . . and know in my own heart that I can rule wisely."

"Then be chief of chiefs until you're sure," Dunbarth urged. "I can accept that."

For the first time in five years, the Great Hall of Audience was packed to capacity when the Council of Thanes assembled there. And for the first time in a century, the great chamber rang with cheers and applause as each order of business was done. Tap Tolec was named to the Council of Thanes, representing Thane Theiwar, and Dunbarth Ironthumb's title was amended on the scrolls, from representative to chieftain of Thane Hylar.

Solemnly, then, the ancient scroll embodying the Covenant of the Forge was produced and read aloud. Following the reading, a single amendment was proposed by Jeron Redleather. The amendment was to delete the passage allowing government by decree only in times of emergency. Such an amendment was necessary to allow for appointment of a regent . . . or for the coronation of a king.

The old treaty was amended by unanimous vote, and Derkin Lawgiver was appointed Regent of Thorbardin to the cheers of tens of thousands of dwarves. As the applause echoed through the great chamber, Helta Graywood entered and walked down the ramp toward the dais, followed by several brilliantly cloaked dwarves carrying an ornate chair. It had once been the chair of state of a human prince, Lord Sakar Kane of Klanath.

Helta directed the dwarves as they set the chair in the center of the dais. Then she turned, suddenly embarrassed by the tens of thousands of pairs of eyes watching her every move.

"It's . . . ah, this is Derkin's chair," she explained. "He has grown fond of it, so I had it brought along."

Derkin chuckled in surprise, and some of the chieftains smiled. In the gathered throng, a moment of puzzled silence passed, and Helta glared around at the huge crowd. Then, placing her fists on her hips, as her husband so often did, she snapped, "Well, a regent can't do everything standing up, you know!"

* * * * *

The regency of Derkin Lawgiver in Thorbardin lasted for thirty-six years. During that time the war of conquest waged by the Daltigothian Empire against the elves and humans of eastern Ergoth finally dragged to a close, with no real victors. The war never again spilled into the dwarven lands, but dwarves were involved in it. Because of the scheming of a Theiwar named Than-Kar, Thorbardin had been demeaned, and the Hylar Chieftain Dunbarth Ironthumb returned to the field several times with Hylar warriors to assist the elves in their battles.

By the time the war finally ended, the western elves were well along on the development of a new elven culture—in truth a new nation—in the land of Qualinesti. Thousands of them also had joined with dwarves in the continued building of a city in Tharkas Pass—Pax Tharkas.

In the thirty-first year of his regency, Derkin Lawgiver left Thorbardin for a time to travel to Pax Tharkas. There he met with the elf leader Kith-Kanan, to formally adopt a permanent treaty between the dwarves and the elves. Joining in the solemn ceremony were the two chief magistrates of Pax Tharkas, the elf Selanas Prill and the dwarf Talon Oakbeard.

The treaty formalized the alliance between dwarves and elves, and dedicated Pax Tharkas as a living monument to that alliance—and to all those who had died in the cause of it.

The treaty was called the Swordsheath Scroll.

It was the last time Derkin Lawgiver would ever leave.

Five years later, he became the first king of Thorbardin—a Thorbardin that was no longer confined to subterranean caverns sealed from the world by impregnable gates, but was now a mighty nation, spanning the mountain lands of old Kal-Thax, from Pax Tharkas to the Thunder Peaks, from Sky's End to the Anviltops—a nation full of dwarven places like Stoneforge and Barter, Herdlinger and Firestone, Redbluff and Split Crag—a kingdom where those who chose the open sky lived as Neidar and those who preferred the comfort of stone lived as Holgar, with the great fortress of Thorbardin as capital of it all.

Derkin the Lawgiver reigned as king in Thorbardin for one hundred and twenty-three years. He was succeeded by his grandson, Damon Stonetooth, who decreed that he and all future kings would be known both by their own names and by a "throne" name, honoring the first of the dwarven kings.

The name was Derkin.